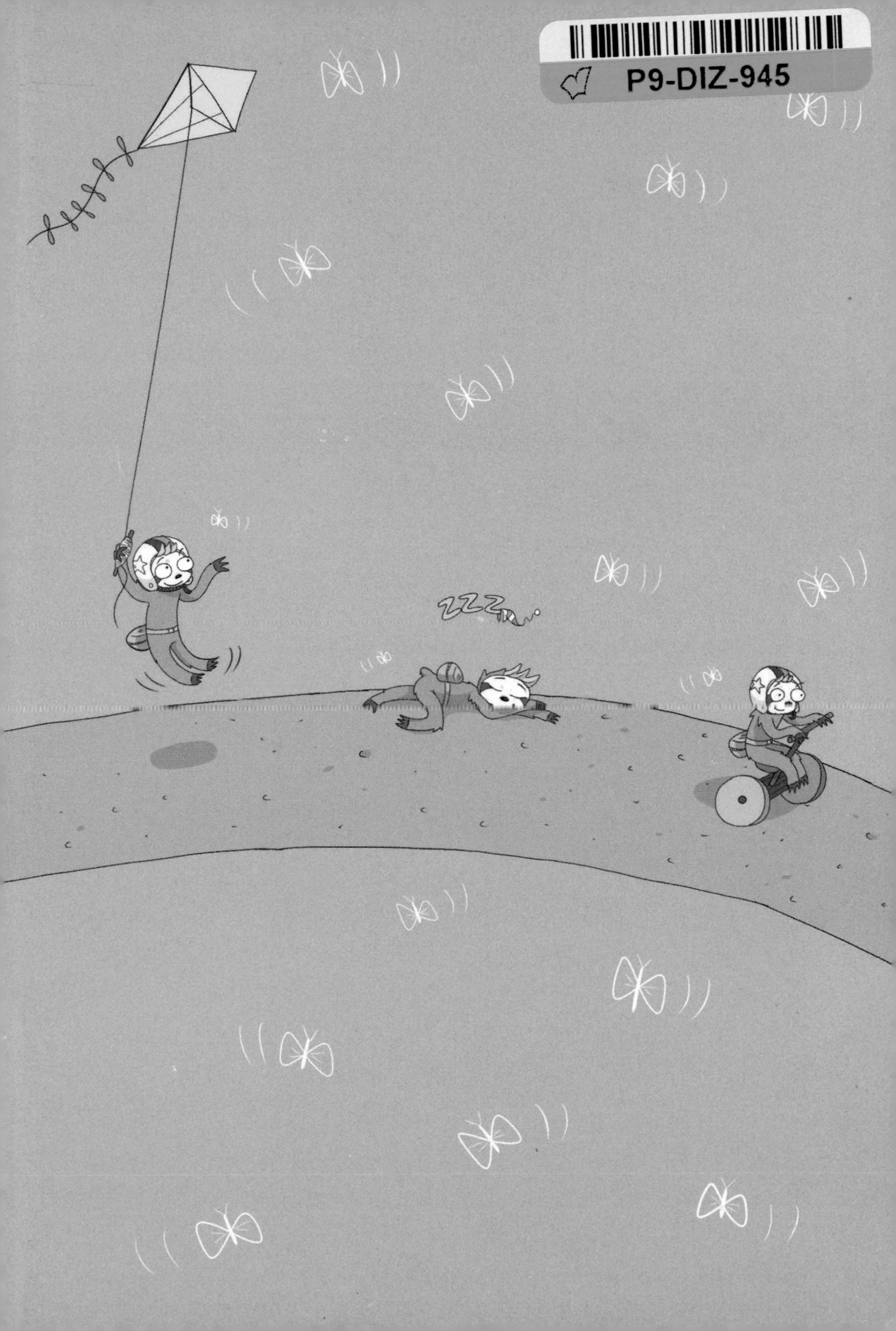
ZZZ

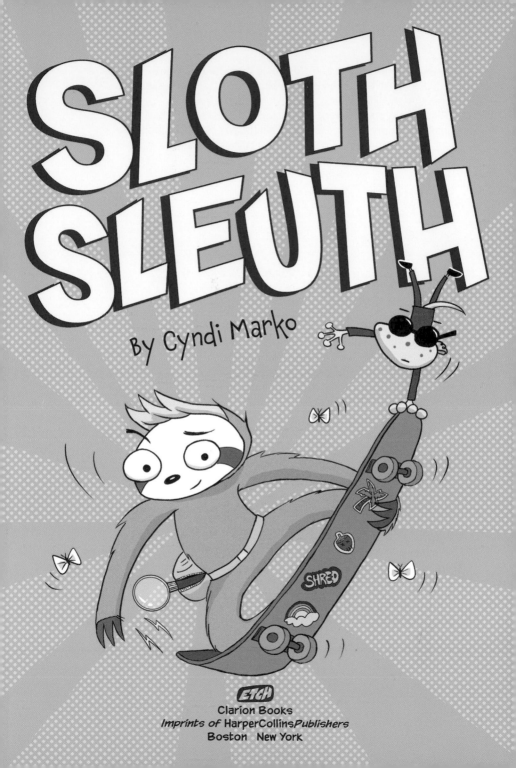

SLOTH SLEUTH

By Cyndi Marko

ETCH
Clarion Books
Imprints of HarperCollinsPublishers
Boston   New York

For my *Shenanigans* writing group. If I ever have to hide out on a tropical isle with a bunch of criminals, I'll pick you guys. ;)

Also, to my editor, Amy; my designer, Celeste; the whole team at Clarion; my agent, Elizabeth; and to my colorist, Jess, who brightened Paz's world—a bazillion thanks.
—C.M.

Etch and Clarion Books are imprints of HarperCollins Publishers.

Sloth Sleuth
 For information address HarperCollins Children's Books, a division of HarperCollins Publishers, 195 Broadway, New York, NY 10007.
clarionbooks.com

Library of Congress Cataloging-in-Publication Data has been applied for.
ISBN: 978-0-35-844893-8

Illustrator: Cyndi Marko
Colorist: Jess Lome
Lettering by Natalie Fondriest
The illustrations in this book were done in Clip Studio.
The text was set in CCYadaYadaYada.
Cover and interior design by Celeste Knudsen

Manufactured in Spain
EST 10 9 8 7 6 5 4 3 2 1
4500844145

First Edition

THE PREAMBLE

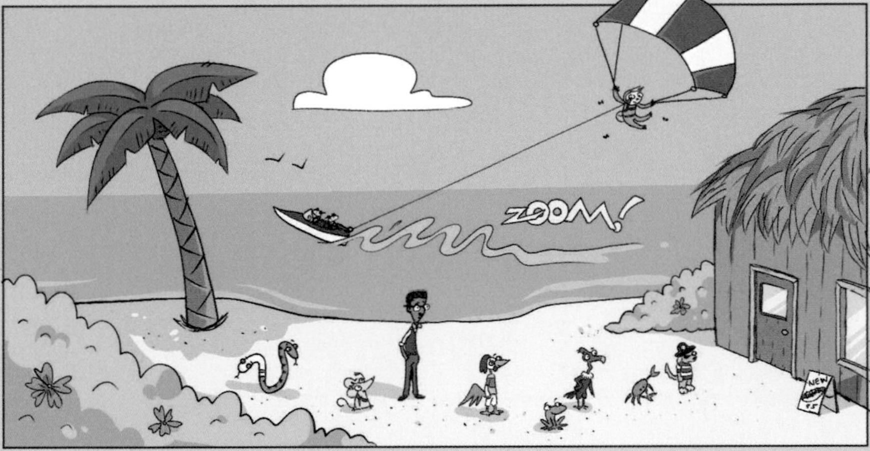
ZOOM!

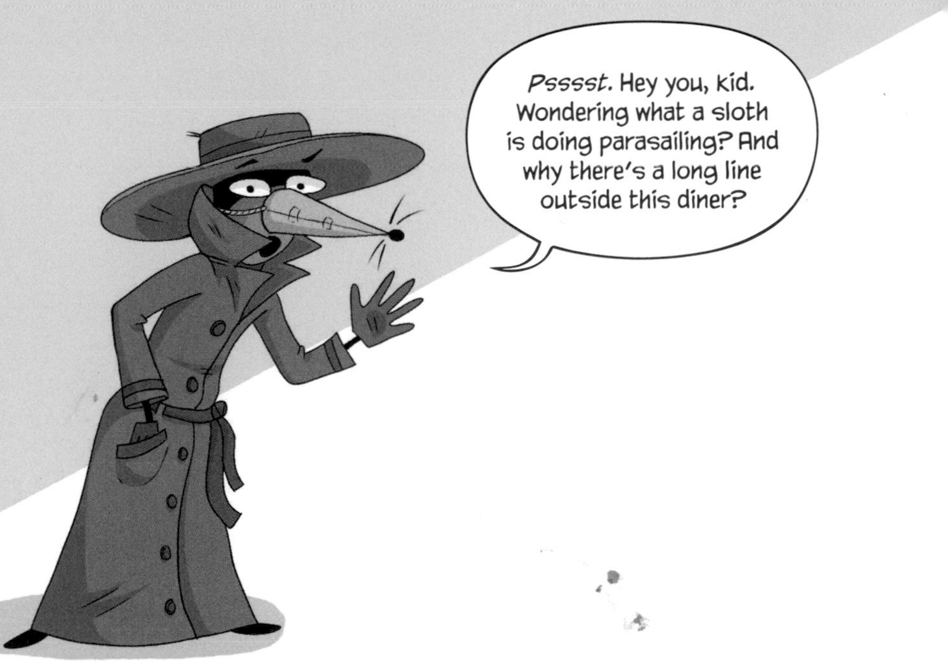
Psssst. Hey you, kid. Wondering what a sloth is doing parasailing? And why there's a long line outside this diner?

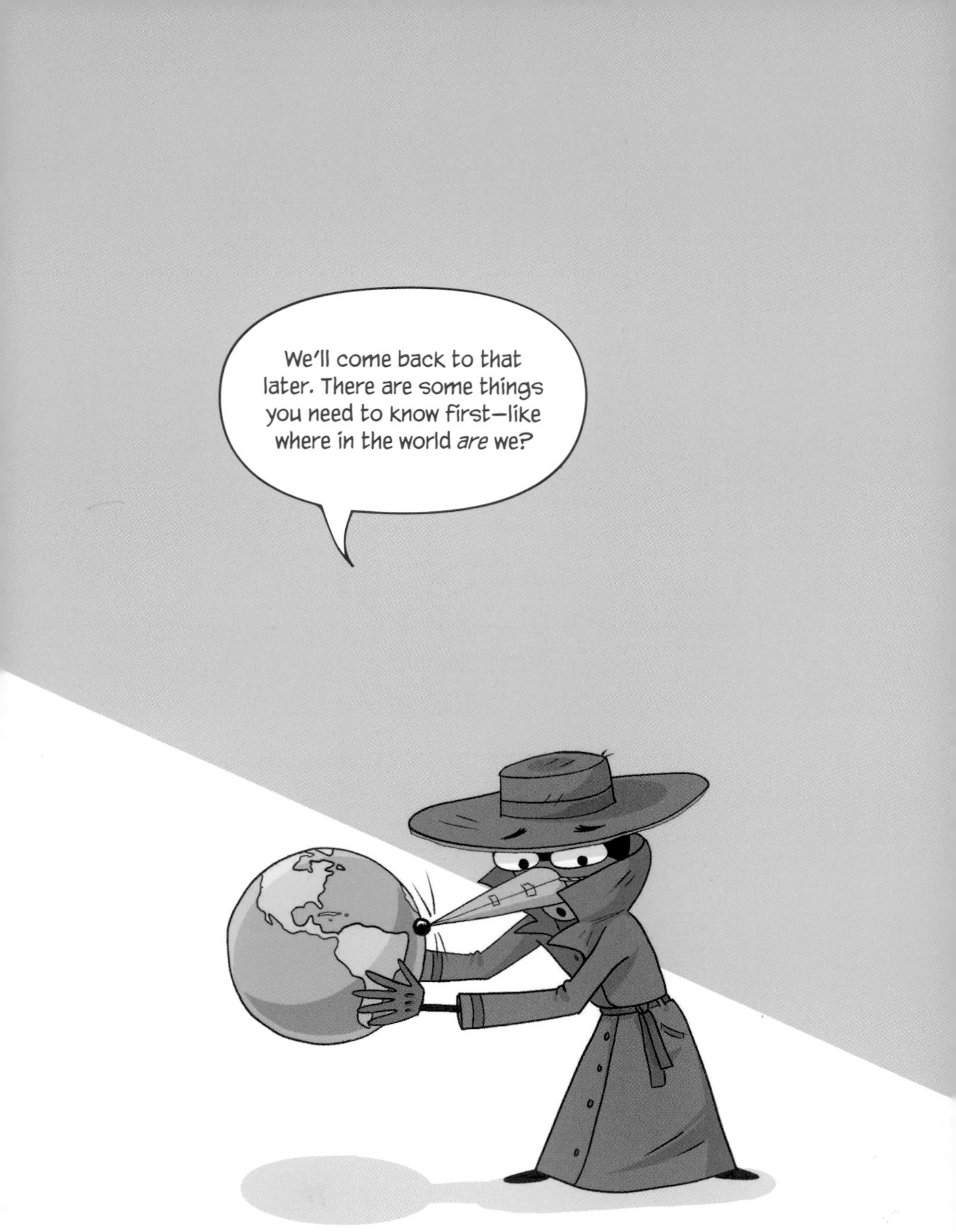
We'll come back to that later. There are some things you need to know first—like where in the world *are* we?

WE ARE HERE

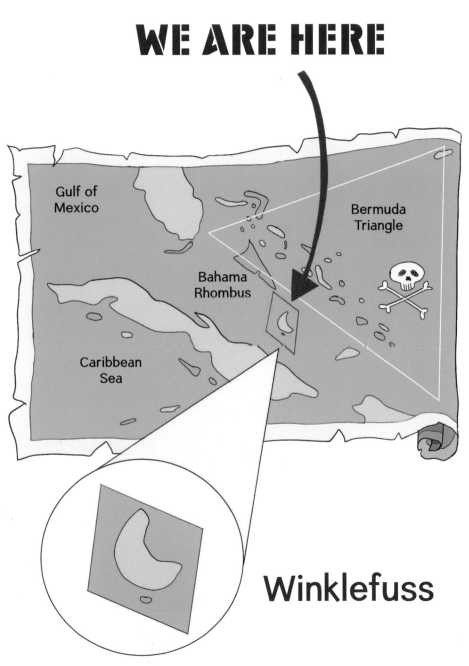

Gulf of Mexico

Bermuda Triangle

Bahama Rhombus

Caribbean Sea

Winklefuss

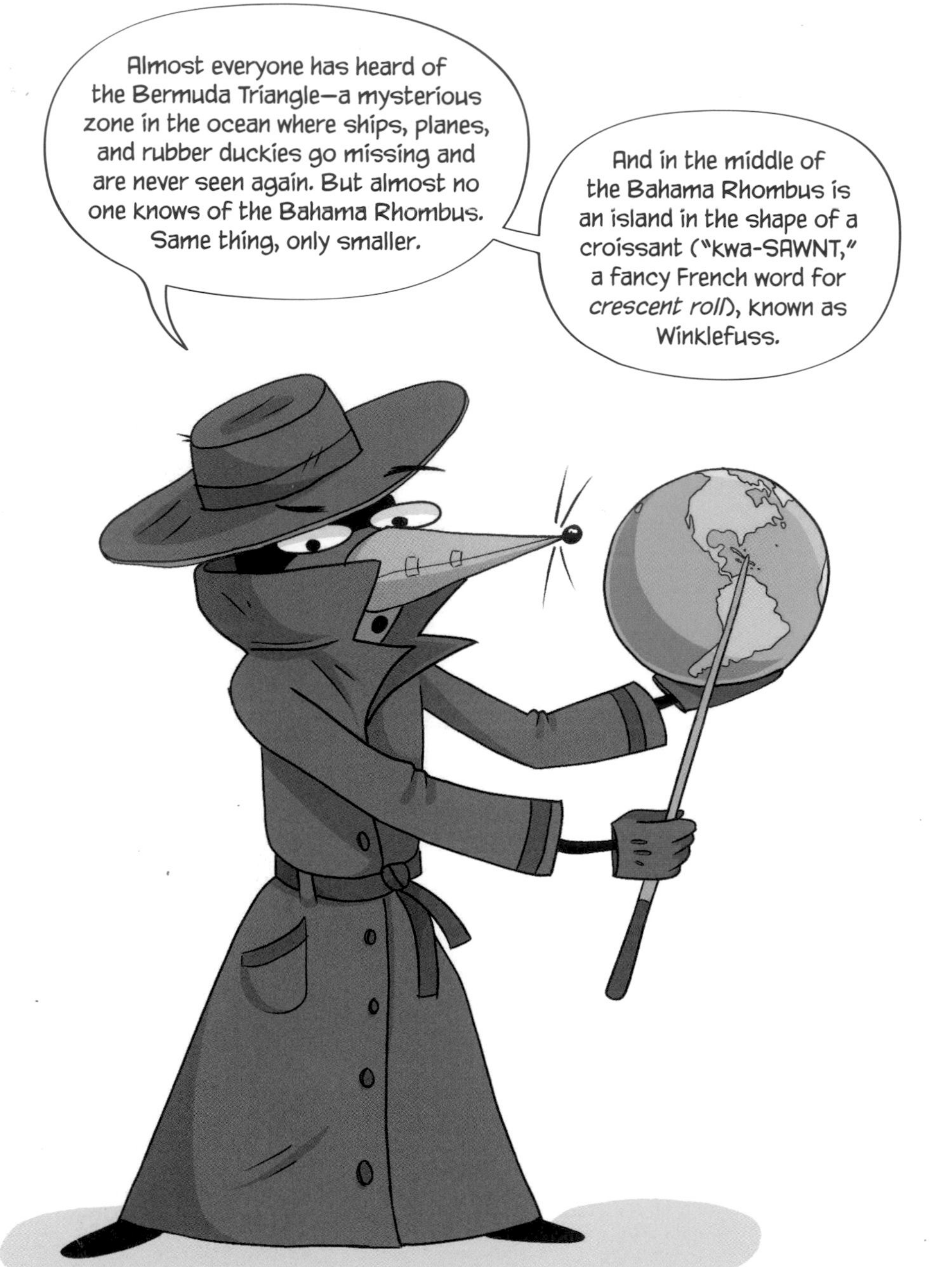
Almost everyone has heard of the Bermuda Triangle—a mysterious zone in the ocean where ships, planes, and rubber duckies go missing and are never seen again. But almost no one knows of the Bahama Rhombus. Same thing, only smaller.
And in the middle of the Bahama Rhombus is an island in the shape of a croissant ("kwa-SAWNT," a fancy French word for crescent roll), known as Winklefuss.

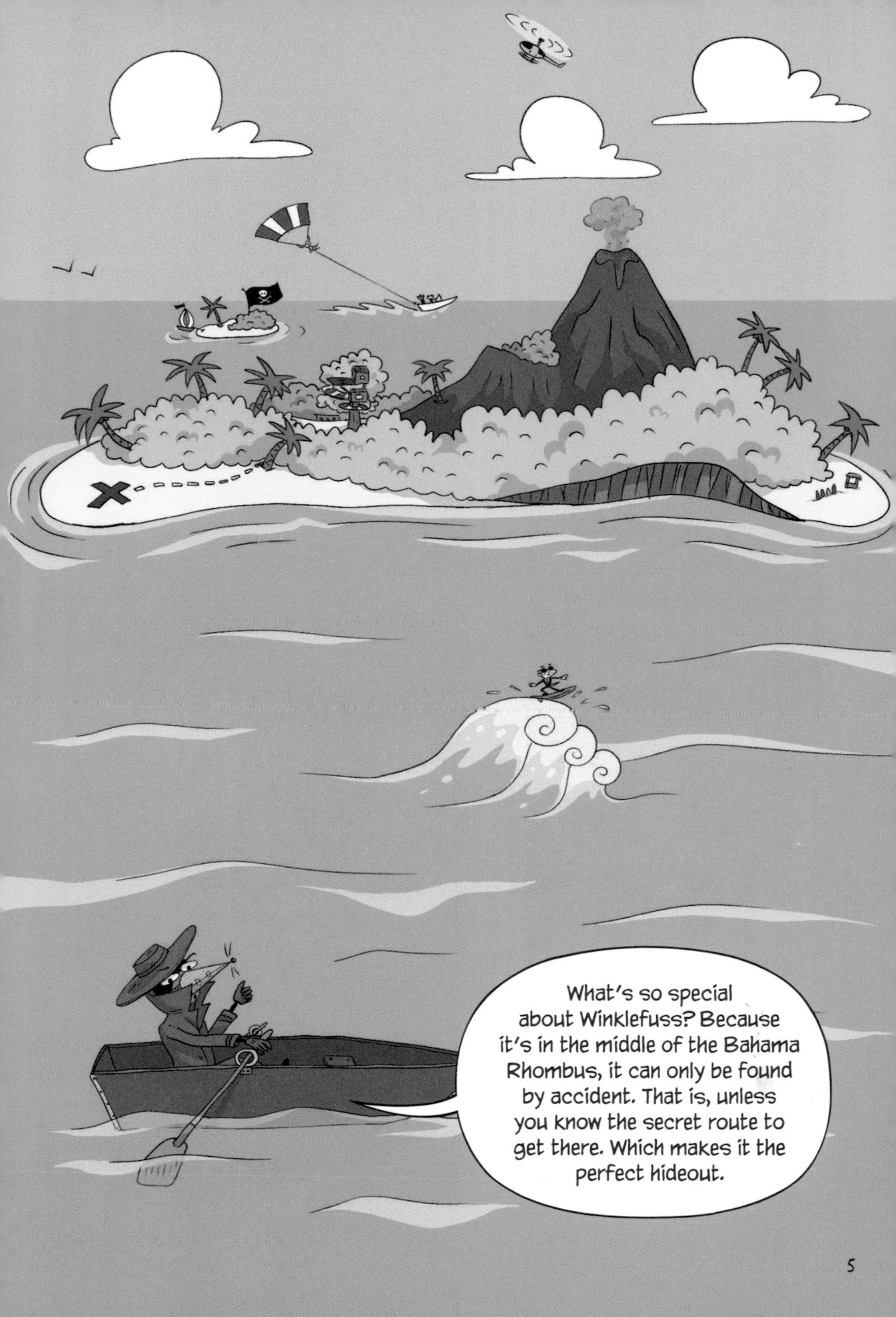
What's so special about Winklefuss? Because it's in the middle of the Bahama Rhombus, it can only be found by accident. That is, unless you know the secret route to get there. Which makes it the perfect hideout.

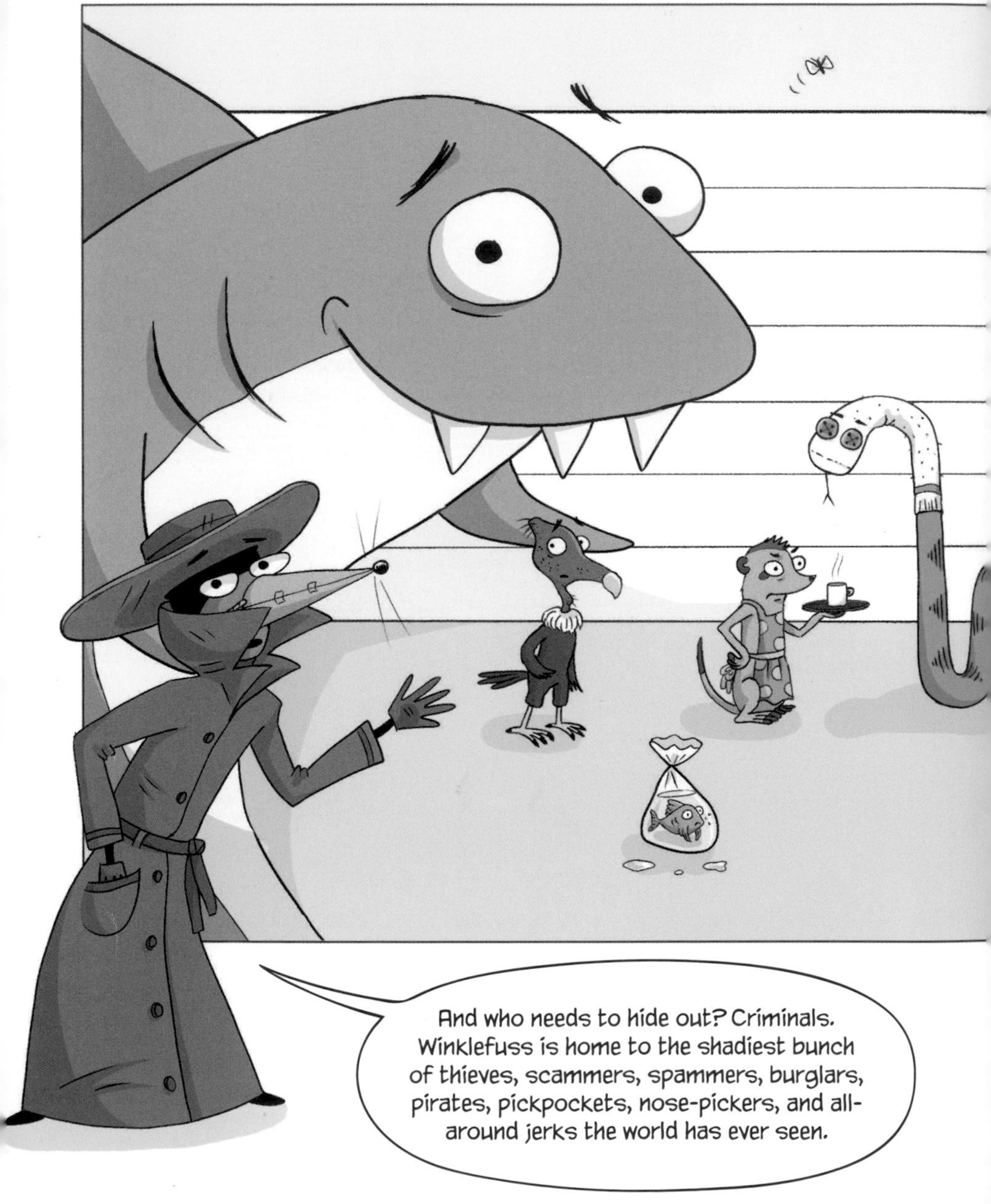
And who needs to hide out? Criminals. Winklefuss is home to the shadiest bunch of thieves, scammers, spammers, burglars, pirates, pickpockets, nose-pickers, and all-around jerks the world has ever seen.

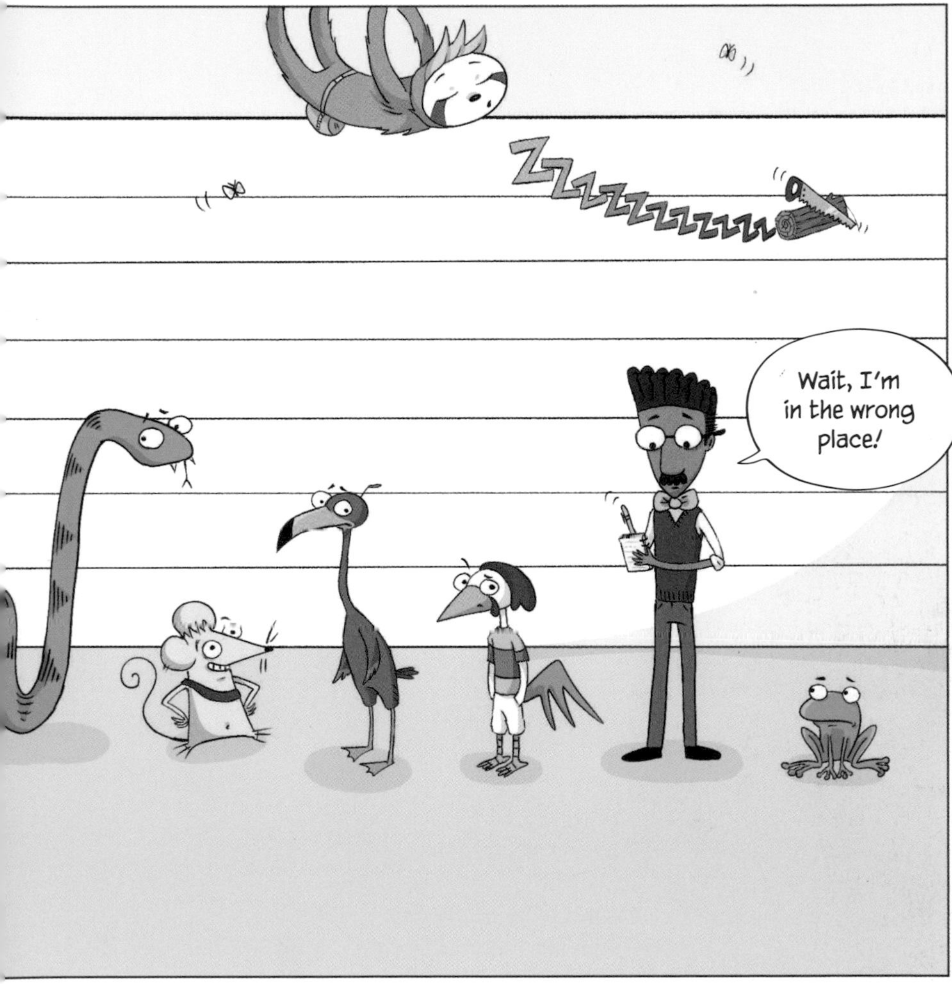
Wait, I'm in the wrong place!

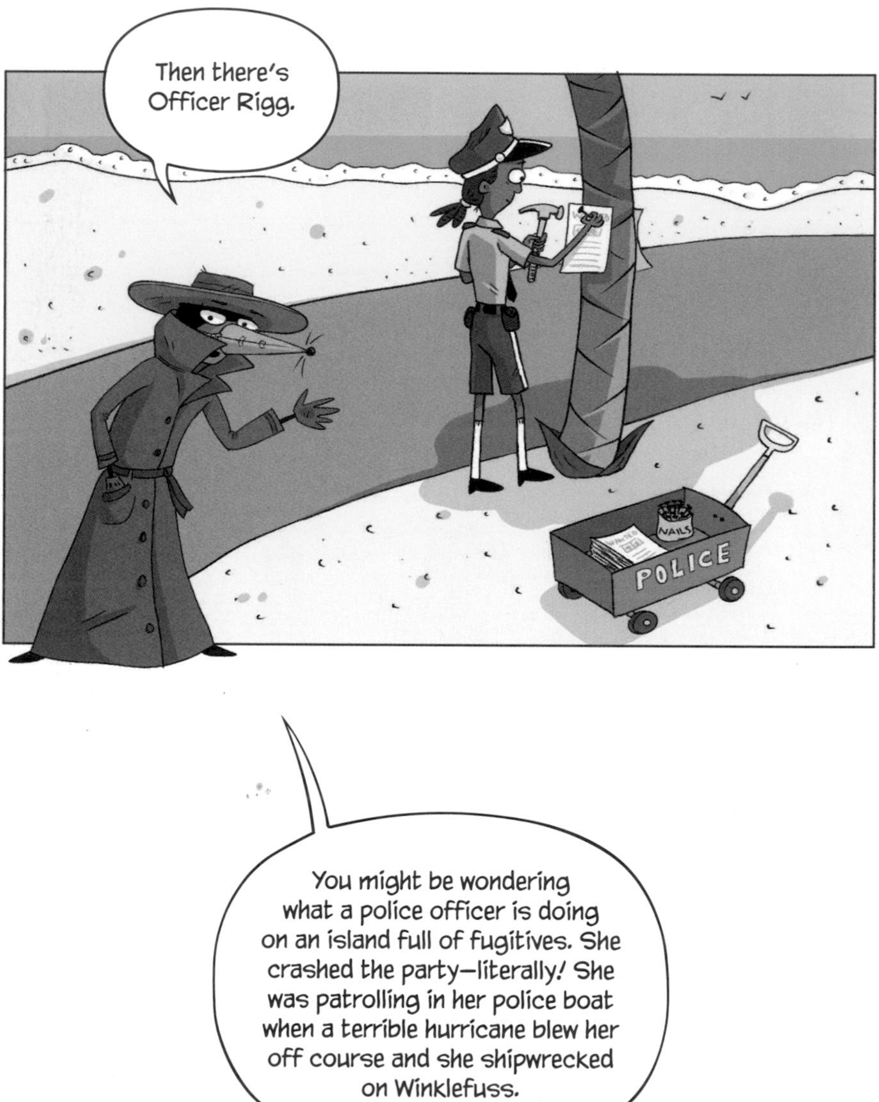
Then there's Officer Rigg.
NAILS
POLICE
You might be wondering what a police officer is doing on an island full of fugitives. She crashed the party—literally! She was patrolling in her police boat when a terrible hurricane blew her off course and she shipwrecked on Winklefuss.

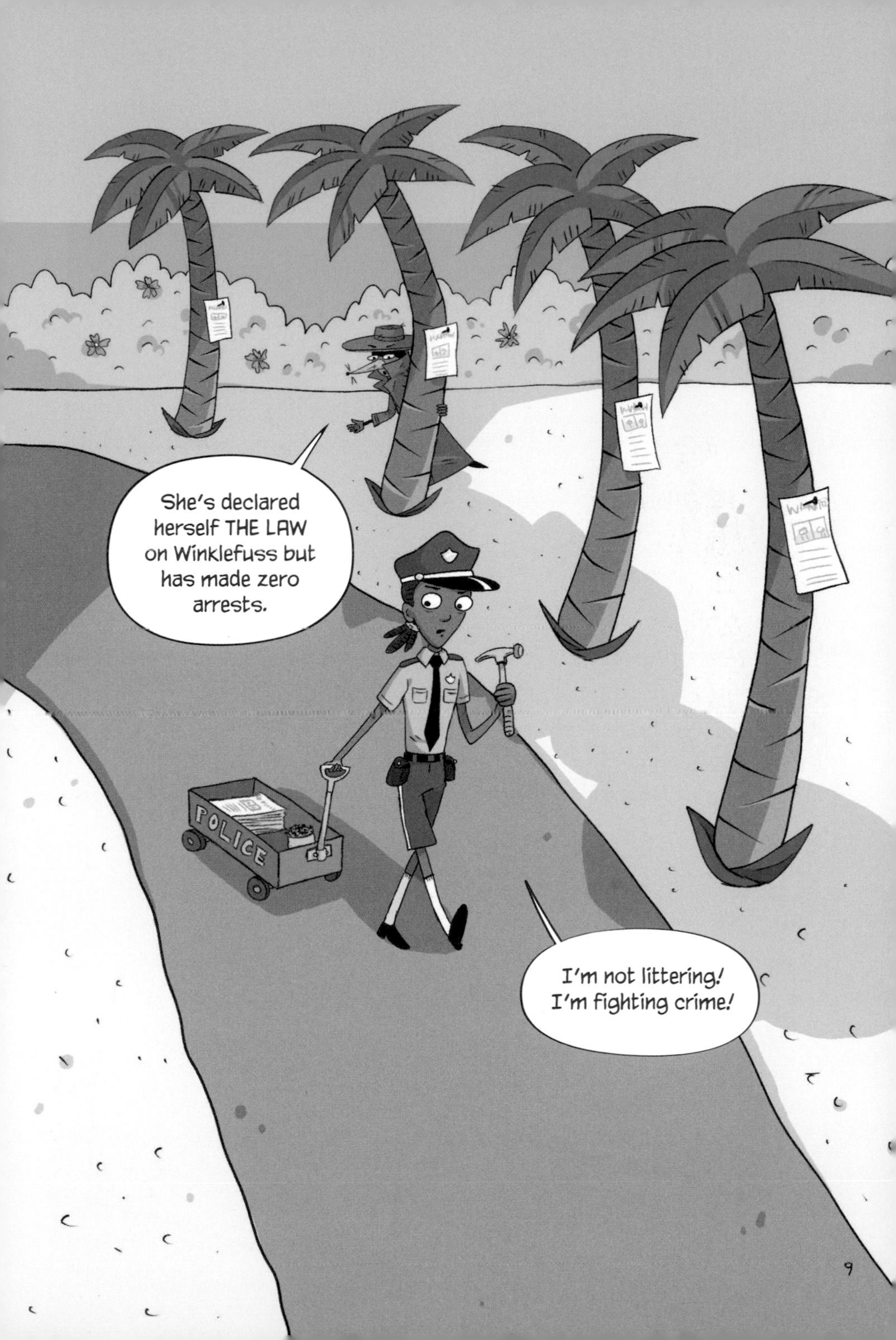
She's declared herself THE LAW on Winklefuss but has made zero arrests.
I'm not littering! I'm fighting crime!
POLICE

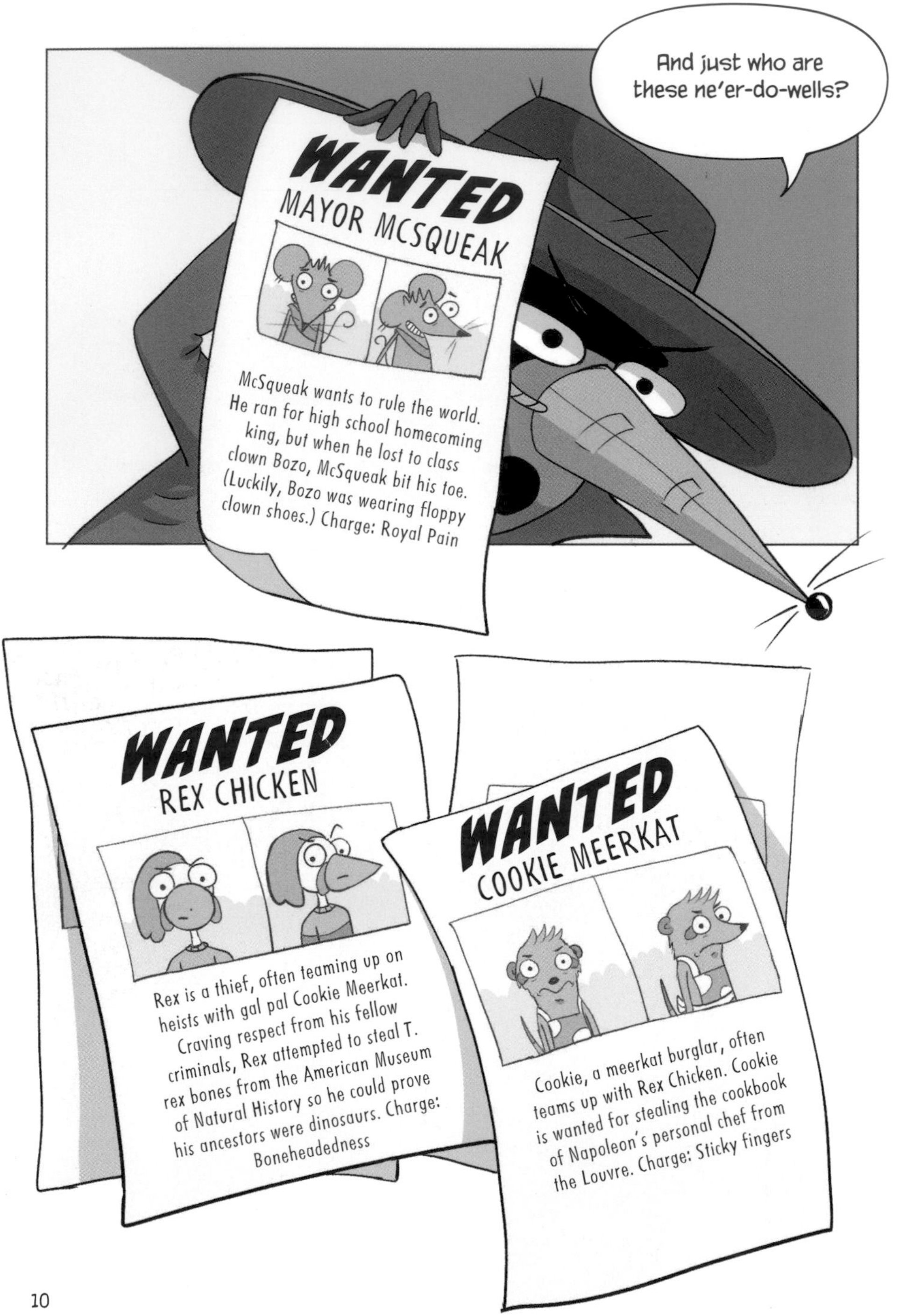
And just who are these ne'er-do-wells?
WANTED
MAYOR MCSQUEAK
McSqueak wants to rule the world. He ran for high school homecoming king, but when he lost to class clown Bozo, McSqueak bit his toe. (Luckily, Bozo was wearing floppy clown shoes.) Charge: Royal Pain
WANTED
REX CHICKEN
Rex is a thief, often teaming up on heists with gal pal Cookie Meerkat. Craving respect from his fellow criminals, Rex attempted to steal T. rex bones from the American Museum of Natural History so he could prove his ancestors were dinosaurs. Charge: Boneheadedness
WANTED
COOKIE MEERKAT
Cookie, a meerkat burglar, often teams up with Rex Chicken. Cookie is wanted for stealing the cookbook of Napoleon's personal chef from the Louvre. Charge: Sticky fingers

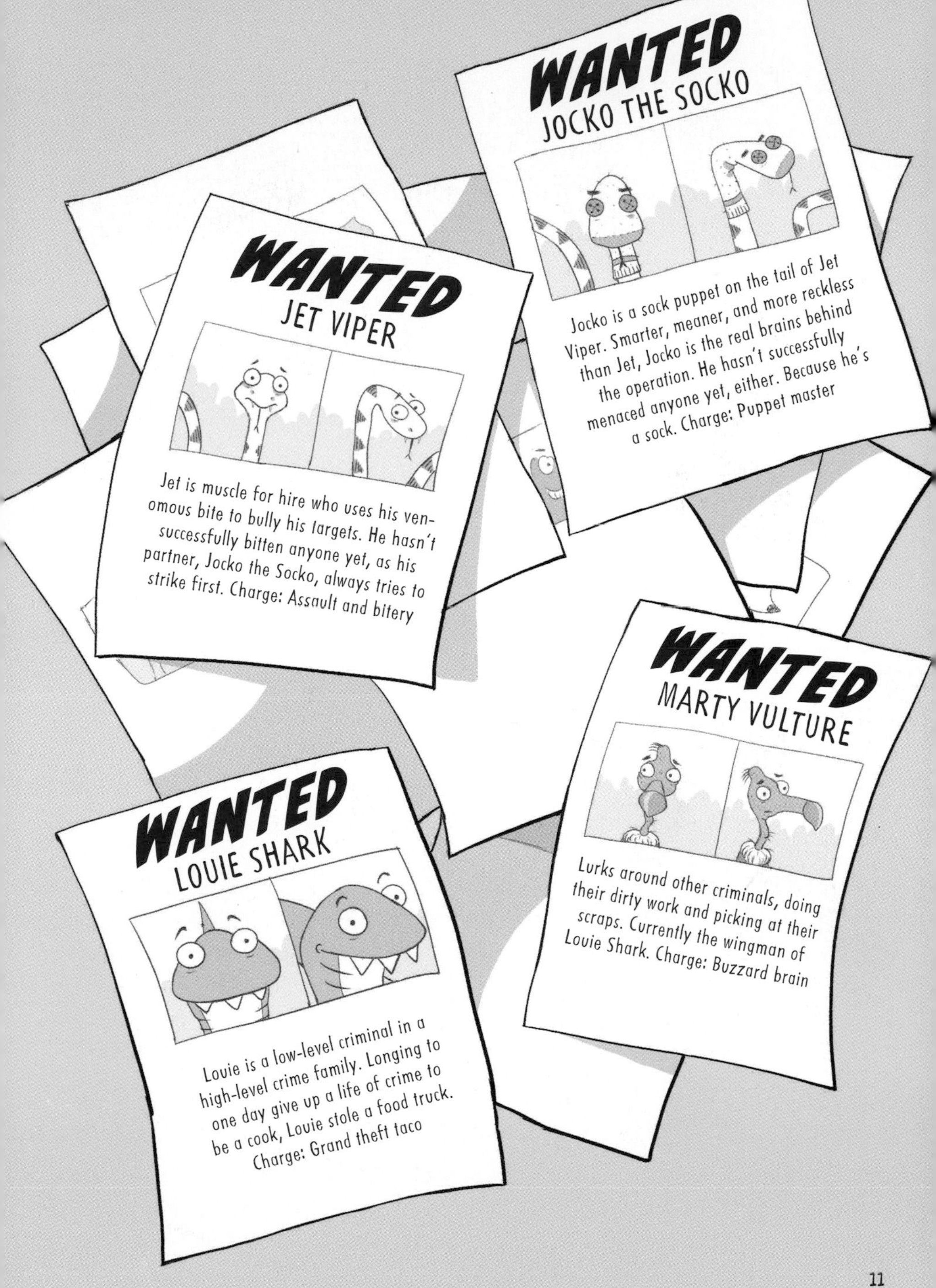
WANTED
JOCKO THE SOCKO
Jocko is a sock puppet on the tail of Jet Viper. Smarter, meaner, and more reckless than Jet, Jocko is the real brains behind the operation. He hasn't successfully menaced anyone yet, either. Because he's a sock. Charge: Puppet master
WANTED
JET VIPER
Jet is muscle for hire who uses his venomous bite to bully his targets. He hasn't successfully bitten anyone yet, as his partner, Jocko the Socko, always tries to strike first. Charge: Assault and bitery
WANTED
MARTY VULTURE
Lurks around other criminals, doing their dirty work and picking at their scraps. Currently the wingman of Louie Shark. Charge: Buzzard brain
WANTED
LOUIE SHARK
Louie is a low-level criminal in a high-level crime family. Longing to one day give up a life of crime to be a cook, Louie stole a food truck. Charge: Grand theft taco

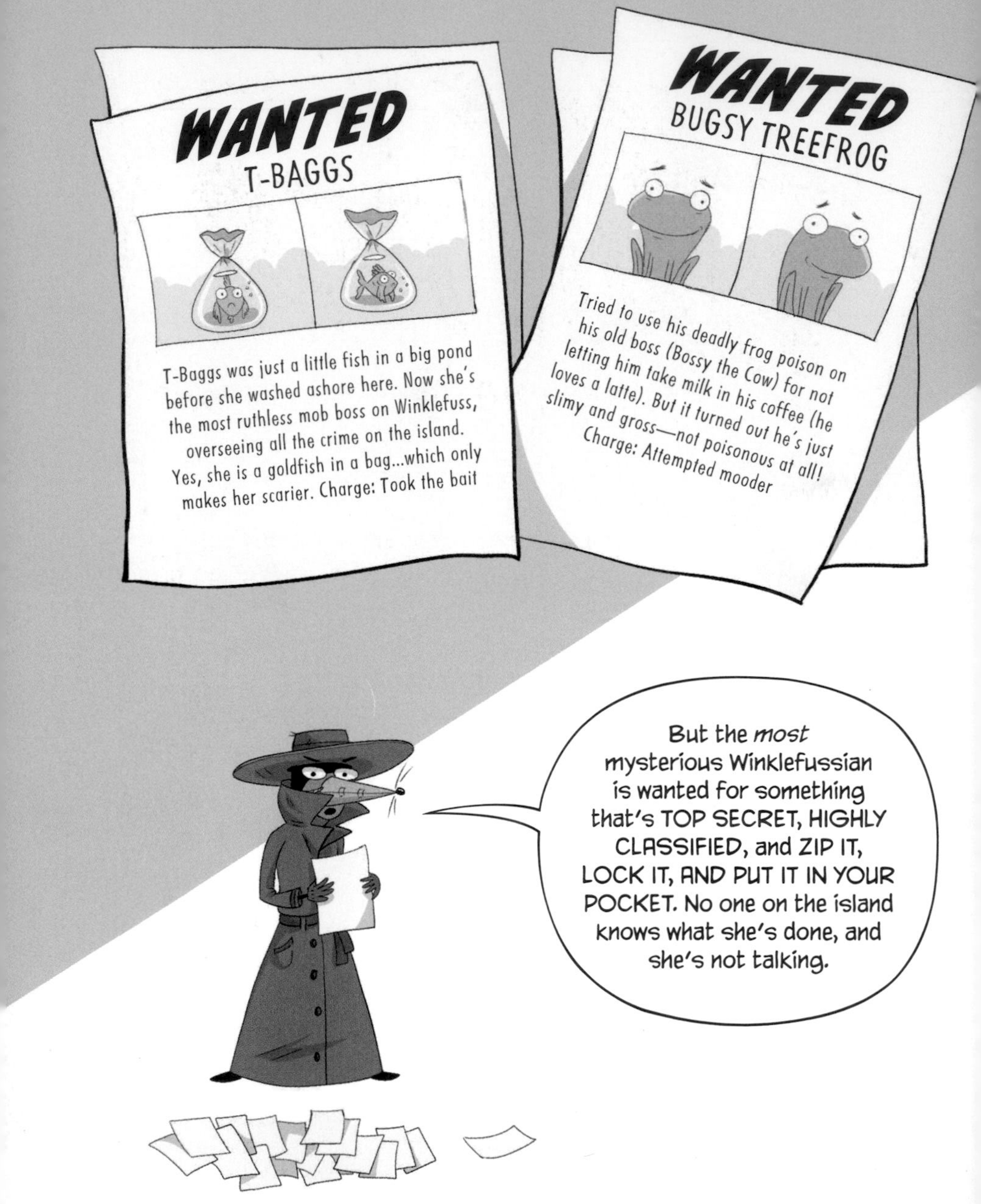
WANTED
T-BAGGS
T-Baggs was just a little fish in a big pond before she washed ashore here. Now she's the most ruthless mob boss on Winklefuss, overseeing all the crime on the island. Yes, she is a goldfish in a bag...which only makes her scarier. Charge: Took the bait
WANTED
BUGSY TREEFROG
Tried to use his deadly frog poison on his old boss (Bossy the Cow) for not letting him take milk in his coffee (he loves a latte). But it turned out he's just slimy and gross—not poisonous at all! Charge: Attempted mooder
But the *most* mysterious Winklefussian is wanted for something that's TOP SECRET, HIGHLY CLASSIFIED, and ZIP IT, LOCK IT, AND PUT IT IN YOUR POCKET. No one on the island knows what she's done, and she's not talking.

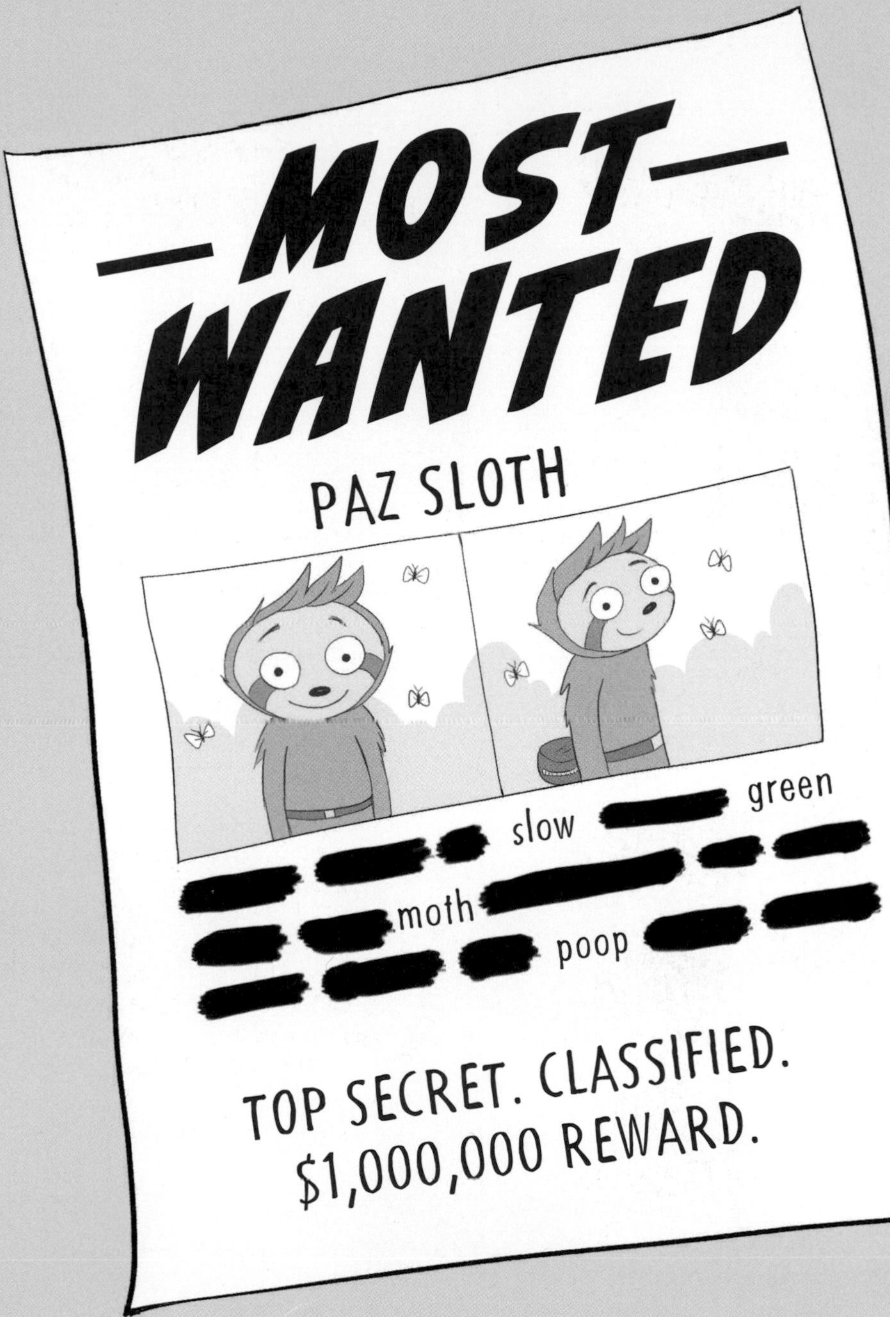
MOST
WANTED
PAZ SLOTH
[redacted] slow [redacted] green [redacted] moth [redacted] poop [redacted]
TOP SECRET. CLASSIFIED.
$1,000,000 REWARD.

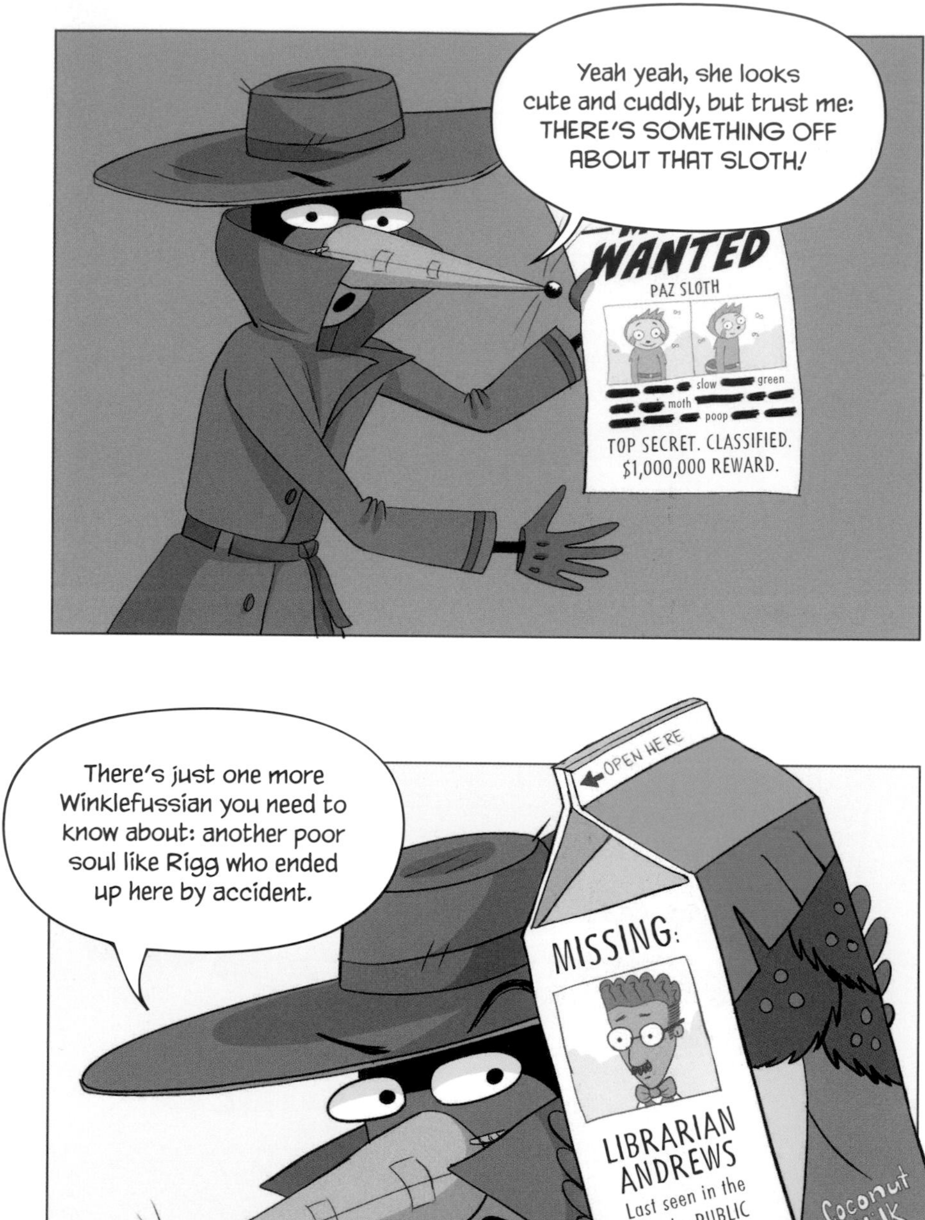
Yeah yeah, she looks cute and cuddly, but trust me: THERE'S SOMETHING OFF ABOUT THAT SLOTH!
WANTED
PAZ SLOTH
[redacted] slow [redacted] green
[redacted] moth [redacted]
[redacted] poop [redacted]
TOP SECRET. CLASSIFIED.
$1,000,000 REWARD.
There's just one more Winklefussian you need to know about: another poor soul like Rigg who ended up here by accident.
OPEN HERE
MISSING:
LIBRARIAN ANDREWS
Last seen in the Topeka PUBLIC LIBRARY spinning out of control in the eye of a tornado.
Coconut Milk

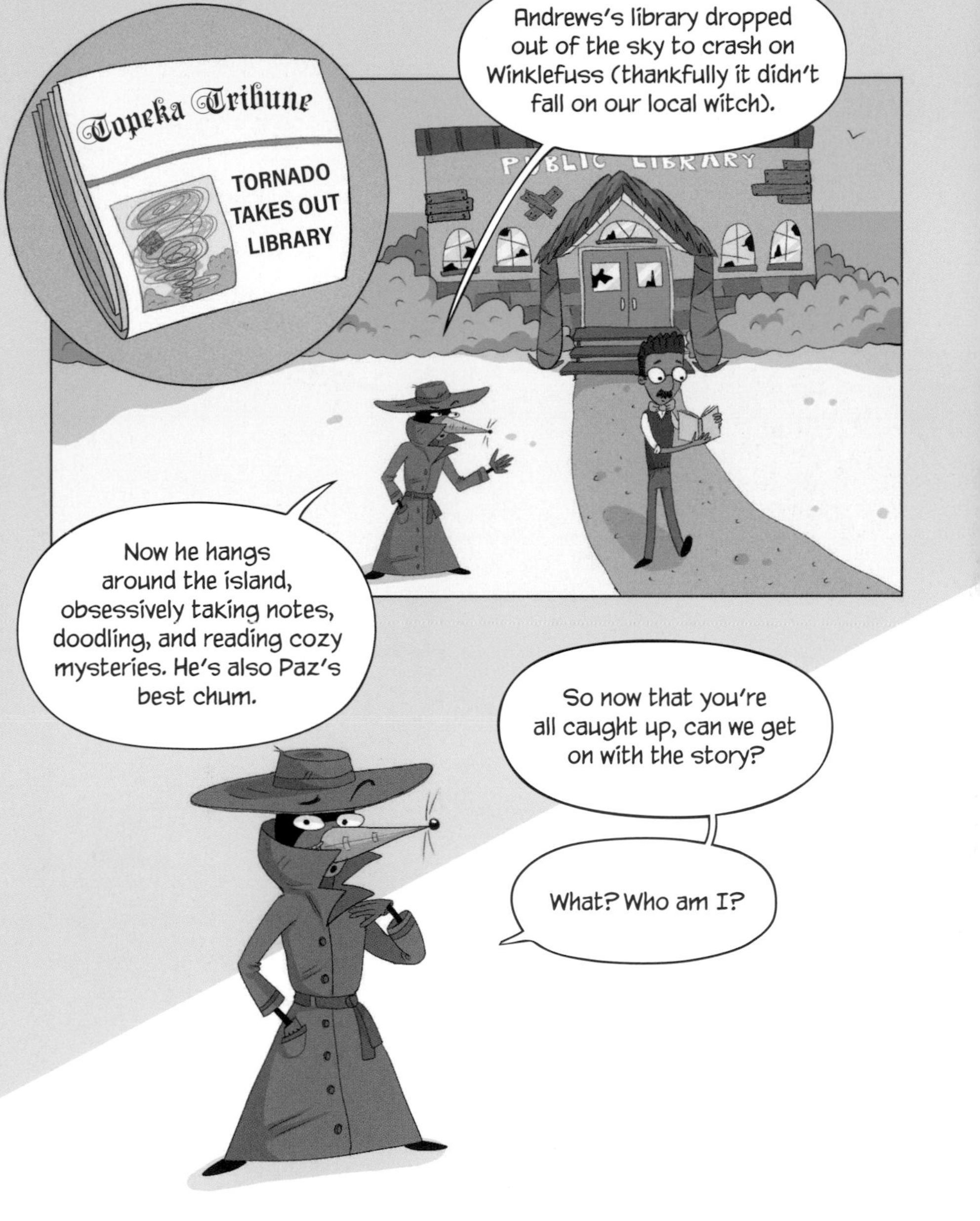
Topeka Tribune
TORNADO TAKES OUT LIBRARY
Andrews's library dropped out of the sky to crash on Winklefuss (thankfully it didn't fall on our local witch).
PUBLIC LIBRARY
Now he hangs around the island, obsessively taking notes, doodling, and reading cozy mysteries. He's also Paz's best chum.
So now that you're all caught up, can we get on with the story?
What? Who am I?

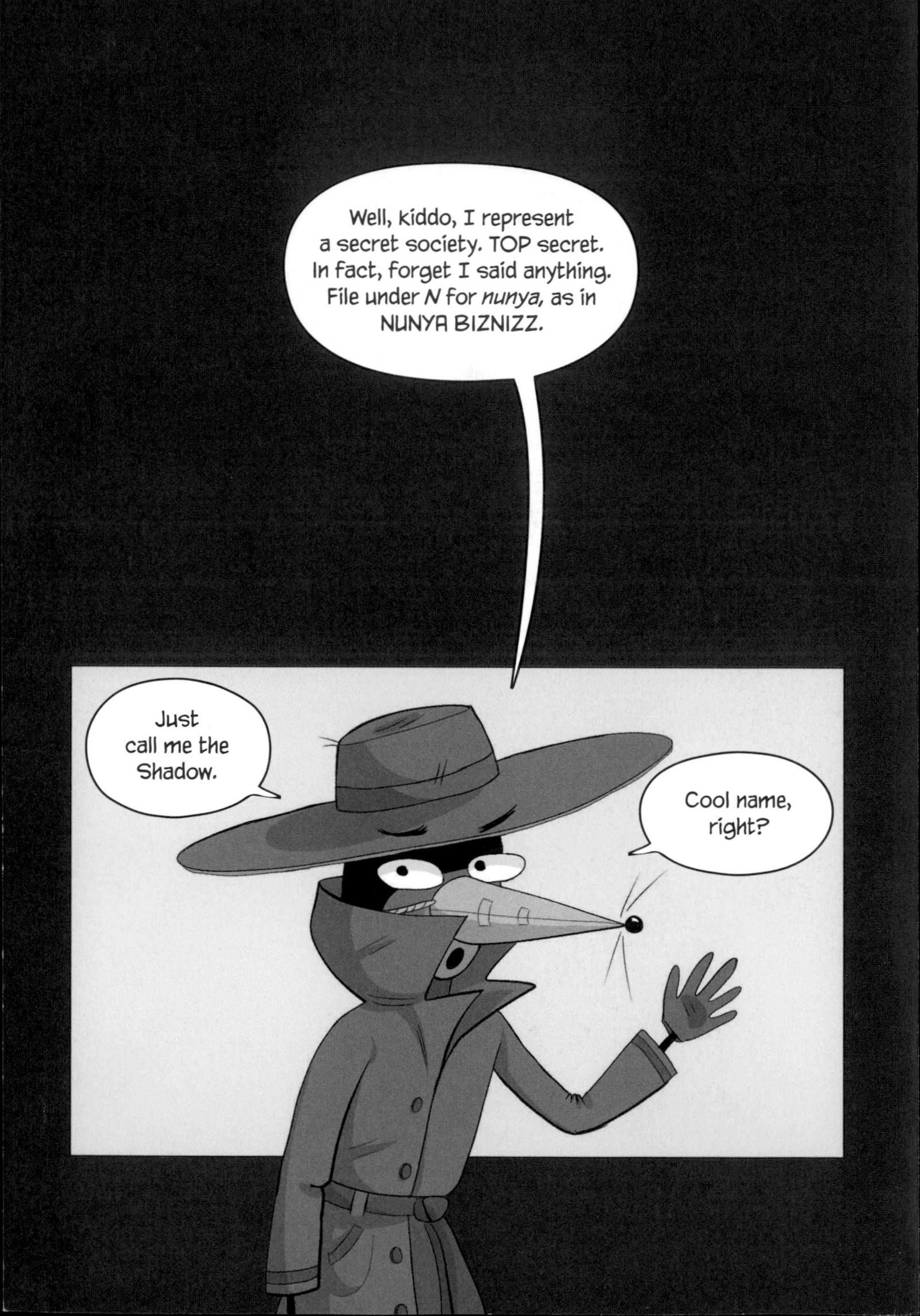

Well, kiddo, I represent a secret society. TOP secret. In fact, forget I said anything. File under *N* for *nunya,* as in NUNYA BIZNIZZ.
Just call me the Shadow.
Cool name, right?

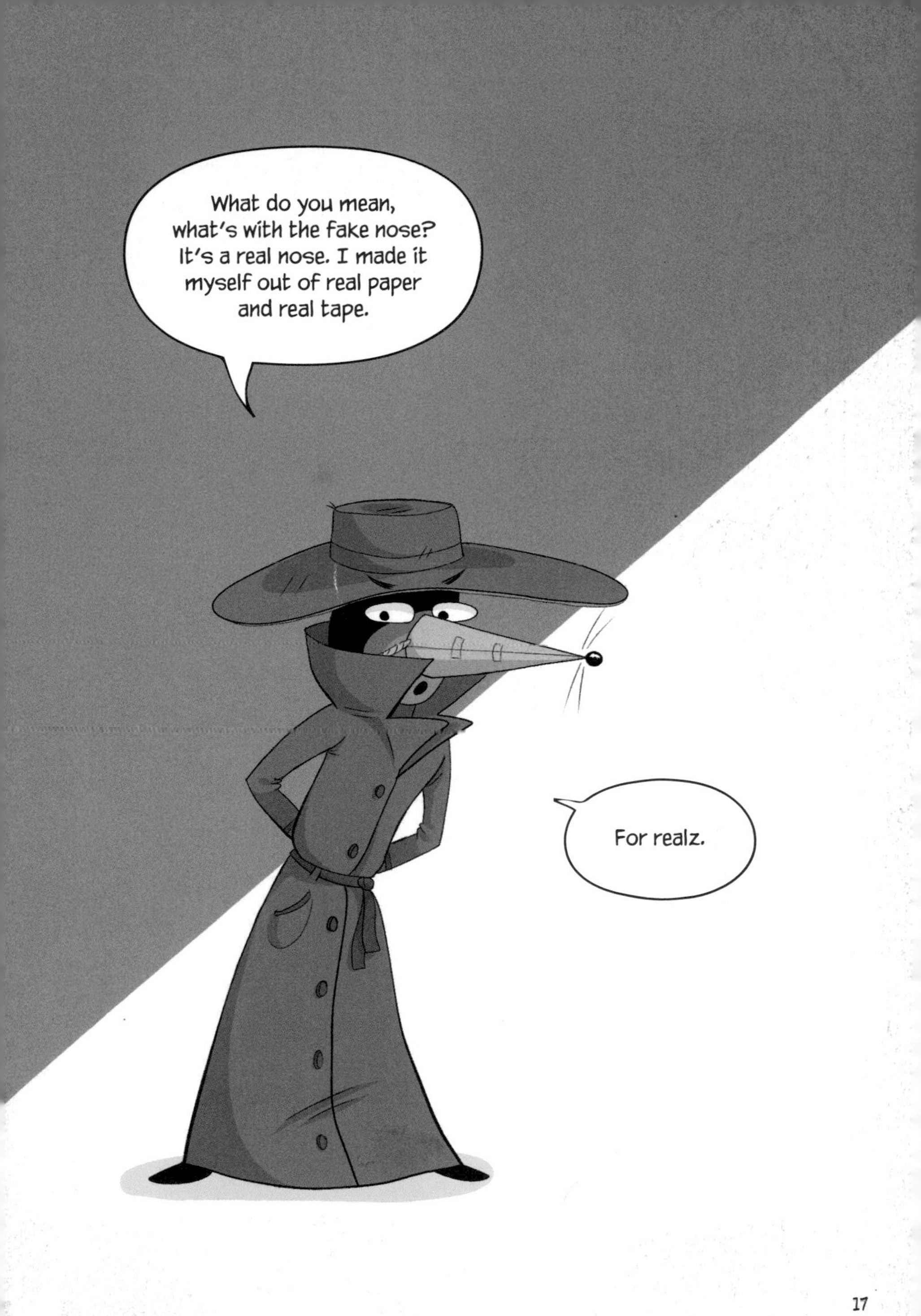
What do you mean, what's with the fake nose? It's a real nose. I made it myself out of real paper and real tape.
For realz.

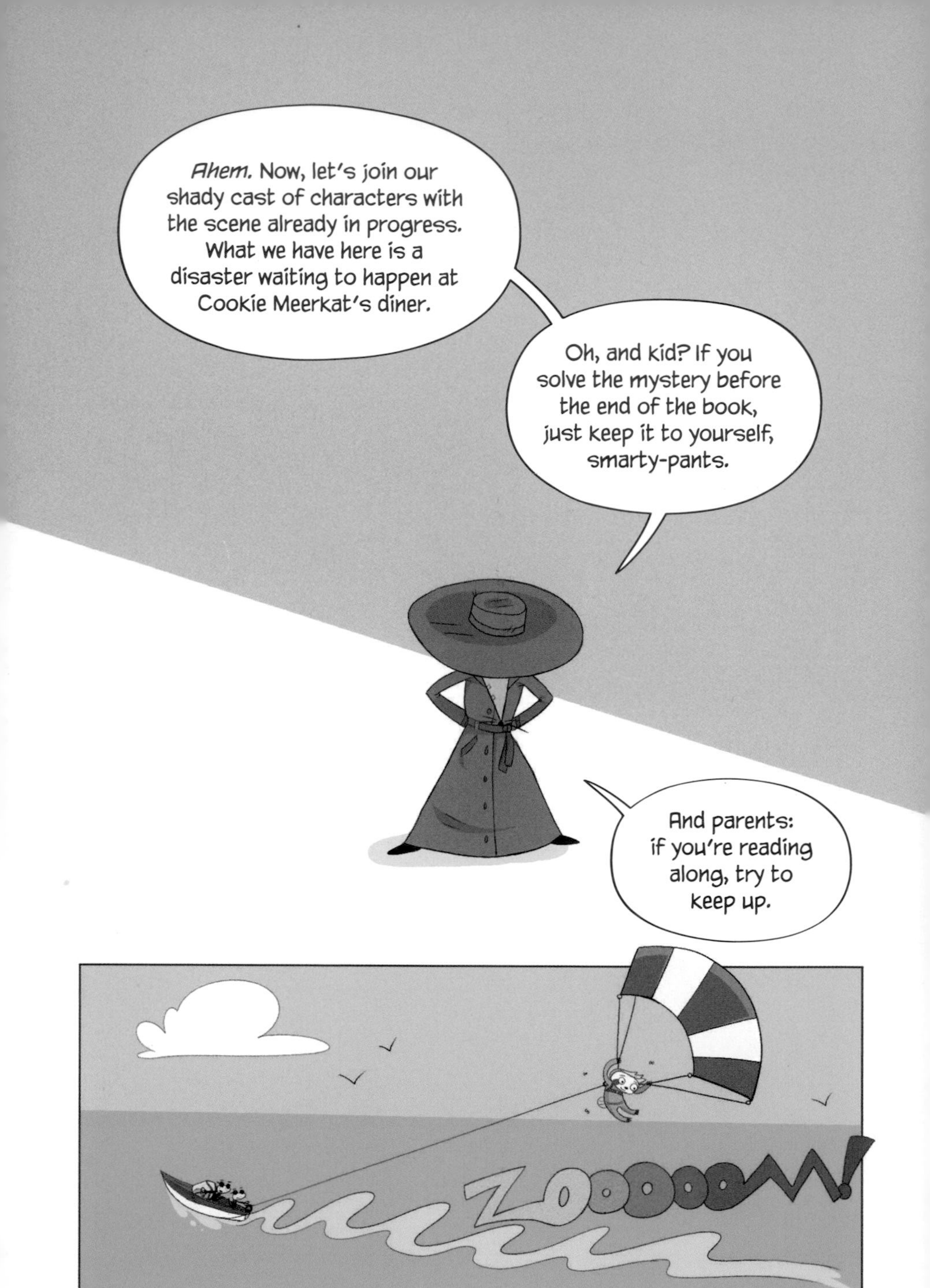
Ahem. Now, let's join our shady cast of characters with the scene already in progress. What we have here is a disaster waiting to happen at Cookie Meerkat's diner.
Oh, and kid? If you solve the mystery before the end of the book, just keep it to yourself, smarty-pants.
And parents: if you're reading along, try to keep up.
ZOOOOOM!

CHAPTER 1

MONDAY. MIDMORNING.
HANGING OUT BY THE SEASHORE.

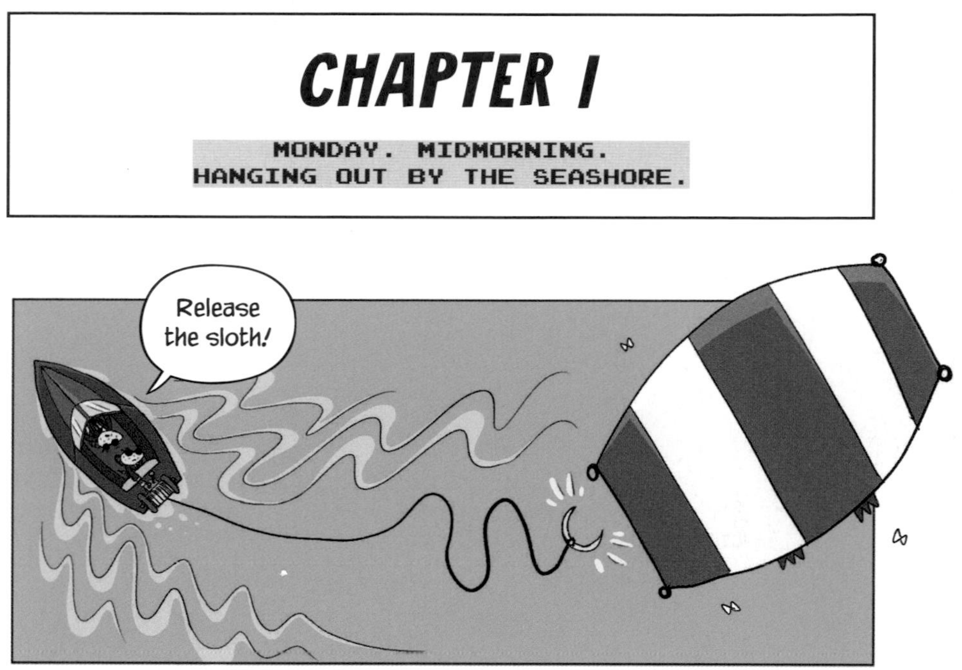
Release the sloth!

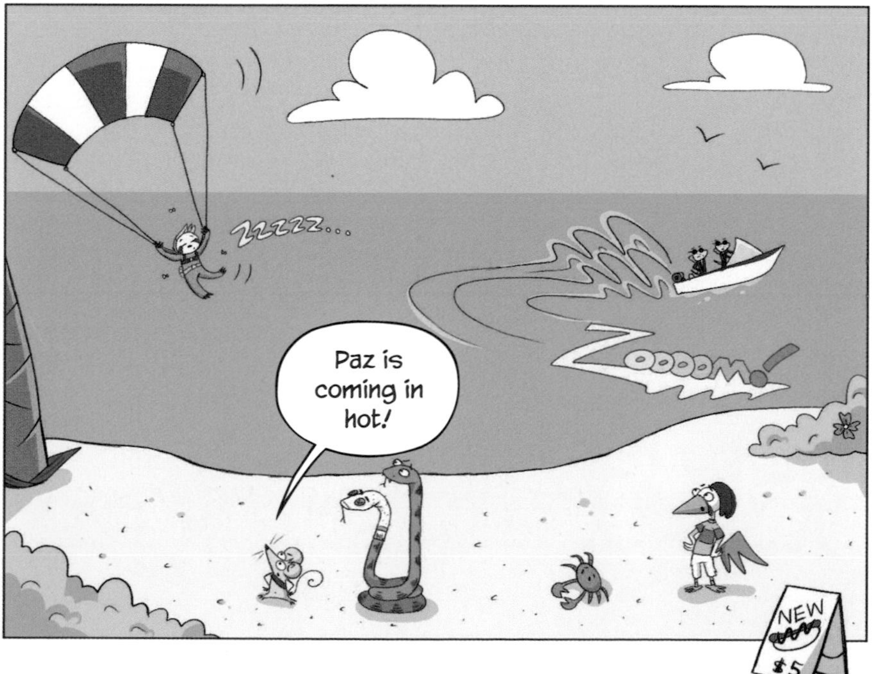
ZZZZZ...
ZOOOOM!
Paz is coming in hot!
NEW
$5

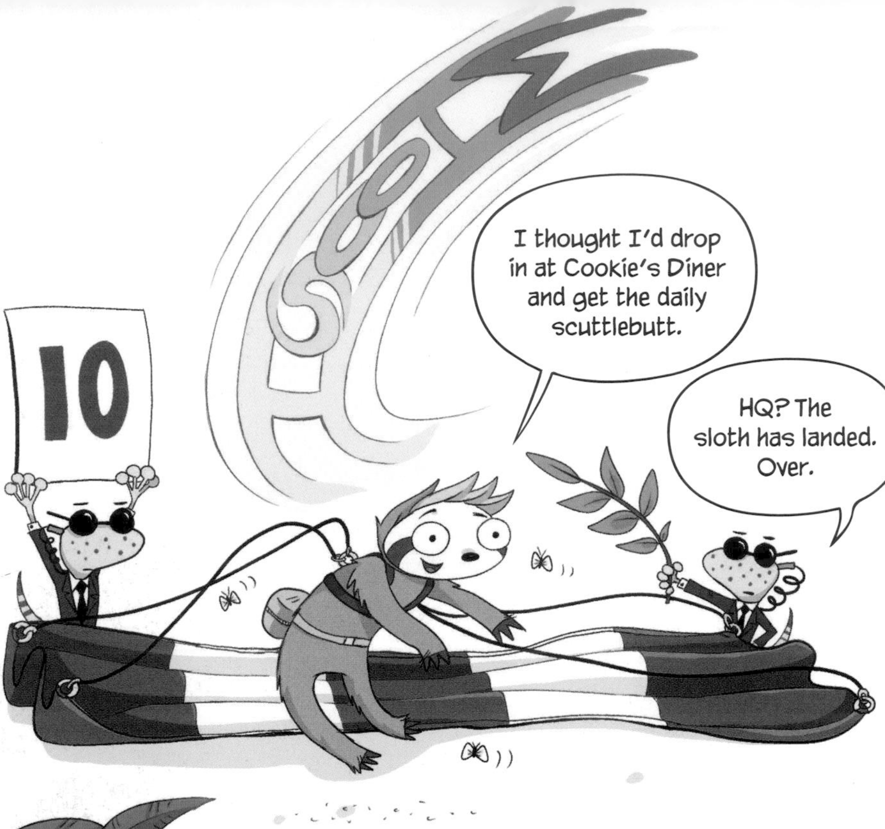
10
I thought I'd drop in at Cookie's Diner and get the daily scuttlebutt.
HQ? The sloth has landed. Over.

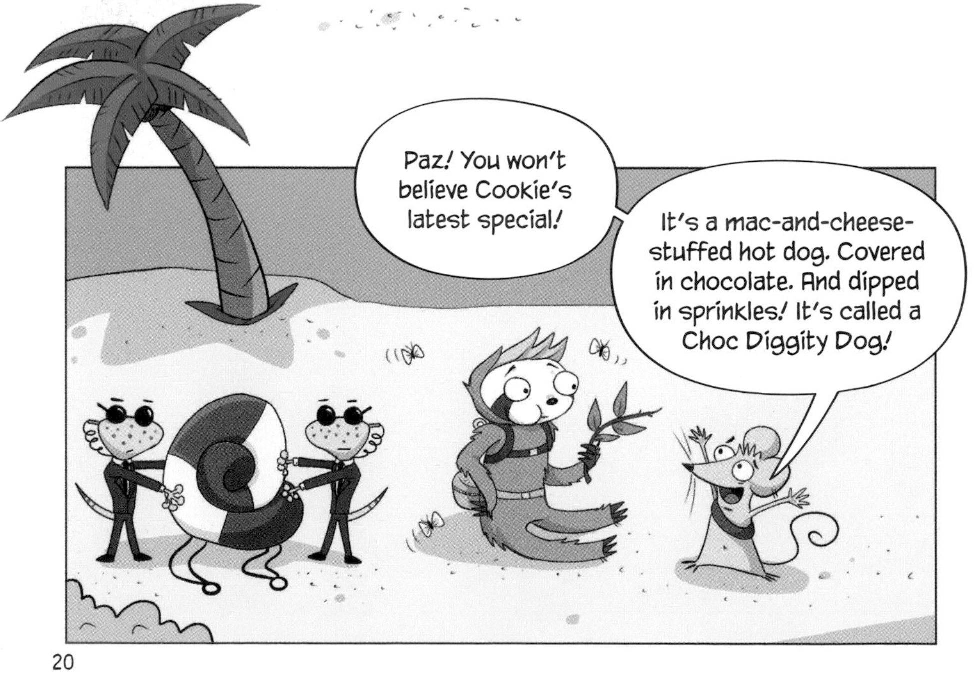
Paz! You won't believe Cookie's latest special!
It's a mac-and-cheese-stuffed hot dog. Covered in chocolate. And dipped in sprinkles! It's called a Choc Diggity Dog!

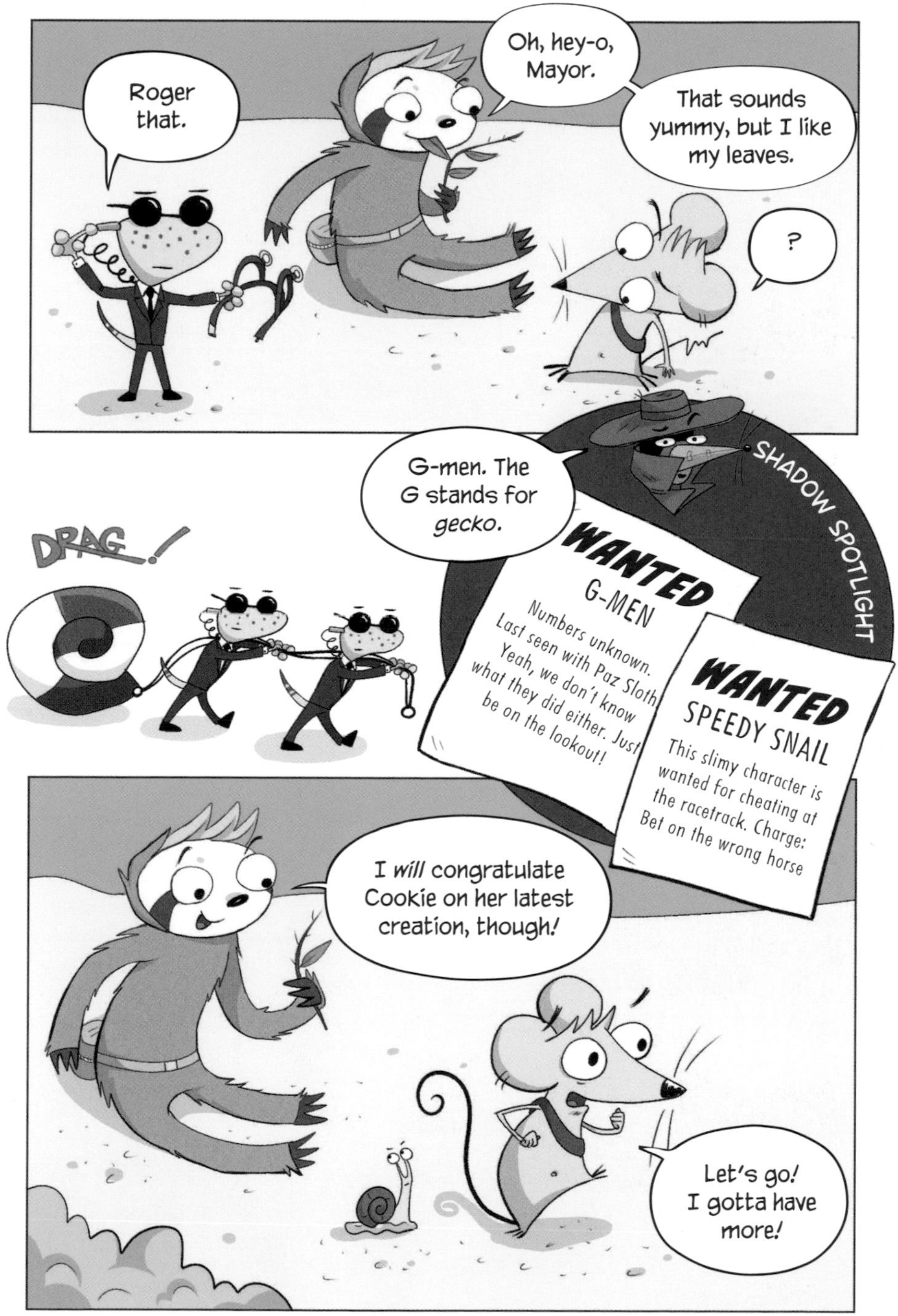
Roger that.
Oh, hey-o, Mayor.
That sounds yummy, but I like my leaves.
?
DRAG!
G-men. The G stands for *gecko*.
SHADOW SPOTLIGHT
WANTED
G-MEN
Numbers unknown. Last seen with Paz Sloth. Yeah, we don't know what they did either. Just be on the lookout!
WANTED
SPEEDY SNAIL
This slimy character is wanted for cheating at the racetrack. Charge: Bet on the wrong horse
I *will* congratulate Cookie on her latest creation, though!
Let's go! I gotta have more!

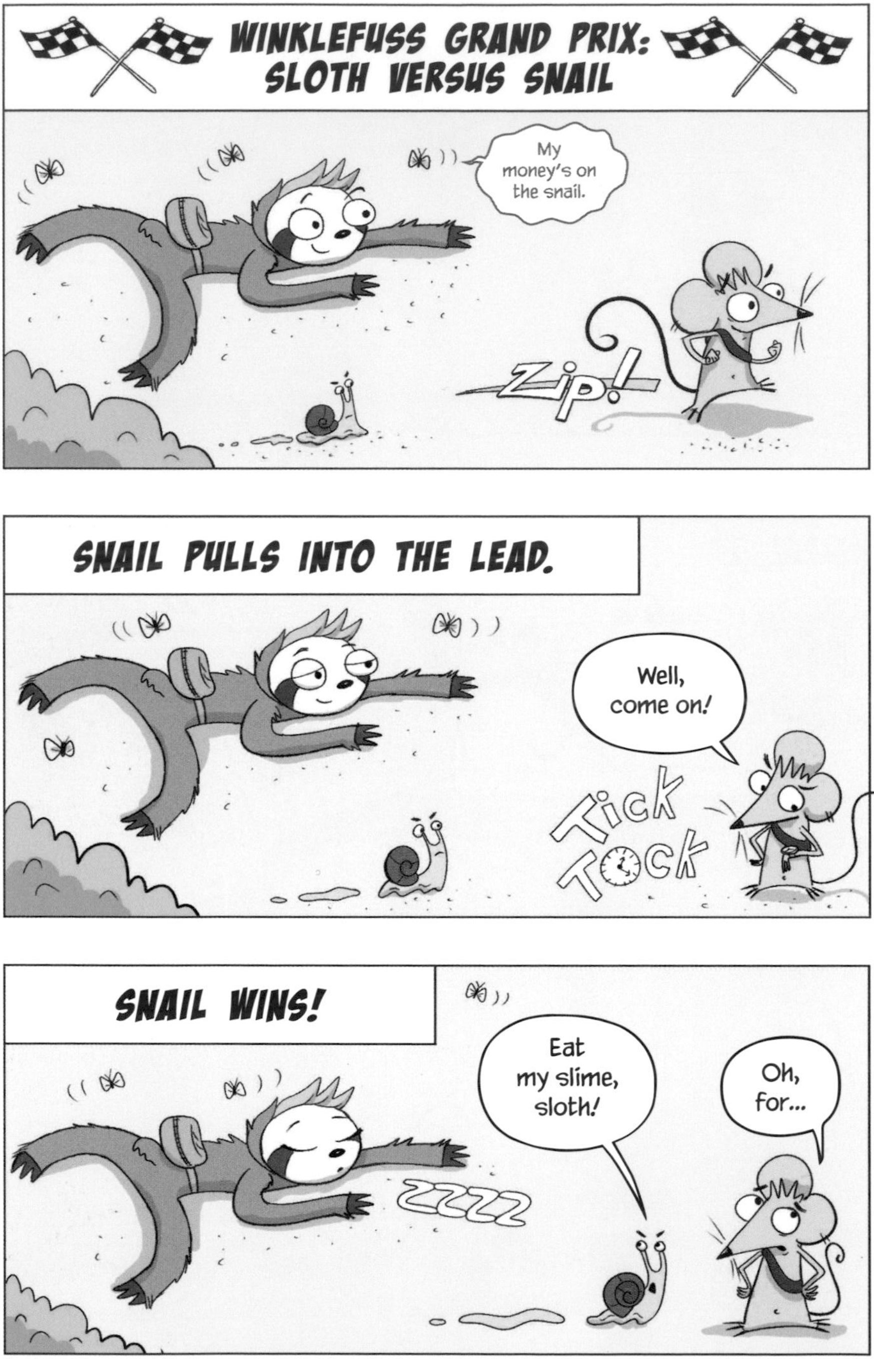
WINKLEFUSS GRAND PRIX: SLOTH VERSUS SNAIL
My money's on the snail.
ZIP!
SNAIL PULLS INTO THE LEAD.
Well, come on!
TICK TOCK
SNAIL WINS!
Eat my slime, sloth!
Oh, for...
ZZZZ

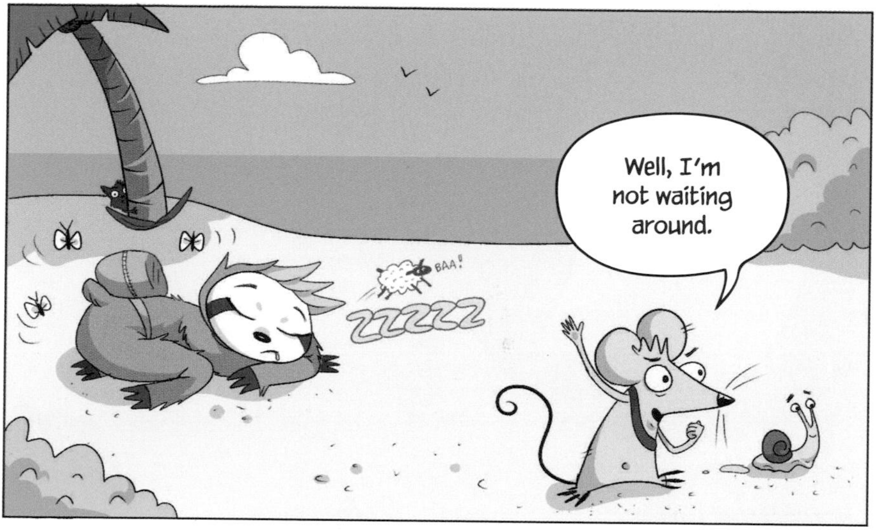
BAA!
ZZZZZZ
Well, I'm not waiting around.

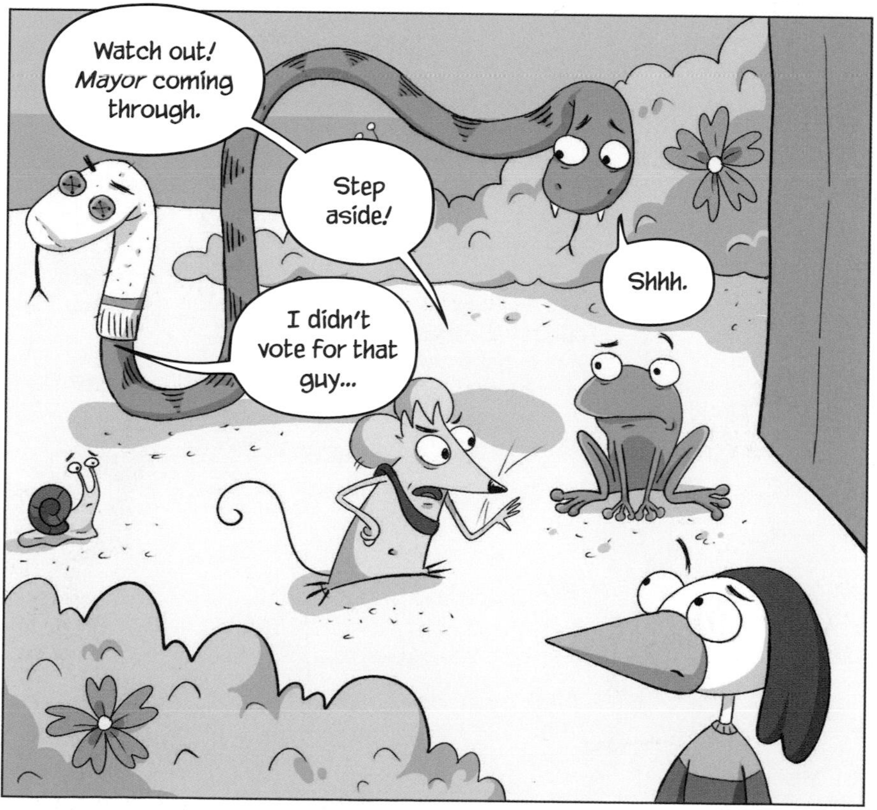
Watch out! *Mayor* coming through.
Step aside!
Shhh.
I didn't vote for that guy...

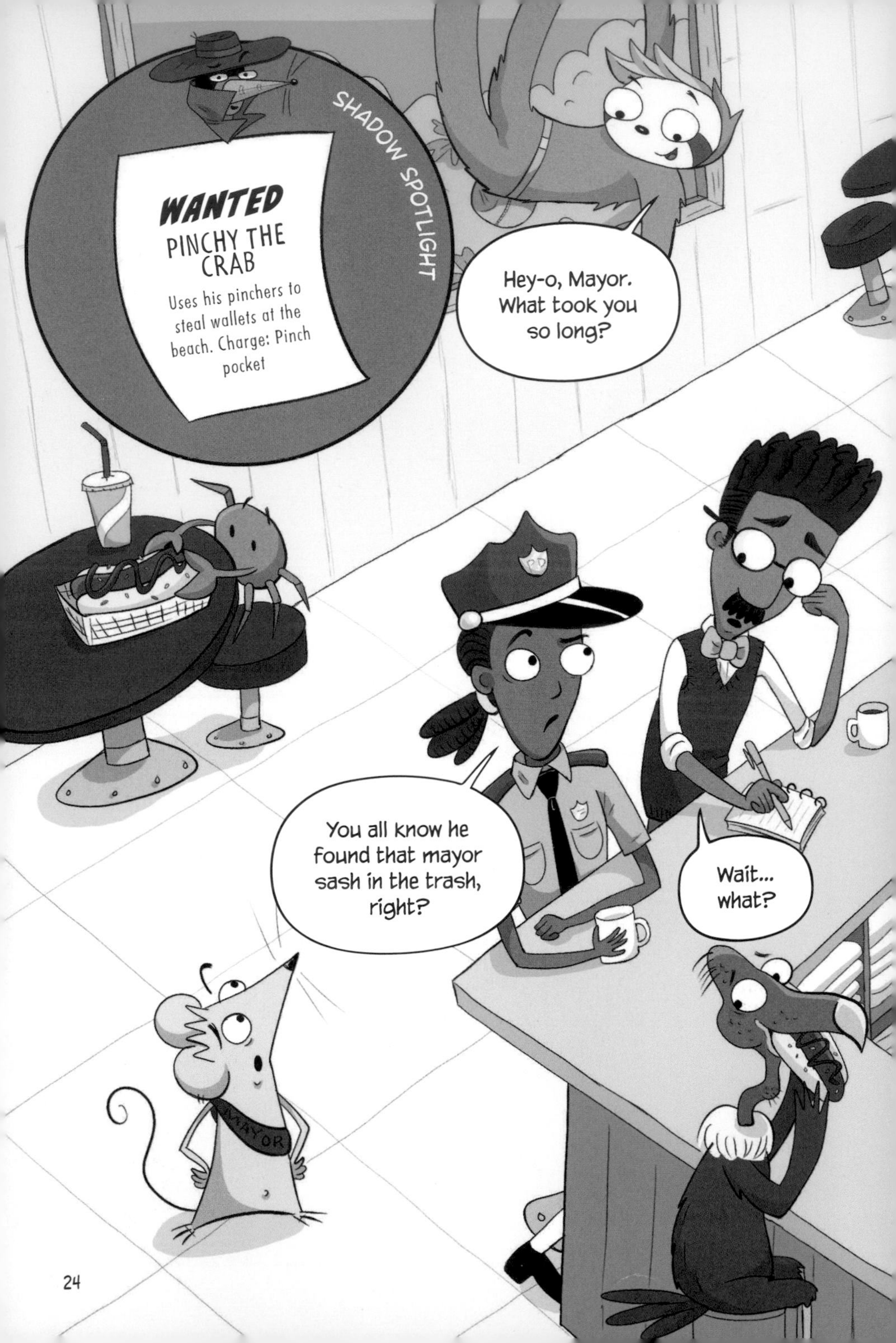
SHADOW SPOTLIGHT
WANTED
PINCHY THE CRAB
Uses his pinchers to steal wallets at the beach. Charge: Pinch pocket
Hey-o, Mayor. What took you so long?
You all know he found that mayor sash in the trash, right?
Wait... what?
MAYOR

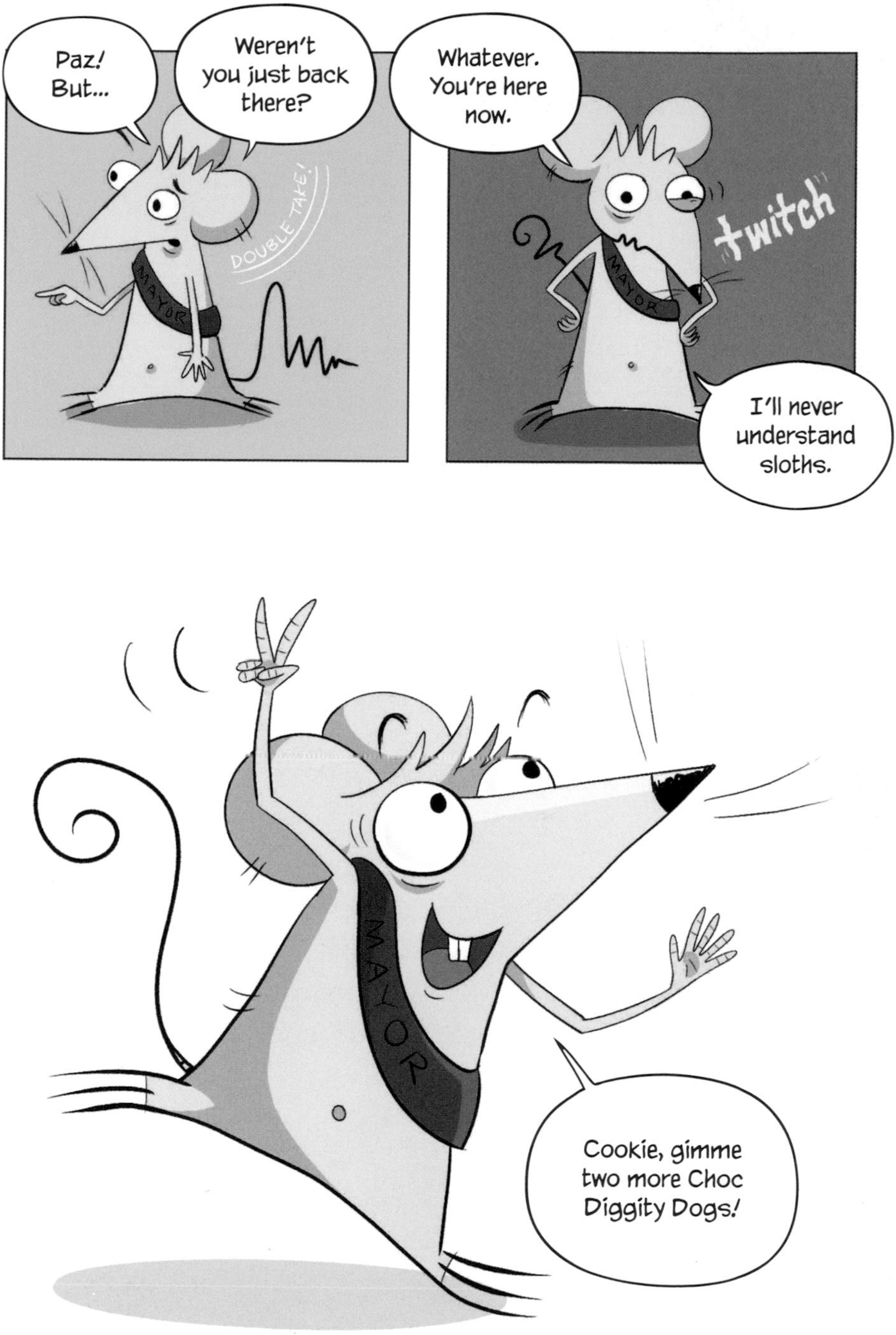
Paz! But...
Weren't you just back there?
MAYOR
DOUBLE TAKE!
Whatever. You're here now.
MAYOR
twitch
I'll never understand sloths.
MAYOR
Cookie, gimme two more Choc Diggity Dogs!

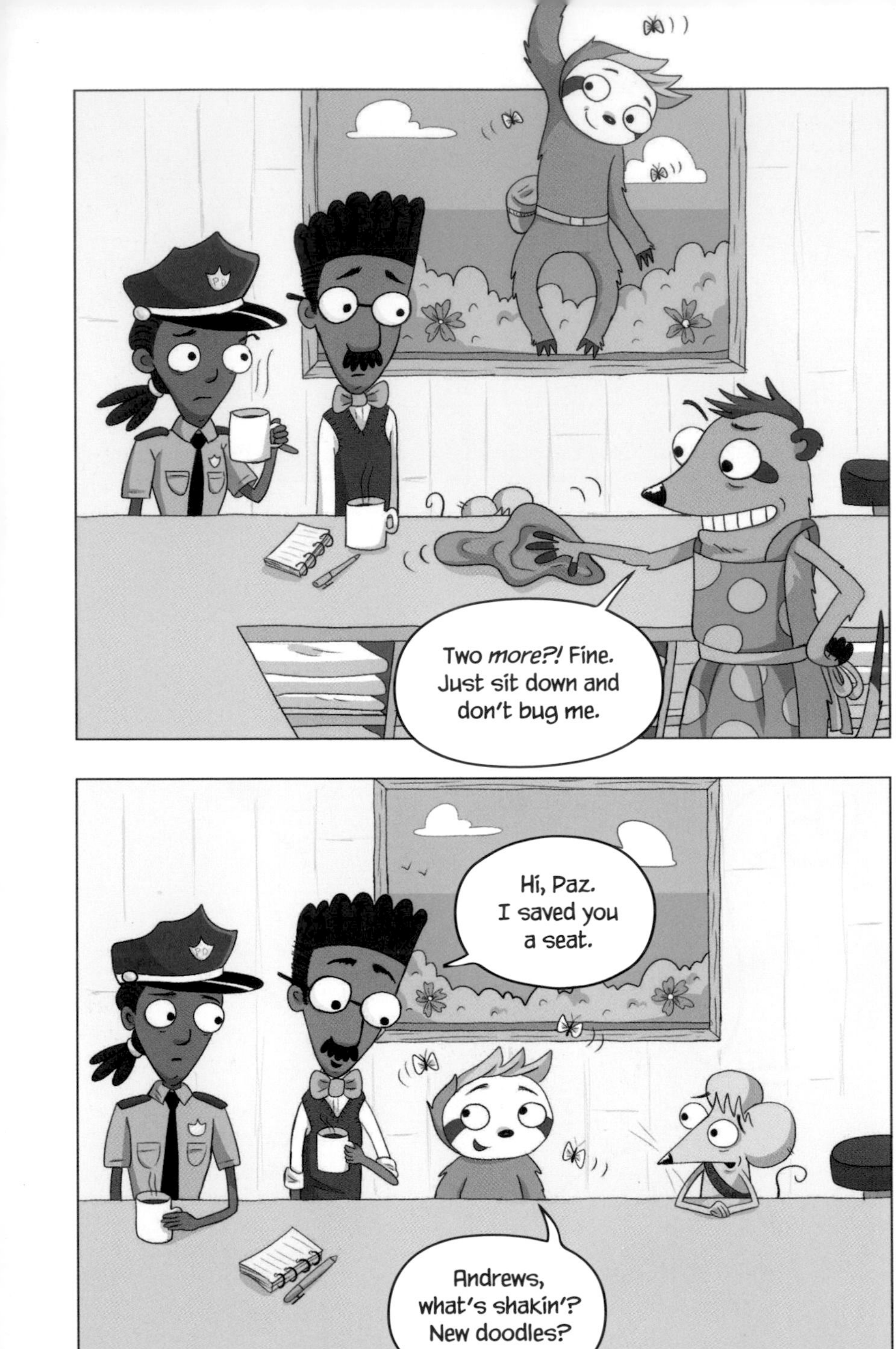
Two *more?!* Fine.
Just sit down and
don't bug me.
Hi, Paz.
I saved you
a seat.
Andrews,
what's shakin'?
New doodles?

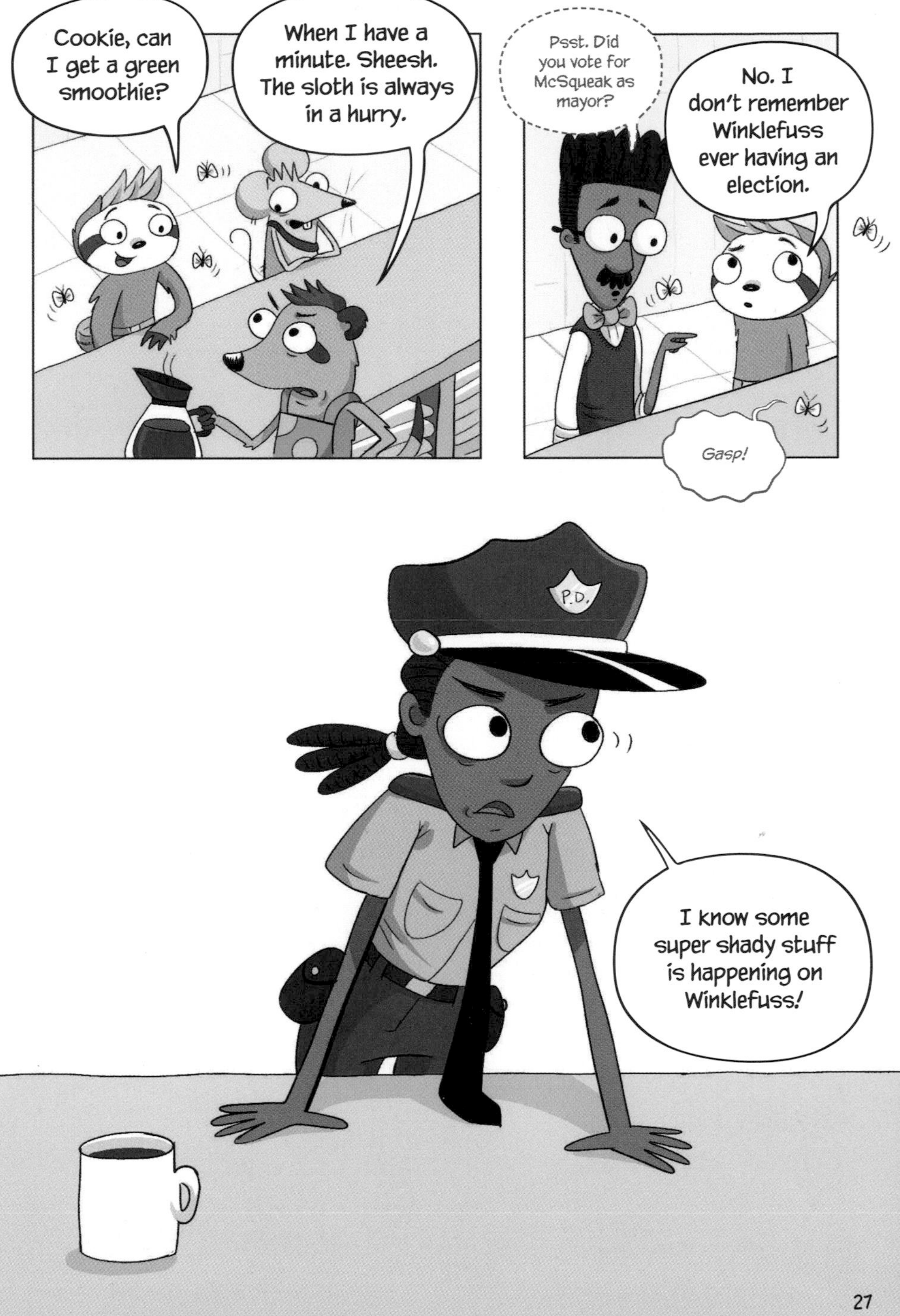
Cookie, can I get a green smoothie?
When I have a minute. Sheesh. The sloth is always in a hurry.
Psst. Did you vote for McSqueak as mayor?
No. I don't remember Winklefuss ever having an election.
Gasp!
P.D.
I know some super shady stuff is happening on Winklefuss!

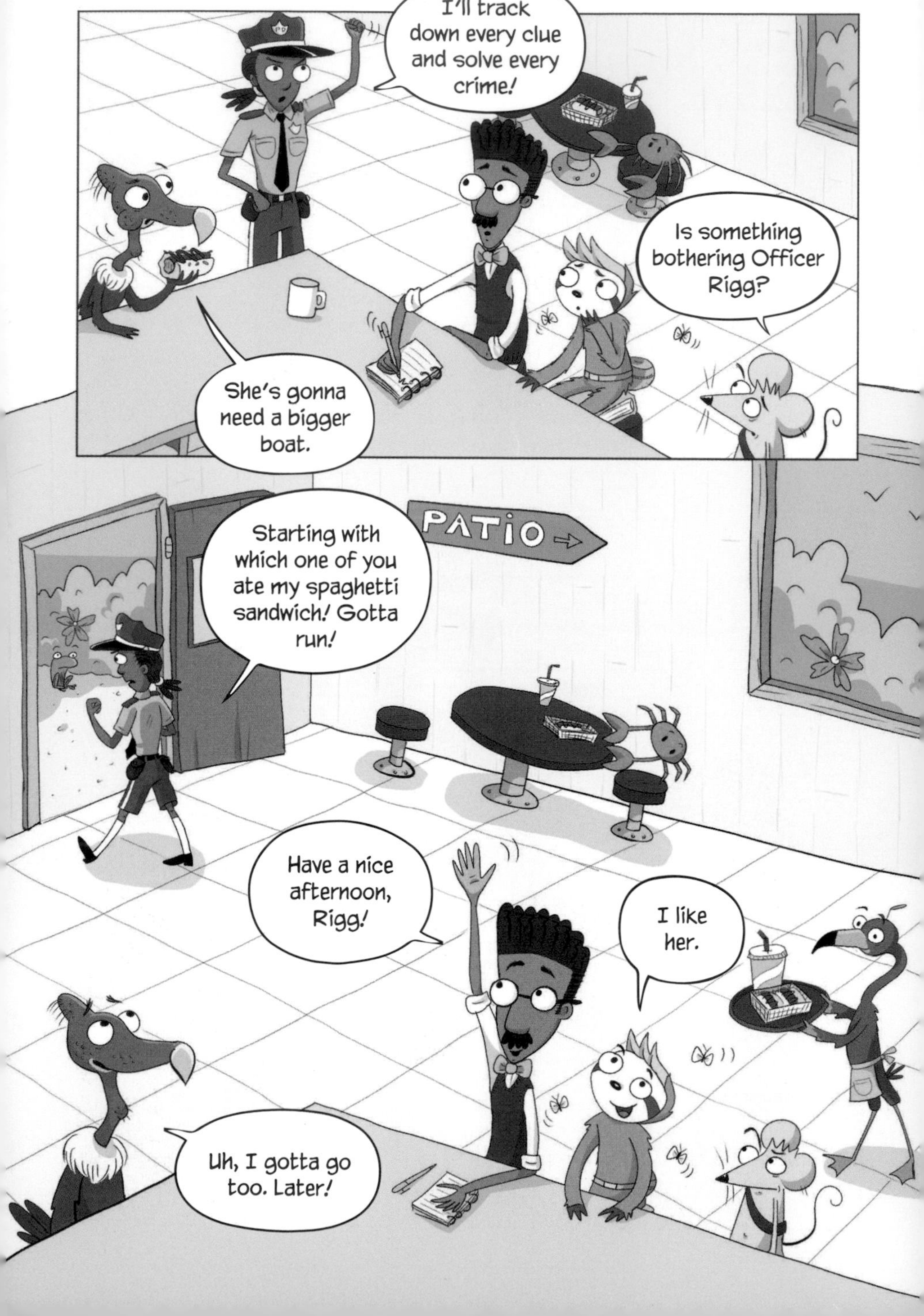

I'll track down every clue and solve every crime!
Is something bothering Officer Rigg?
She's gonna need a bigger boat.
PATIO
Starting with which one of you ate my spaghetti sandwich! Gotta run!
Have a nice afternoon, Rigg!
I like her.
Uh, I gotta go too. Later!

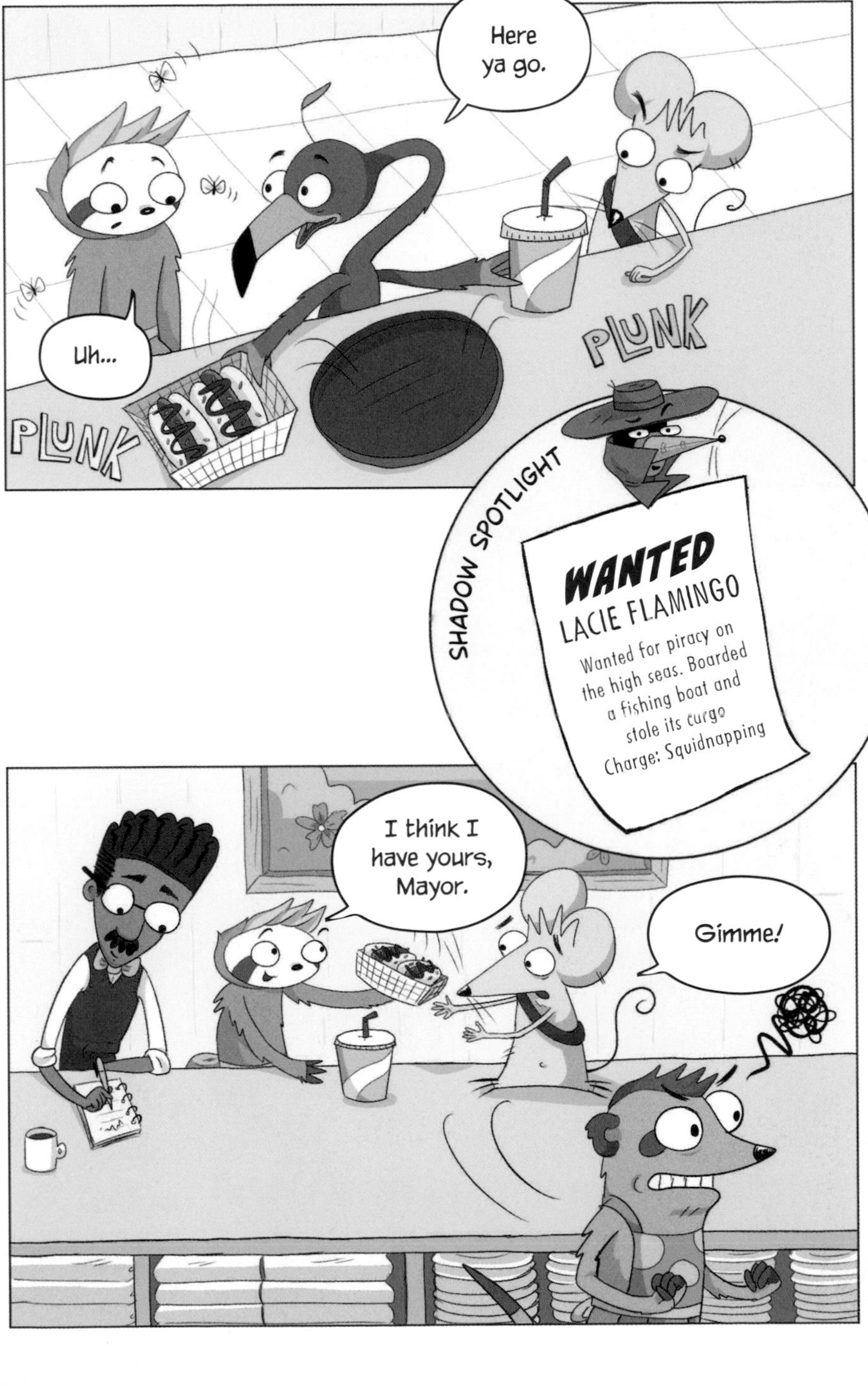
Here ya go.
Uh...
PLUNK
PLUNK
SHADOW SPOTLIGHT
WANTED
LACIE FLAMINGO
Wanted for piracy on the high seas. Boarded a fishing boat and stole its cargo
Charge: Squidnapping
I think I have yours, Mayor.
Gimme!

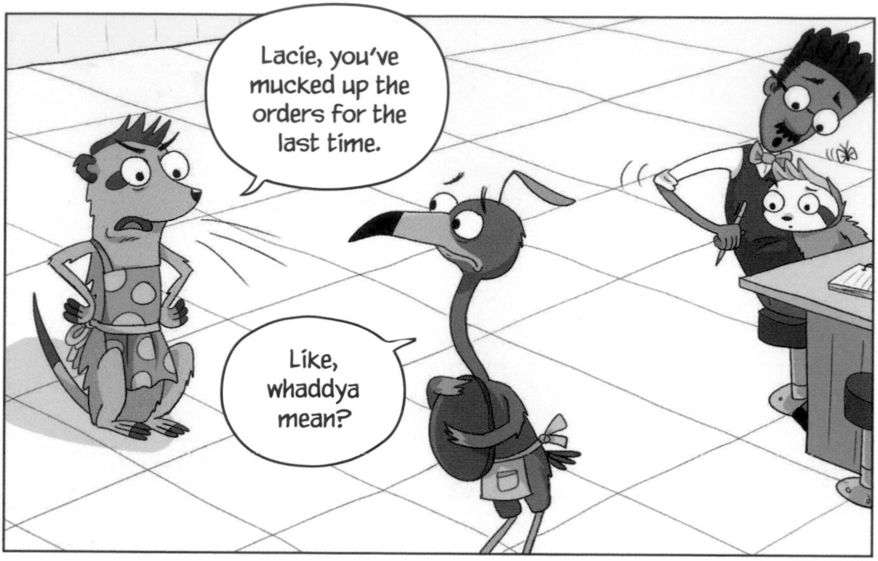
Lacie, you've mucked up the orders for the last time.
Like, whaddya mean?

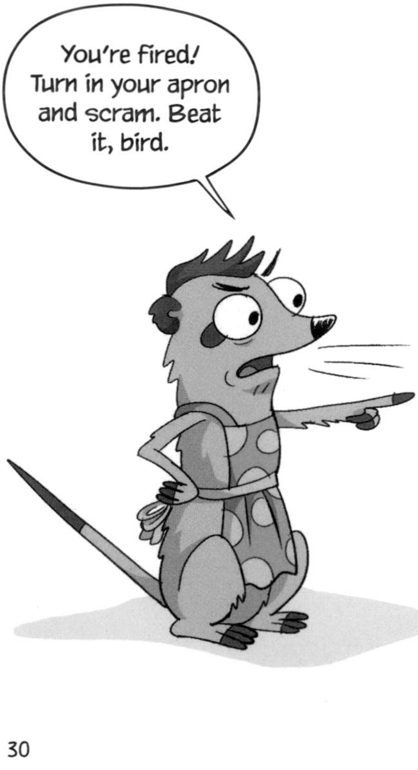
You're fired! Turn in your apron and scram. Beat it, bird.

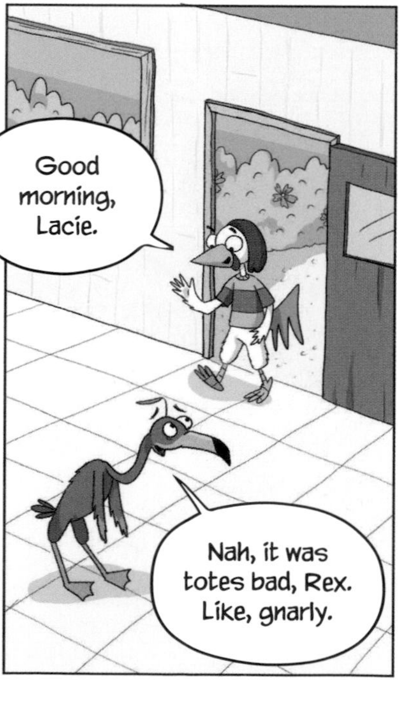
Good morning, Lacie.
Nah, it was totes bad, Rex. Like, gnarly.

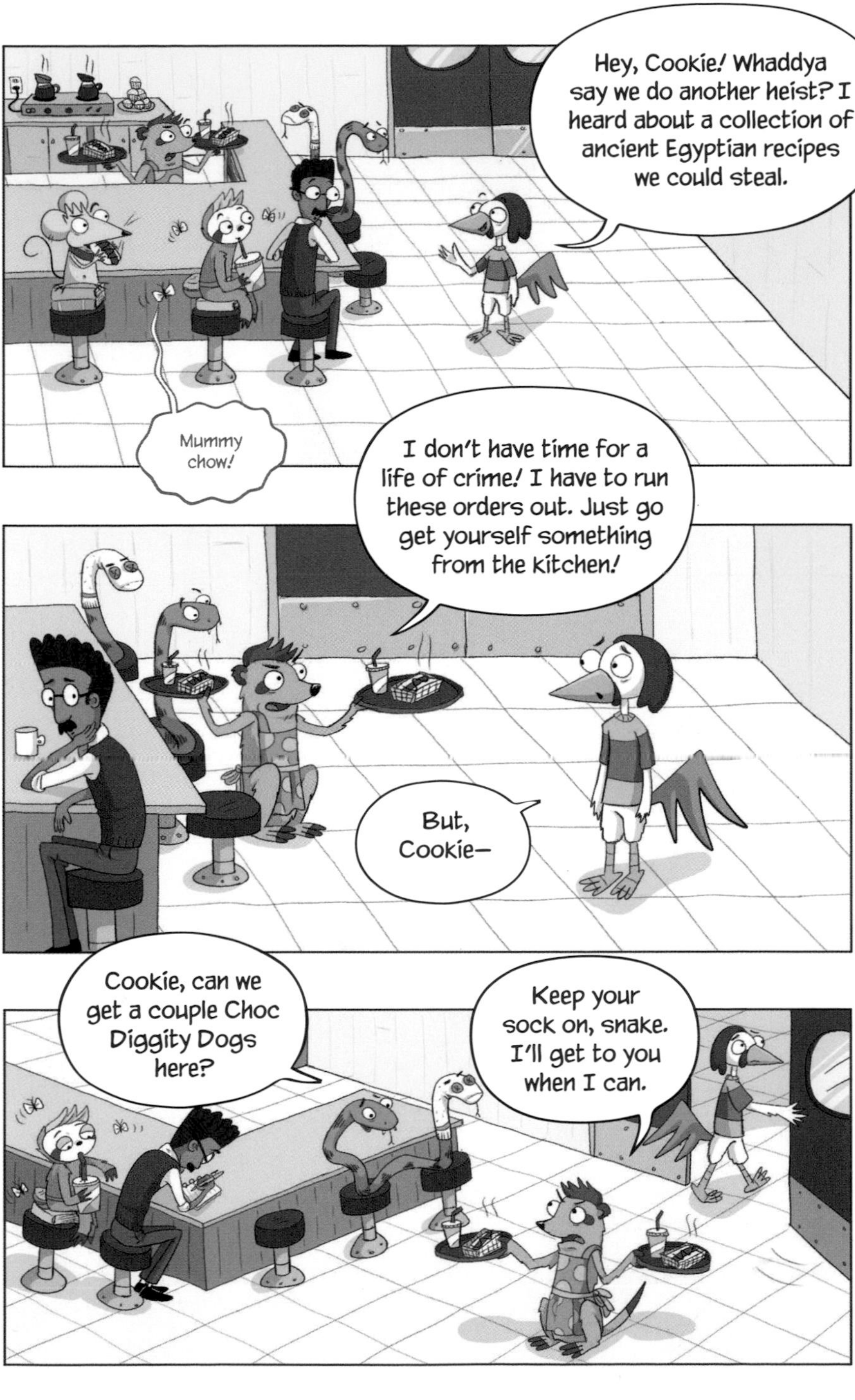
Hey, Cookie! Whaddya say we do another heist? I heard about a collection of ancient Egyptian recipes we could steal.
Mummy chow!
I don't have time for a life of crime! I have to run these orders out. Just go get yourself something from the kitchen!
But, Cookie—
Cookie, can we get a couple Choc Diggity Dogs here?
Keep your sock on, snake. I'll get to you when I can.

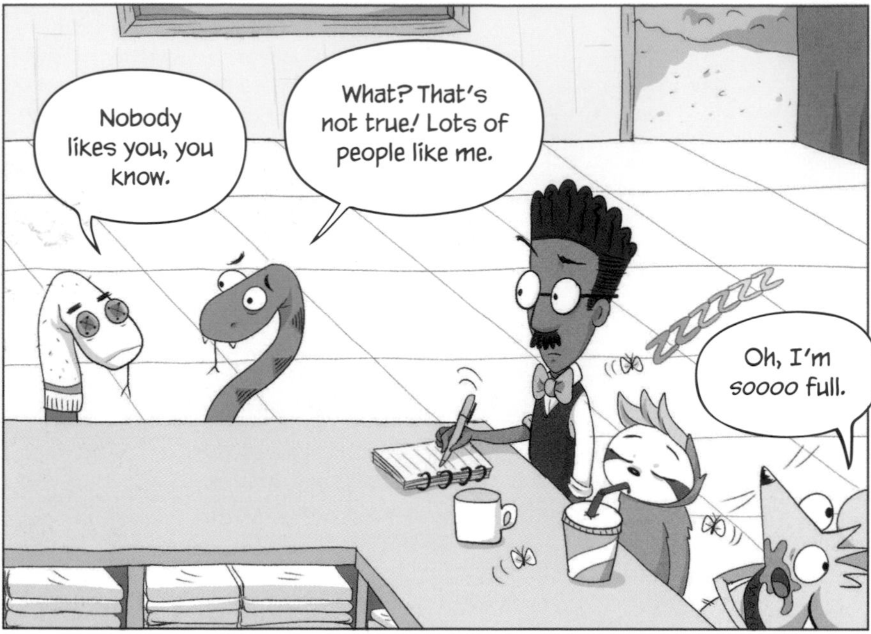
Nobody likes you, you know.
What? That's not true! Lots of people like me.
ZZZZZZ
Oh, I'm *soooo* full.

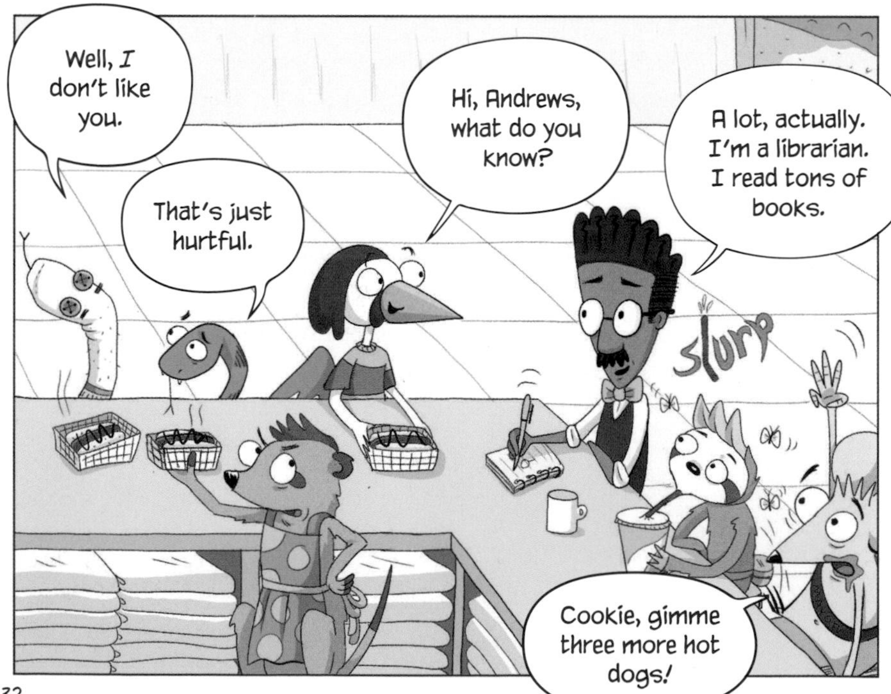
Well, *I* don't like you.
That's just hurtful.
Hi, Andrews, what do you know?
A lot, actually. I'm a librarian. I read tons of books.
slurp
Cookie, gimme three more hot dogs!

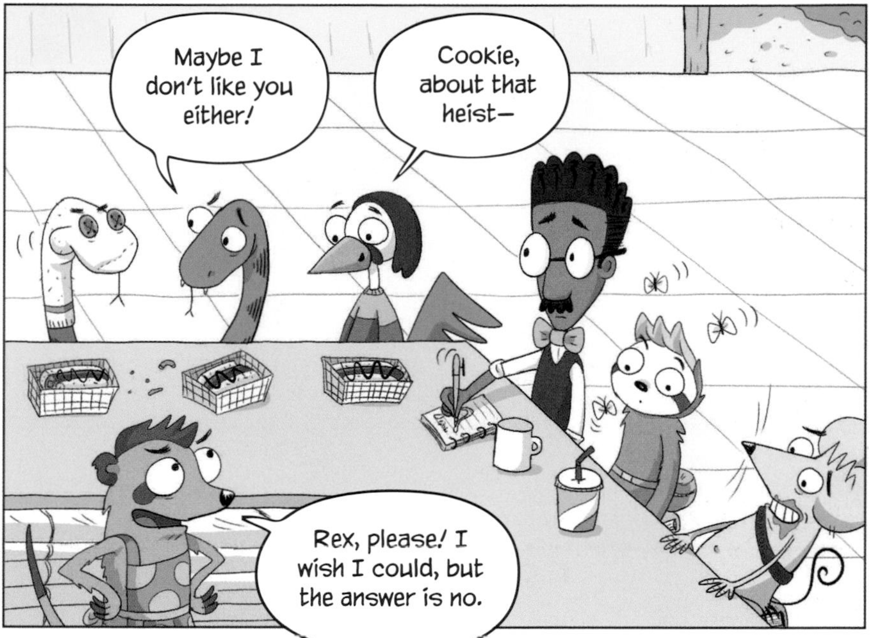
Maybe I don't like you either!
Cookie, about that heist—
Rex, please! I wish I could, but the answer is no.

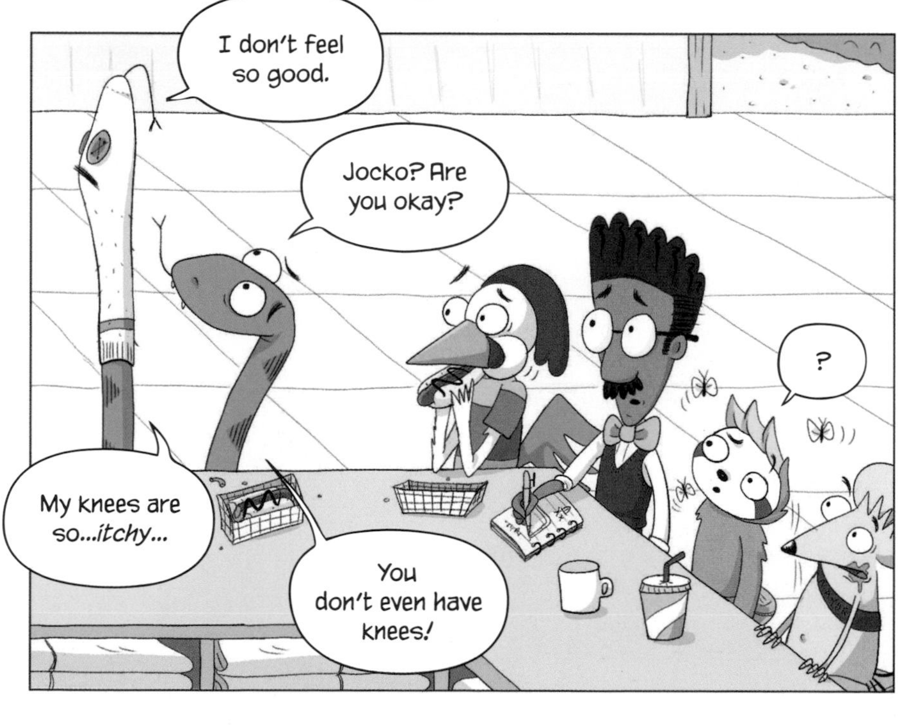
I don't feel so good.
Jocko? Are you okay?
?
My knees are so...*itchy*...
You don't even have knees!

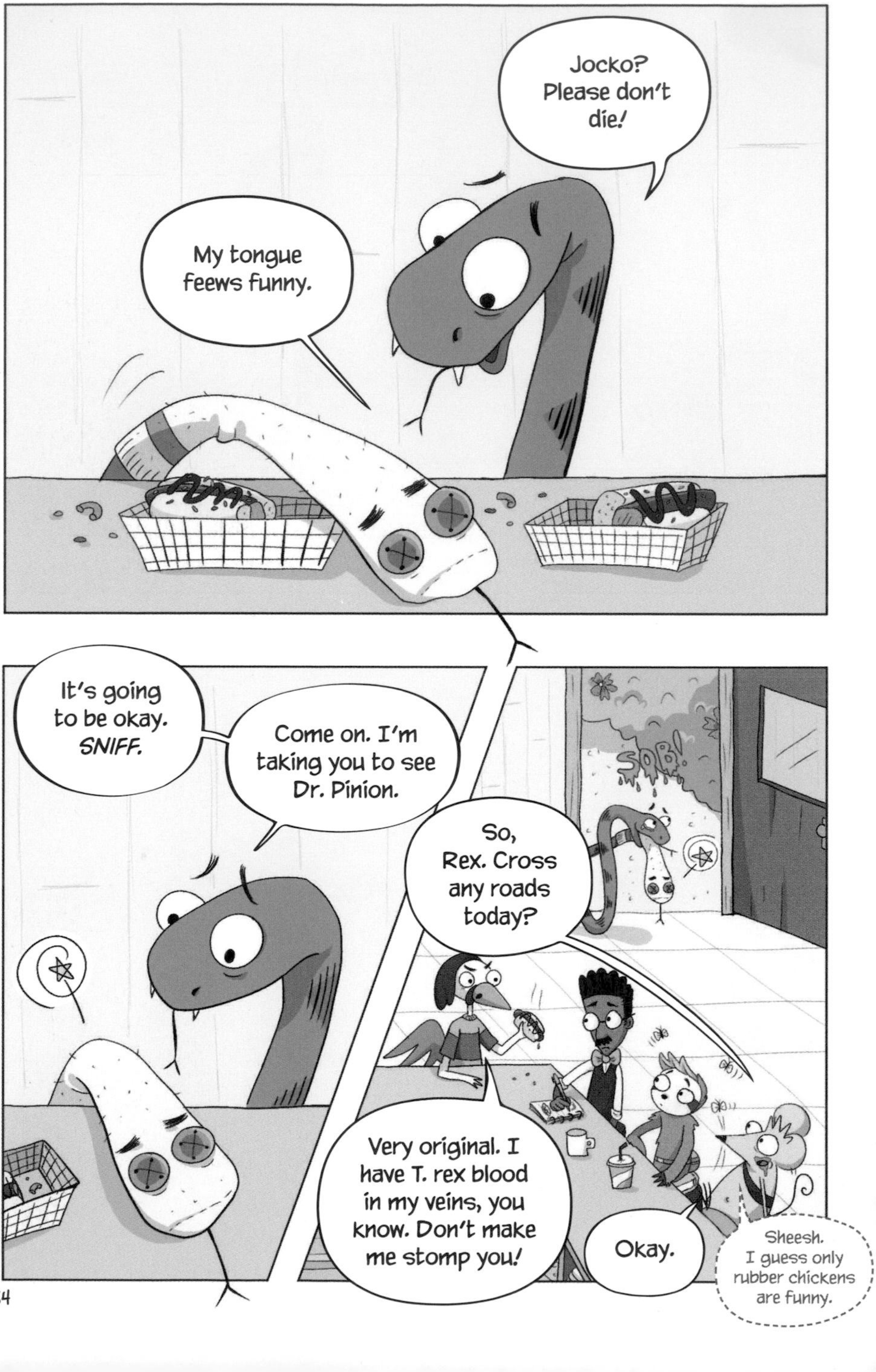
Jocko? Please don't die!
My tongue feews funny.
It's going to be okay. SNIFF.
Come on. I'm taking you to see Dr. Pinion.
SOB!
So, Rex. Cross any roads today?
Very original. I have T. rex blood in my veins, you know. Don't make me stomp you!
Okay.
Sheesh. I guess only rubber chickens are funny.

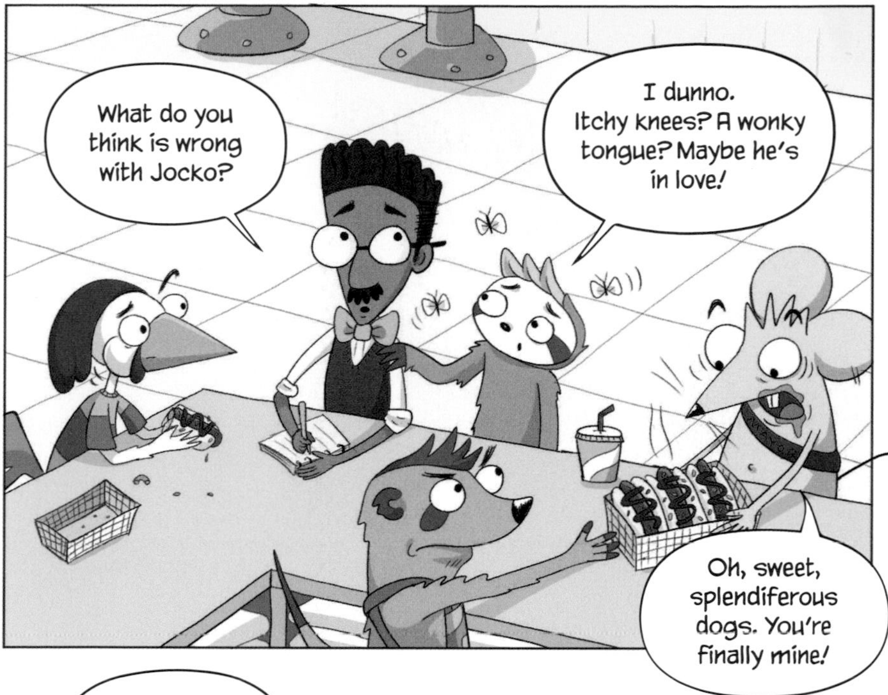
What do you think is wrong with Jocko?
I dunno. Itchy knees? A wonky tongue? Maybe he's in love!
Oh, sweet, splendiferous dogs. You're finally mine!

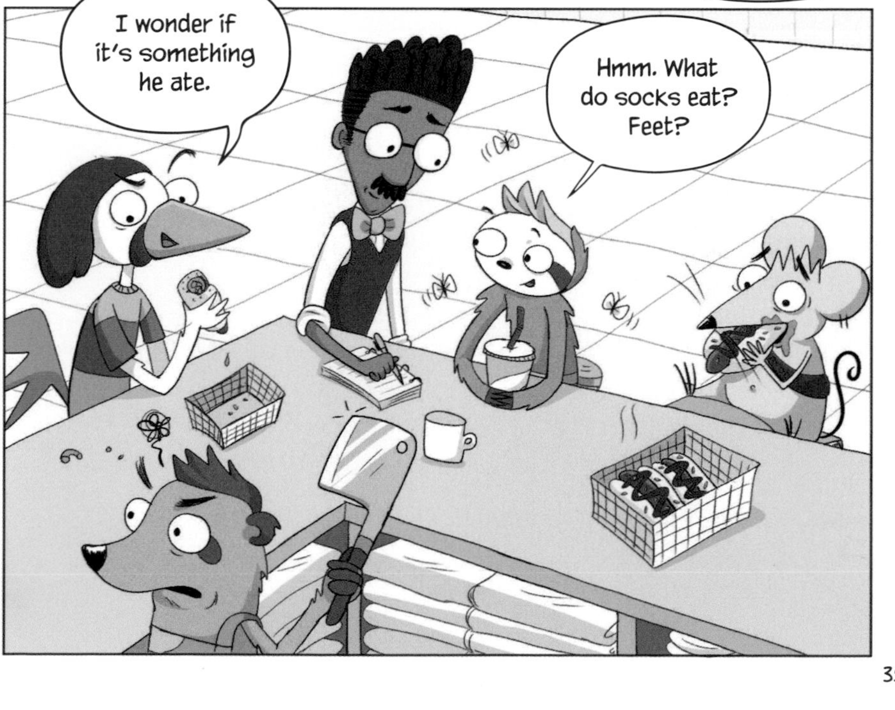
I wonder if it's something he ate.
Hmm. What do socks eat? Feet?

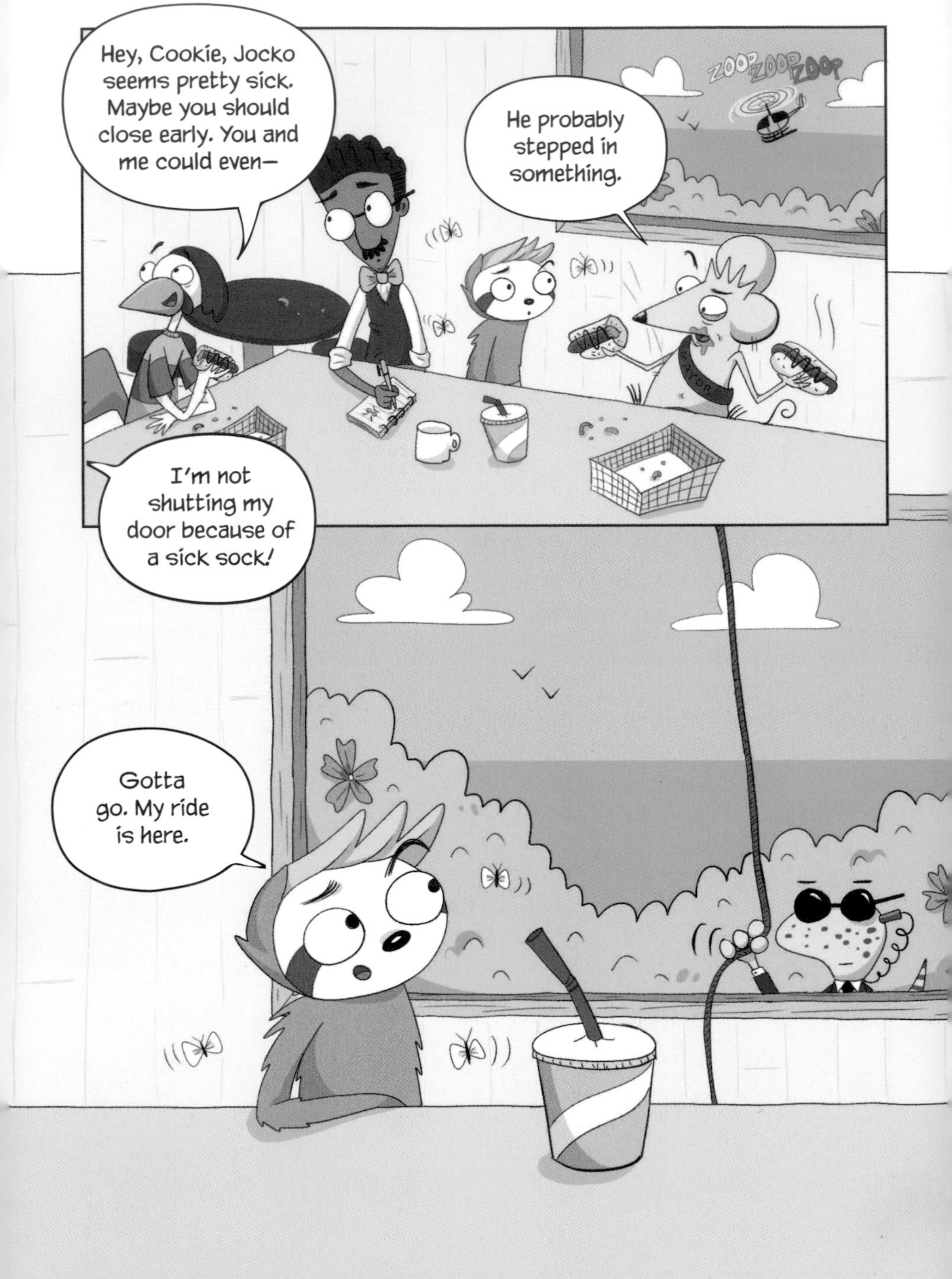
Hey, Cookie, Jocko seems pretty sick. Maybe you should close early. You and me could even—
ZOOP ZOOP ZOOP
He probably stepped in something.
I'm not shutting my door because of a sick sock!
Gotta go. My ride is here.

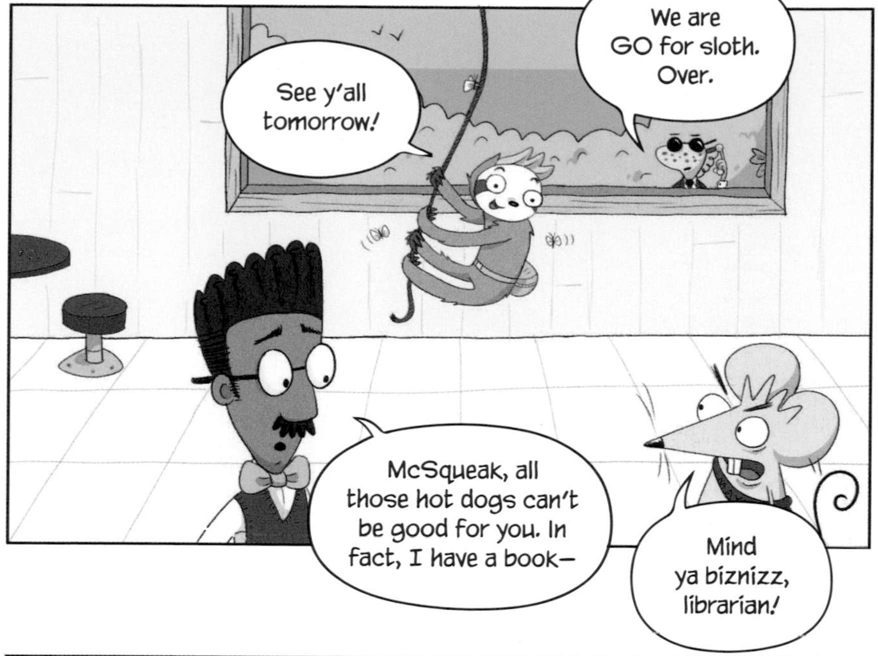
See y'all tomorrow!
We are GO for sloth. Over.
McSqueak, all those hot dogs can't be good for you. In fact, I have a book—
Mind ya biznizz, librarian!

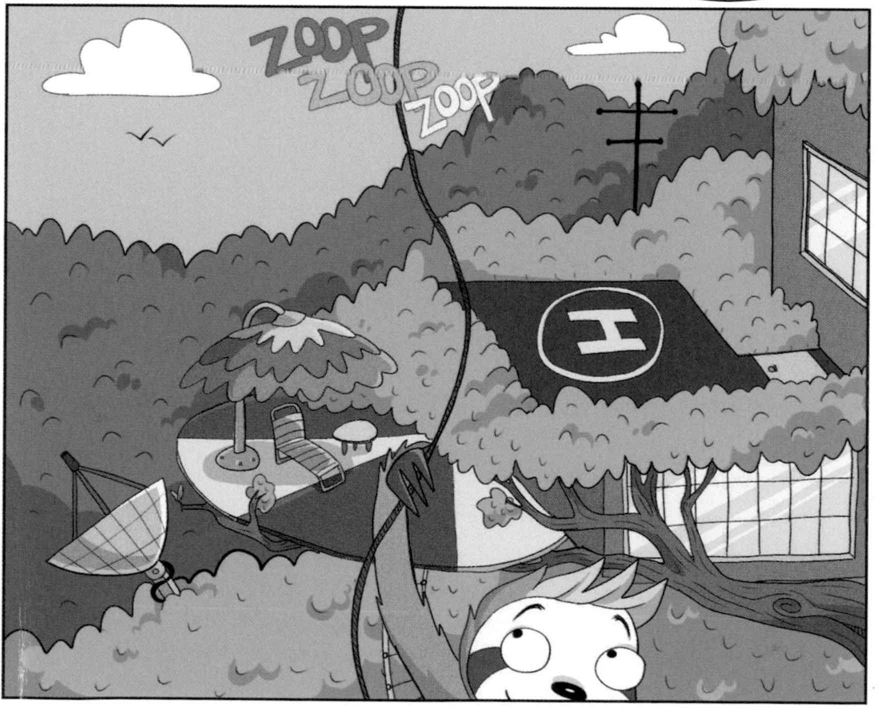
ZOOP
ZOOP
ZOOP

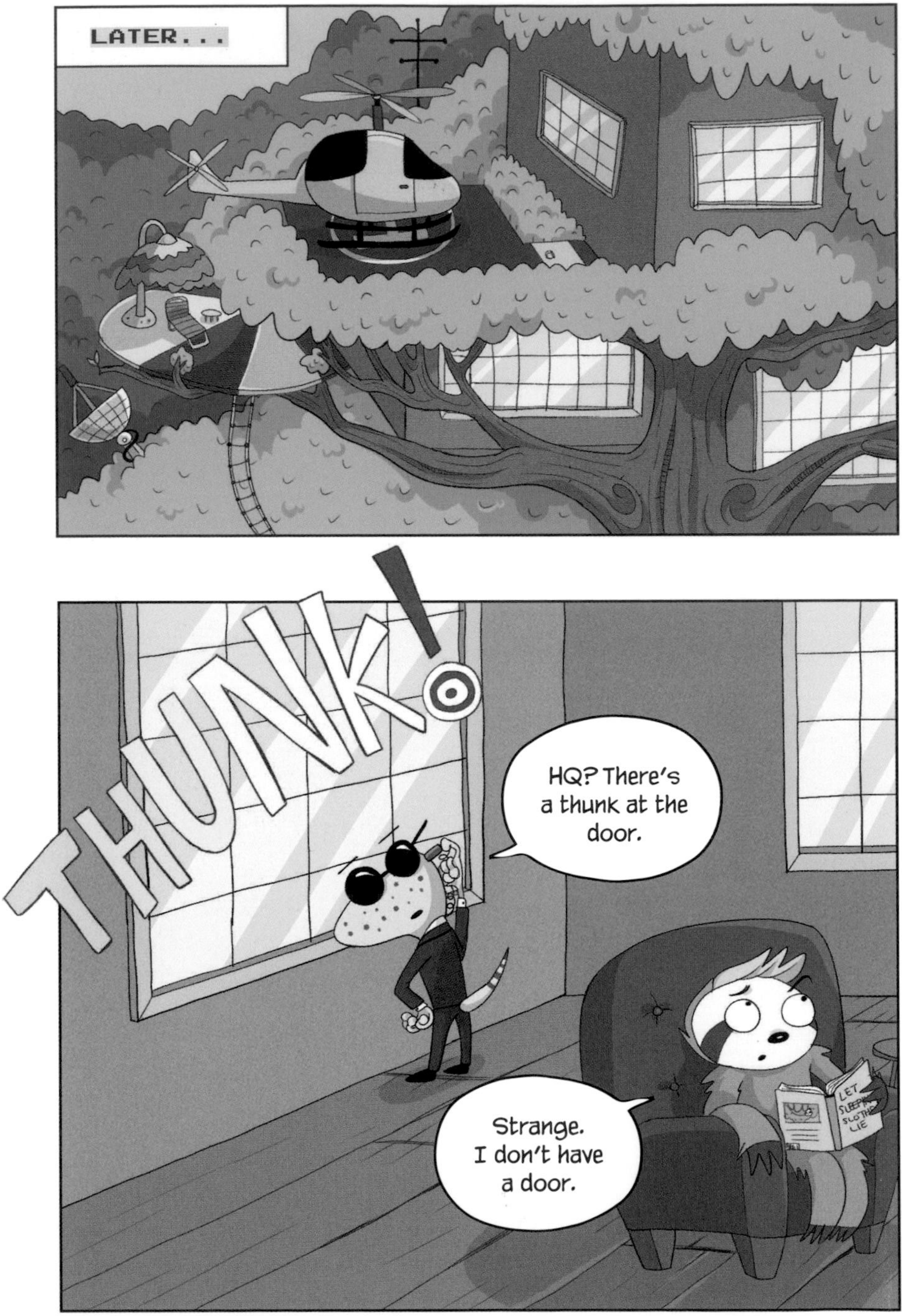
LATER...
THUNK!
HQ? There's a thunk at the door.
Strange. I don't have a door.

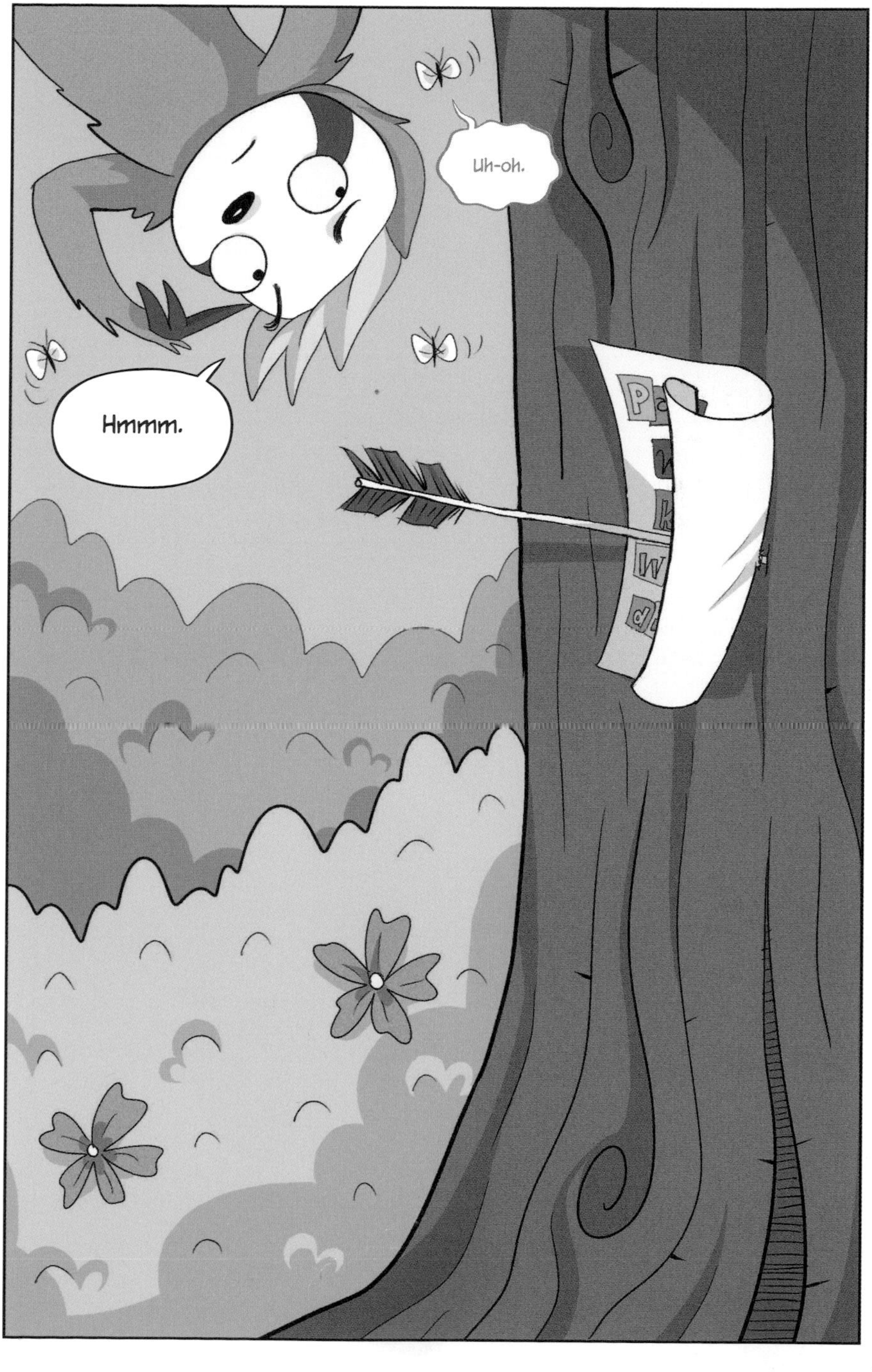
Uh-oh.
Hmmm.

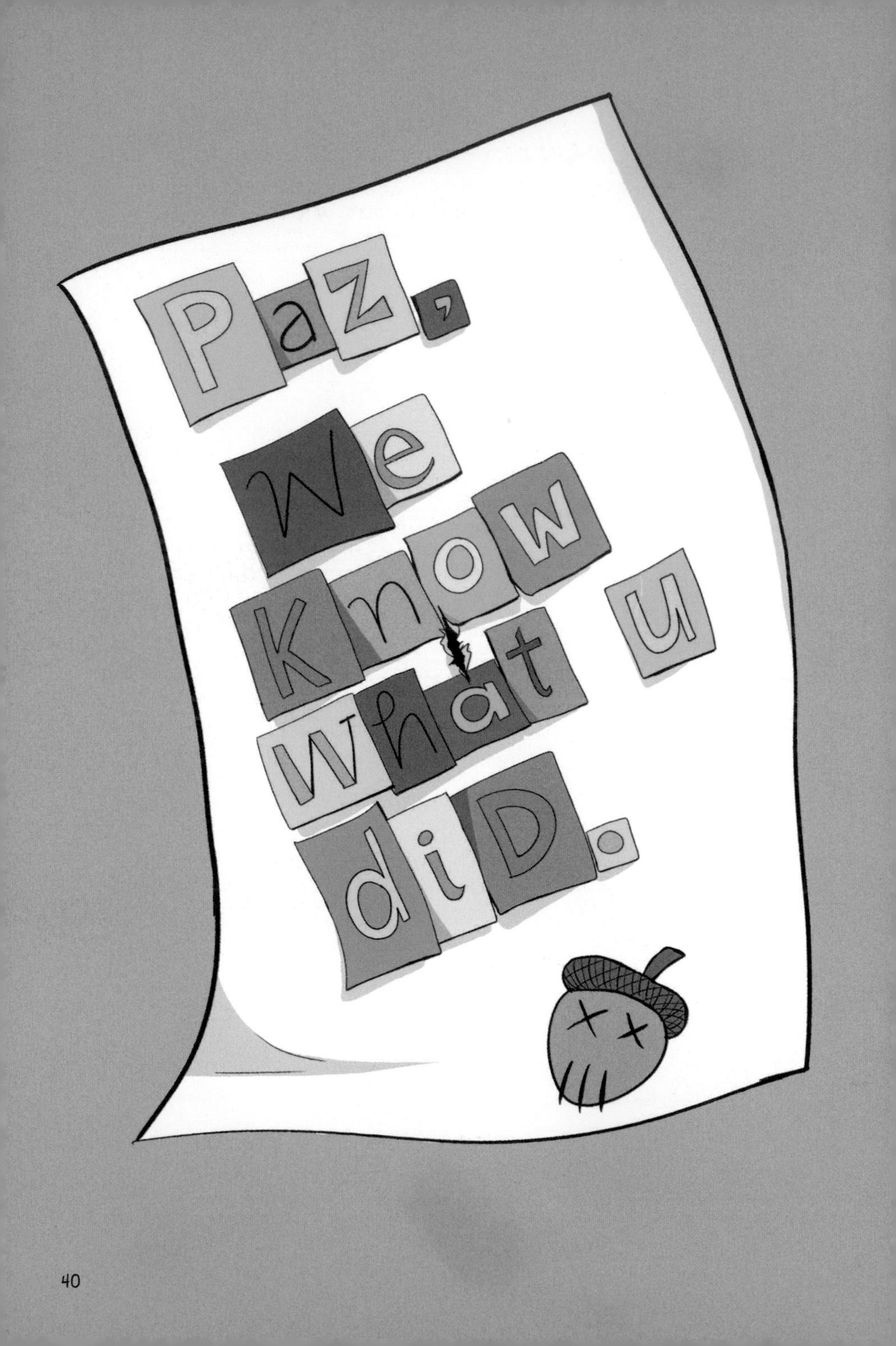
PaZ,
We Know
What u
diD.

CHAPTER 2

TUESDAY. EARLY MORNING.
HANGING OUT IN THE TREEHOUSE.

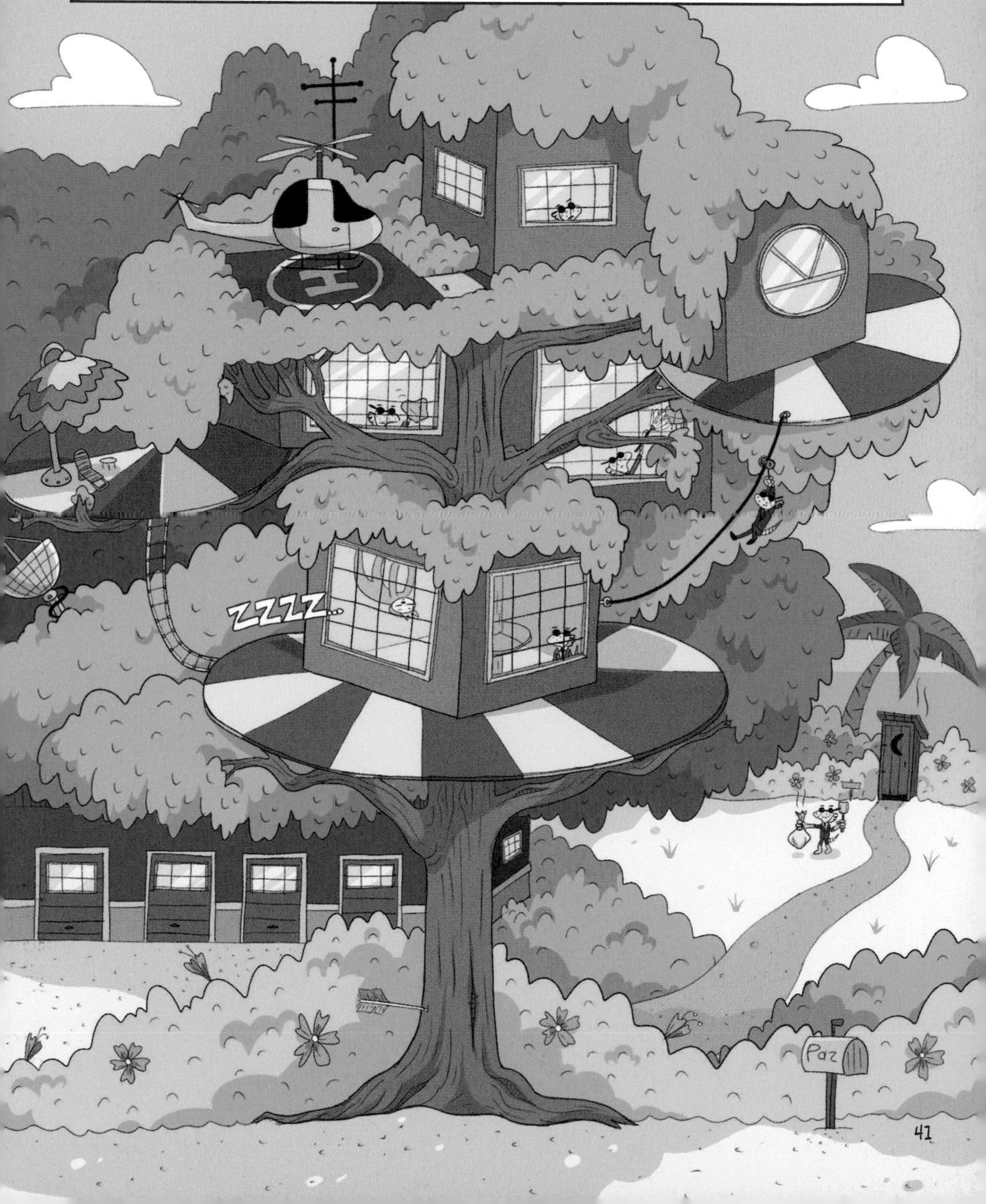
ZZZZ...
Paz

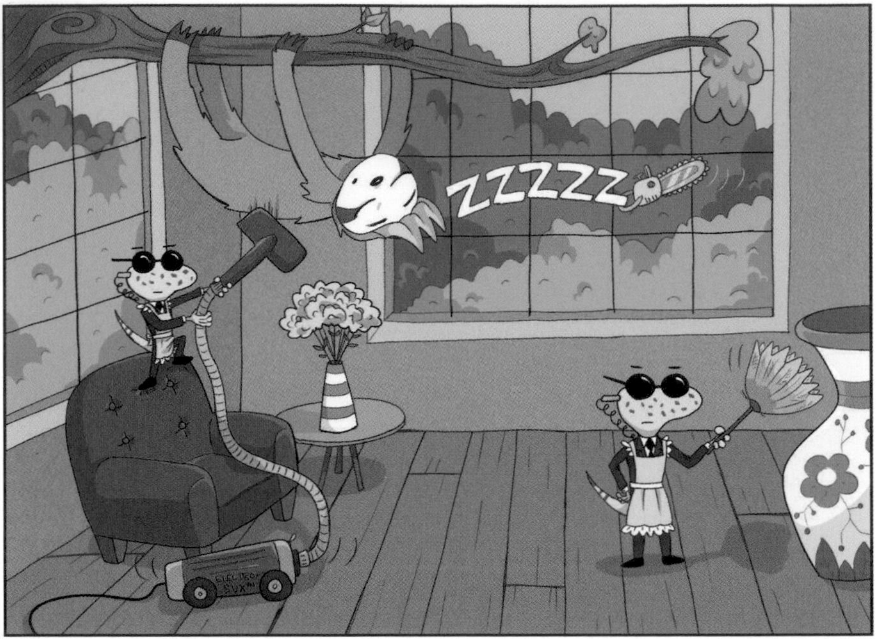
ZZZZZ

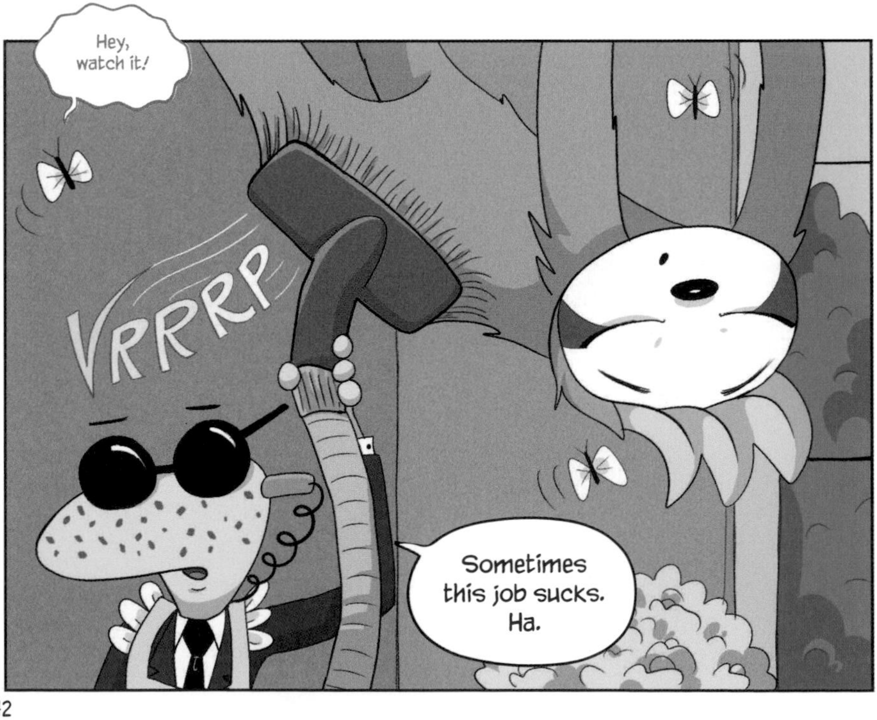
Hey, watch it!
VRRRP
Sometimes this job sucks. Ha.

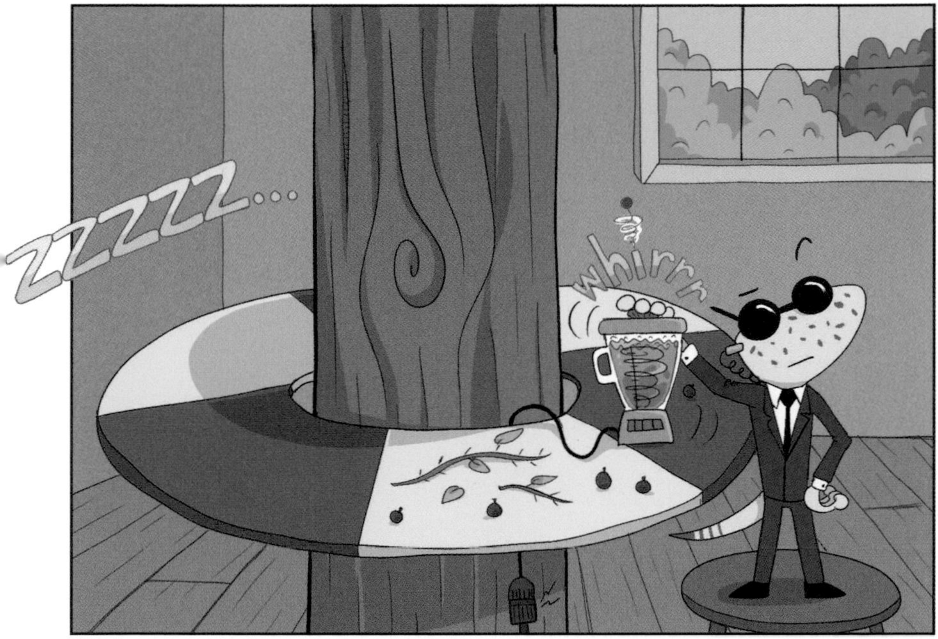
ZZZZZZ...
whirrrr

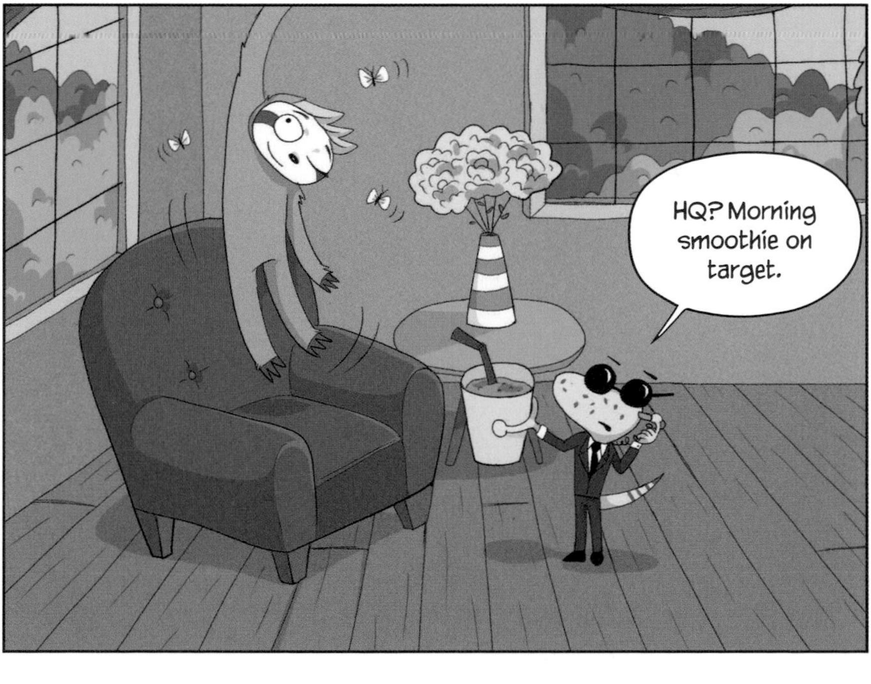
HQ? Morning smoothie on target.

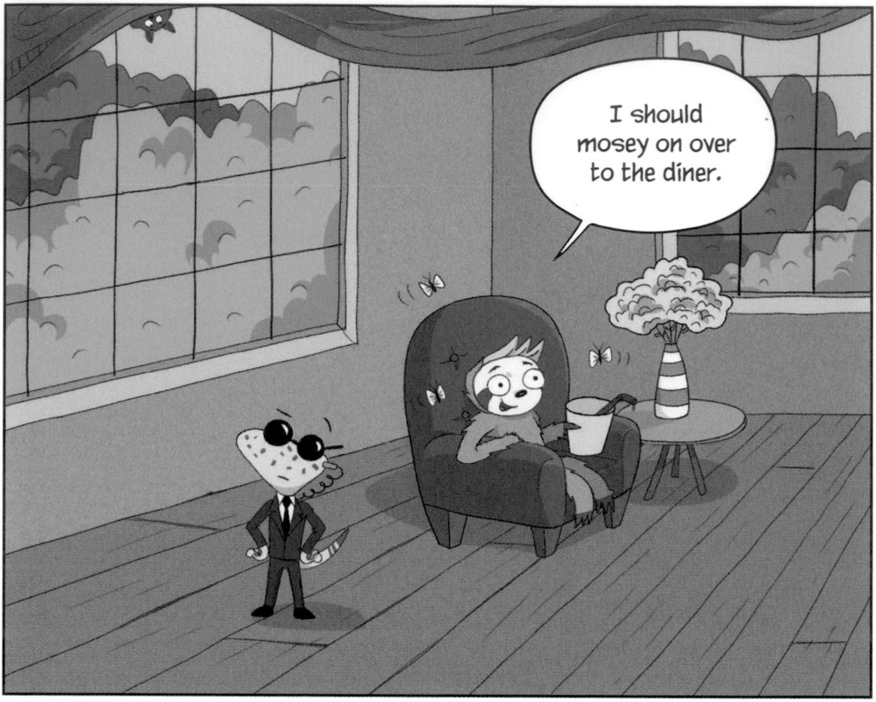
I should mosey on over to the diner.

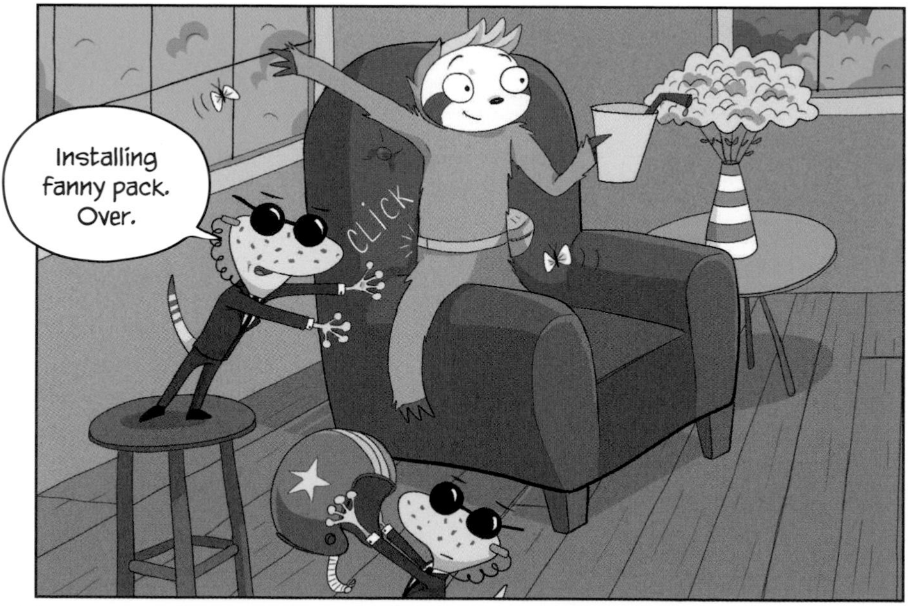
Installing fanny pack. Over.
CLICK

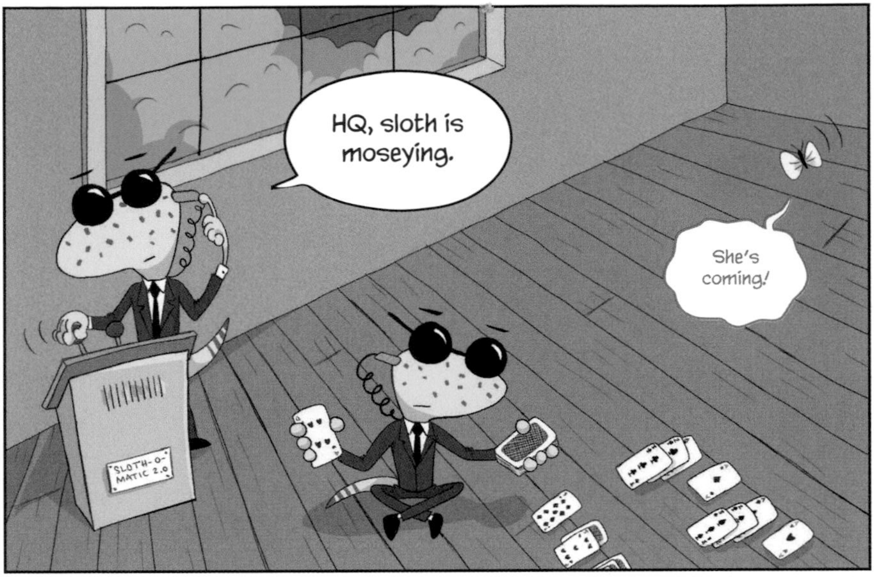
HQ, sloth is moseying.
She's coming!
SLOTH-O-MATIC 2.0

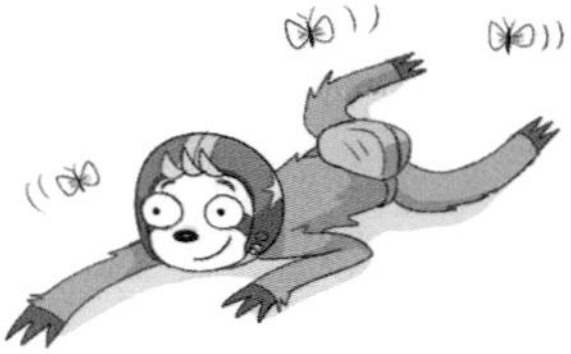

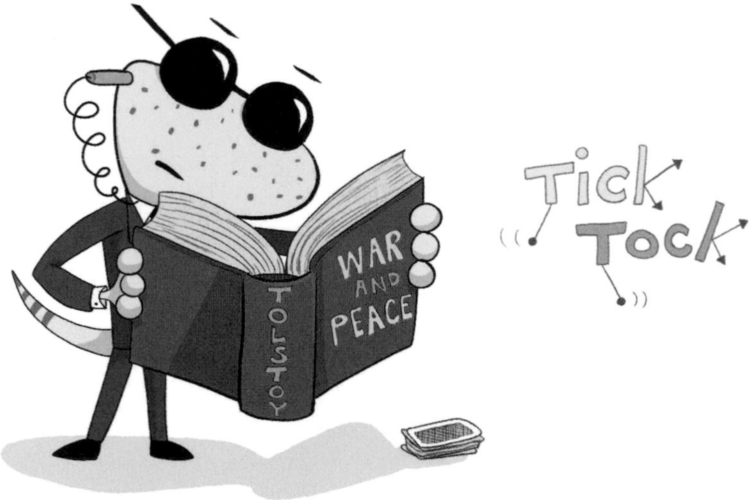
WAR AND PEACE
TOLSTOY
Tick
Tock

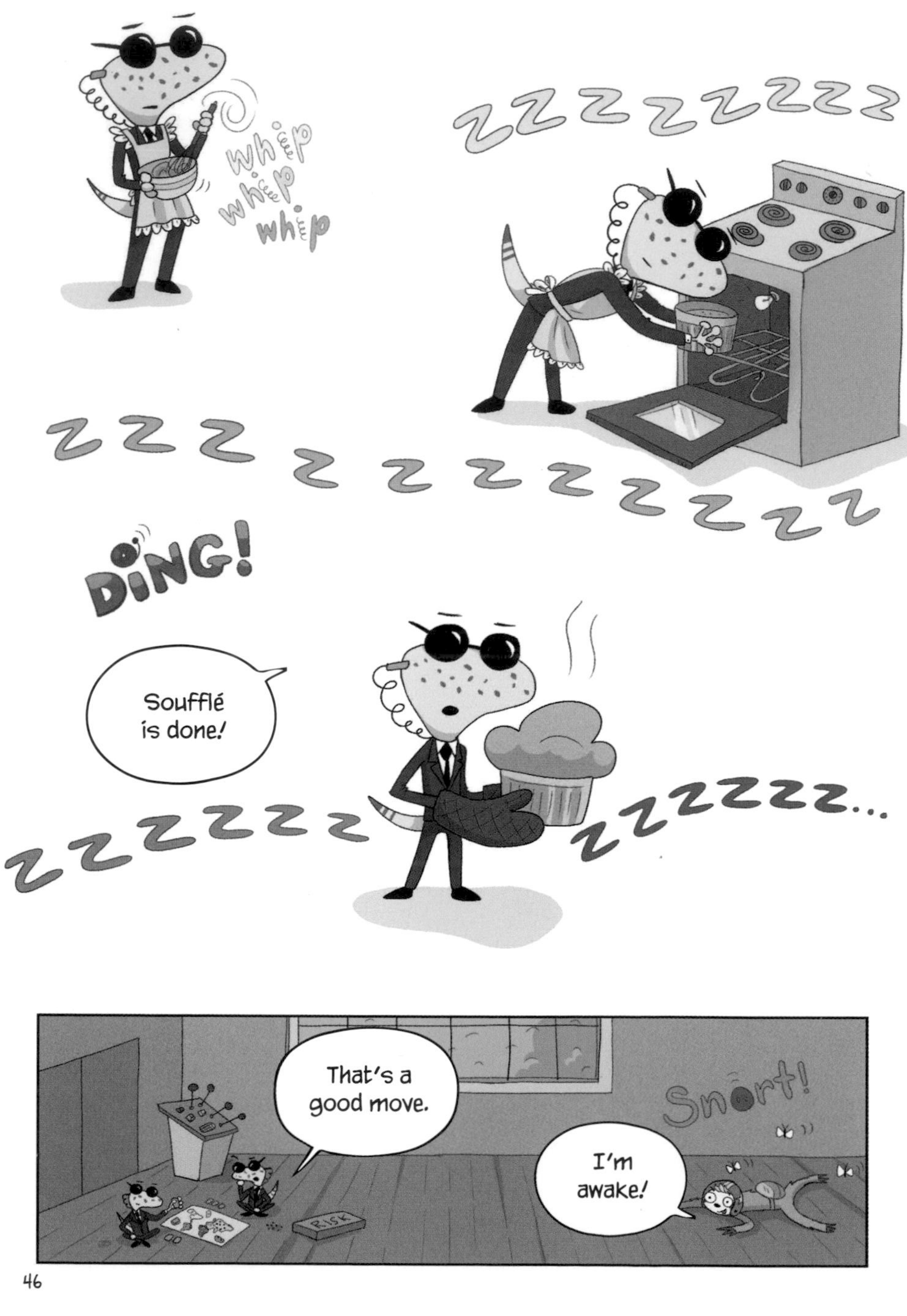
whip
whip
whip
ZZZZZZZZZ
ZZZZZZZZZZZZZZ
DING!
Soufflé is done!
ZZZZZZZZZZZZZZ...
That's a good move.
Snort!
I'm awake!

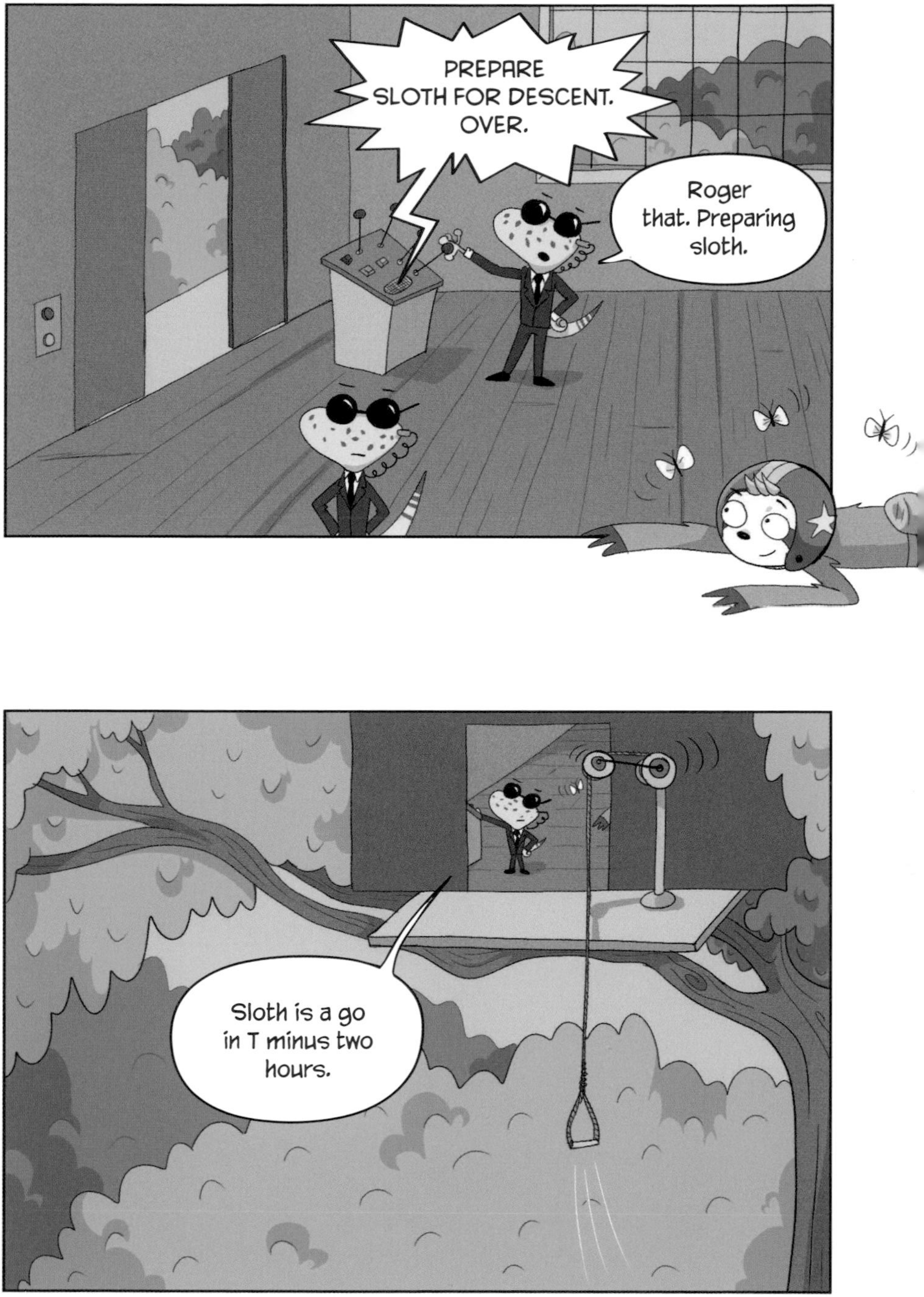
PREPARE SLOTH FOR DESCENT. OVER.
Roger that. Preparing sloth.
Sloth is a go in T minus two hours.

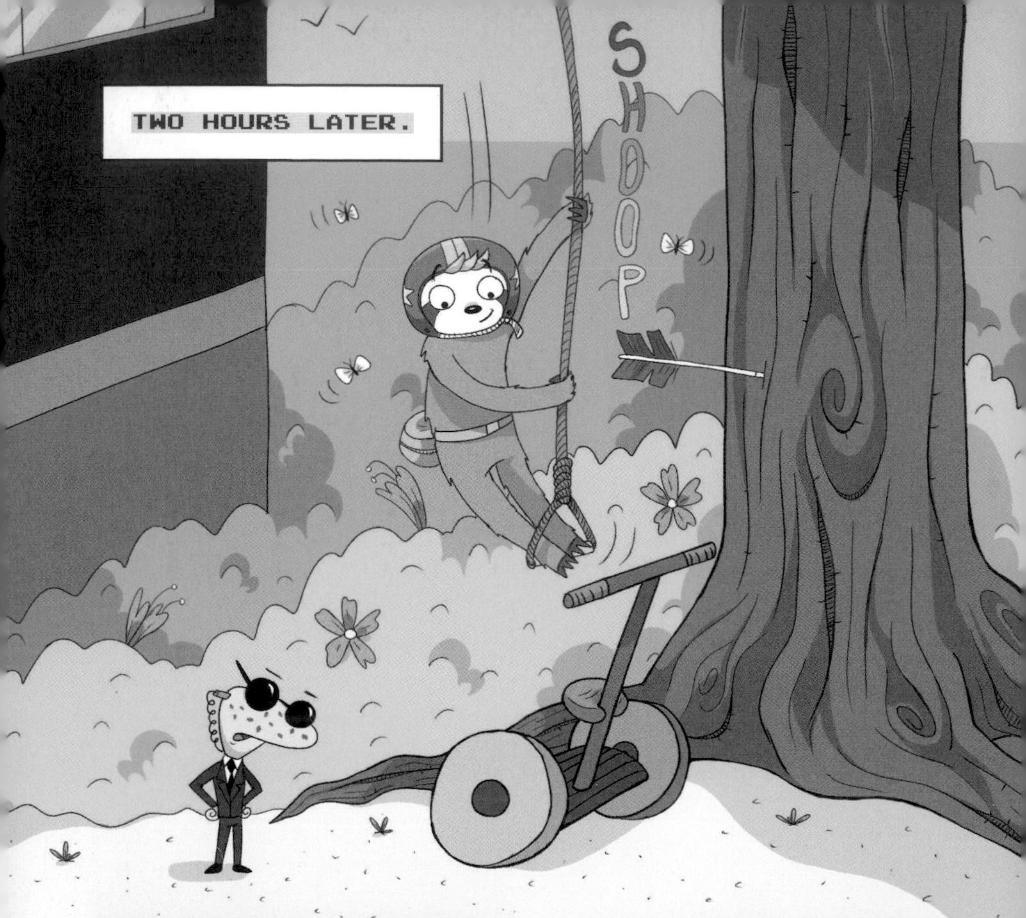
TWO HOURS LATER.
SHOOP

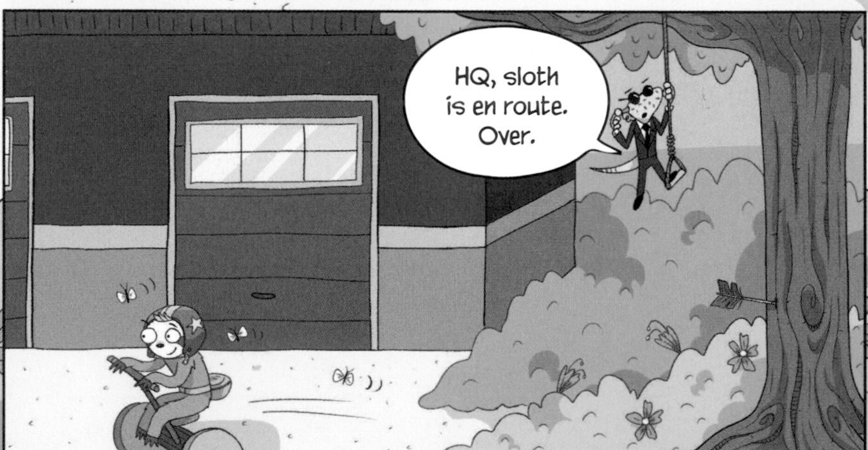
HQ, sloth is en route. Over.

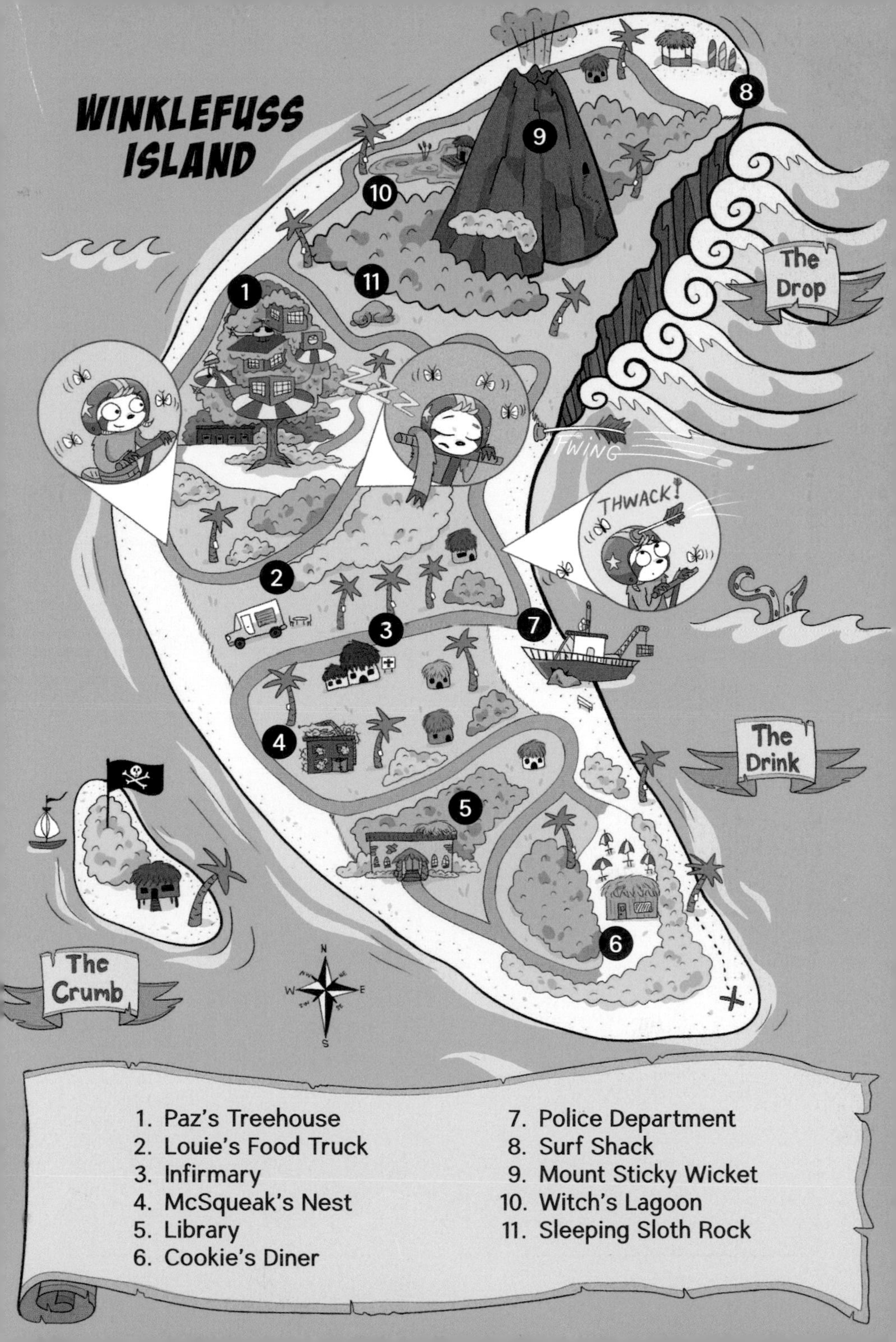
WINKLEFUSS ISLAND
The Drop
The Drink
The Crumb
FWING
THWACK!
N
S
E
W
1. Paz's Treehouse
2. Louie's Food Truck
3. Infirmary
4. McSqueak's Nest
5. Library
6. Cookie's Diner
7. Police Department
8. Surf Shack
9. Mount Sticky Wicket
10. Witch's Lagoon
11. Sleeping Sloth Rock

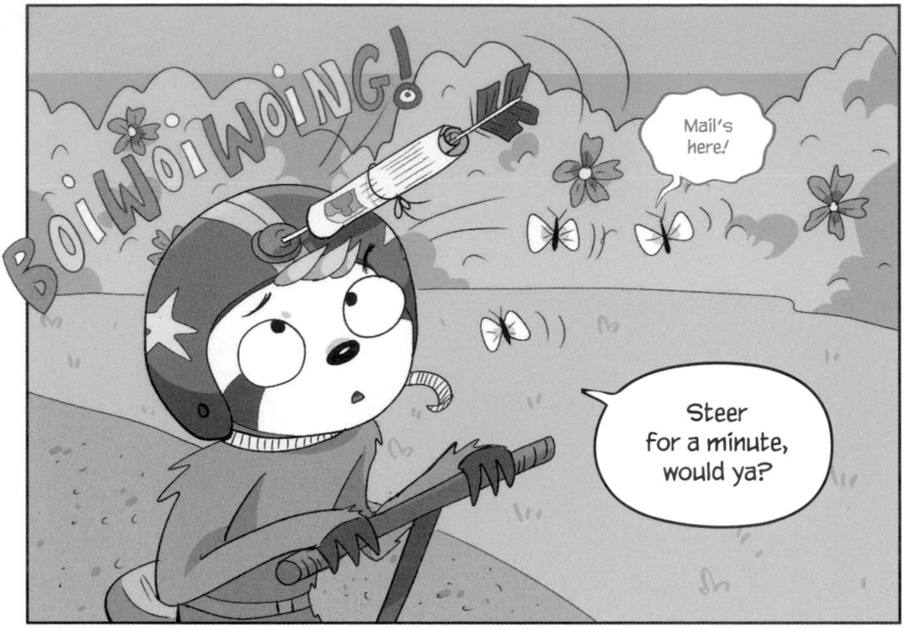
BOIWOIWOING!
Mail's here!
Steer for a minute, would ya?

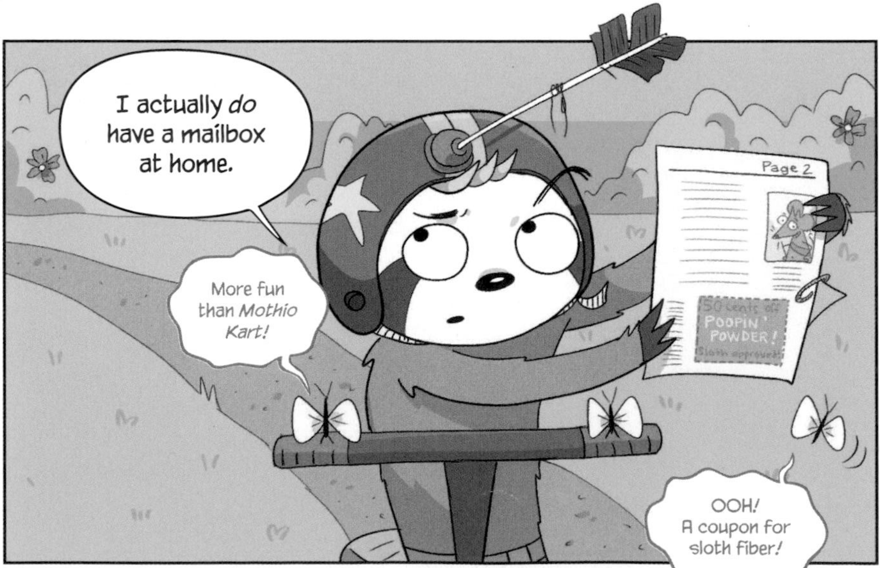
I actually *do* have a mailbox at home.
More fun than *Mothio Kart!*
Page 2
50 cents off
POOPIN' POWDER!
Sloth approved!
OOH! A coupon for sloth fiber!

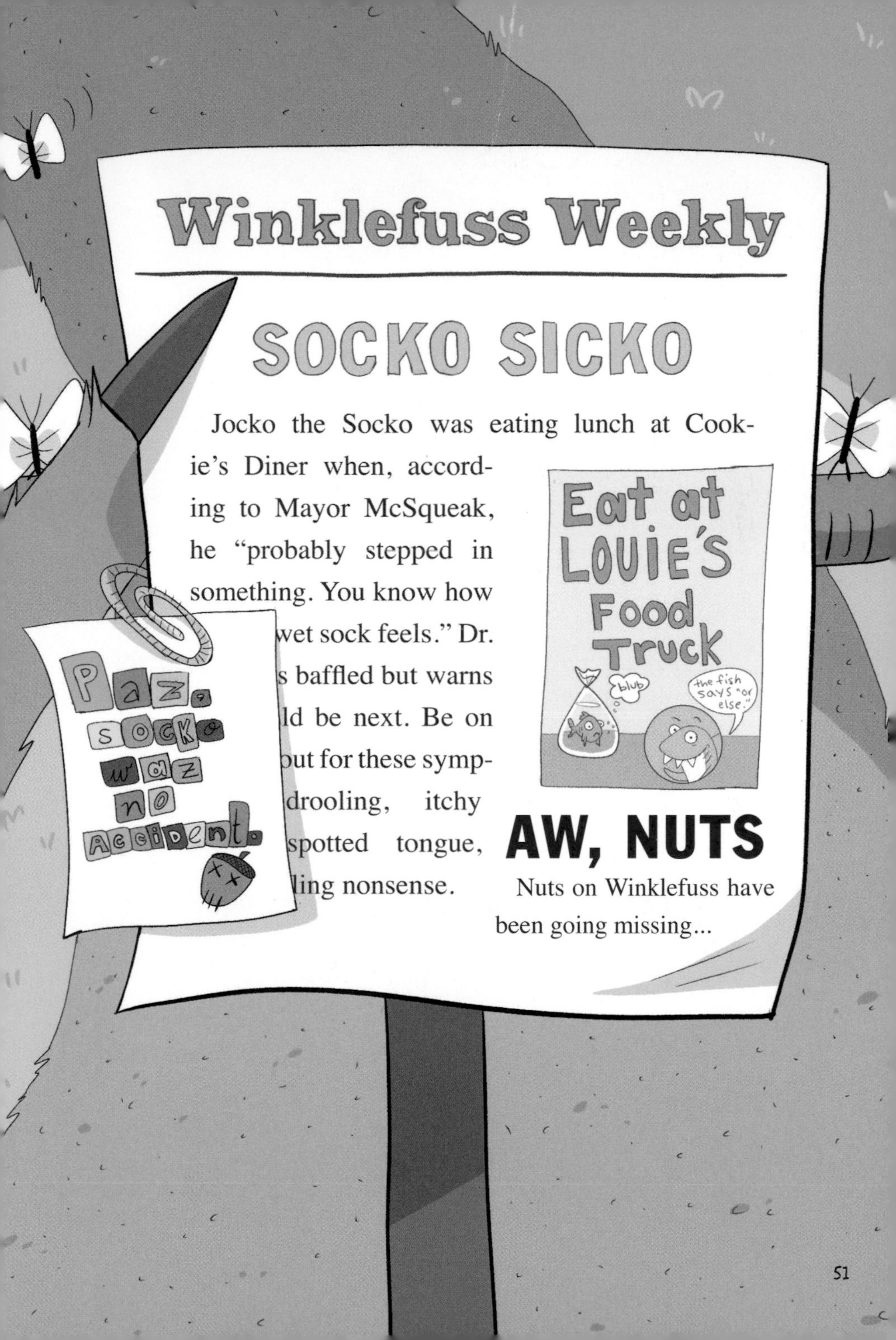
Winklefuss Weekly
SOCKO SICKO
Jocko the Socko was eating lunch at Cookie's Diner when, according to Mayor McSqueak, he "probably stepped in something. You know how
wet sock feels." Dr.
s baffled but warns
ld be next. Be on
out for these symp-
drooling, itchy
spotted tongue,
ling nonsense.
Eat at LOUIE'S Food Truck
blub
the fish says "or else."
AW, NUTS
Nuts on Winklefuss have been going missing...
Paz, socko waz no accident.

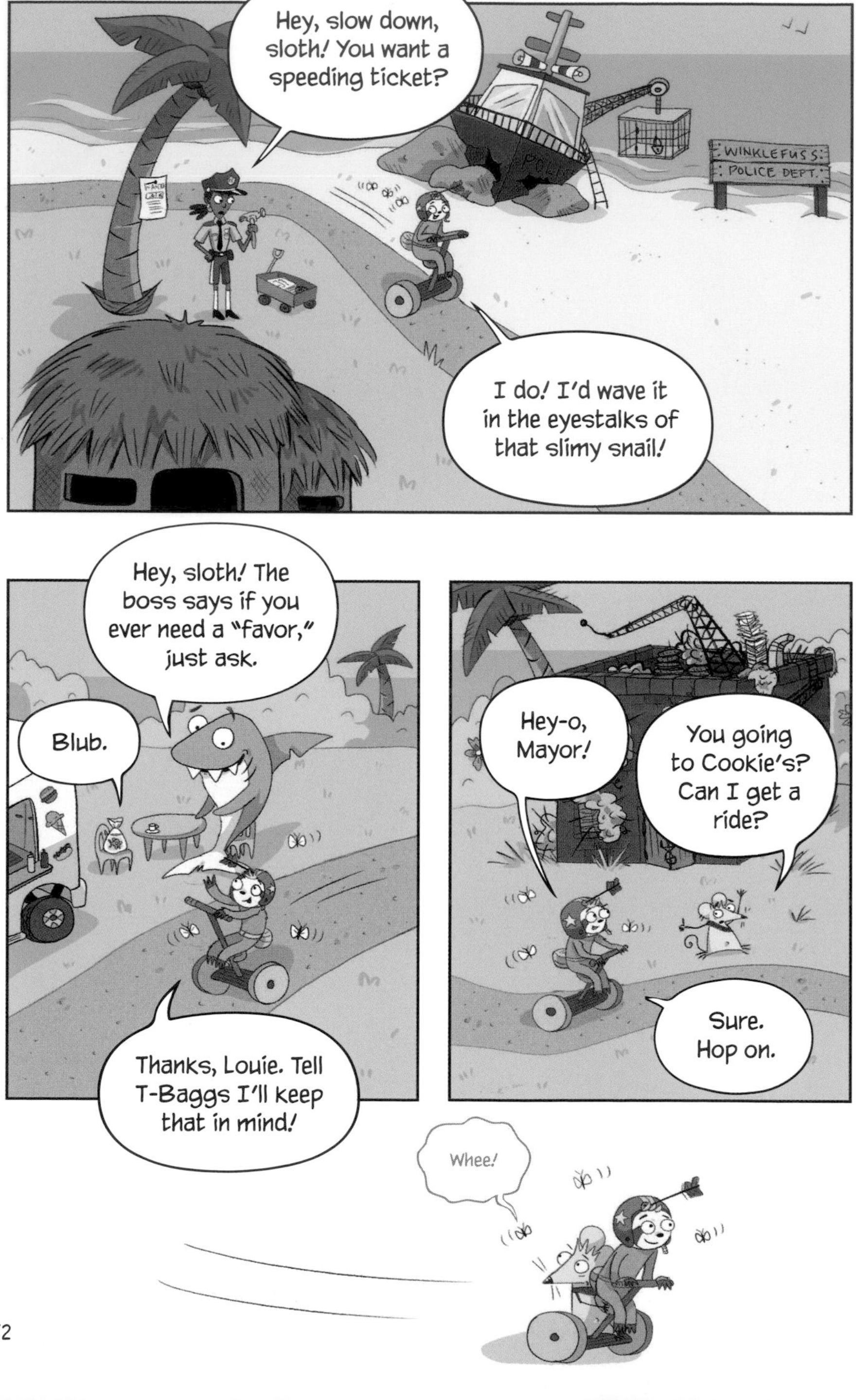
Hey, slow down, sloth! You want a speeding ticket?
WINKLEFUSS POLICE DEPT.
I do! I'd wave it in the eyestalks of that slimy snail!
Hey, sloth! The boss says if you ever need a "favor," just ask.
Blub.
Thanks, Louie. Tell T-Baggs I'll keep that in mind!
Hey-o, Mayor!
You going to Cookie's? Can I get a ride?
Sure. Hop on.
Whee!

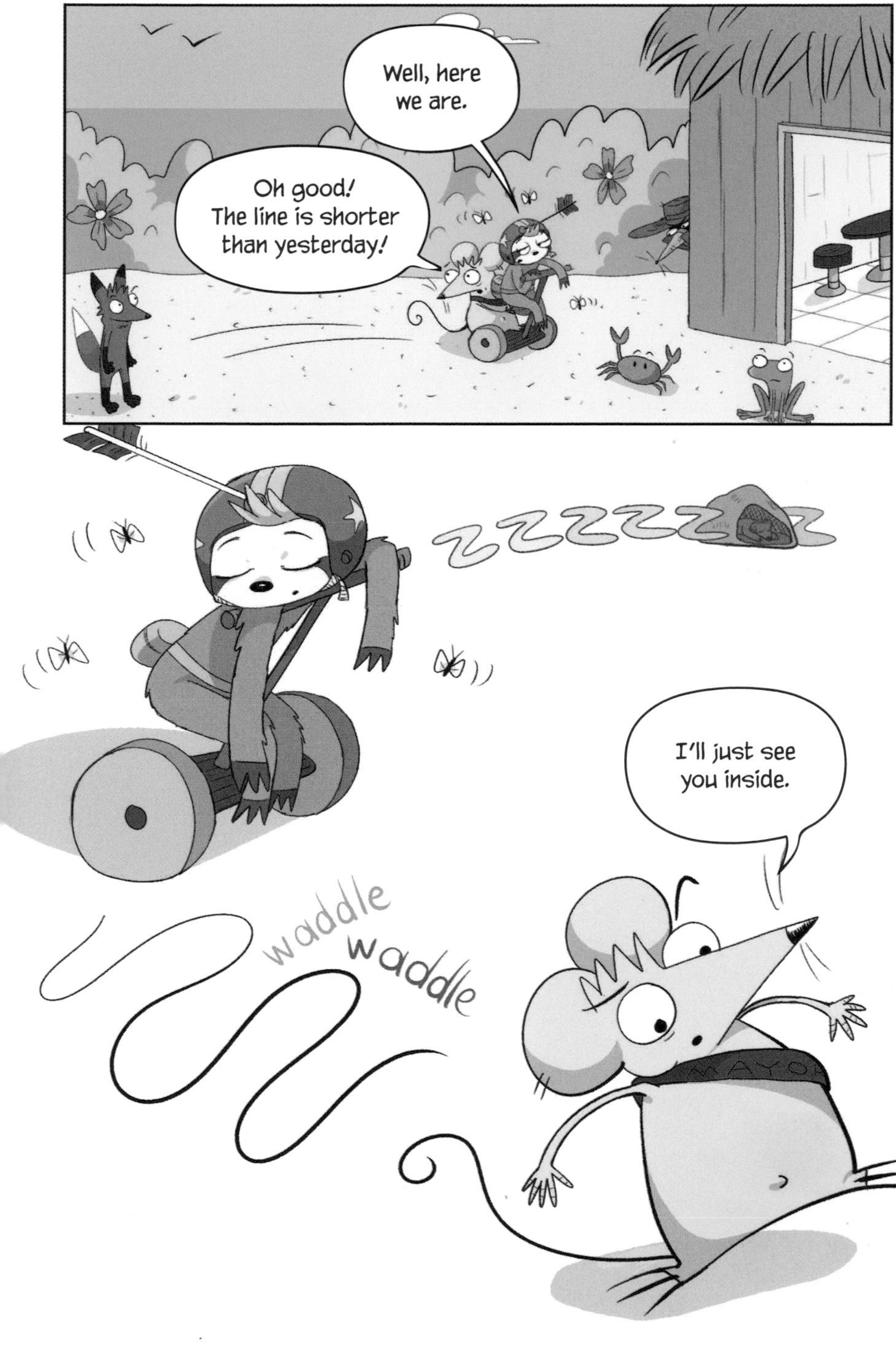
Well, here we are.
Oh good! The line is shorter than yesterday!
ZZZZZZZ
I'll just see you inside.
waddle waddle
MAYO

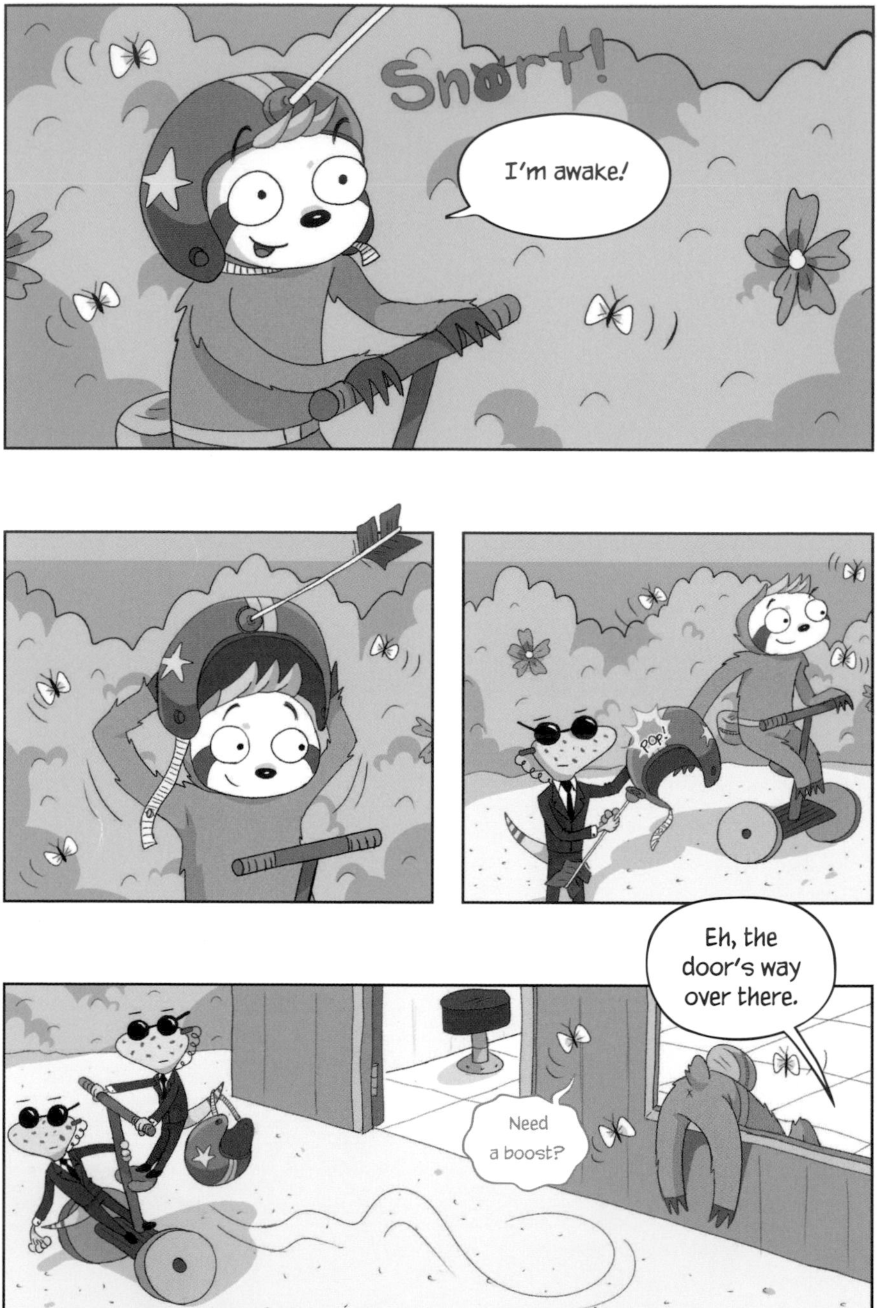
Snort!
I'm awake!
POP!
Eh, the door's way over there.
Need a boost?

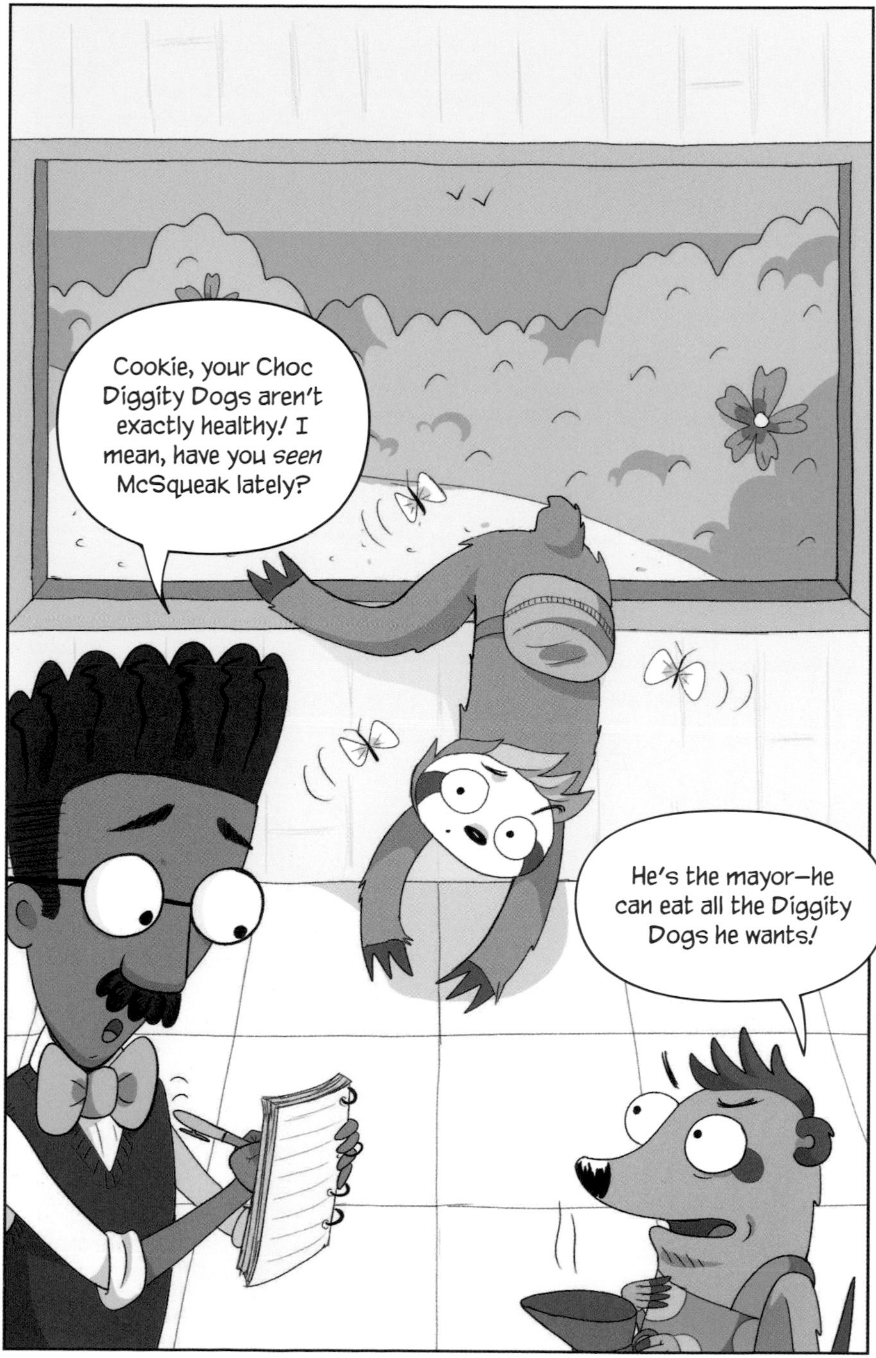
Cookie, your Choc Diggity Dogs aren't exactly healthy! I mean, have you *seen* McSqueak lately?
He's the mayor—he can eat all the Diggity Dogs he wants!

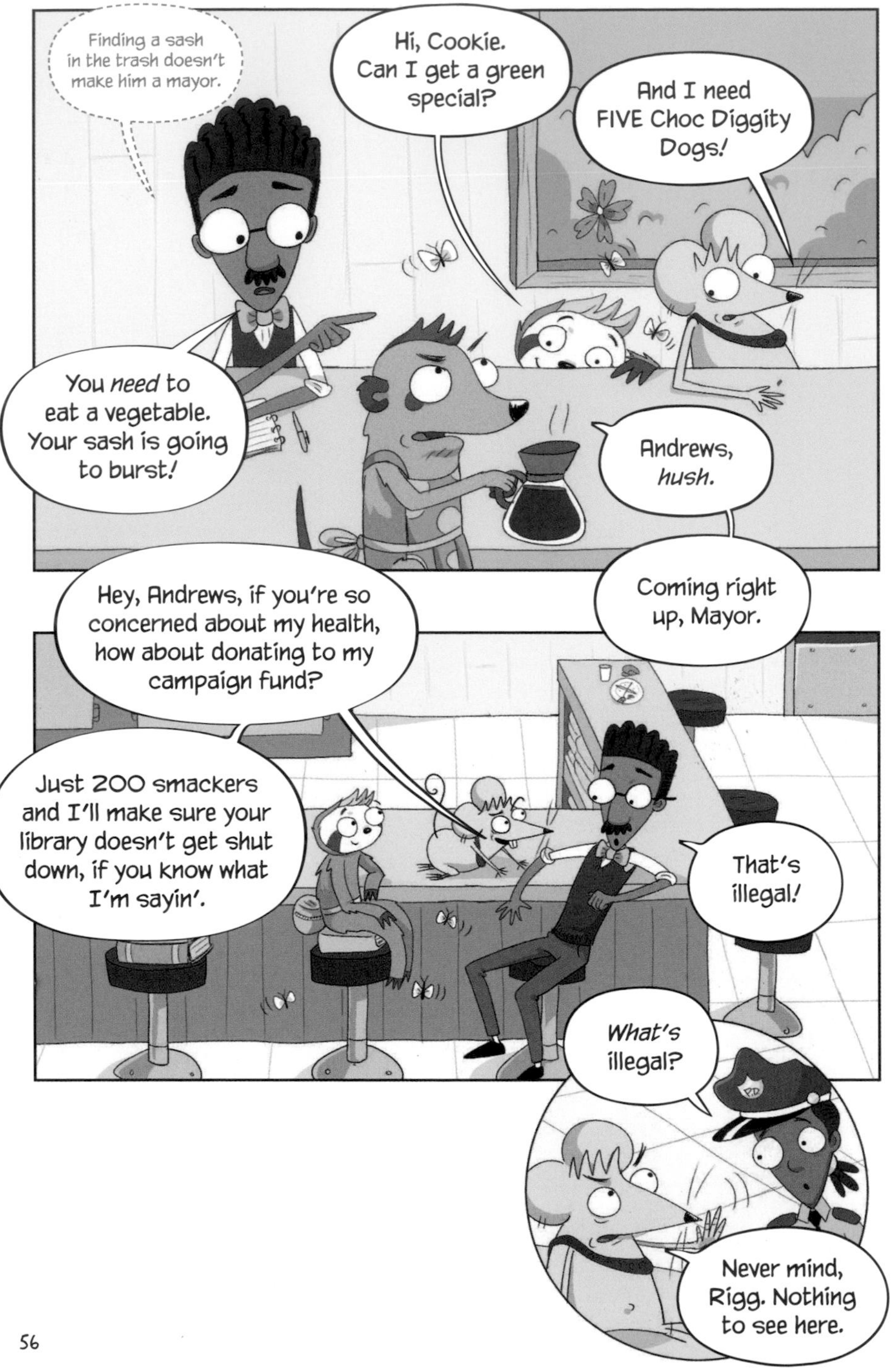

Finding a sash in the trash doesn't make him a mayor.
Hi, Cookie. Can I get a green special?
And I need FIVE Choc Diggity Dogs!
You *need* to eat a vegetable. Your sash is going to burst!
Andrews, *hush*.
Coming right up, Mayor.
Hey, Andrews, if you're so concerned about my health, how about donating to my campaign fund?
Just 200 smackers and I'll make sure your library doesn't get shut down, if you know what I'm sayin'.
That's illegal!
What's illegal?
Never mind, Rigg. Nothing to see here.

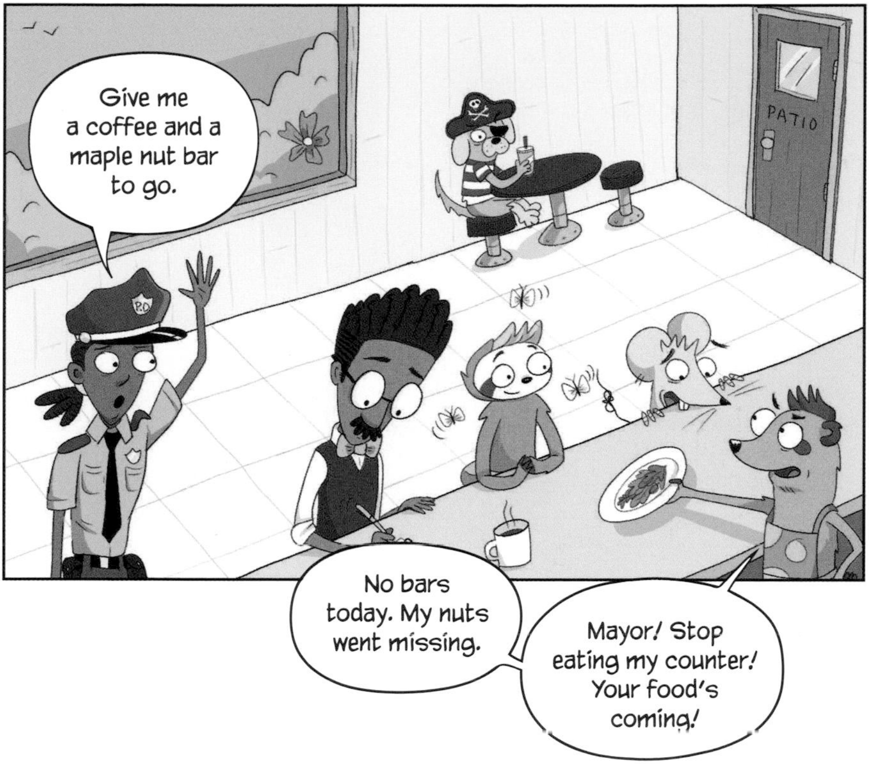
Give me a coffee and a maple nut bar to go.
PATIO
No bars today. My nuts went missing.
Mayor! Stop eating my counter! Your food's coming!

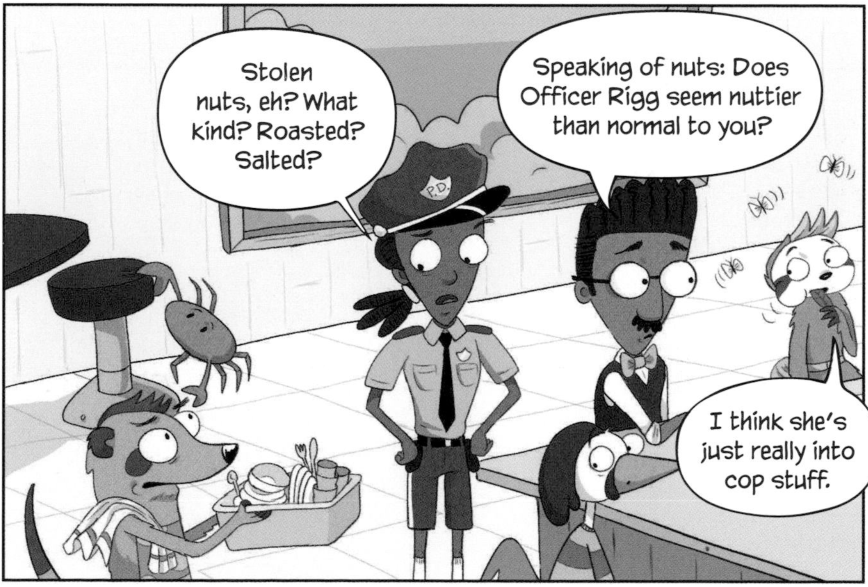
Stolen nuts, eh? What kind? Roasted? Salted?
Speaking of nuts: Does Officer Rigg seem nuttier than normal to you?
I think she's just really into cop stuff.

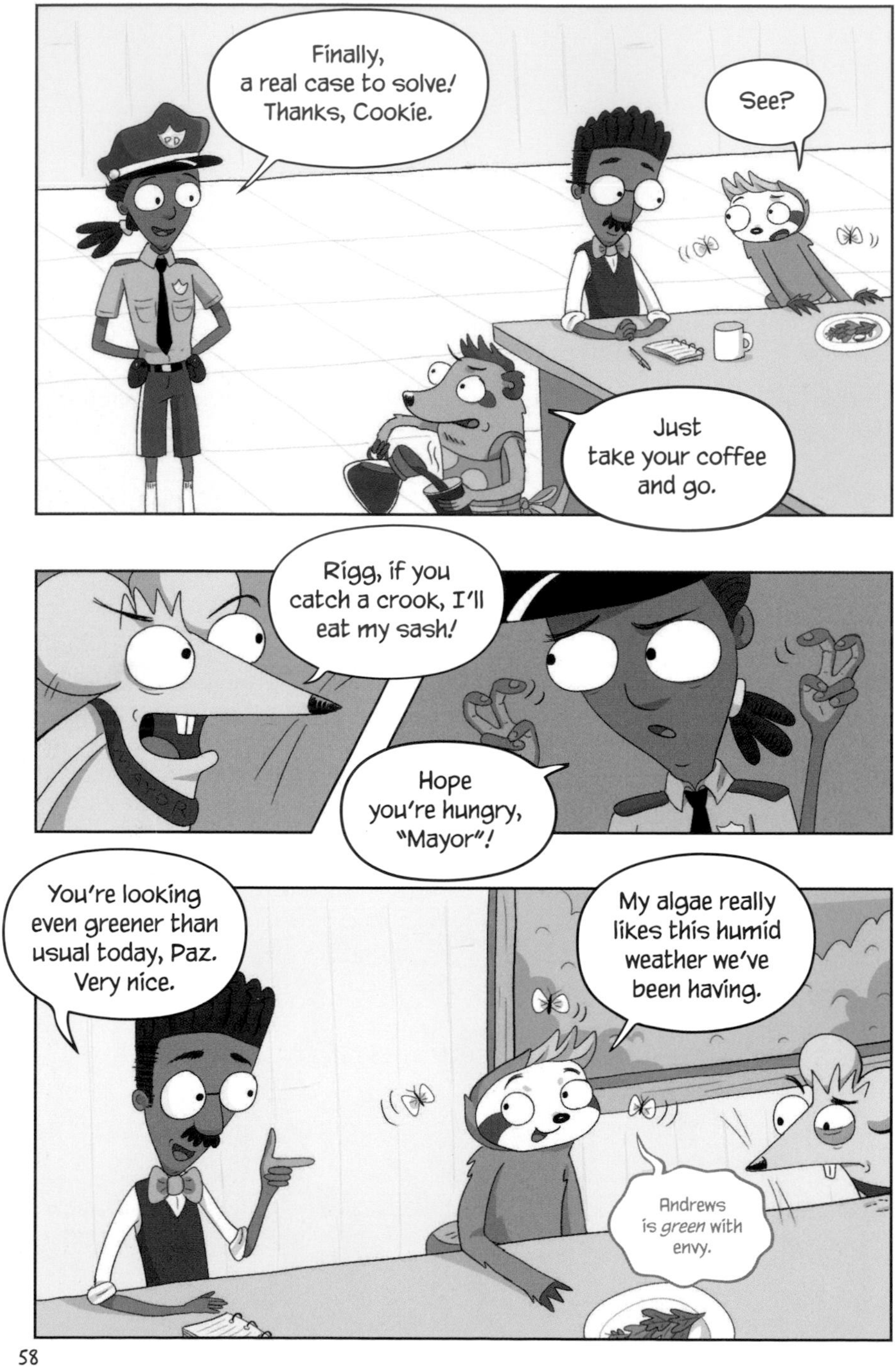
Finally, a real case to solve! Thanks, Cookie.
See?
Just take your coffee and go.
Rigg, if you catch a crook, I'll eat my sash!
MAYOR
Hope you're hungry, "Mayor"!
You're looking even greener than usual today, Paz. Very nice.
My algae really likes this humid weather we've been having.
Andrews is *green* with envy.

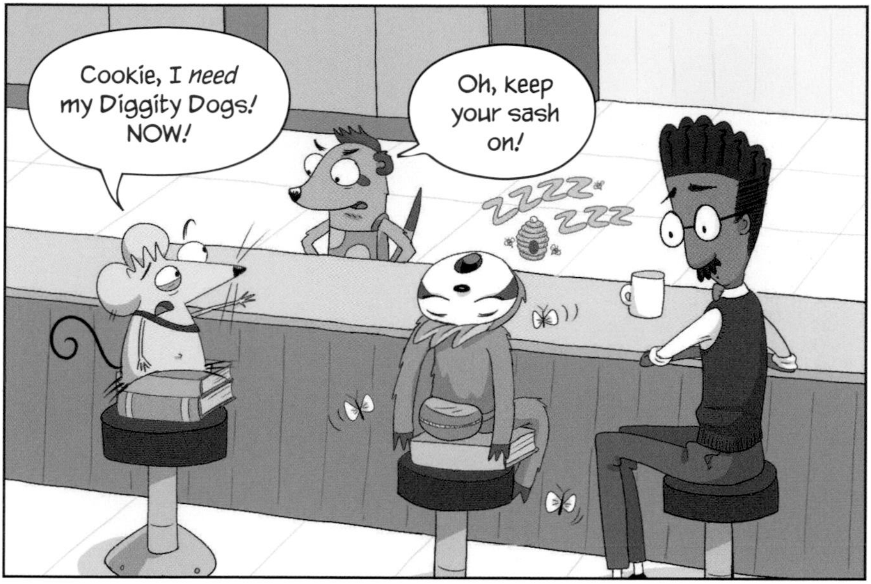
Cookie, I *need* my Diggity Dogs! NOW!
Oh, keep your sash on!
ZZZZZ ZZZ

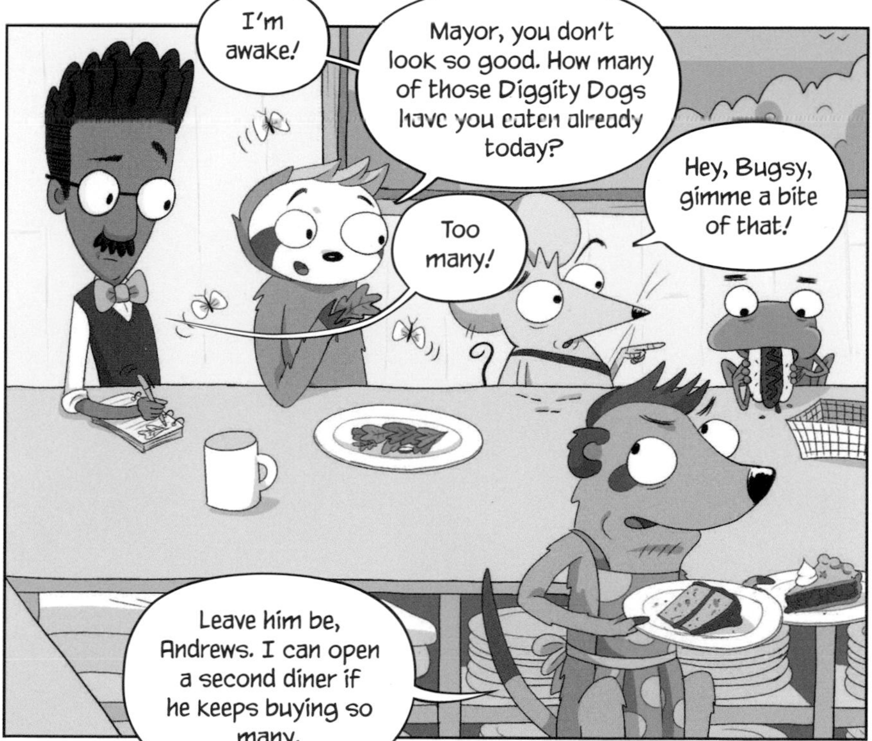
I'm awake!
Mayor, you don't look so good. How many of those Diggity Dogs have you eaten already today?
Too many!
Hey, Bugsy, gimme a bite of that!
Leave him be, Andrews. I can open a second diner if he keeps buying so many.

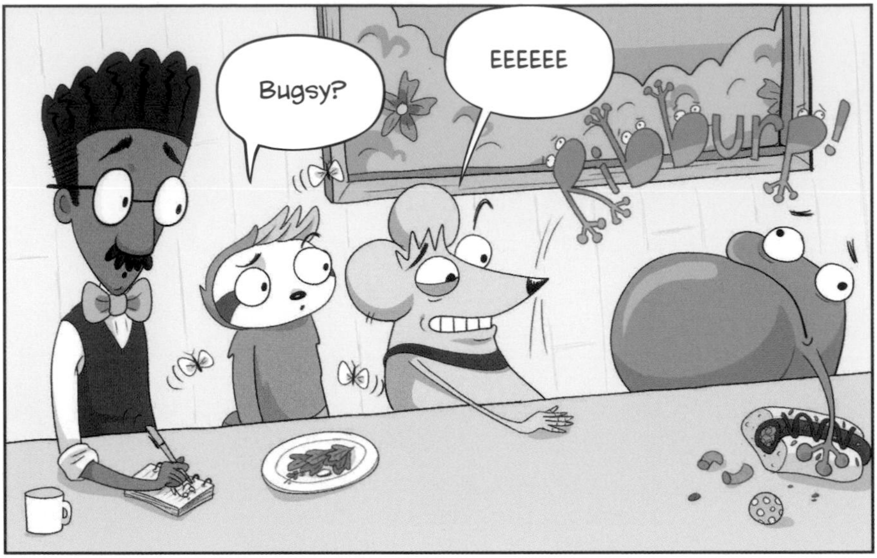
Bugsy?
EEEEEE
burp!

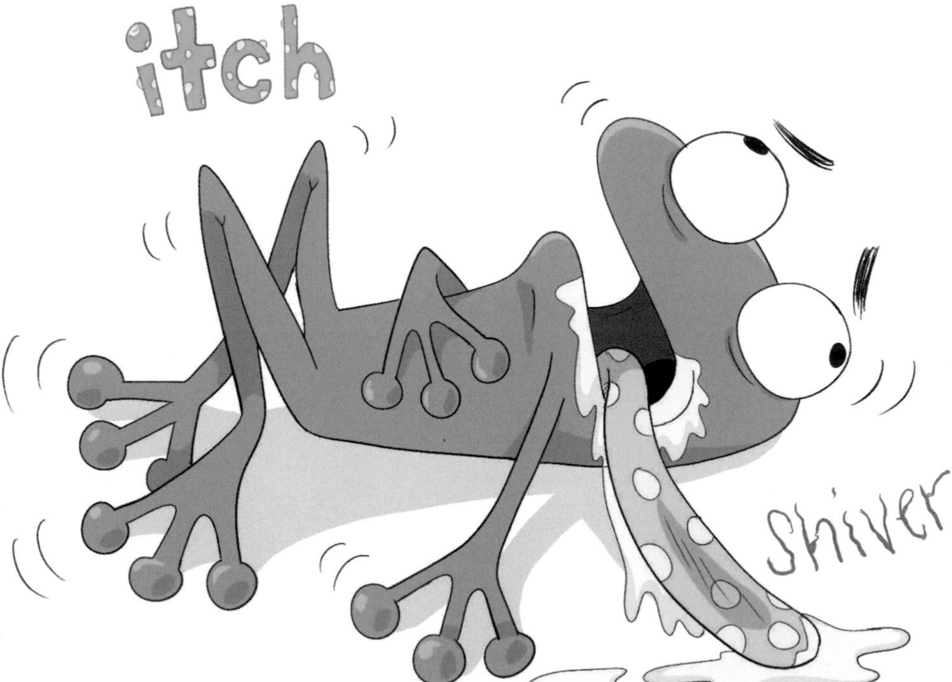
itch
shiver

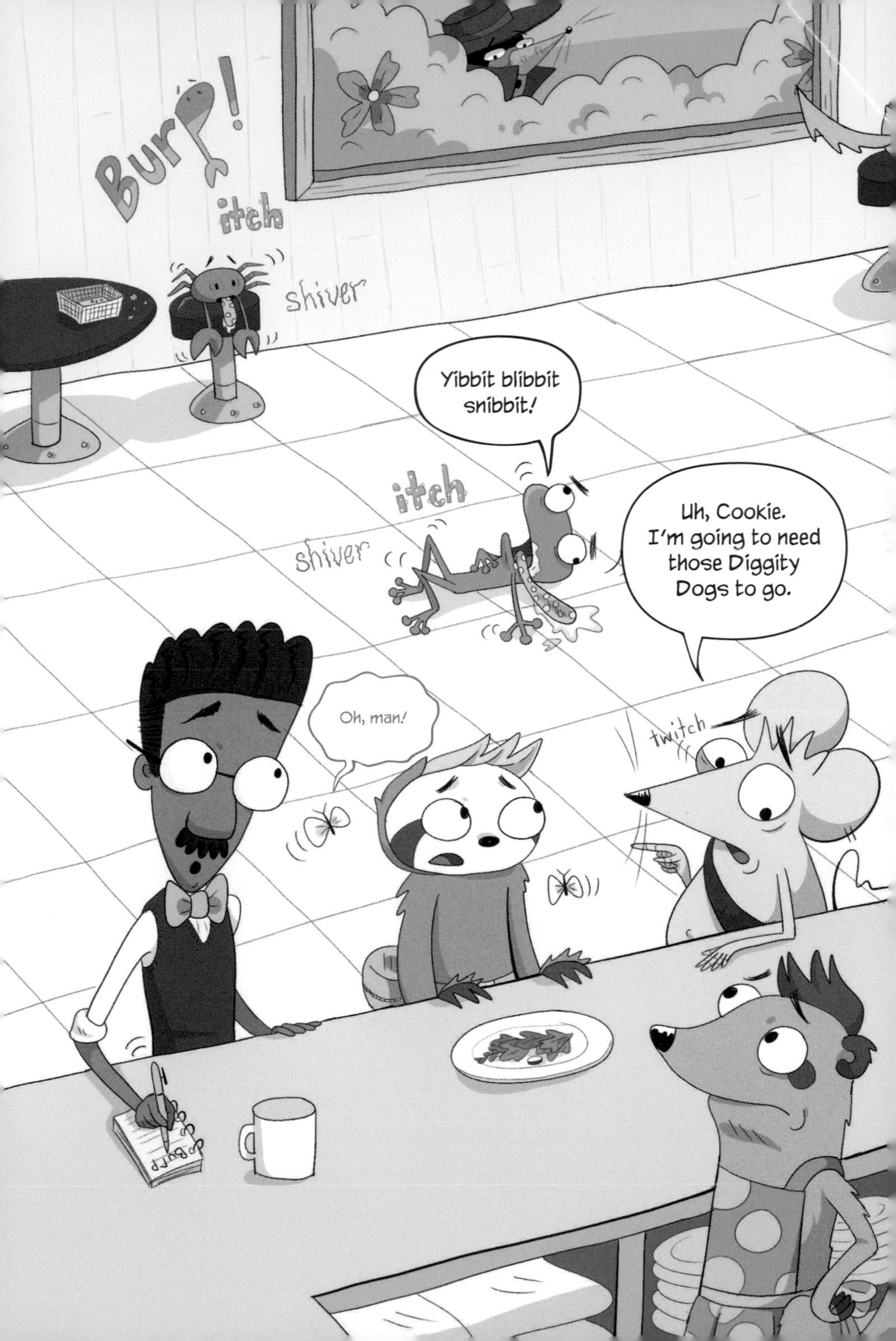
Burp!
itch
shiver
Yibbit blibbit snibbit!
itch
shiver
Uh, Cookie. I'm going to need those Diggity Dogs to go.
Oh, man!
twitch

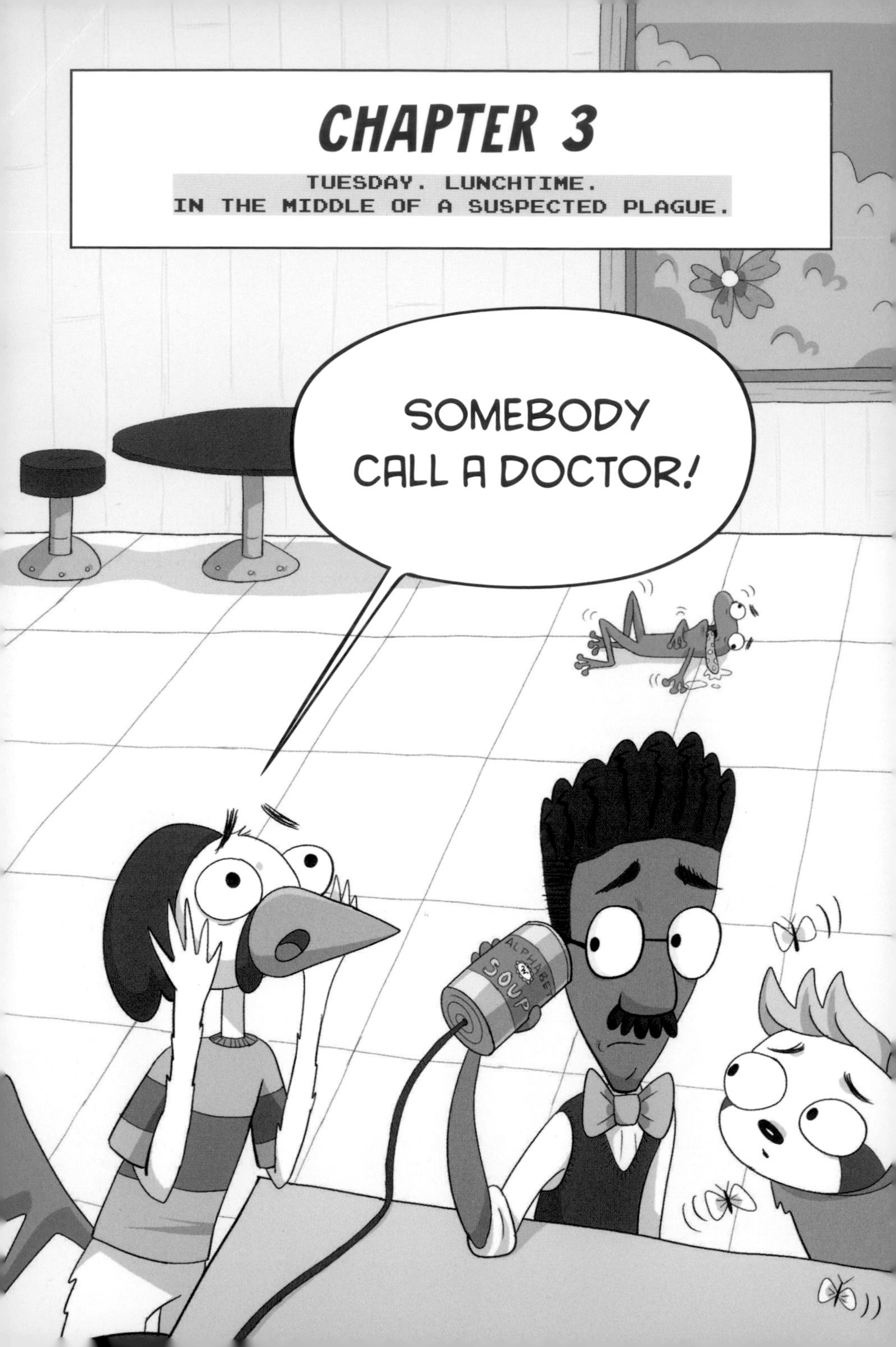
CHAPTER 3
TUESDAY. LUNCHTIME.
IN THE MIDDLE OF A SUSPECTED PLAGUE.
SOMEBODY CALL A DOCTOR!
ALPHABET SOUP

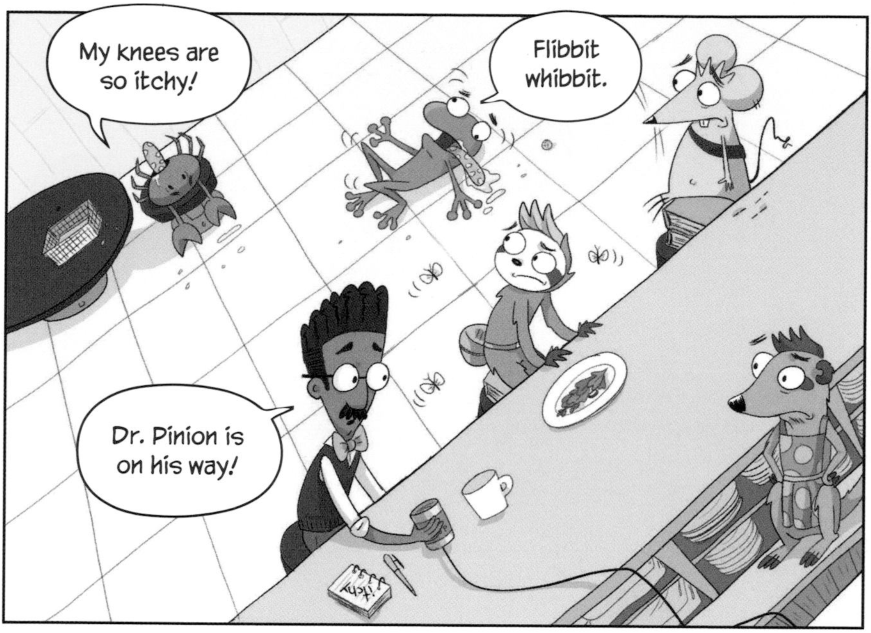
My knees are so itchy!
Flibbit whibbit.
Dr. Pinion is on his way!

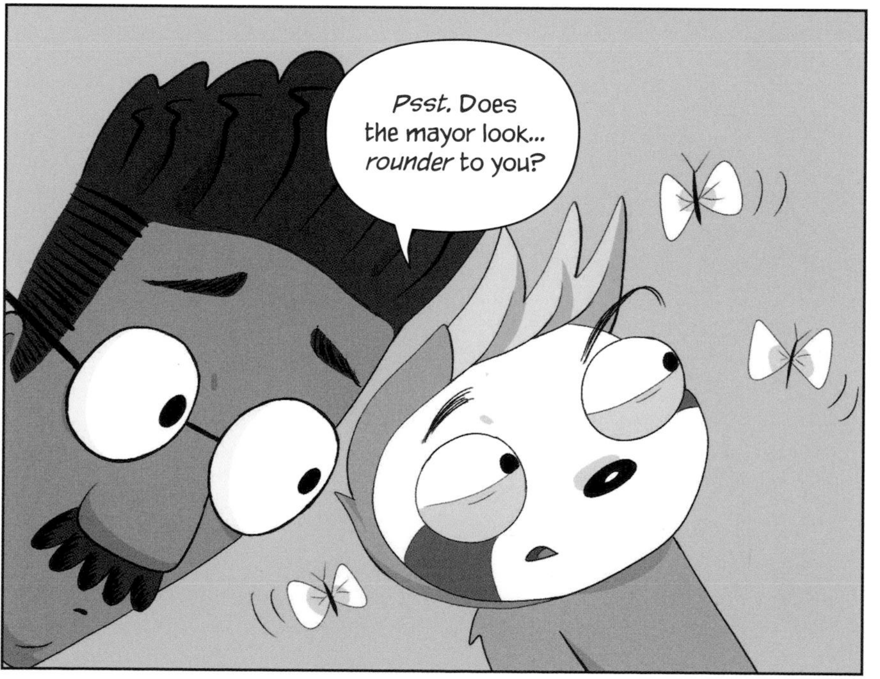
Psst. Does the mayor look... *rounder* to you?

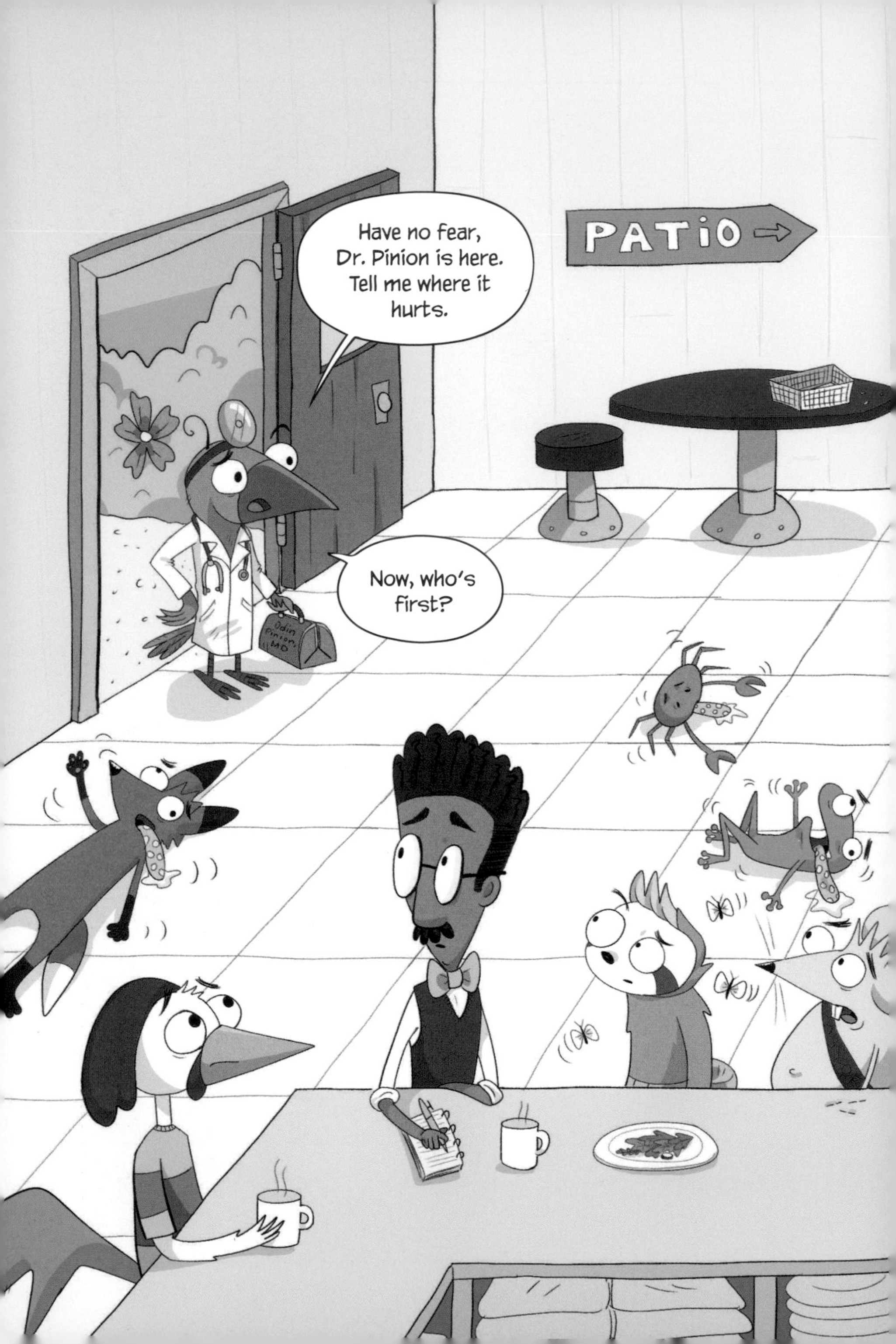
Have no fear, Dr. Pinion is here. Tell me where it hurts.
PATIO
Odin Pinion, MD
Now, who's first?

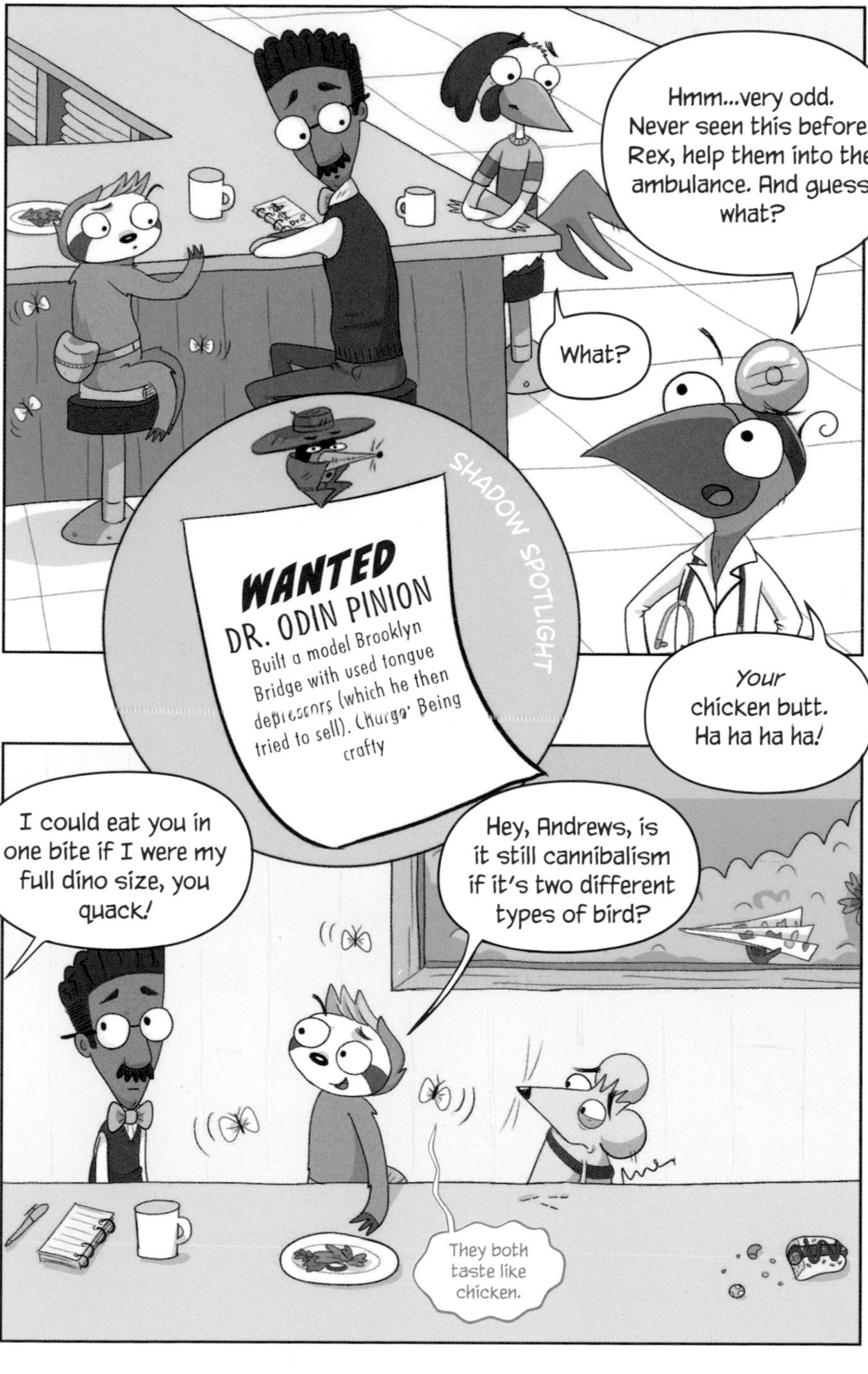
Hmm...very odd. Never seen this before. Rex, help them into the ambulance. And guess what?
What?
Your chicken butt. Ha ha ha ha!
SHADOW SPOTLIGHT
WANTED
DR. ODIN PINION
Built a model Brooklyn Bridge with used tongue depressors (which he then tried to sell). Charge: Being crafty
I could eat you in one bite if I were my full dino size, you quack!
Hey, Andrews, is it still cannibalism if it's two different types of bird?
They both taste like chicken.

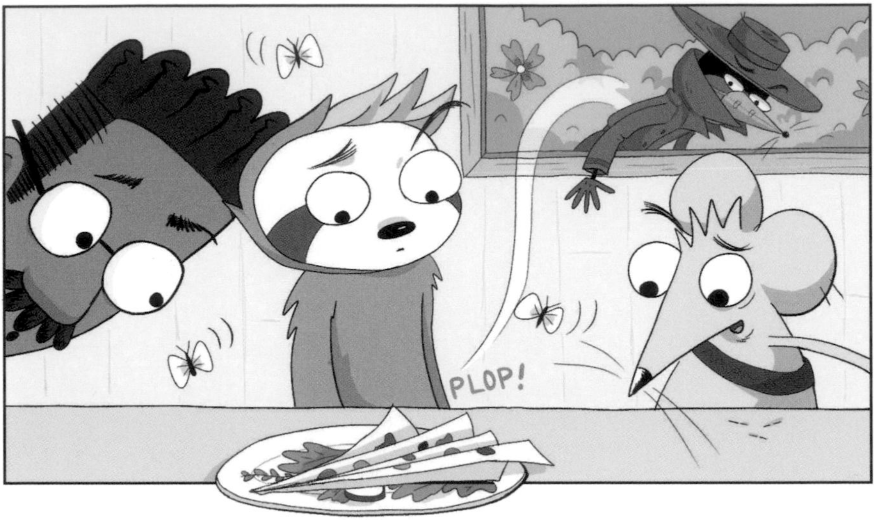
PLOP!

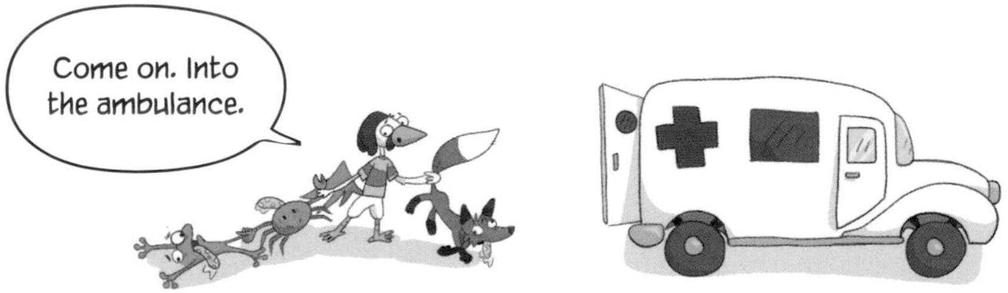
Come on. Into the ambulance.

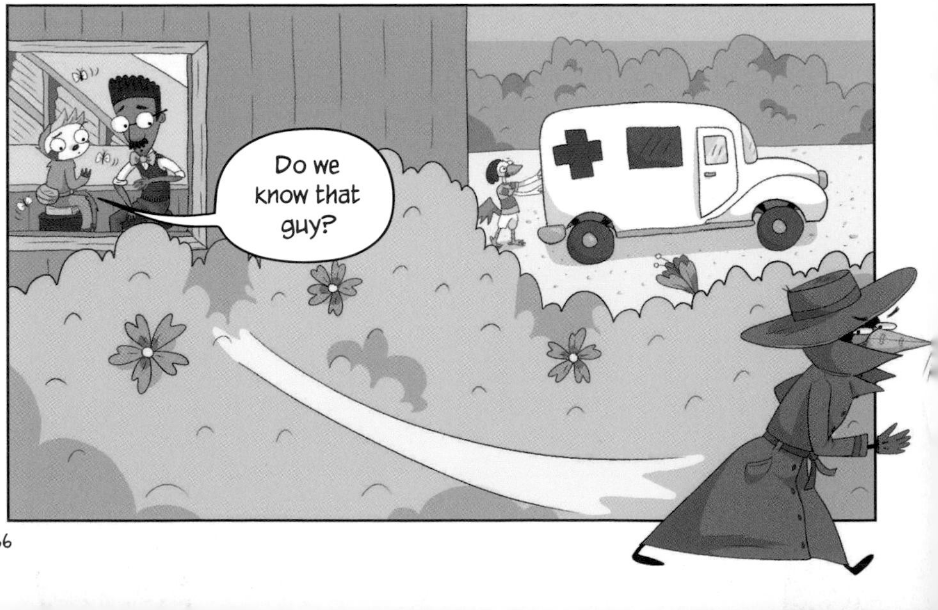
Do we know that guy?

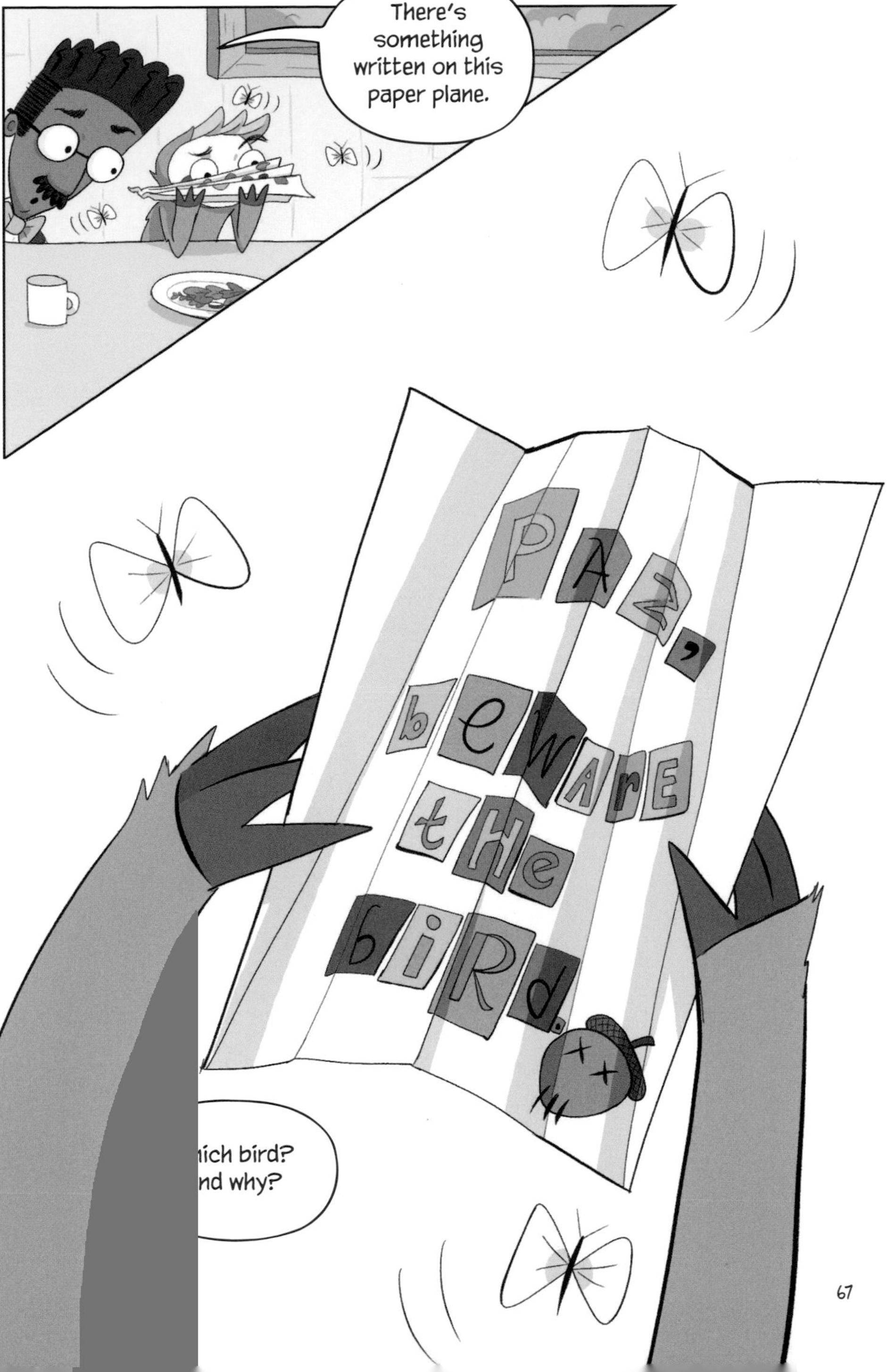
There's something written on this paper plane.
PAZ, beware the bird.
ich bird?
nd why?

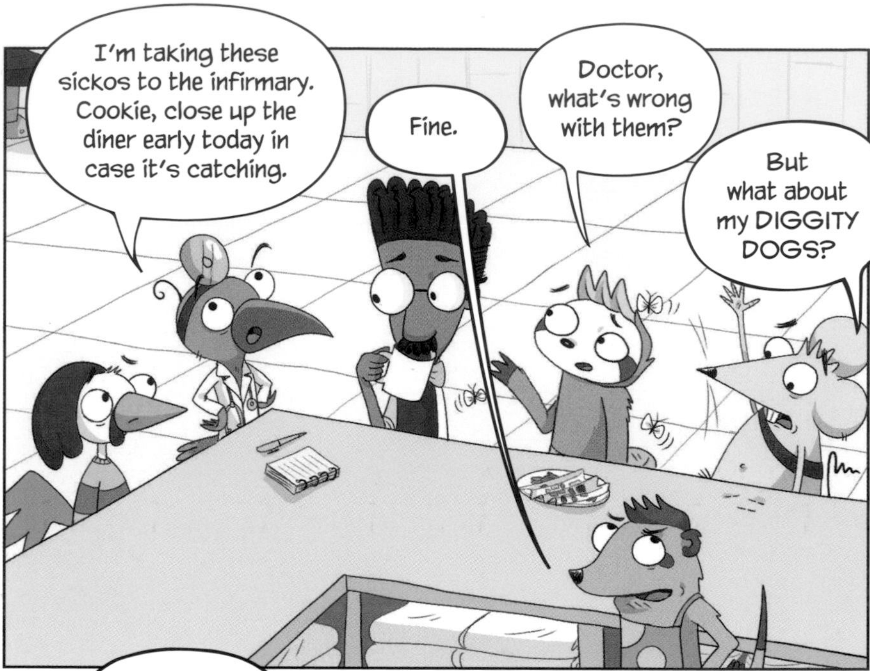
I'm taking these sickos to the infirmary. Cookie, close up the diner early today in case it's catching.
Fine.
Doctor, what's wrong with them?
But what about my DIGGITY DOGS?

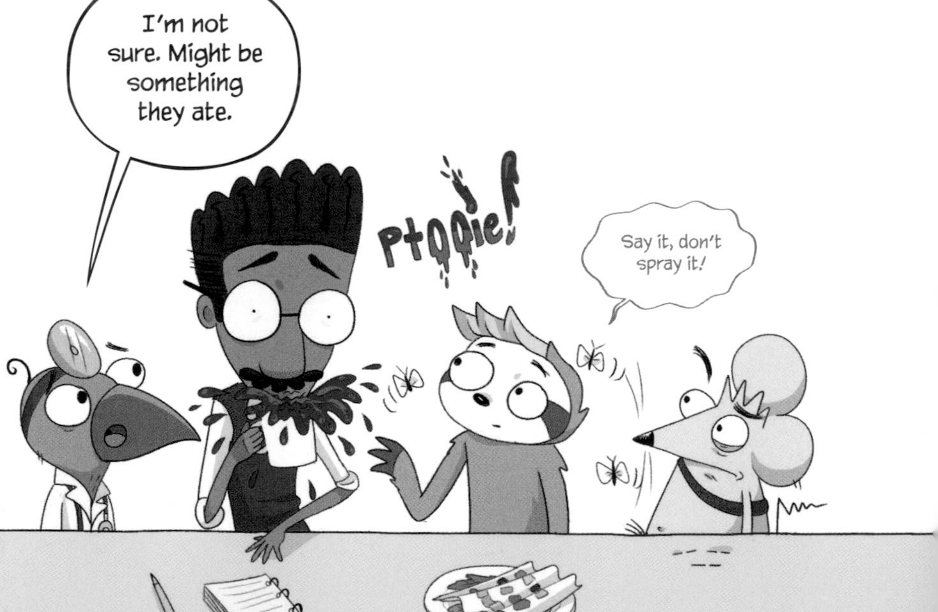
I'm not sure. Might be something they ate.
Ptooie!
Say it, don't spray it!

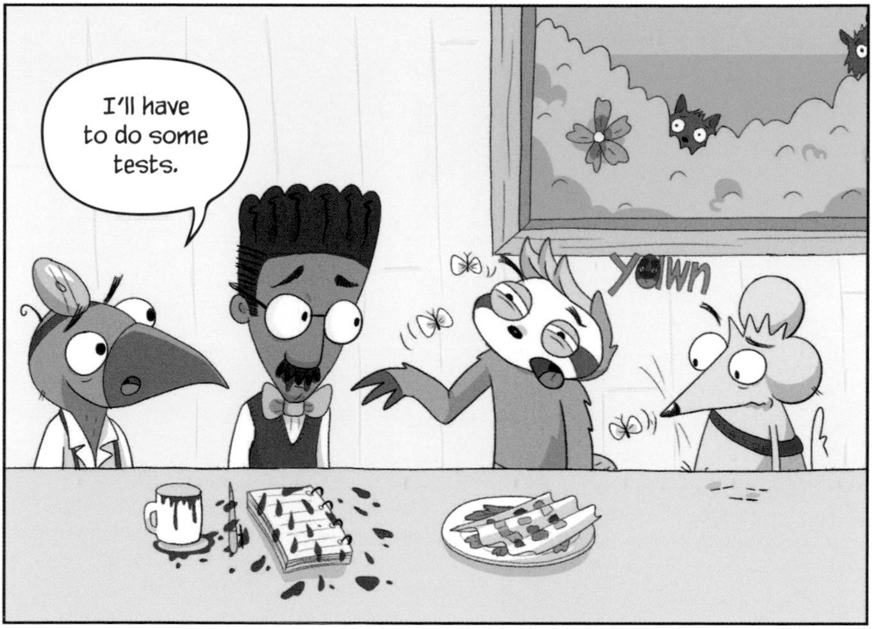
I'll have to do some tests.
YAWN

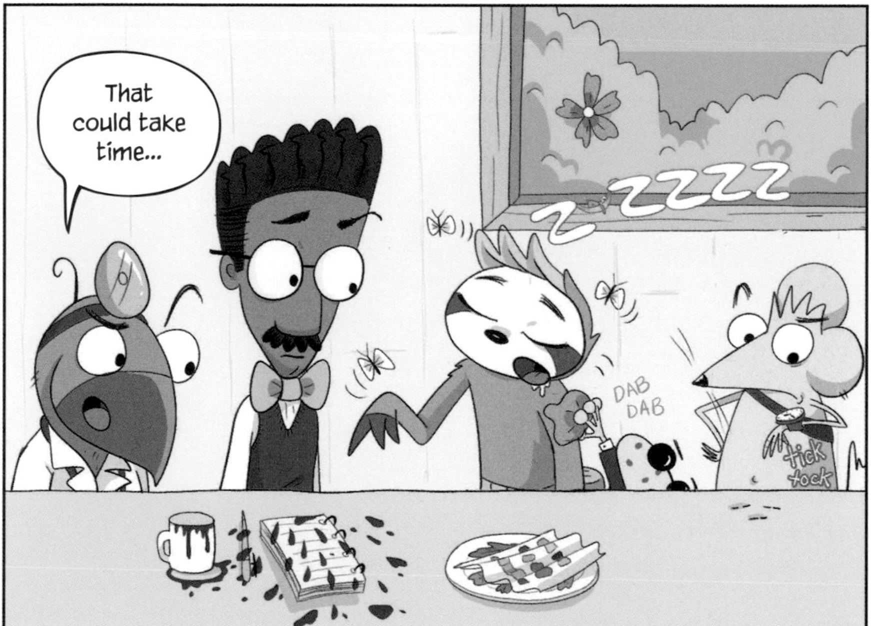
That could take time...
ZZZZZZ
DAB DAB
tick tock

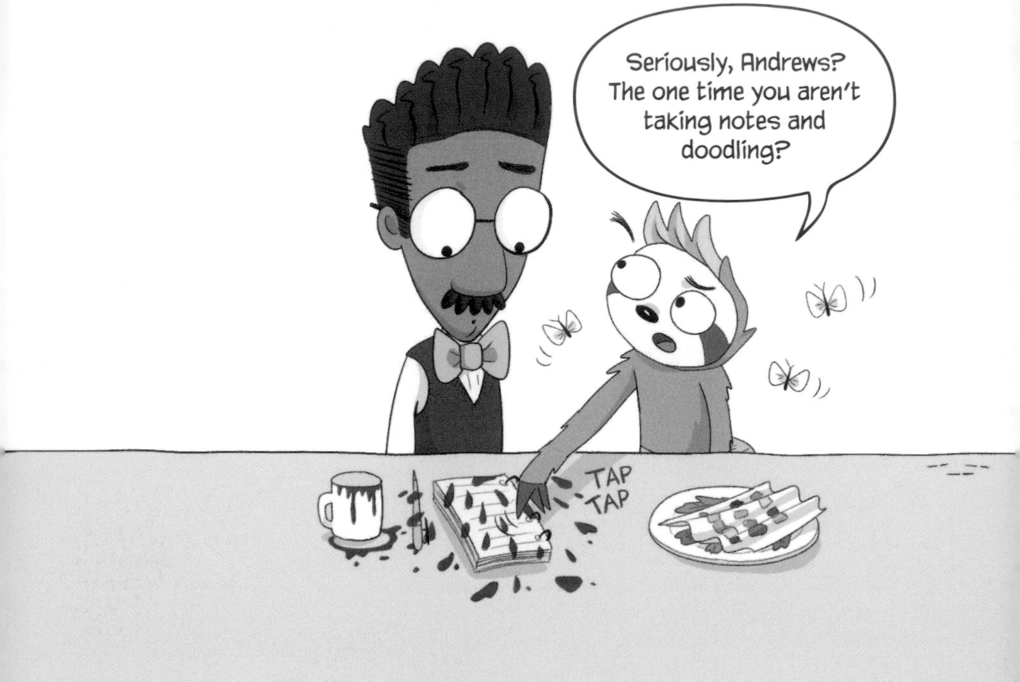
Seriously, Andrews? The one time you aren't taking notes and doodling?
TAP
TAP

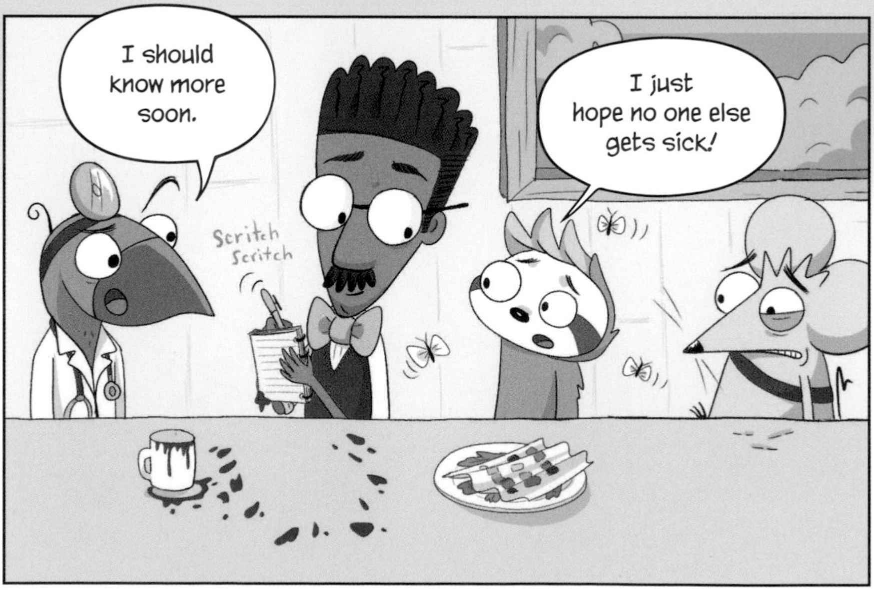
I should know more soon.
Scritch
Scritch
I just hope no one else gets sick!

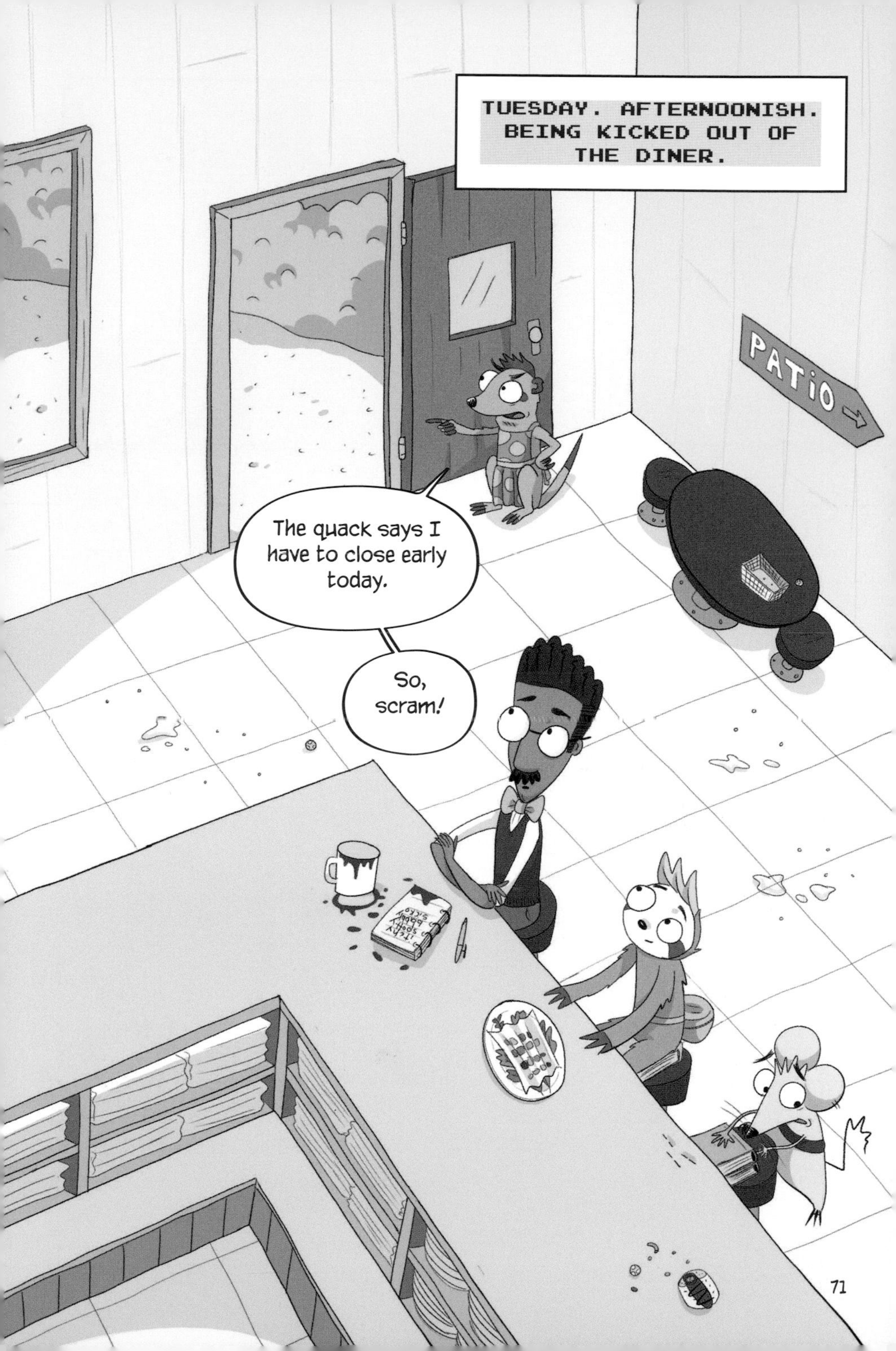
TUESDAY. AFTERNOONISH. BEING KICKED OUT OF THE DINER.
PATIO
The quack says I have to close early today.
So, scram!

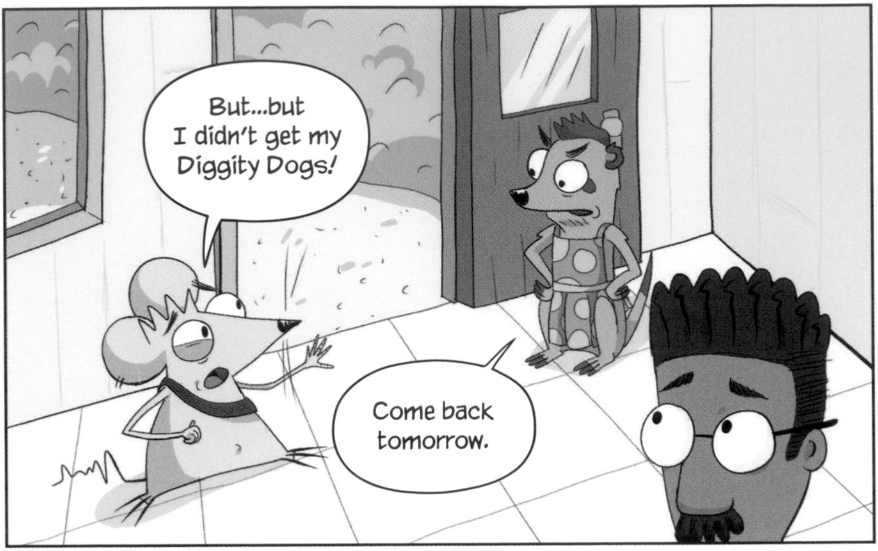
But...but I didn't get my Diggity Dogs!
Come back tomorrow.

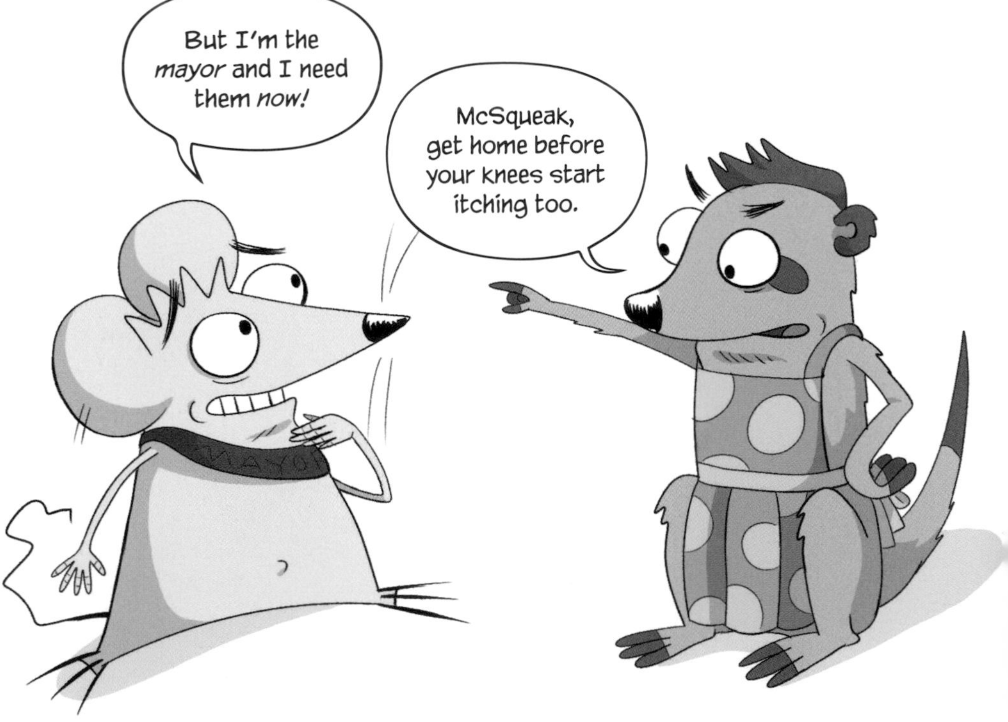
But I'm the *mayor* and I need them *now!*
McSqueak, get home before your knees start itching too.
MAYOR

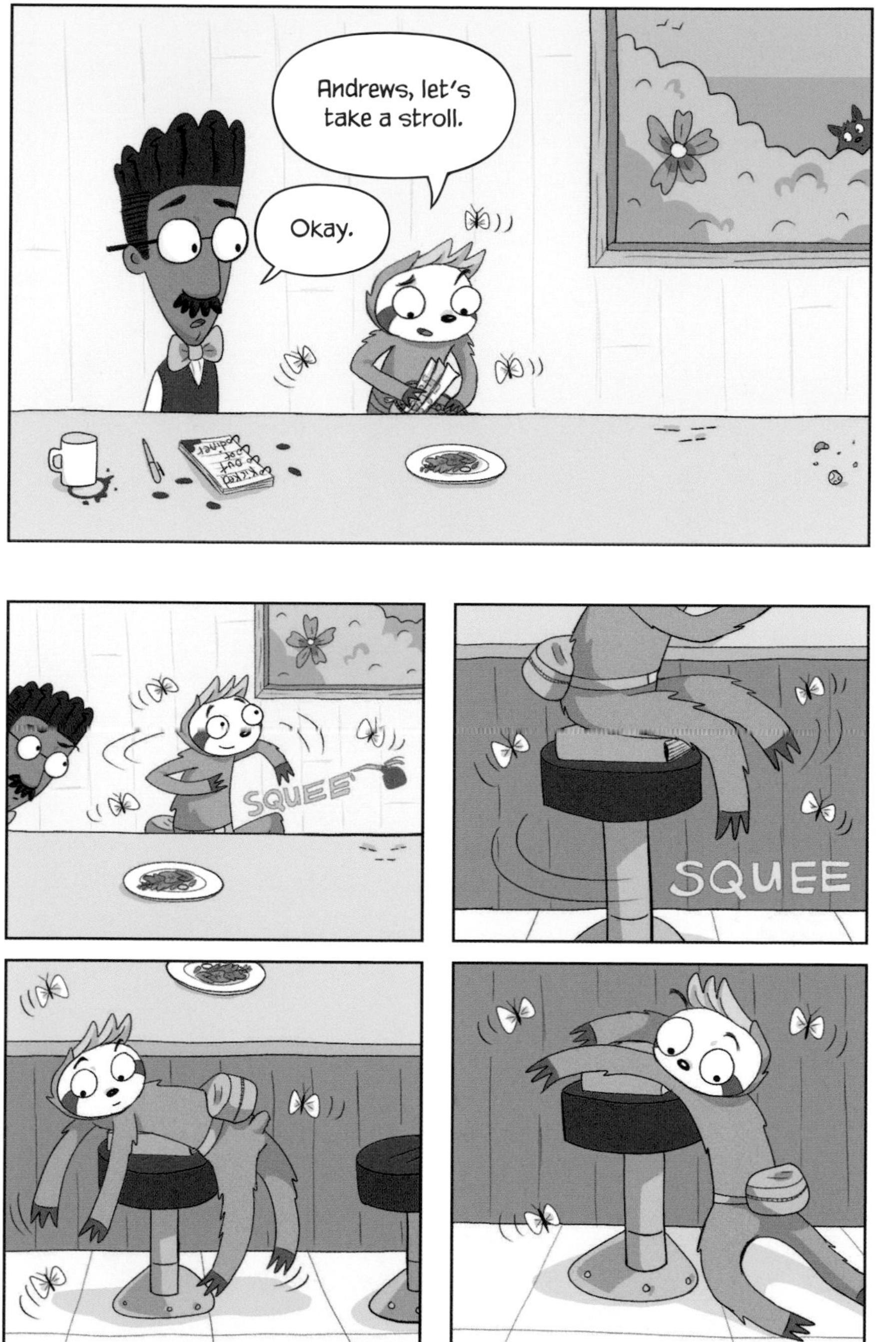
Andrews, let's take a stroll.
Okay.
SQUEE
SQUEE

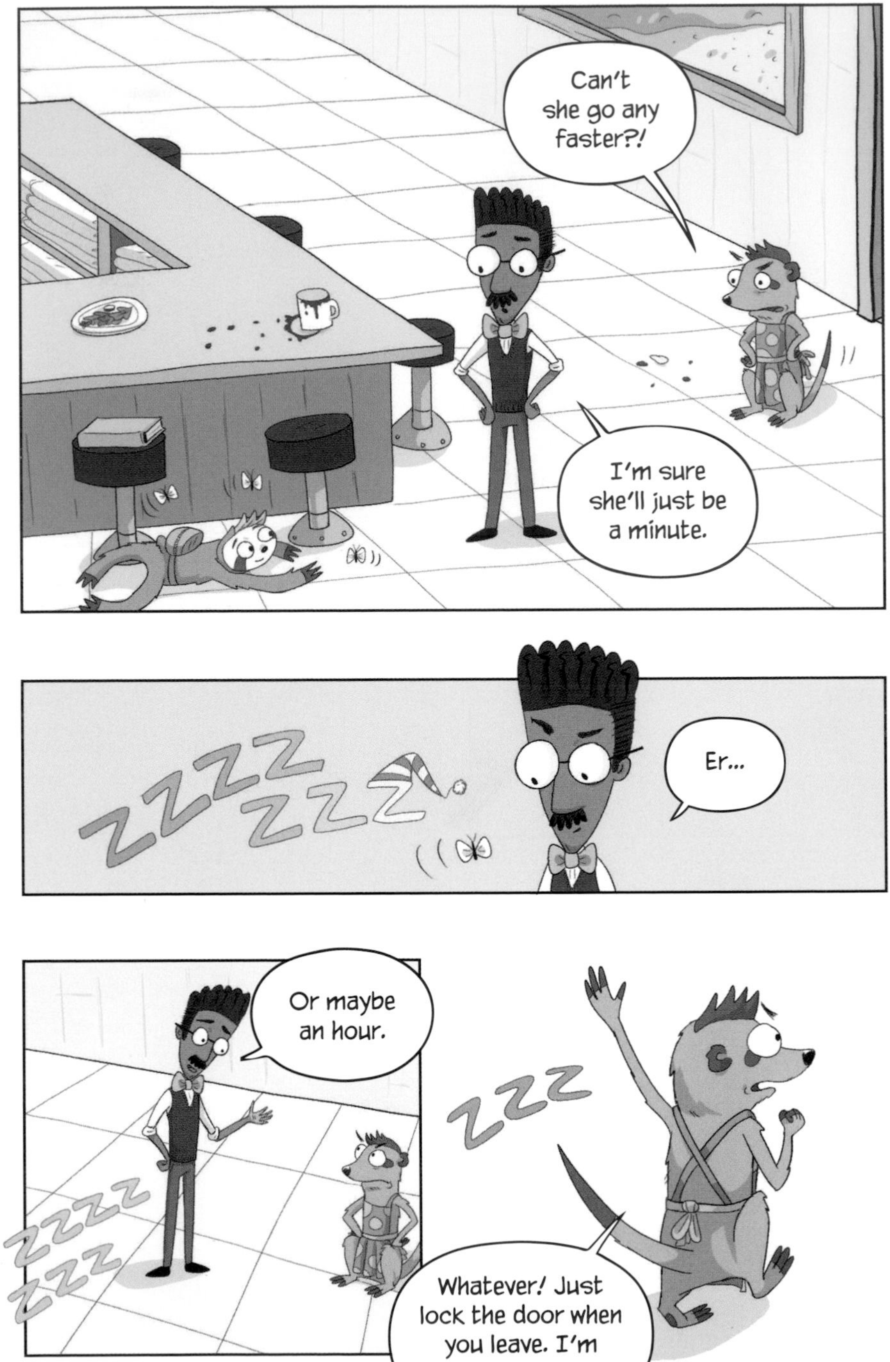
Can't she go any faster?!
I'm sure she'll just be a minute.
Er...
Or maybe an hour.
Whatever! Just lock the door when you leave. I'm going home.

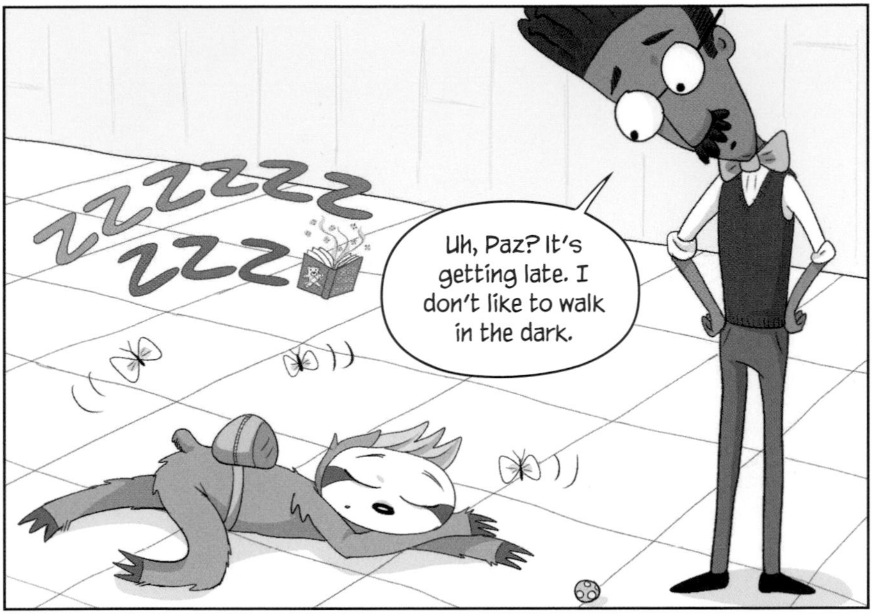
ZZZZZZZ
ZZZ
Uh, Paz? It's getting late. I don't like to walk in the dark.

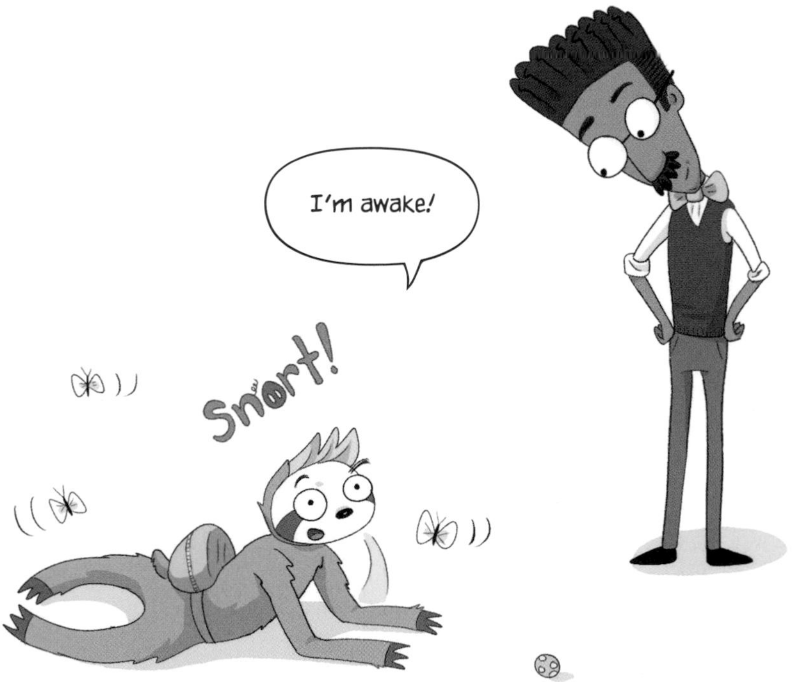
I'm awake!
Snort!

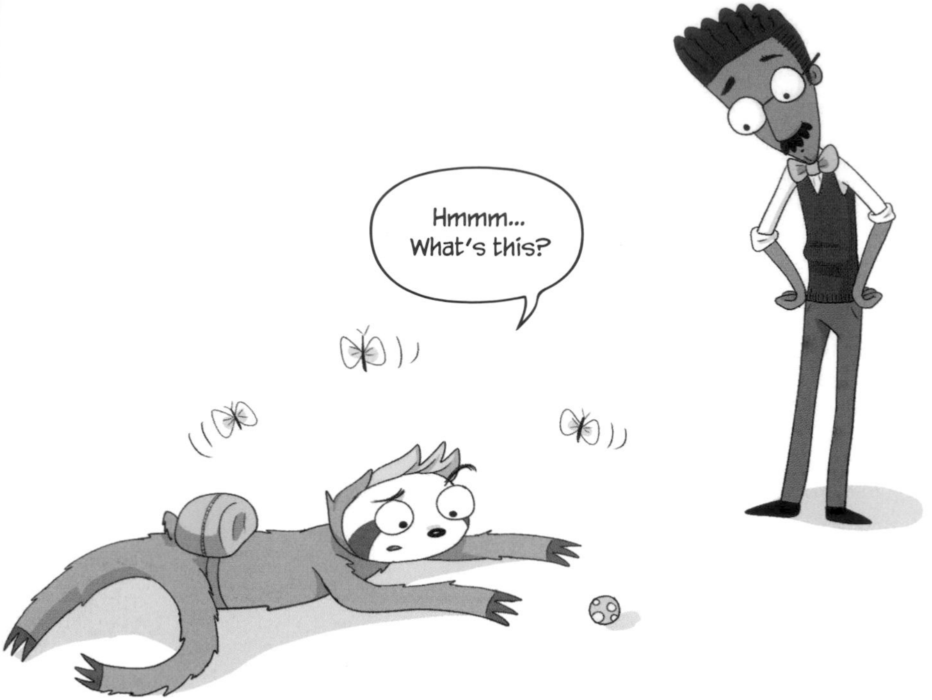
Hmmm...
What's this?

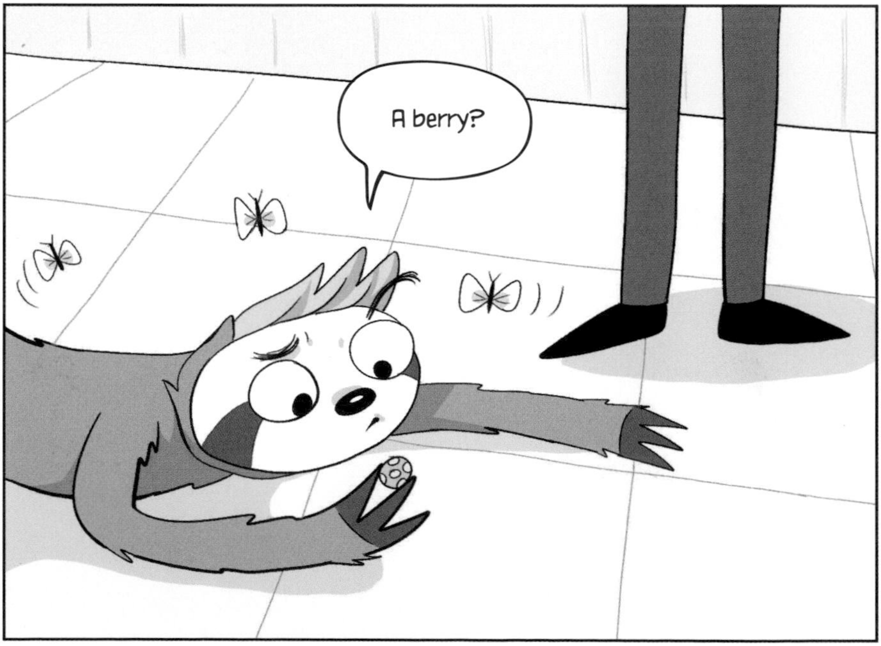
A berry?

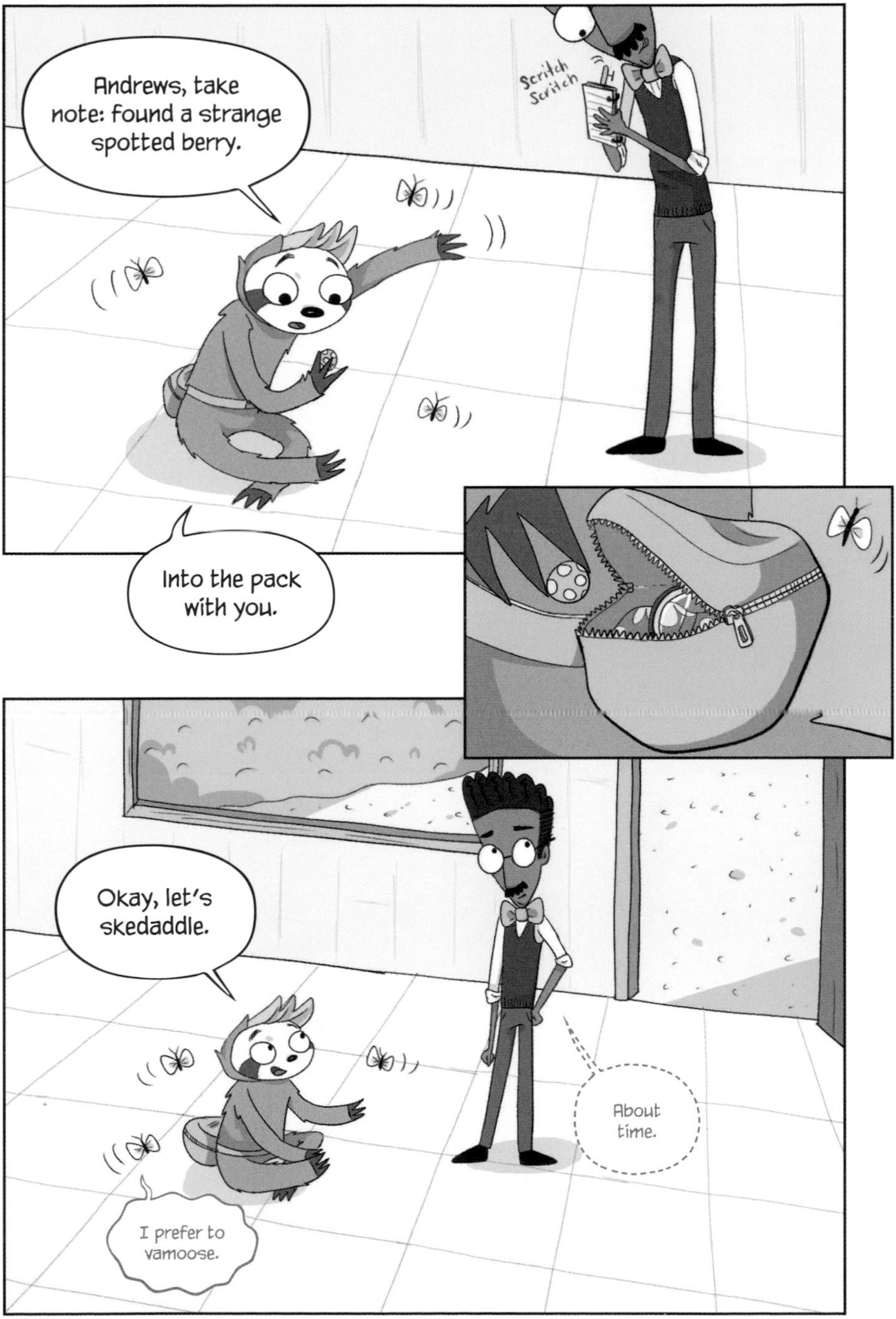
Andrews, take note: found a strange spotted berry.
Scritch Scritch
Into the pack with you.
Okay, let's skedaddle.
About time.
I prefer to vamoose.

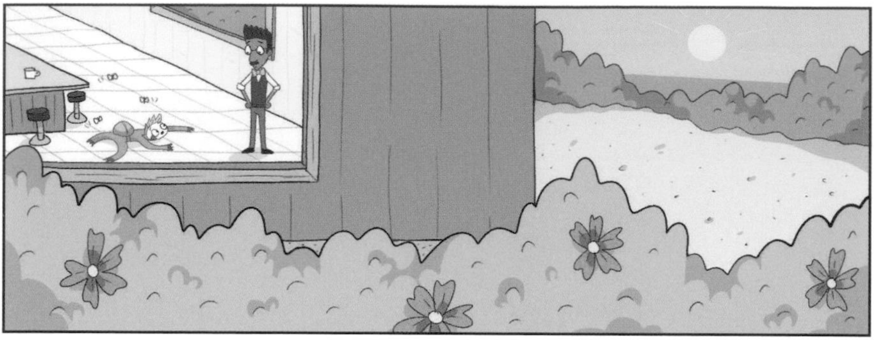

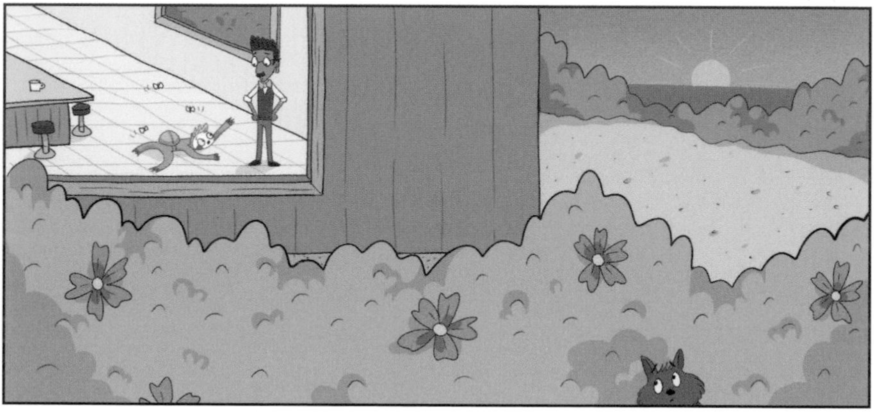

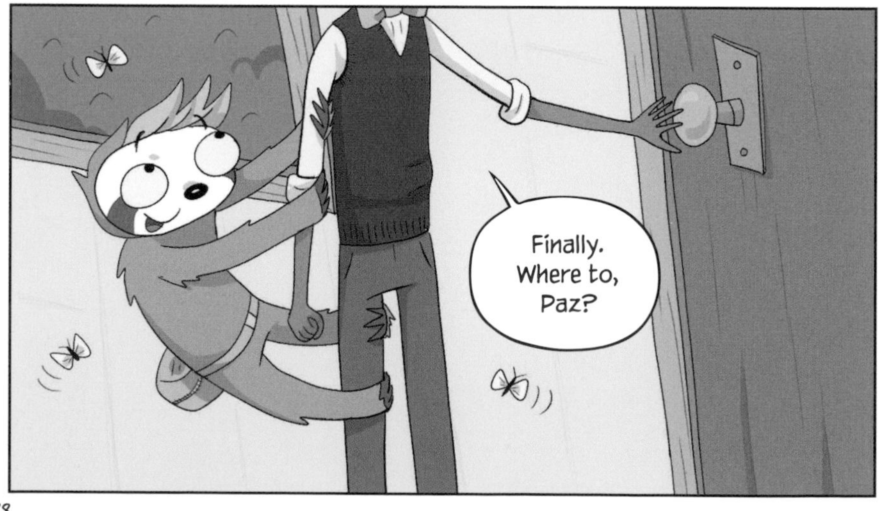
Finally. Where to, Paz?

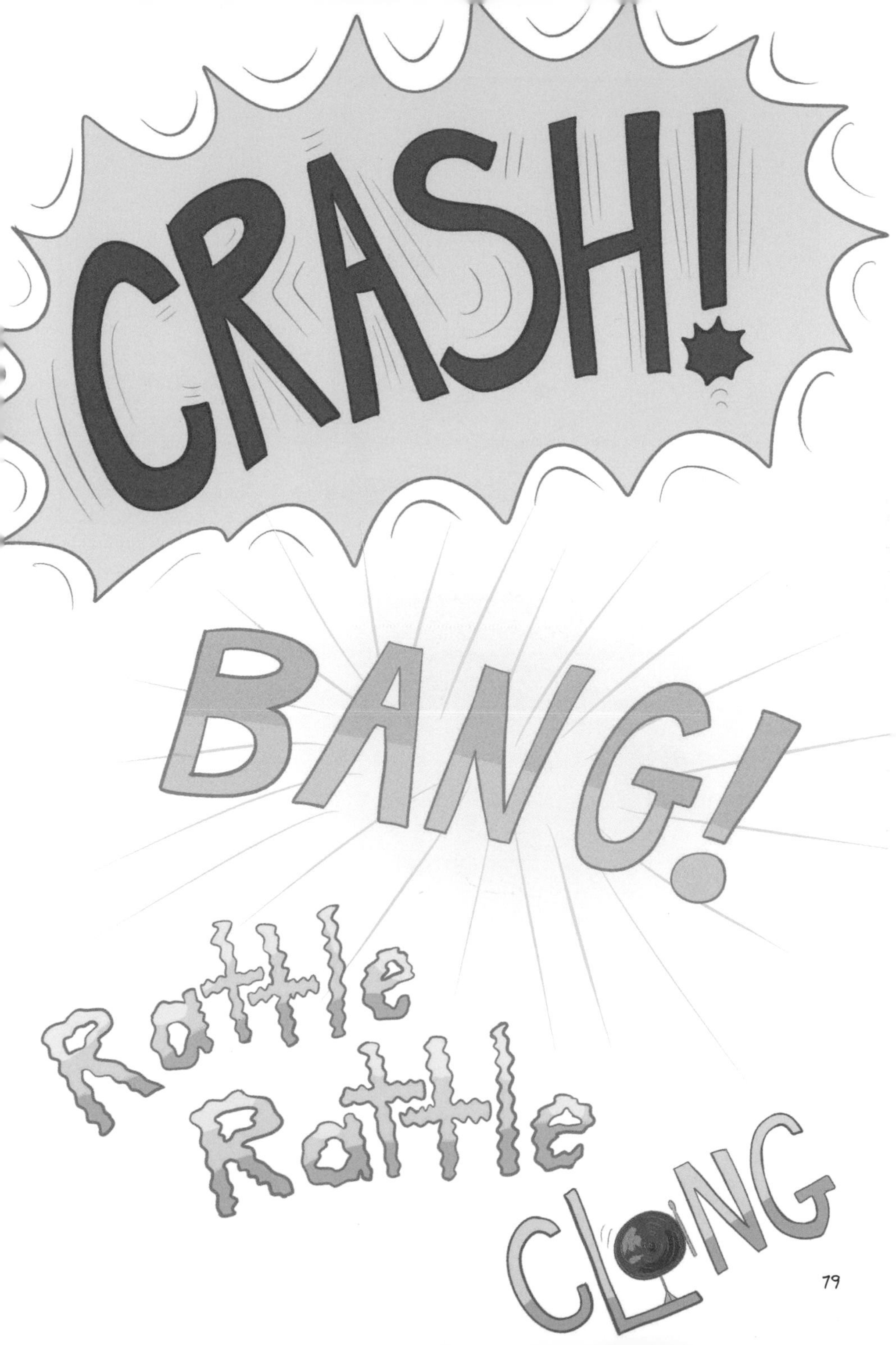
CRASH!
BANG!
Rattle
Rattle
CLING

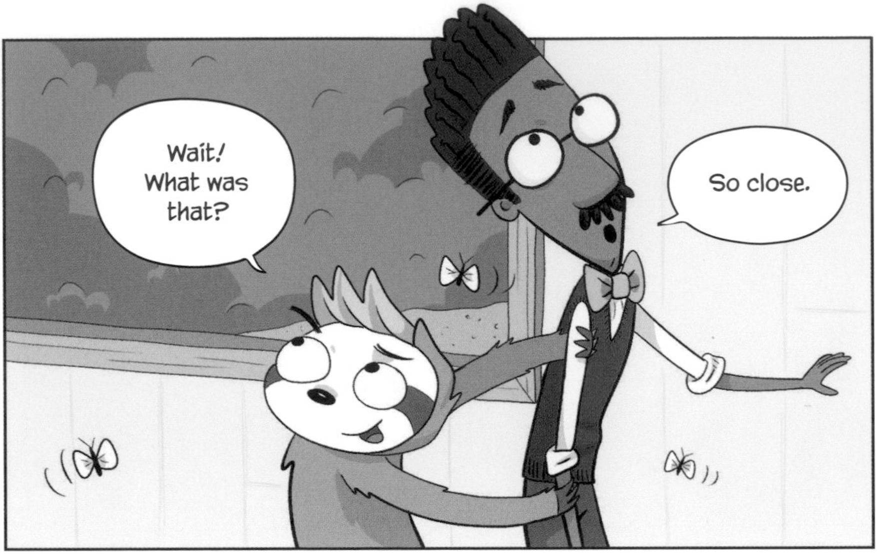
Wait!
What was
that?
So close.

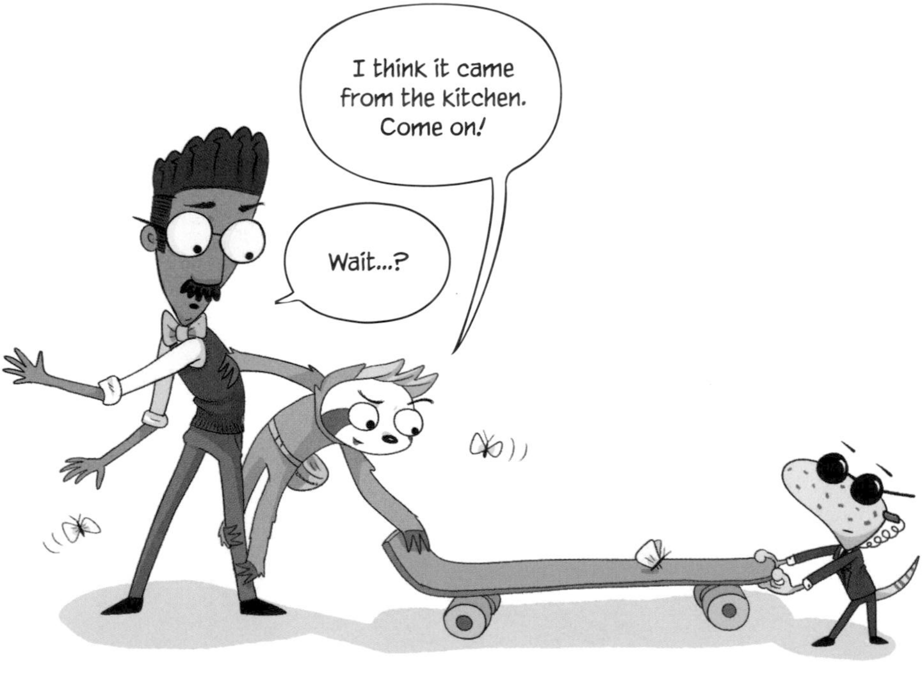
I think it came
from the kitchen.
Come on!
Wait...?

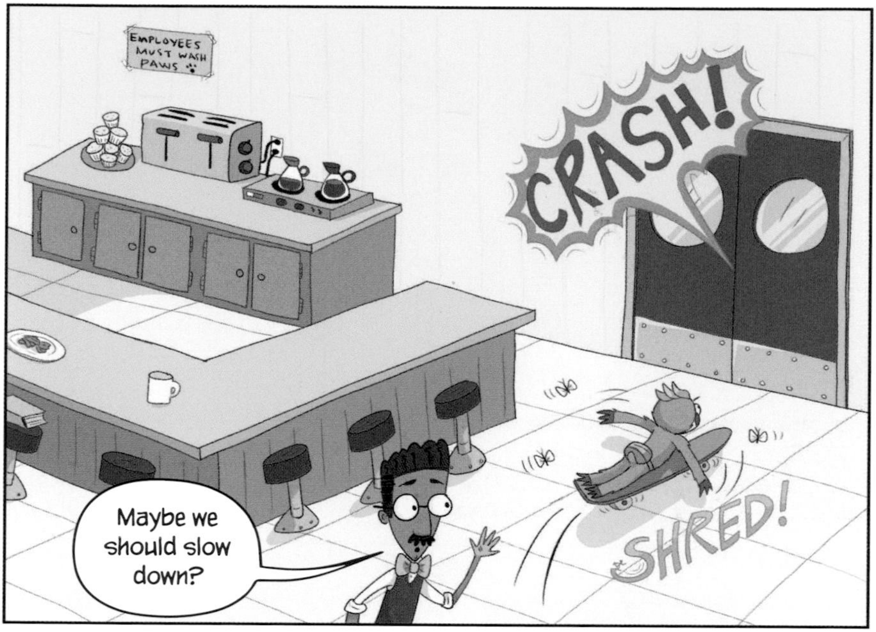
EMPLOYEES MUST WASH PAWS
CRASH!
SHRED!
Maybe we should slow down?

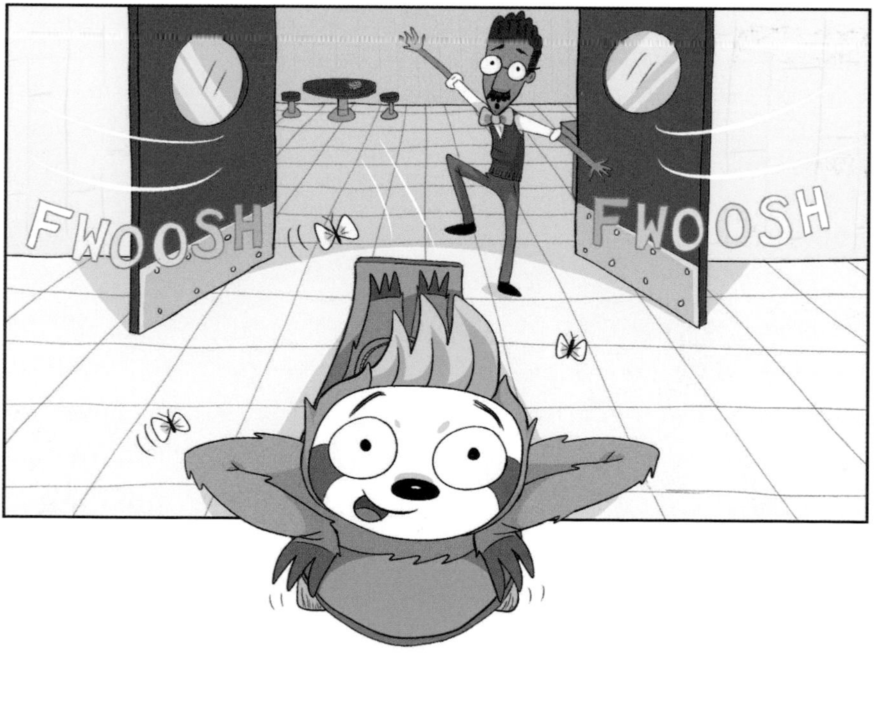
FWOOSH
FWOOSH

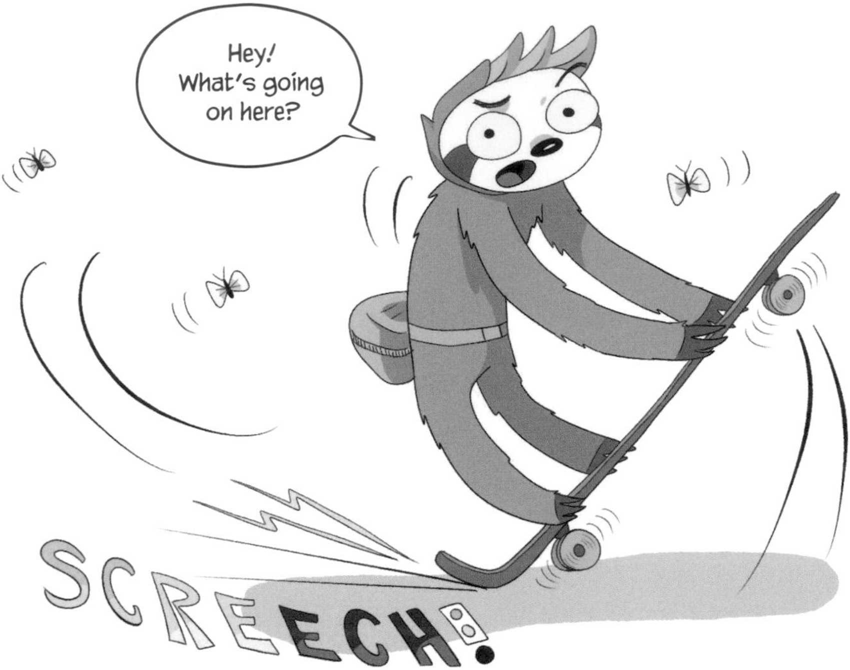
Hey! What's going on here?
SCREECH!

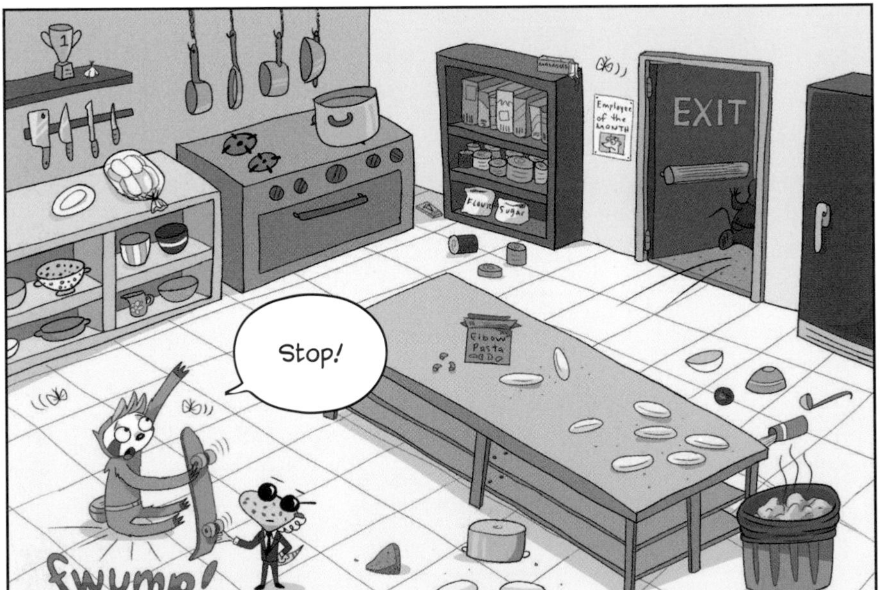
EXIT
Employee of the MONTH
Flour
Sugar
Elbow Pasta
Stop!
fwump!

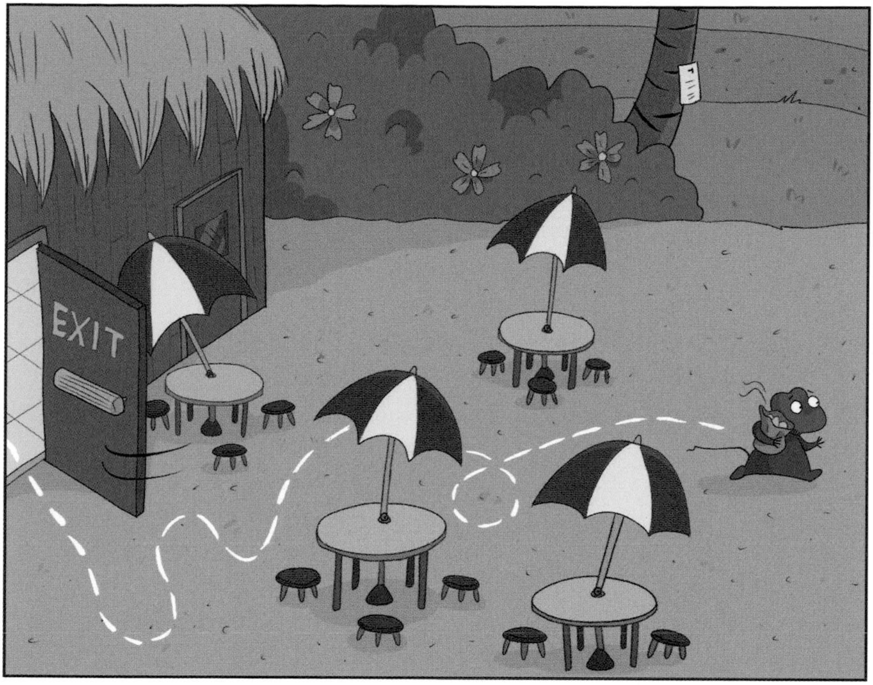
EXIT

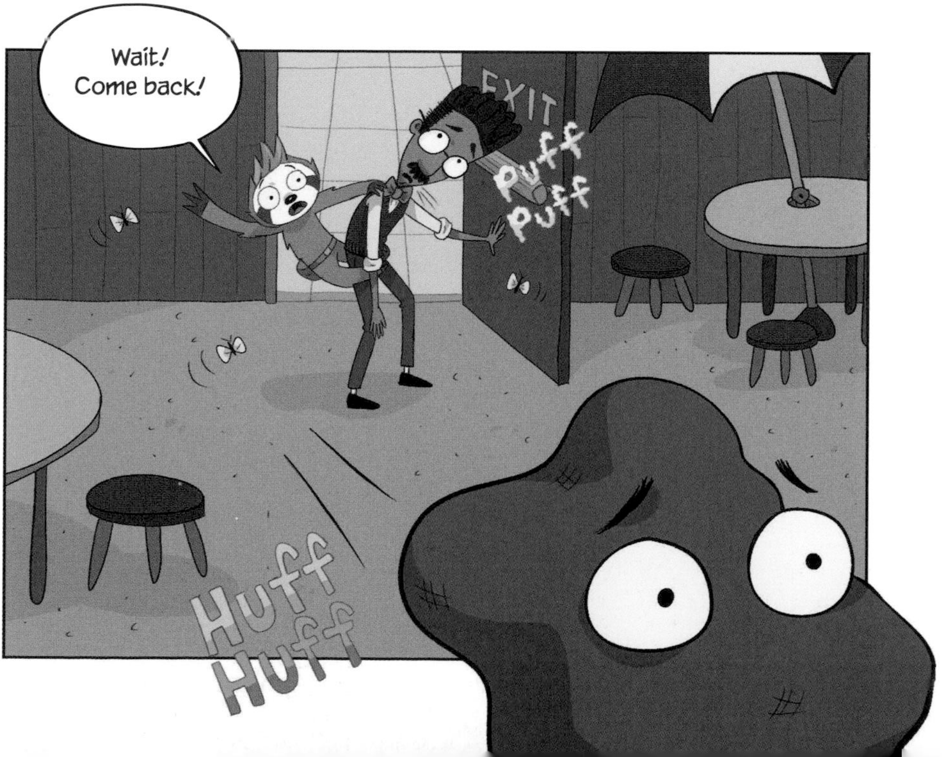
Wait!
Come back!
EXIT
puff
puff
Huff
Huff

CHAPTER 4

TUESDAY. CLOSE TO BEDTIME.
CHASING AFTER A BURGLAR.

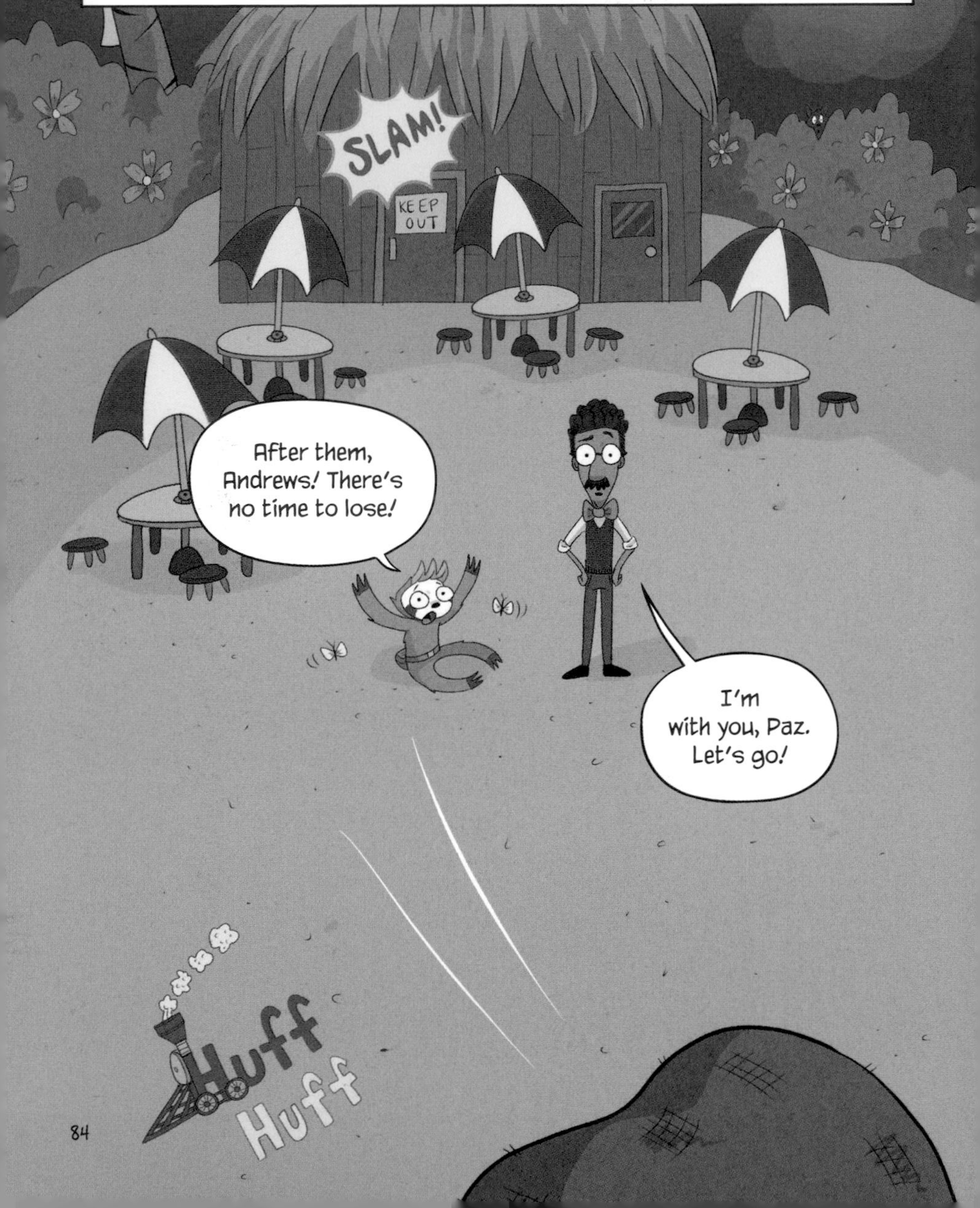
SLAM!
KEEP OUT
After them, Andrews! There's no time to lose!
I'm with you, Paz. Let's go!
Huff
Huff

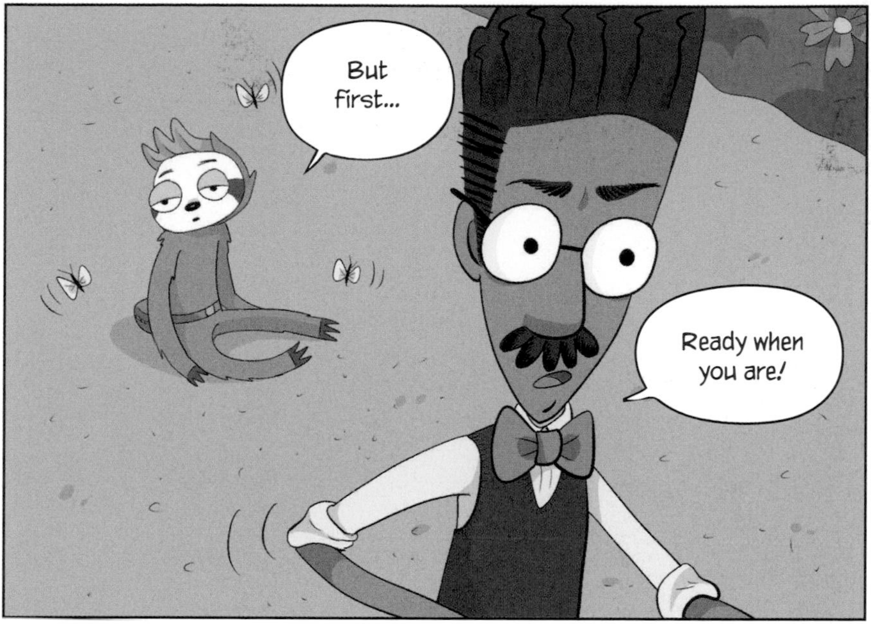
But first...
Ready when you are!

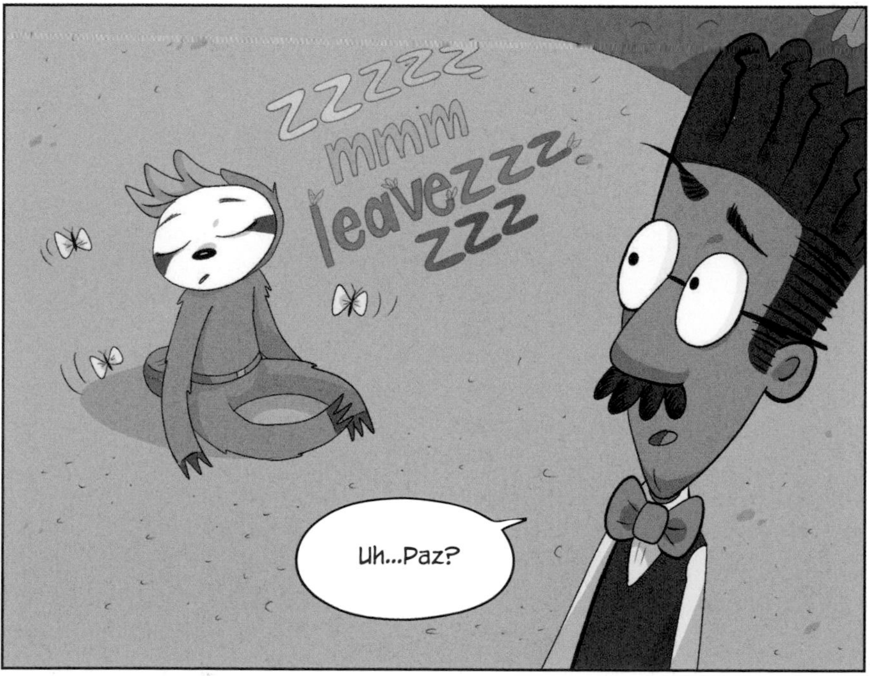
ZZZZZ
mmm
leavezzz
zzz
Uh...Paz?

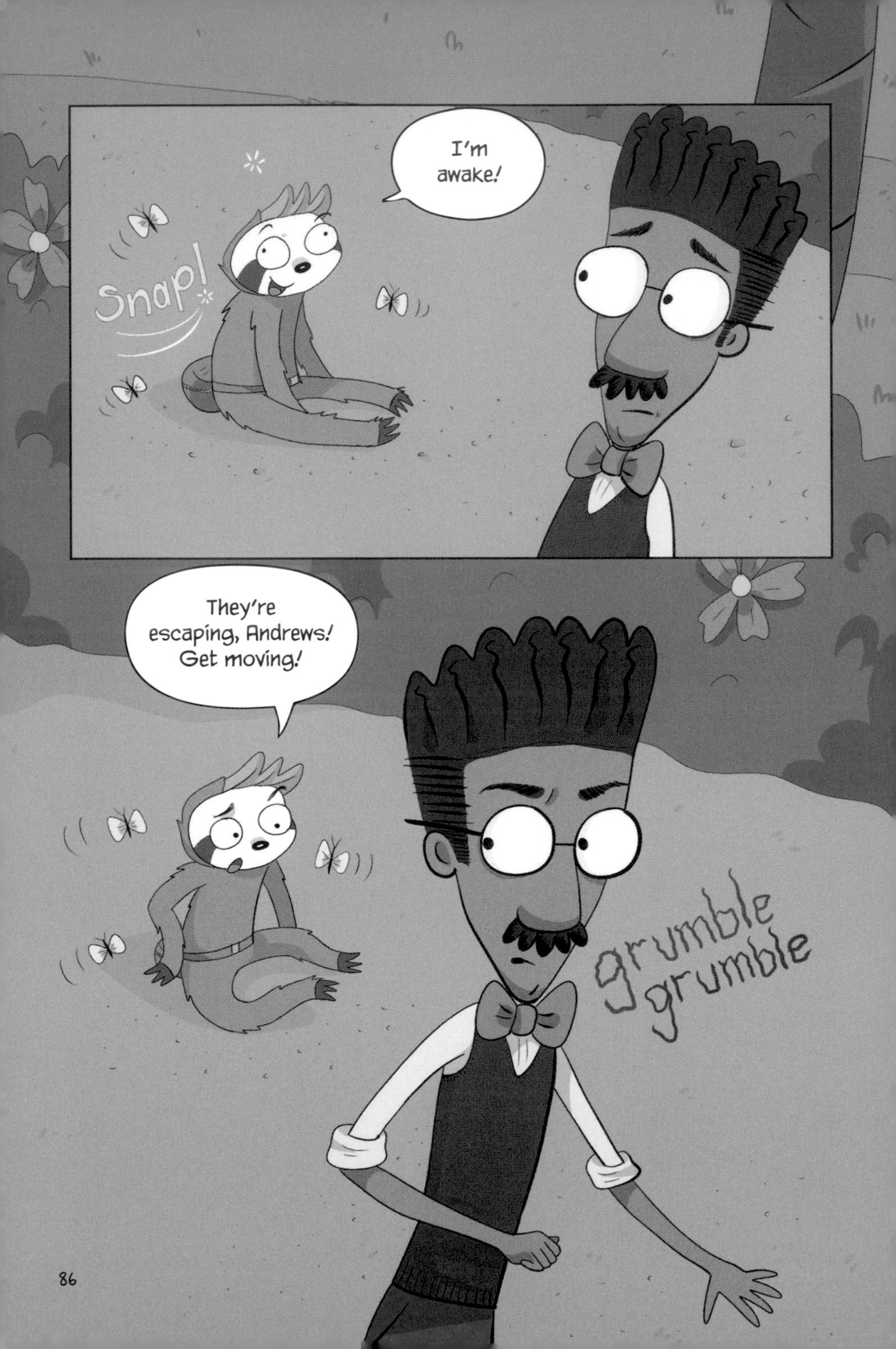
I'm awake!
Snap!
They're escaping, Andrews! Get moving!
grumble grumble

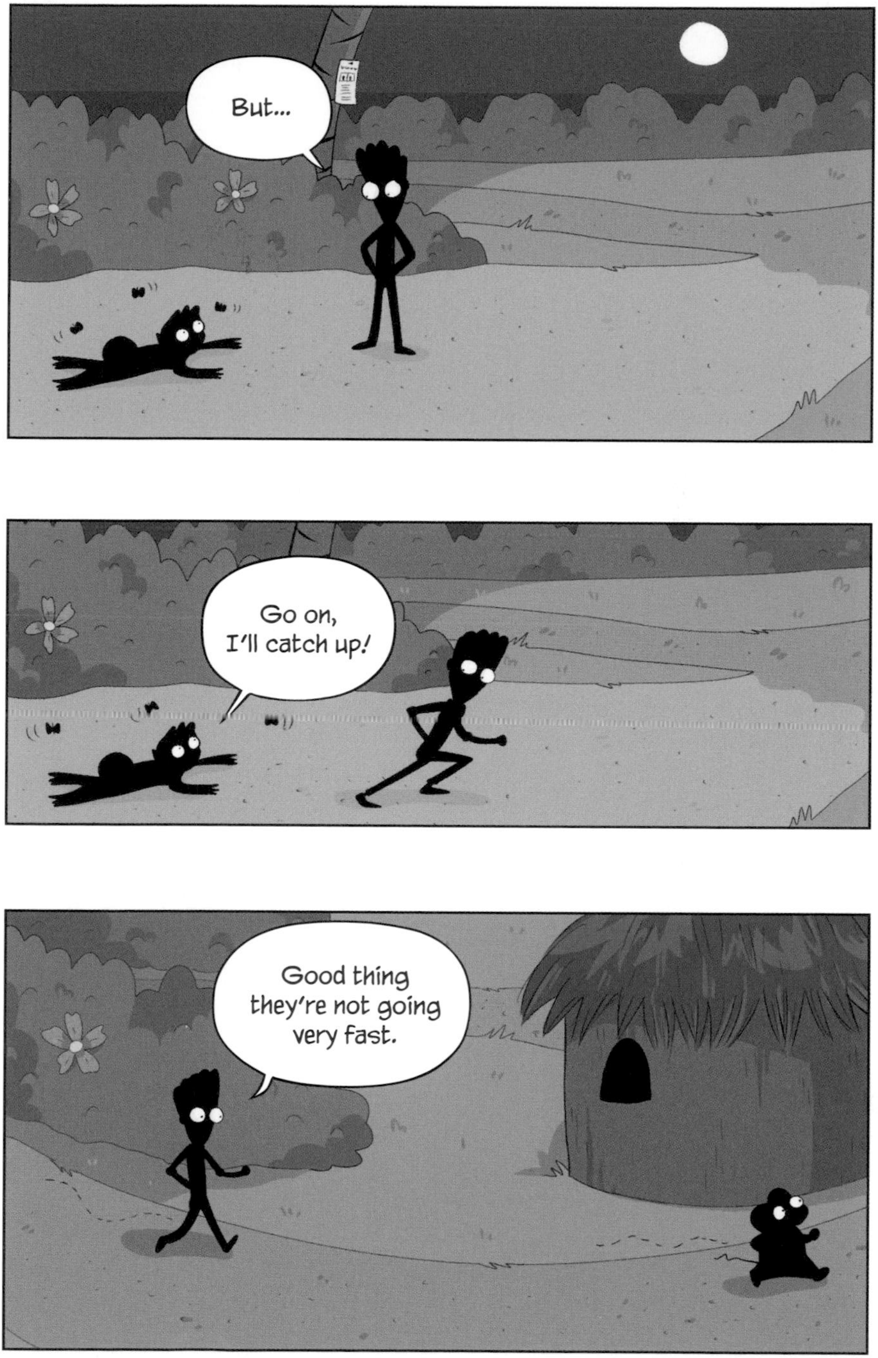
But...
Go on,
I'll catch up!
Good thing
they're not going
very fast.

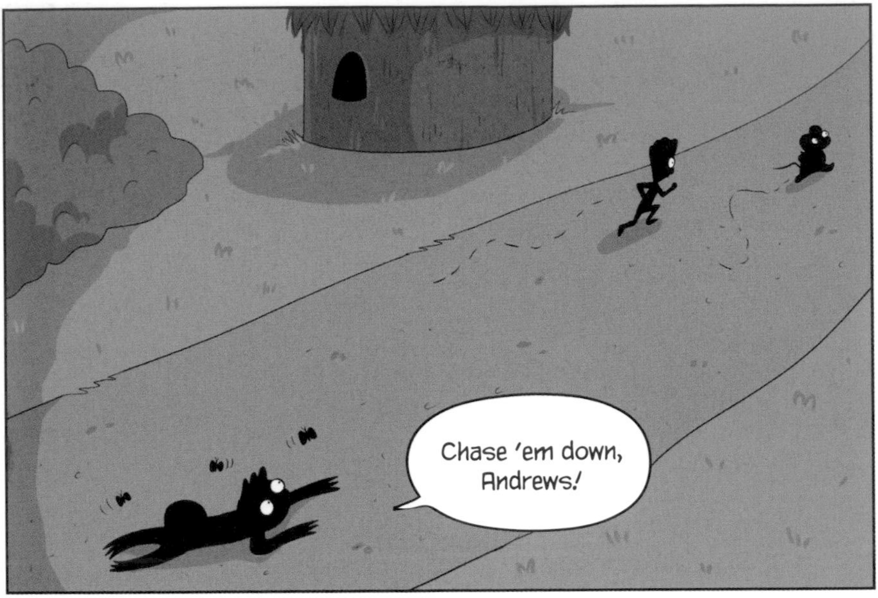
Chase 'em down,
Andrews!

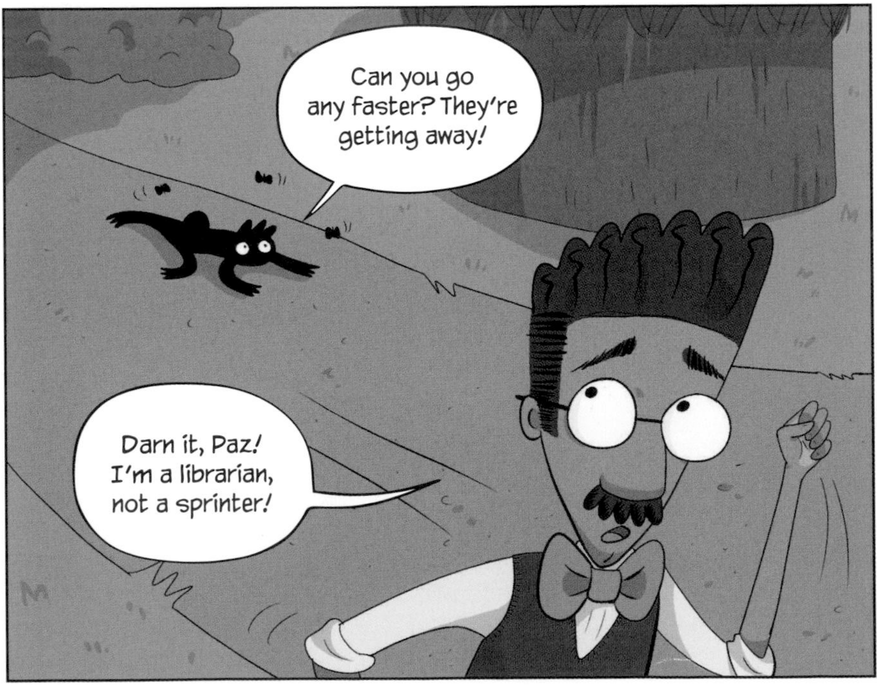
Can you go
any faster? They're
getting away!
Darn it, Paz!
I'm a librarian,
not a sprinter!

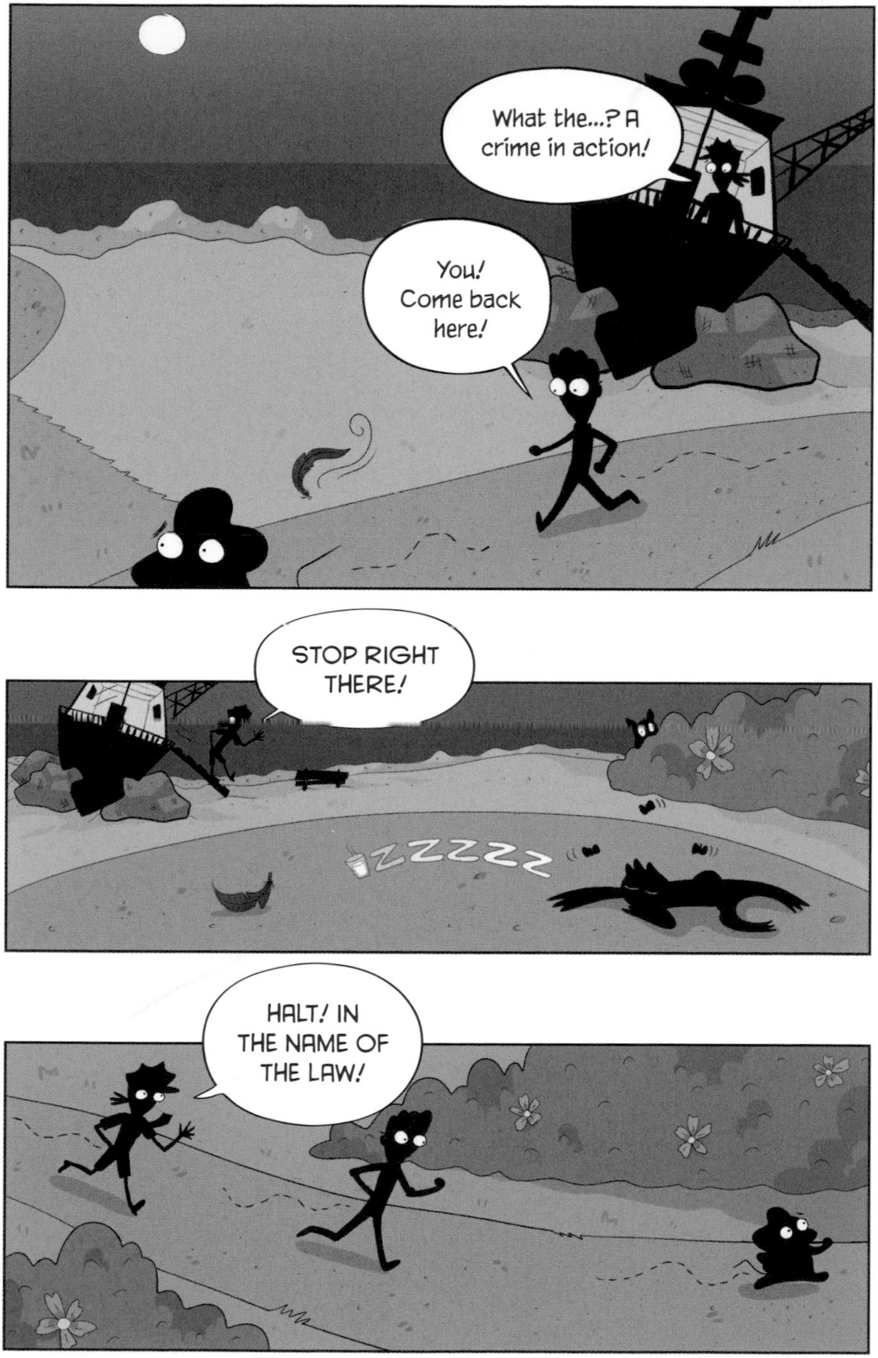
What the...? A crime in action!
You! Come back here!
STOP RIGHT THERE!
HALT! IN THE NAME OF THE LAW!

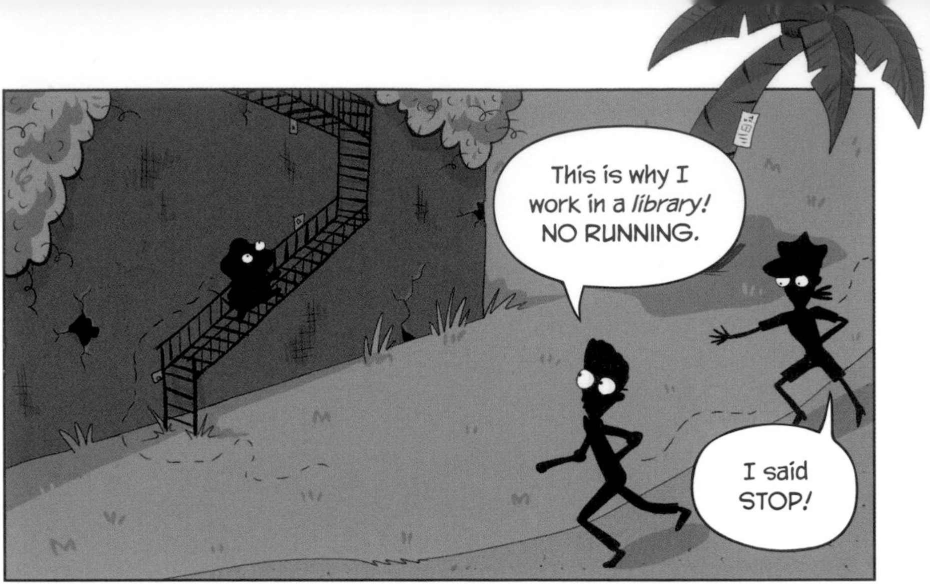
This is why I work in a *library*! NO RUNNING.
I said STOP!

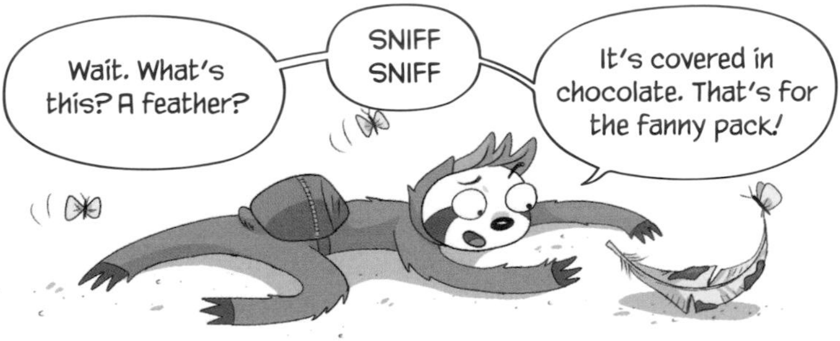
Wait. What's this? A feather?
SNIFF SNIFF
It's covered in chocolate. That's for the fanny pack!

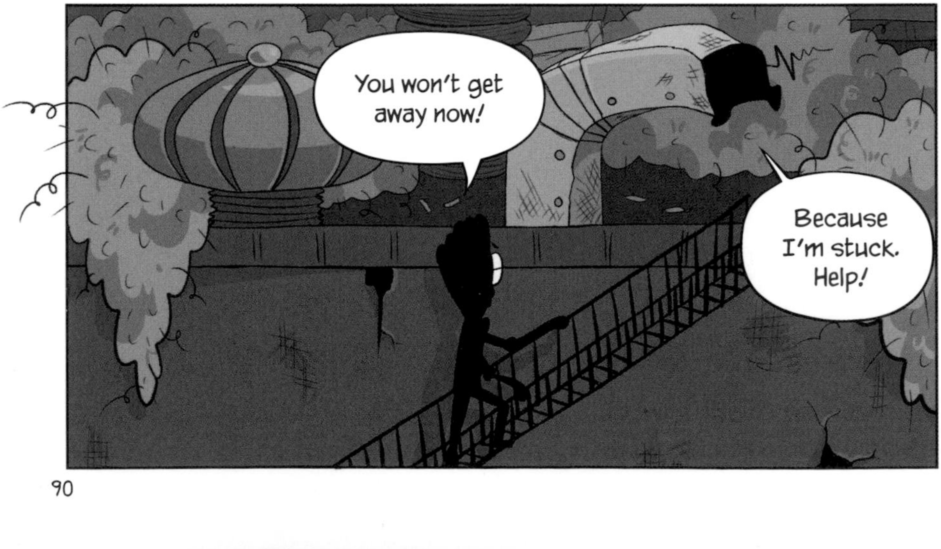
You won't get away now!
Because I'm stuck. Help!

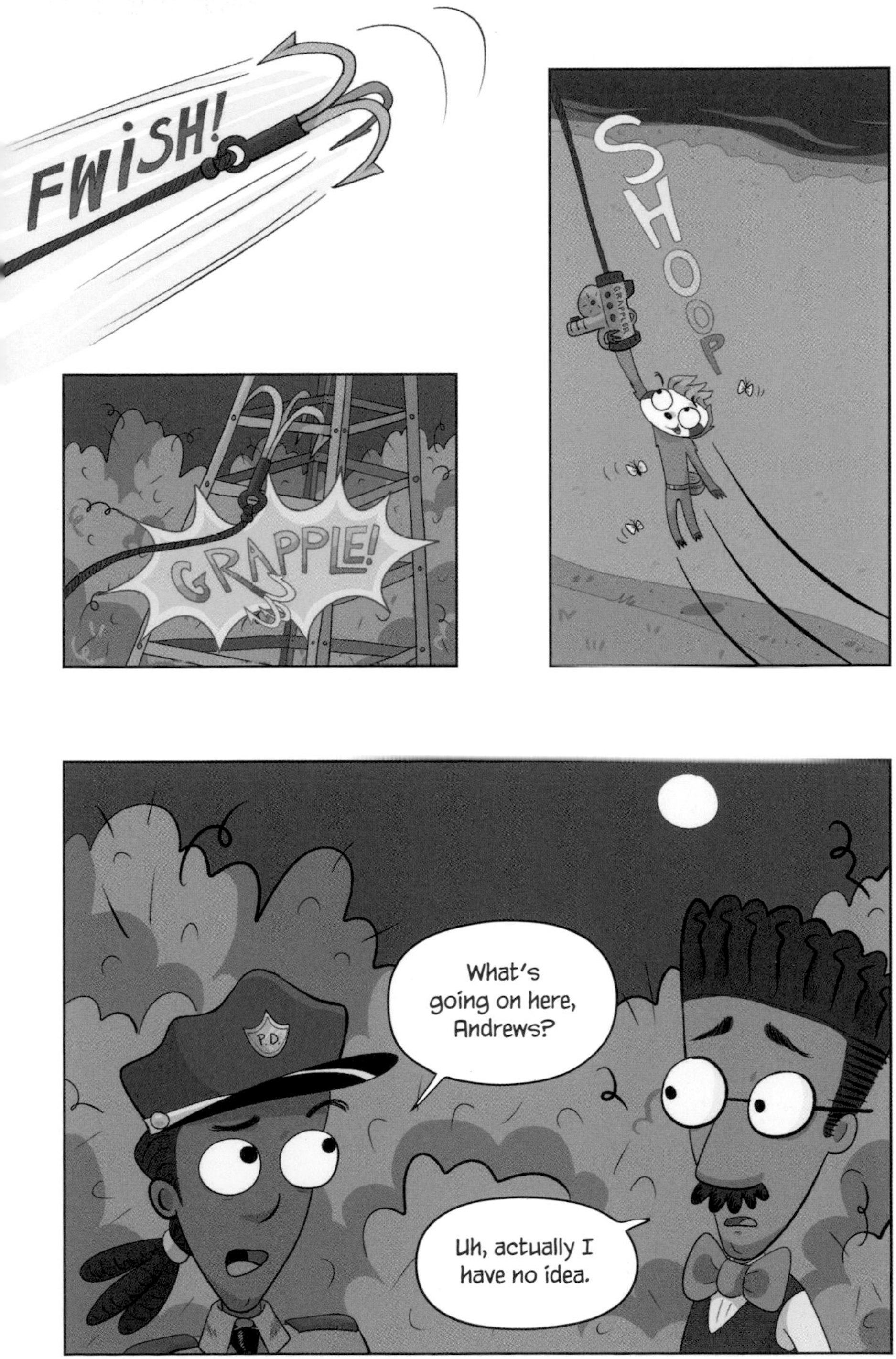
FWiSH!
GRAPPLE!
SHOOP
GRAPPLER
What's going on here, Andrews?
Uh, actually I have no idea.

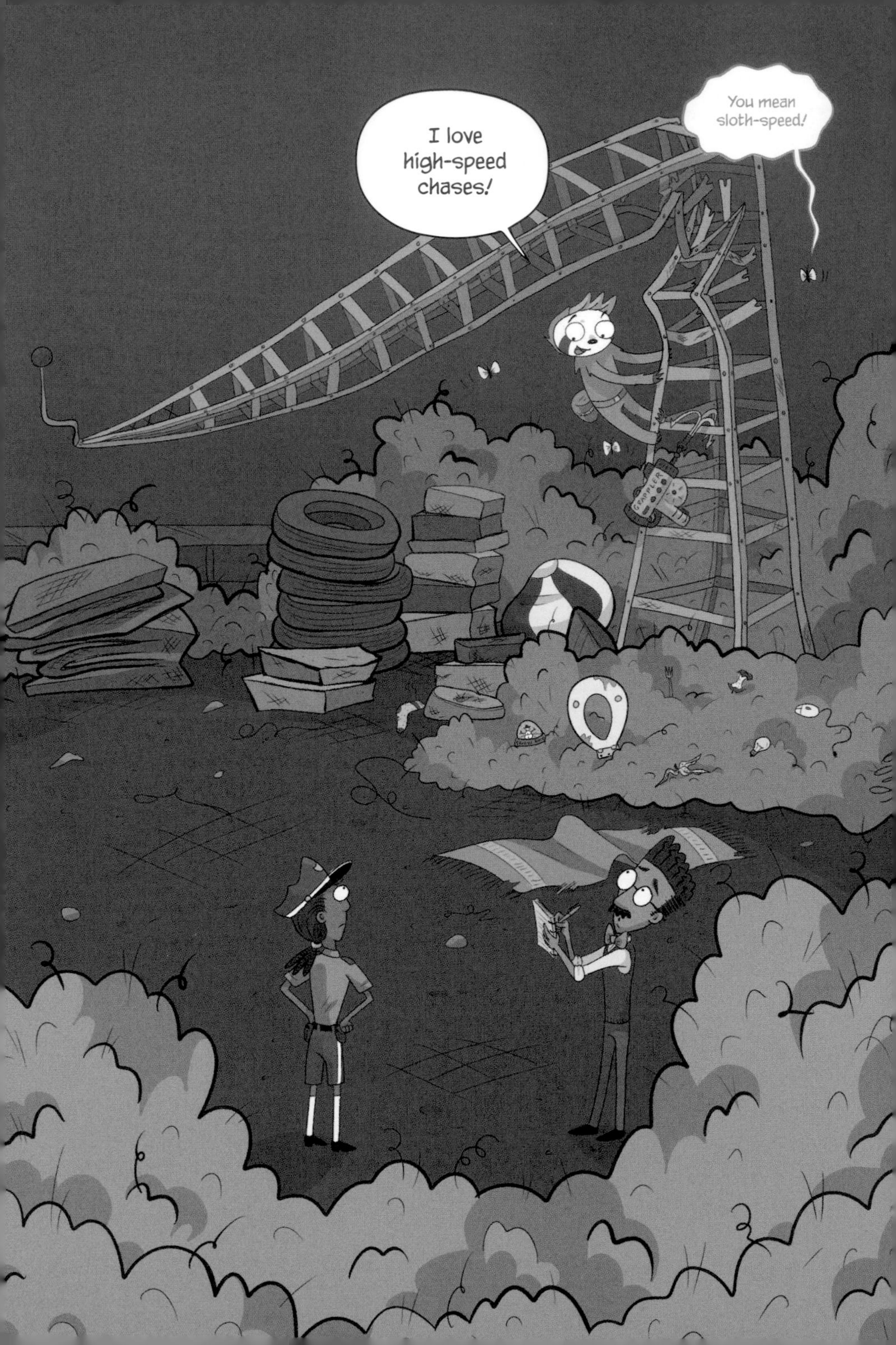
I love high-speed chases!
You mean sloth-speed!

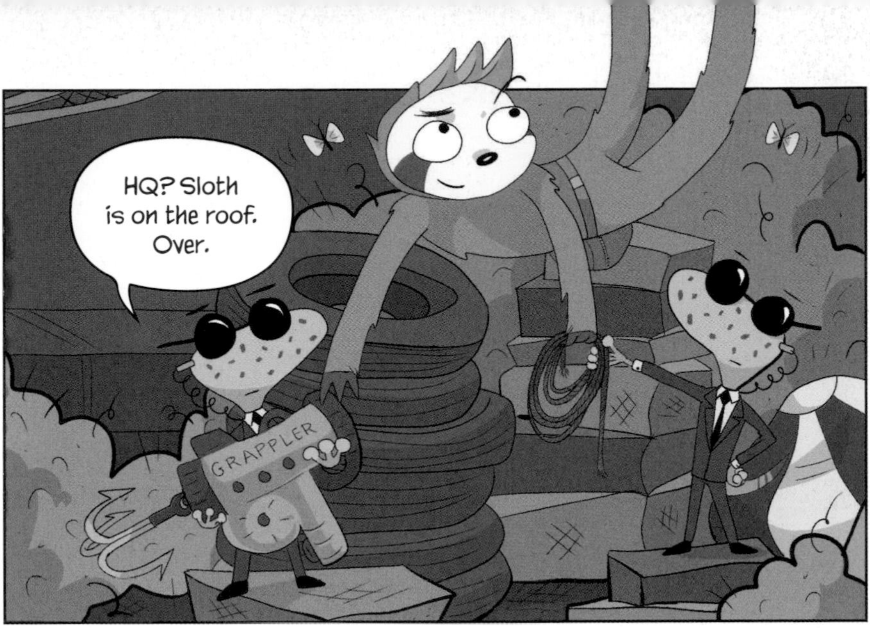
HQ? Sloth
is on the roof.
Over.
GRAPPLER

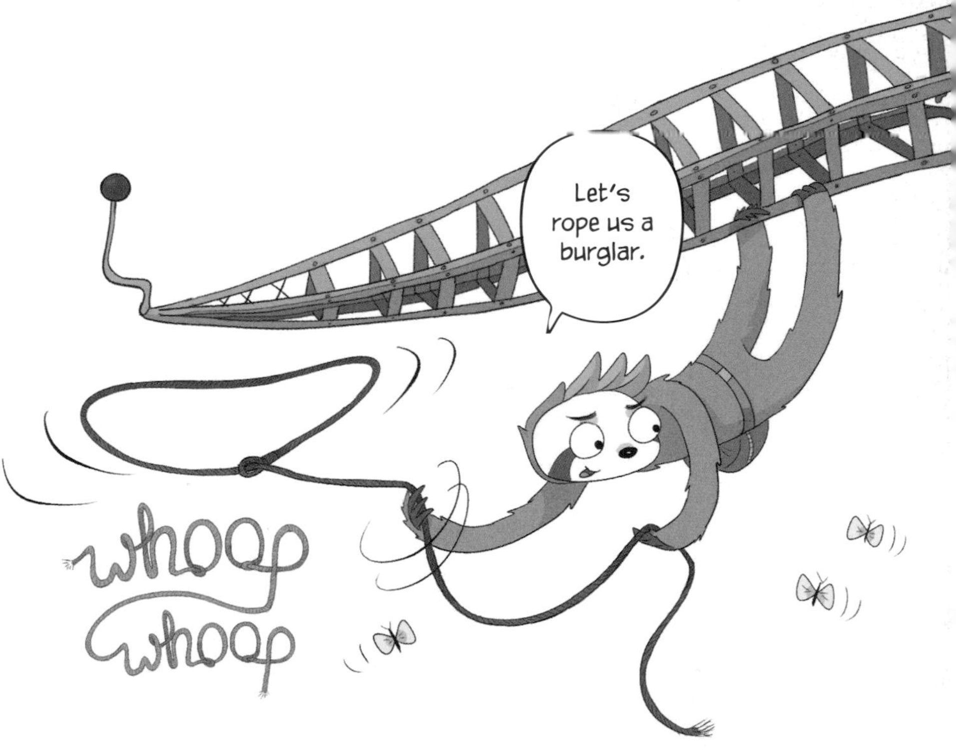
Let's
rope us a
burglar.
whoop
whoop

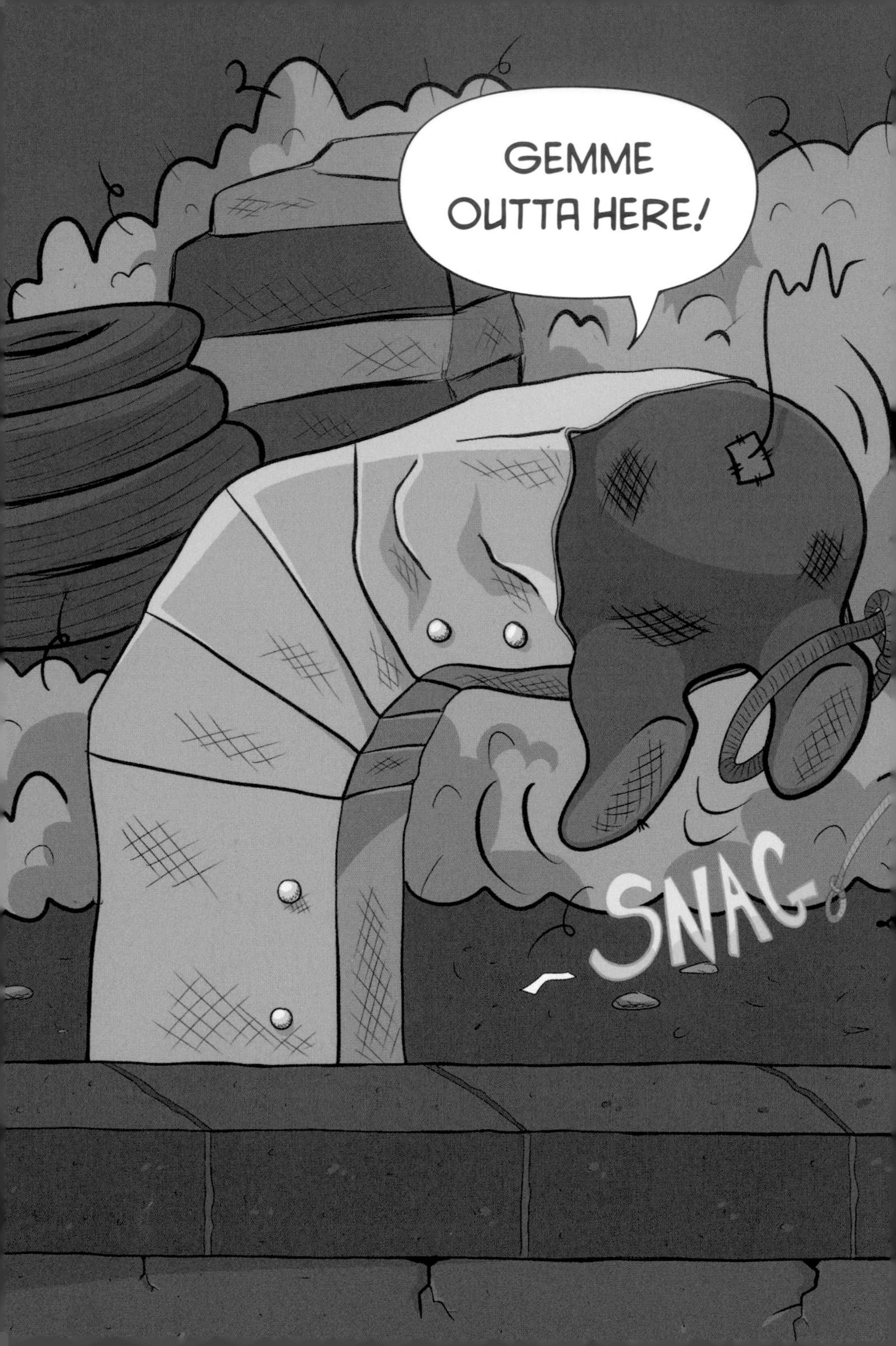
GEMME OUTTA HERE!
SNAG

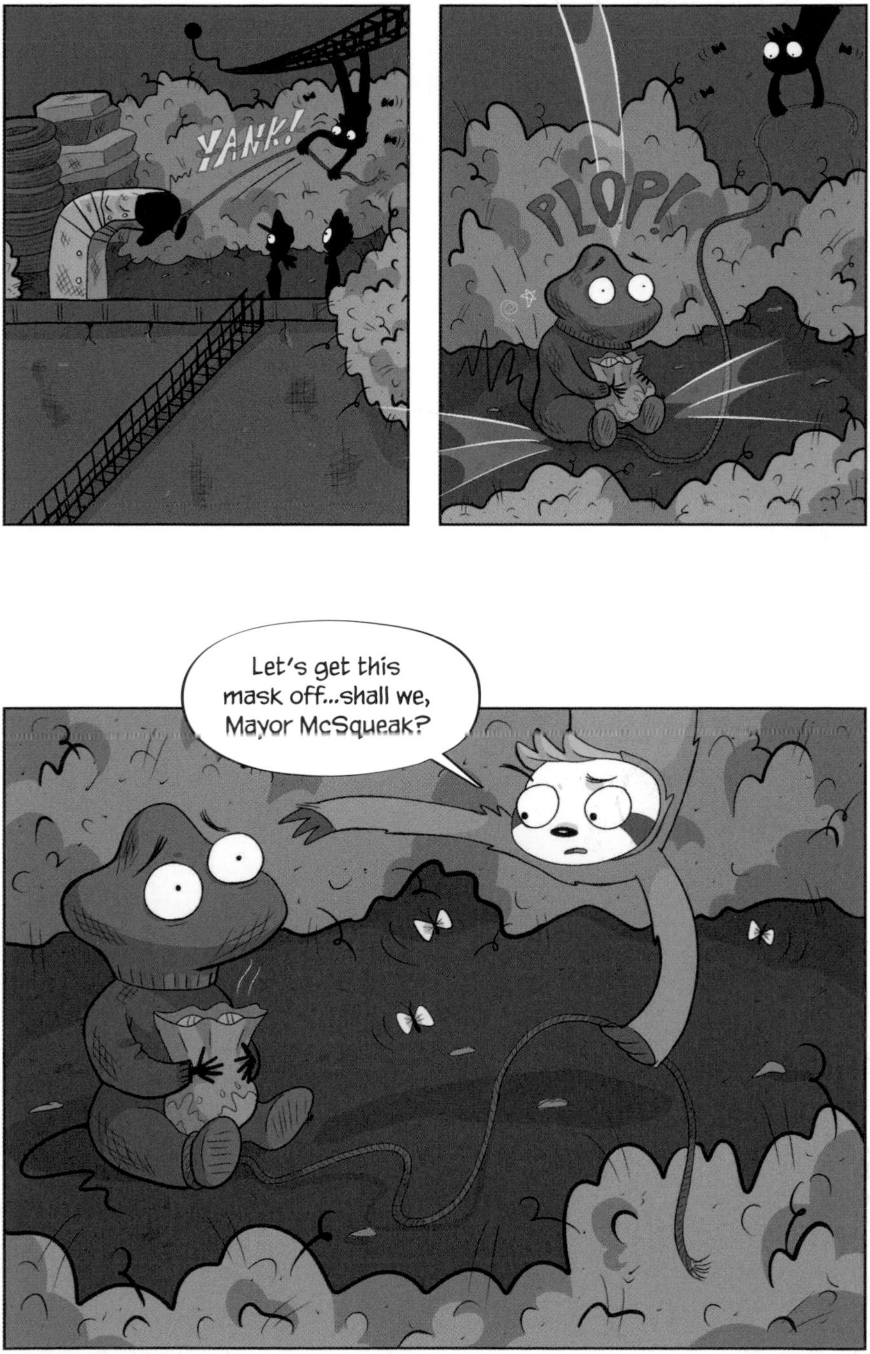
YANK!
PLOP!
Let's get this mask off...shall we, Mayor McSqueak?

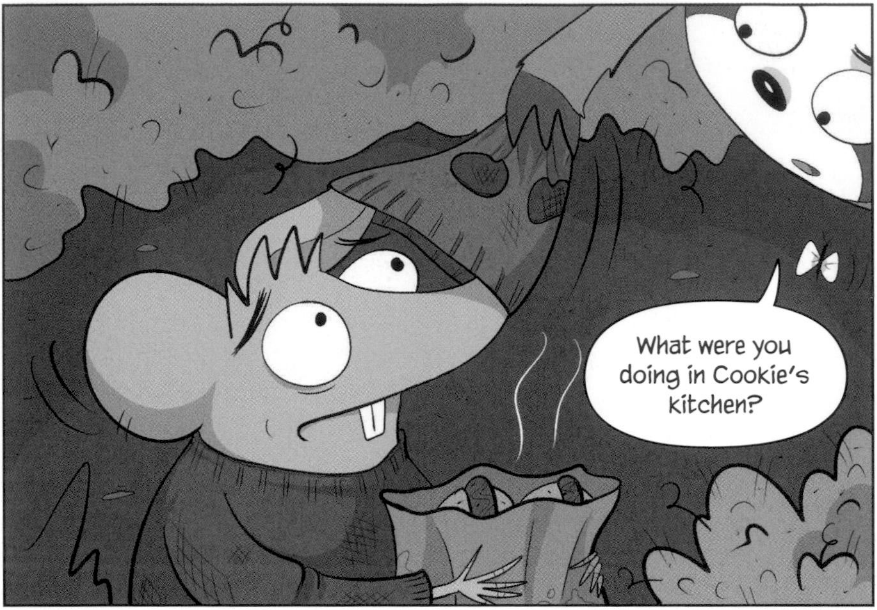
What were you doing in Cookie's kitchen?

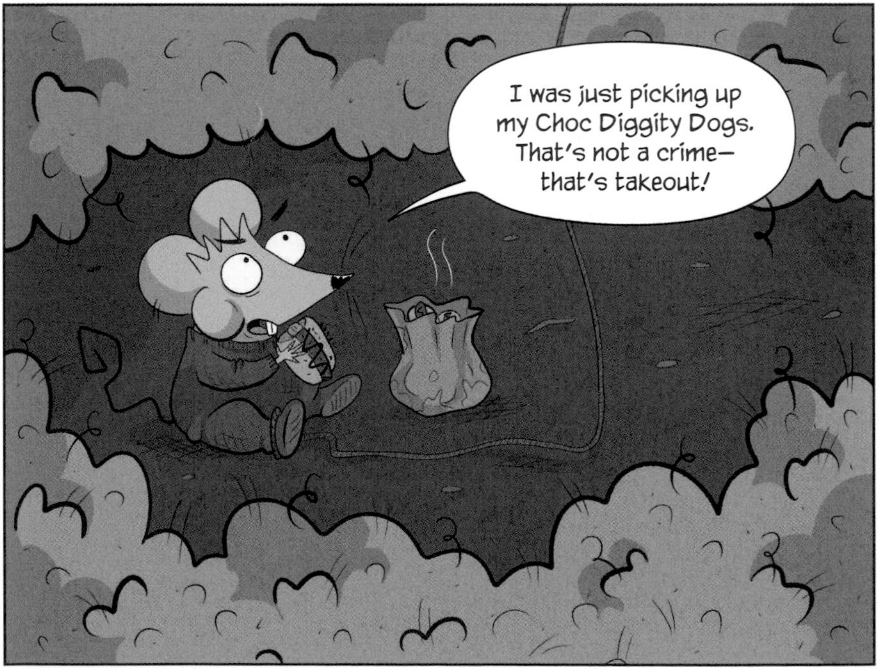
I was just picking up my Choc Diggity Dogs. That's not a crime— that's takeout!

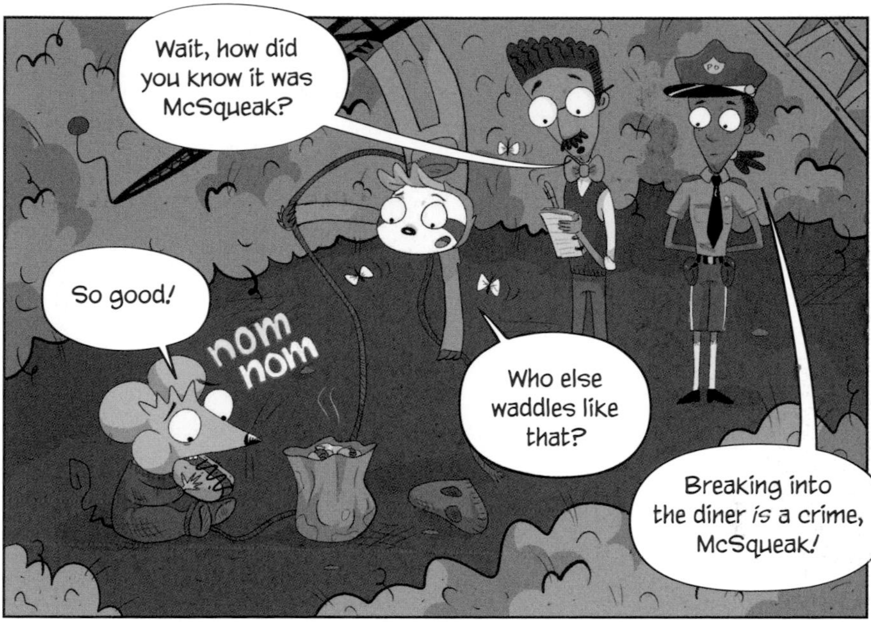
Wait, how did you know it was McSqueak?
So good!
nom nom
Who else waddles like that?
Breaking into the diner *is* a crime, McSqueak!

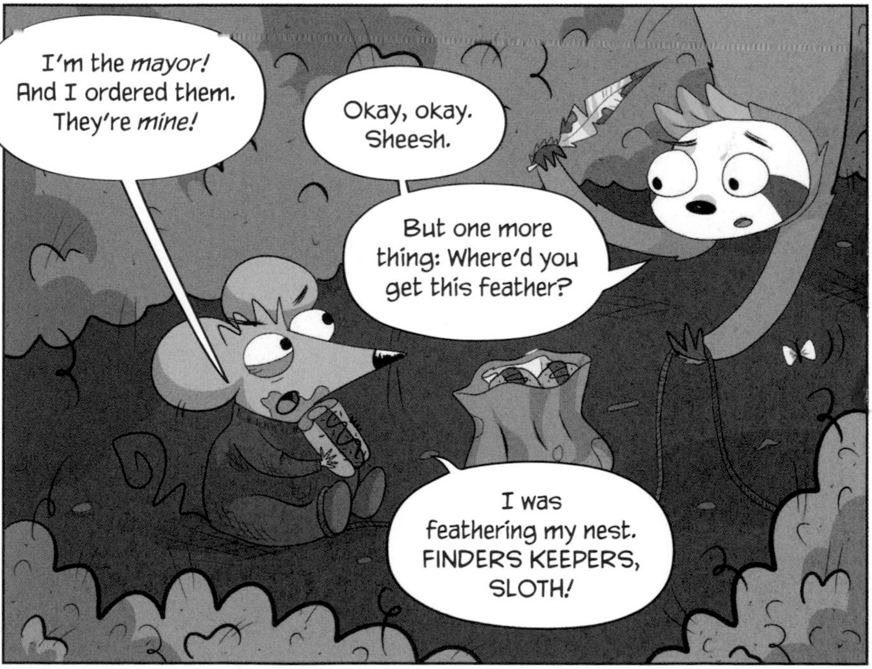
I'm the *mayor!* And I ordered them. They're *mine!*
Okay, okay. Sheesh.
But one more thing: Where'd you get this feather?
I was feathering my nest. FINDERS KEEPERS, SLOTH!

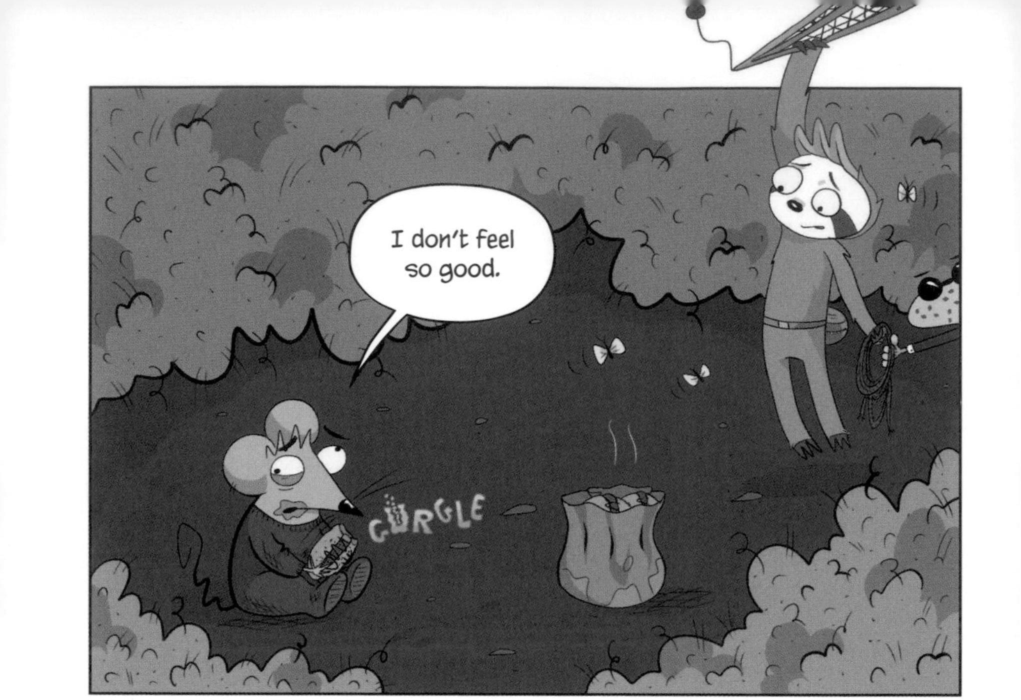
I don't feel so good.
GURGLE

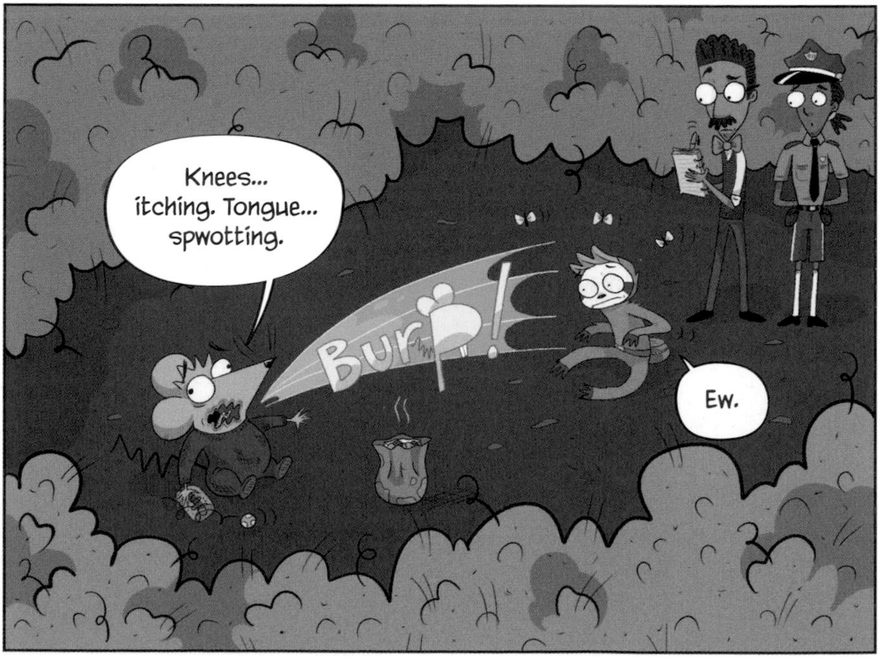
Knees... itching. Tongue... spwotting.
BURP!
Ew.

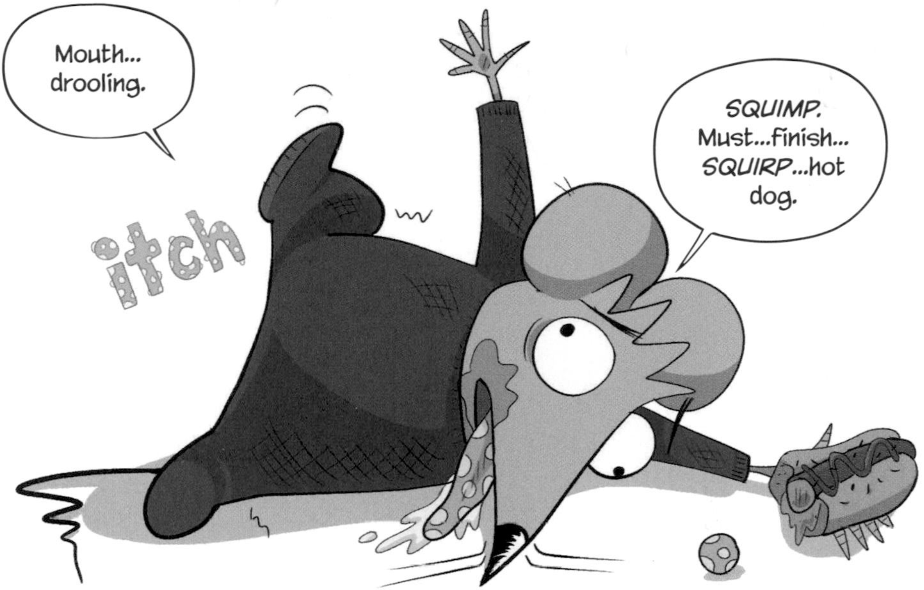
Mouth...
drooling.
itch
SQUIMP. Must...finish... *SQUIRP*...hot dog.

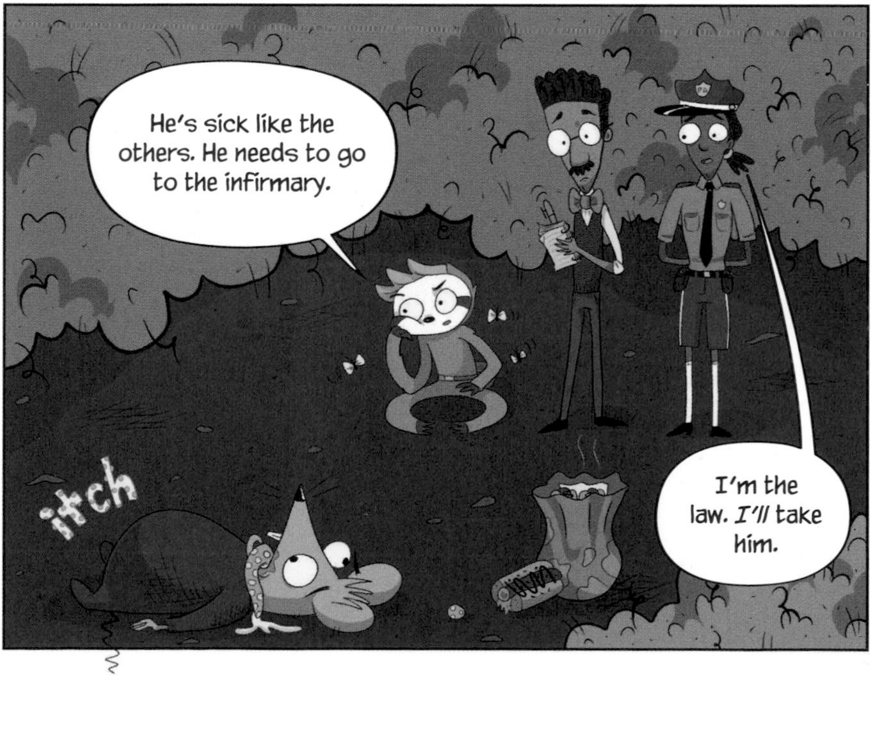
He's sick like the others. He needs to go to the infirmary.
I'm the law. *I'll* take him.
itch

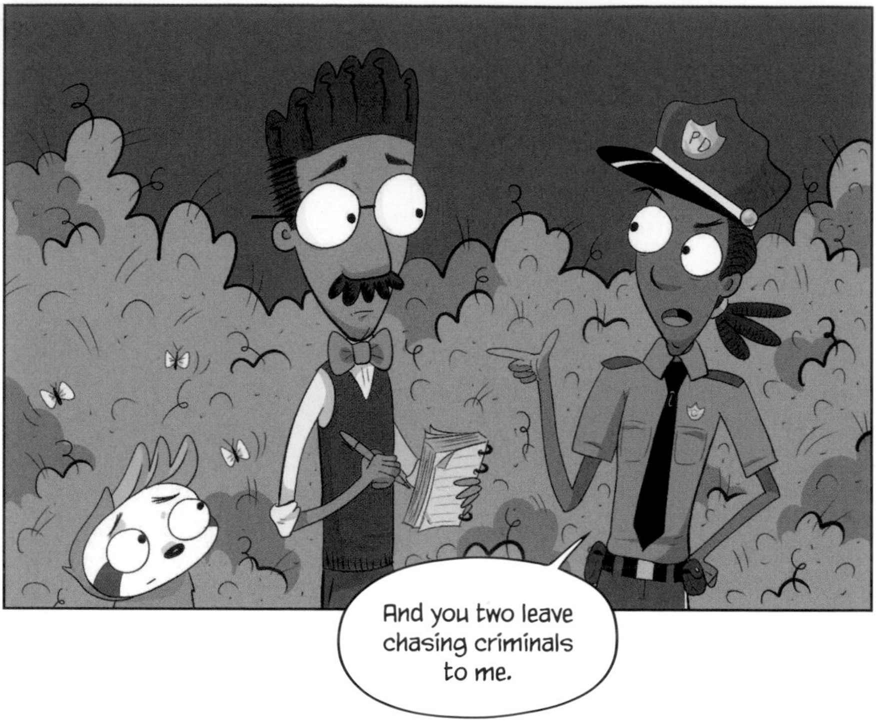
And you two leave chasing criminals to me.

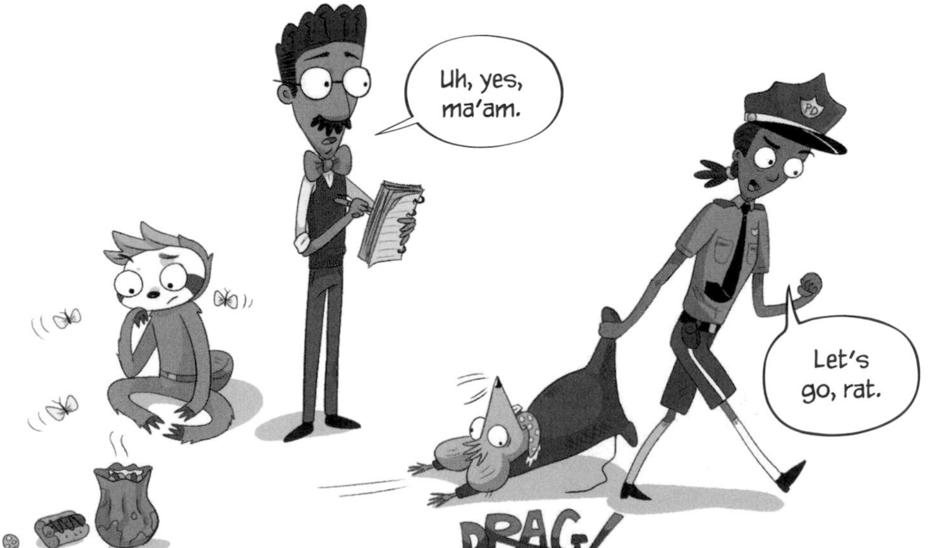
Uh, yes, ma'am.
Let's go, rat.
DRAG!

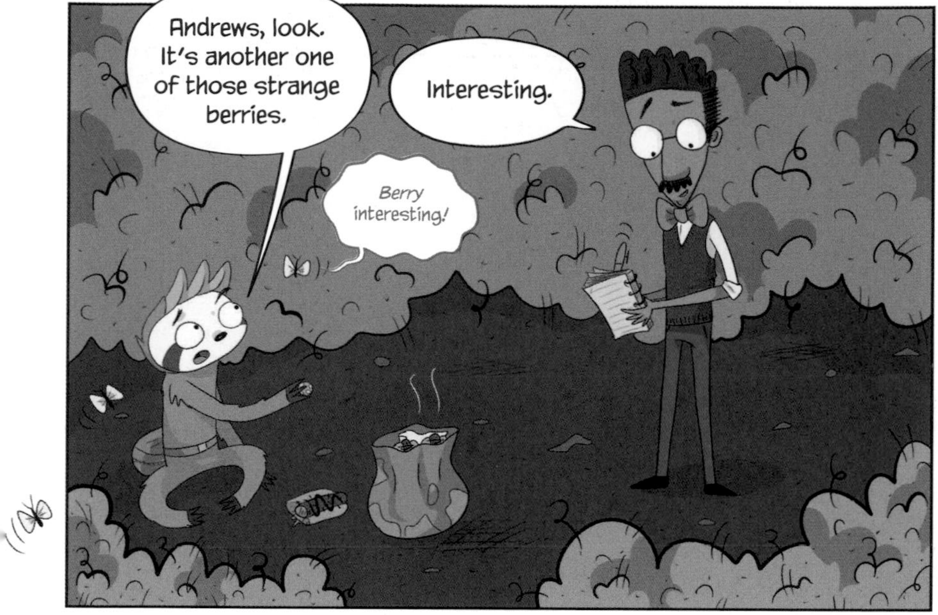
Andrews, look. It's another one of those strange berries.
Interesting.
Berry interesting!

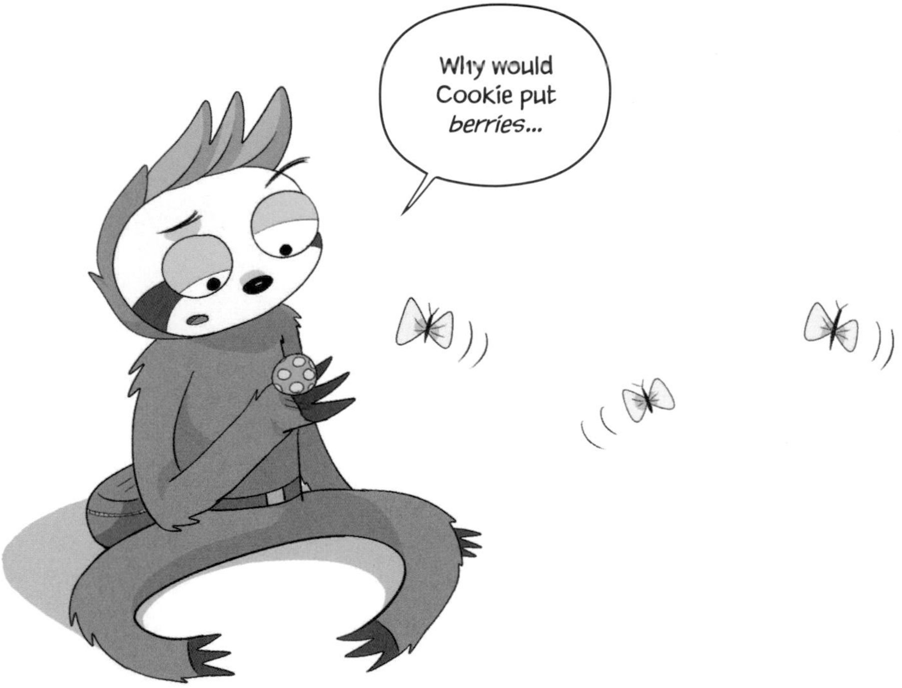
Why would Cookie put *berries...*

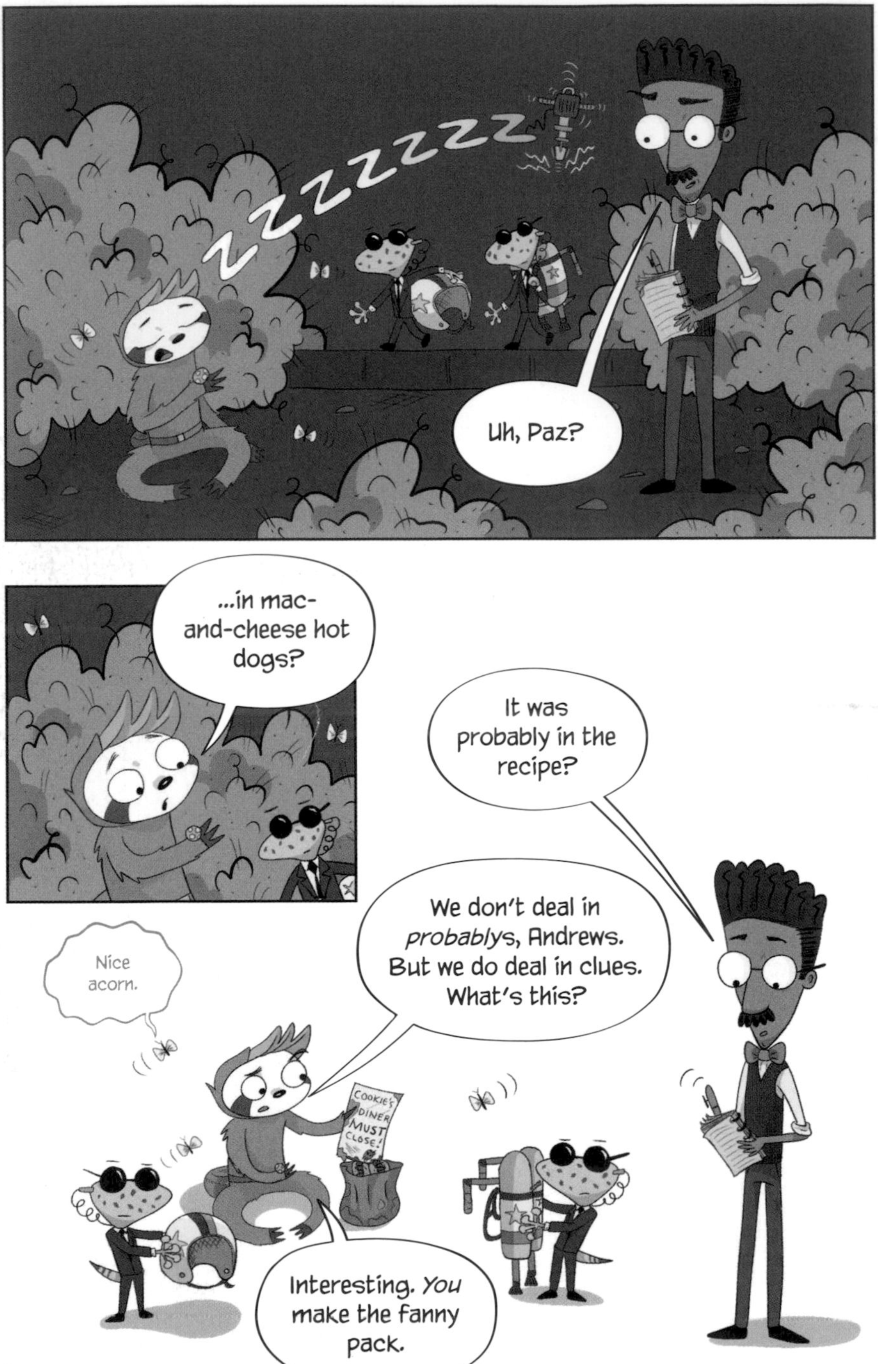
ZZZZZZZZ
Uh, Paz?
...in mac-and-cheese hot dogs?
It was probably in the recipe?
We don't deal in *probablys*, Andrews. But we do deal in clues. What's this?
Nice acorn.
COOKIE'S DINER MUST CLOSE!
Interesting. *You* make the fanny pack.

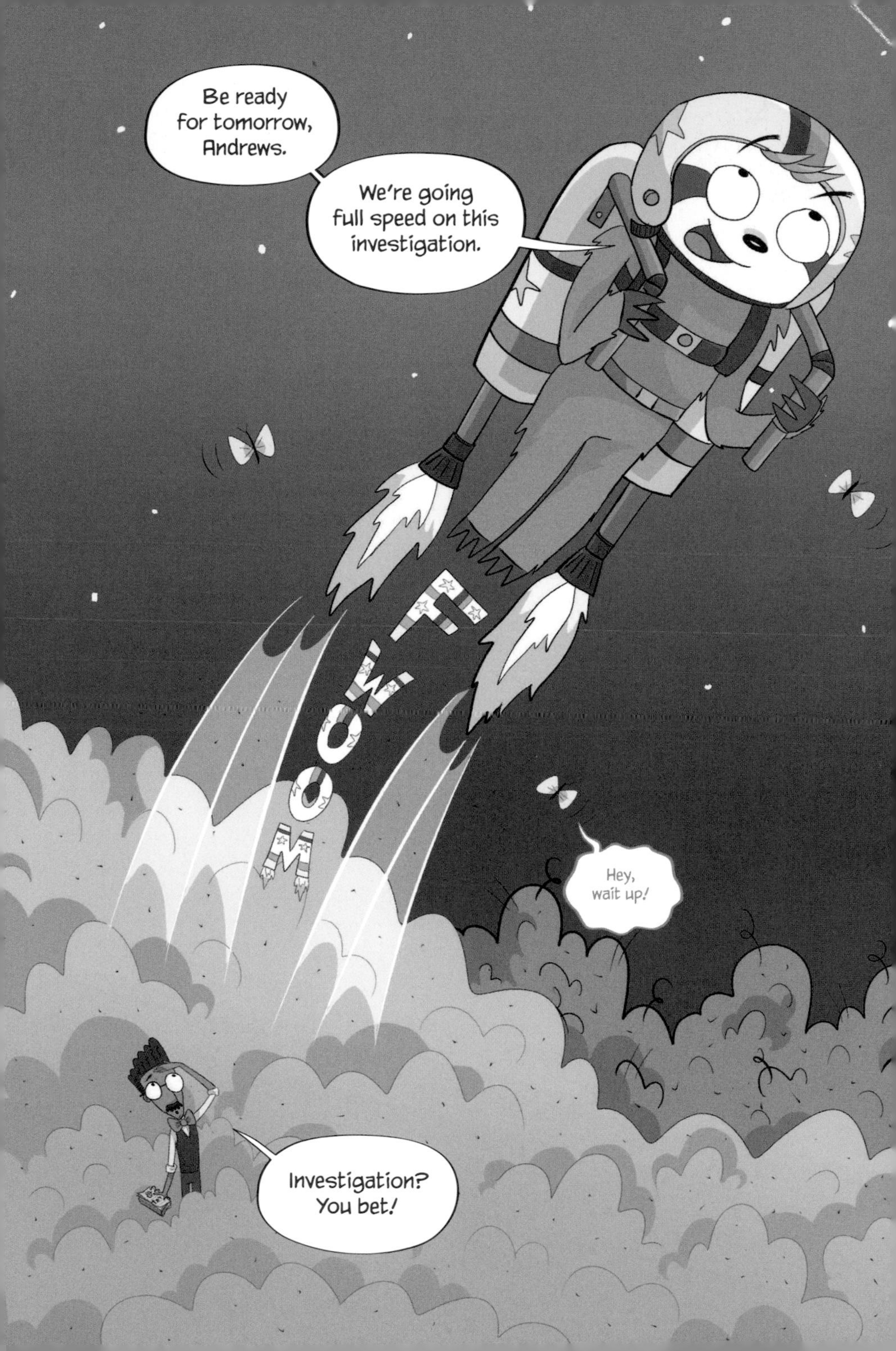
Be ready for tomorrow, Andrews.
We're going full speed on this investigation.
FWOOM
Hey, wait up!
Investigation? You bet!

CHAPTER 5

WEDNESDAY. CRACK OF DAWN.
SNOOZING IN A HAMMOCK.

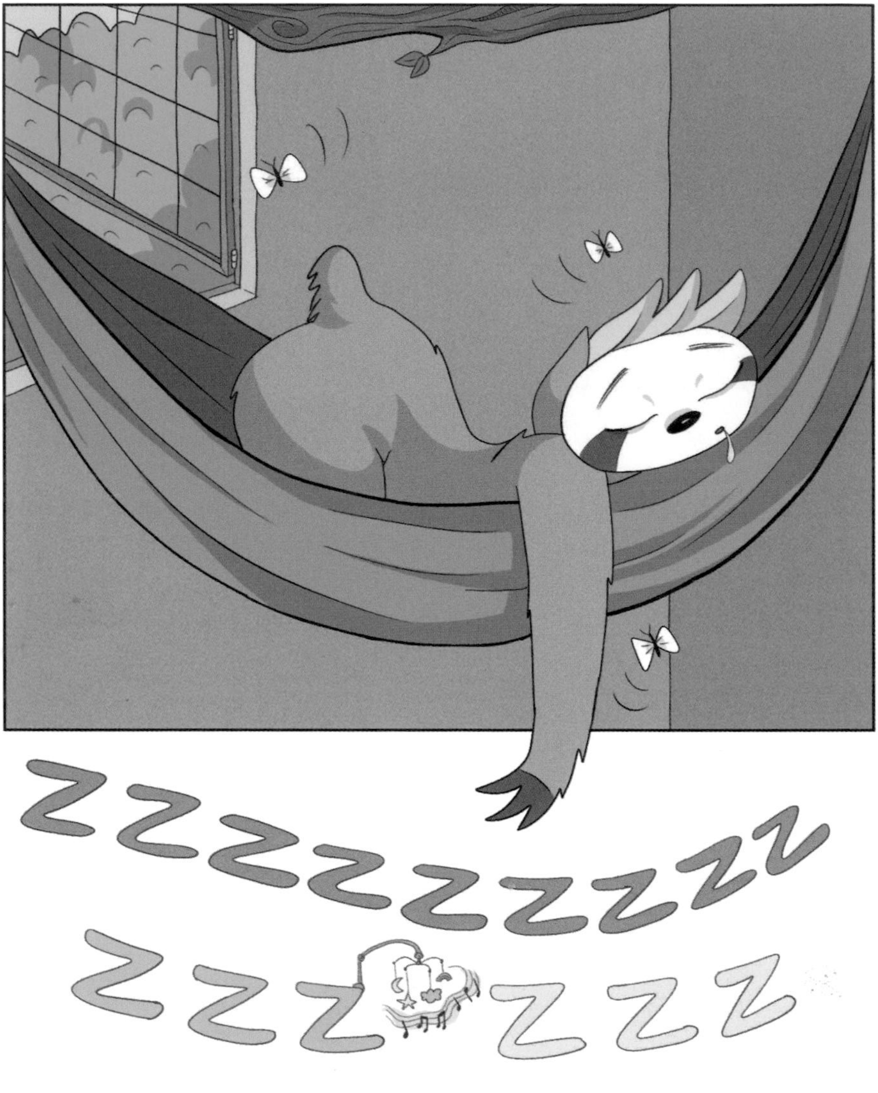
ZZZZZZZZZZ
ZZZZZZ

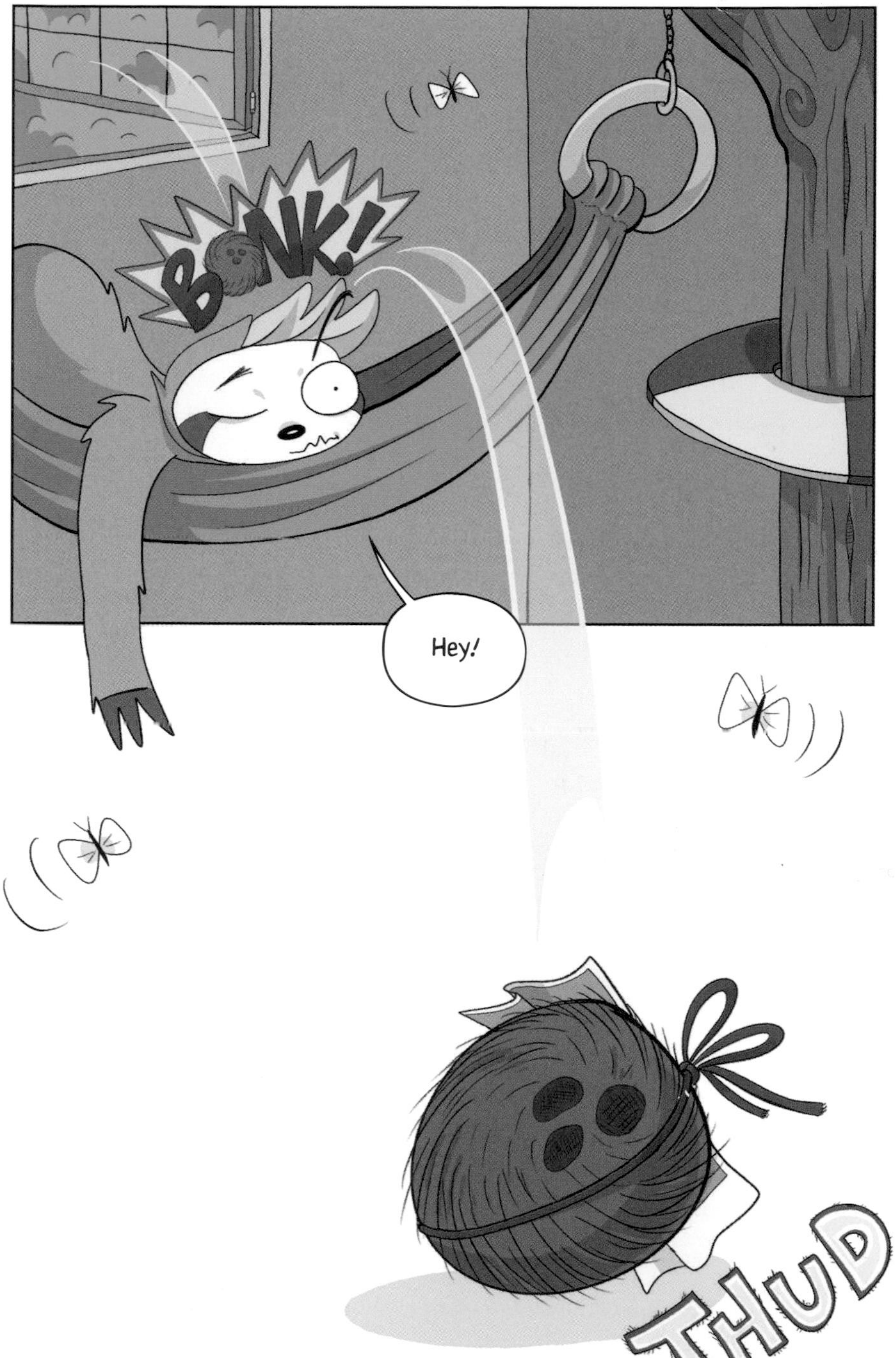
BONK!
Hey!
THUD

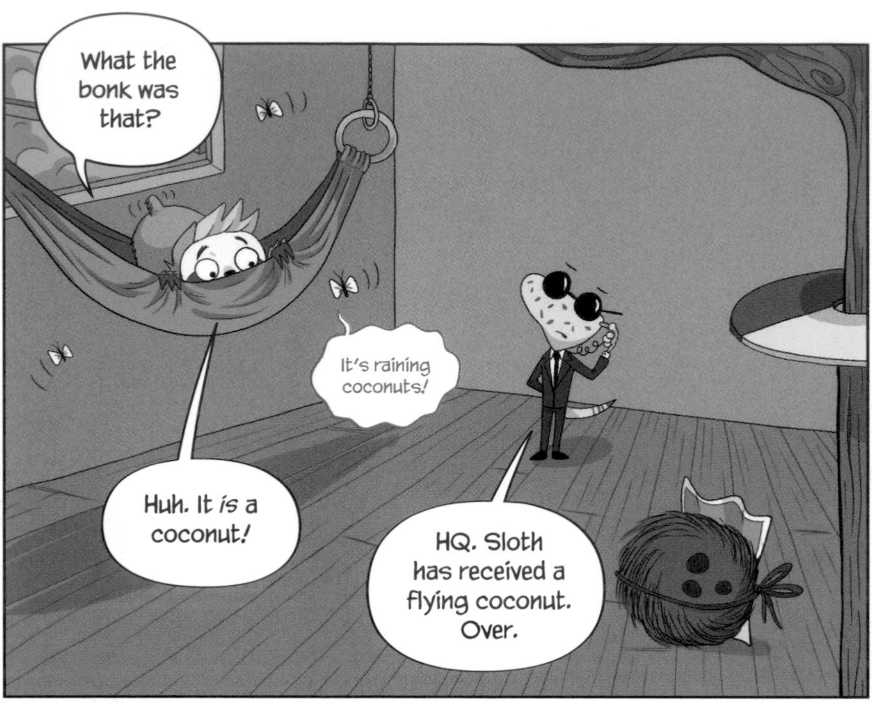
What the bonk was that?
It's raining coconuts!
Huh. It *is* a coconut!
HQ. Sloth has received a flying coconut. Over.

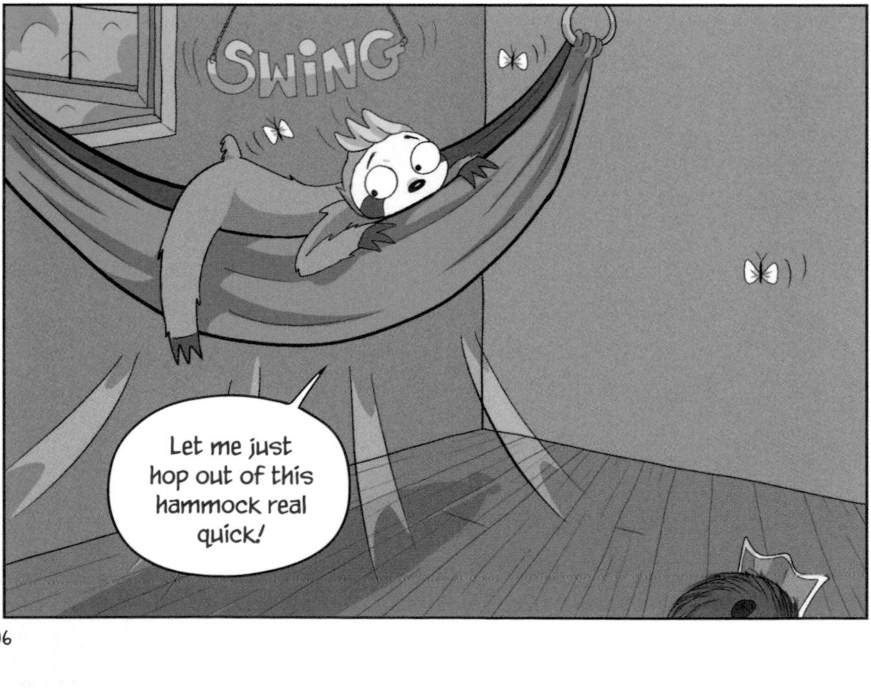
SWING
Let me just hop out of this hammock real quick!

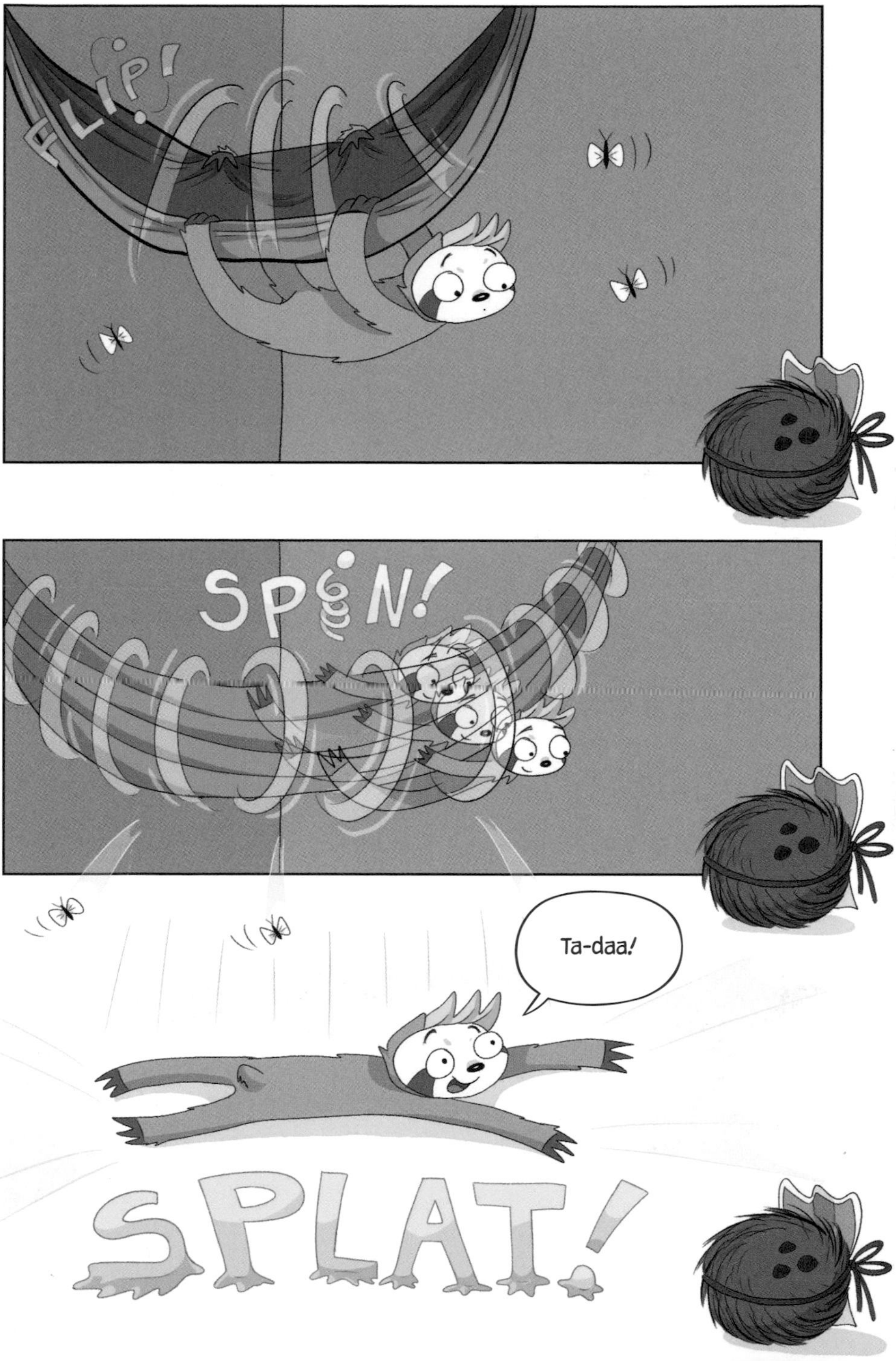
FLIP!
SPIN!
Ta-daa!
SPLAT!

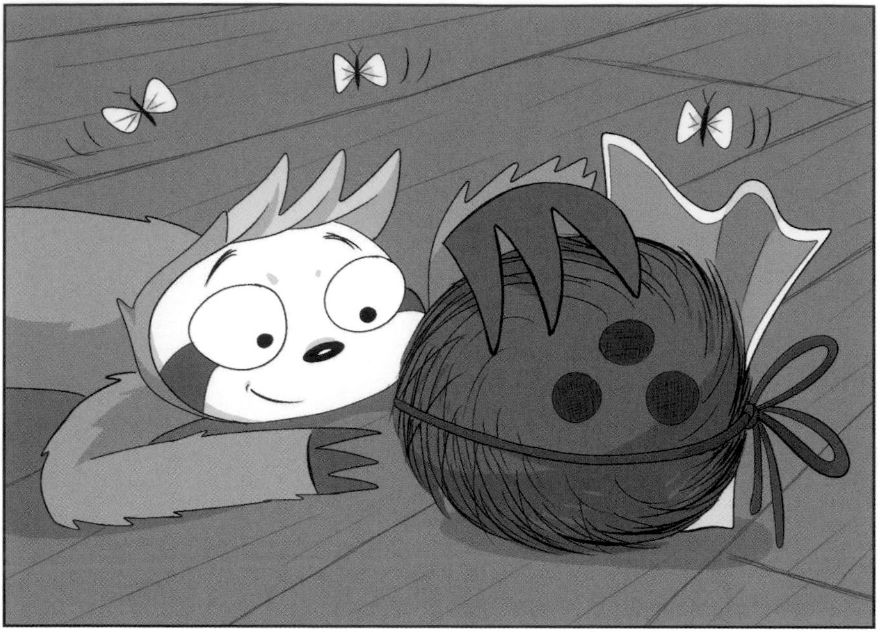

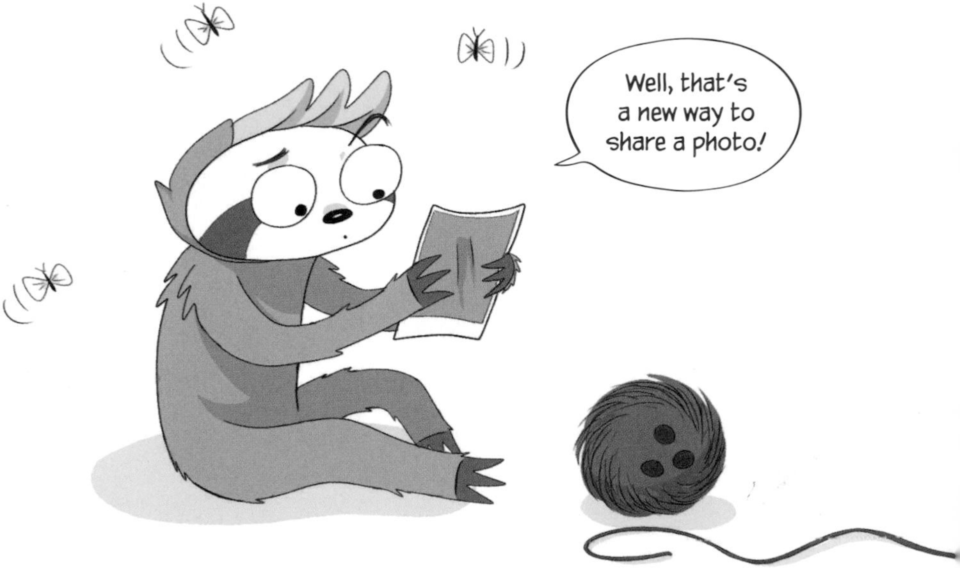
Well, that's a new way to share a photo!

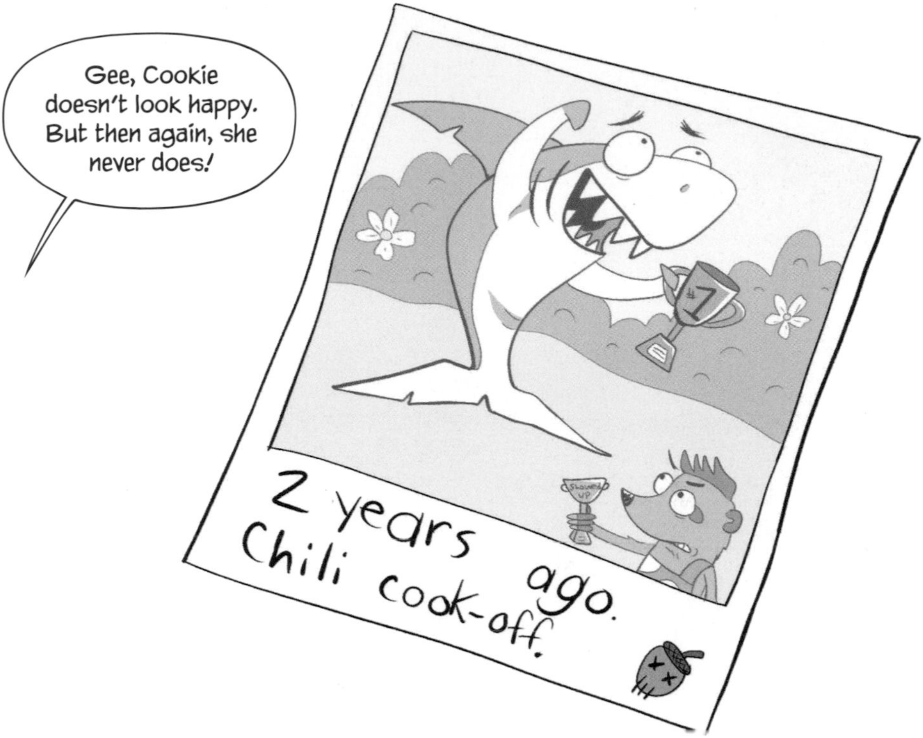
Gee, Cookie doesn't look happy. But then again, she never does!
#1
Showed up
2 years ago.
Chili cook-off.

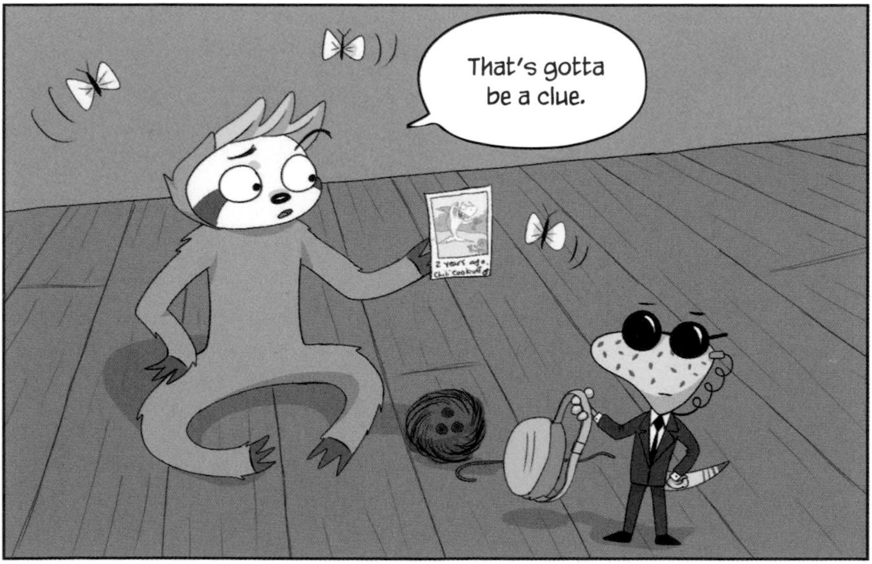
That's gotta be a clue.

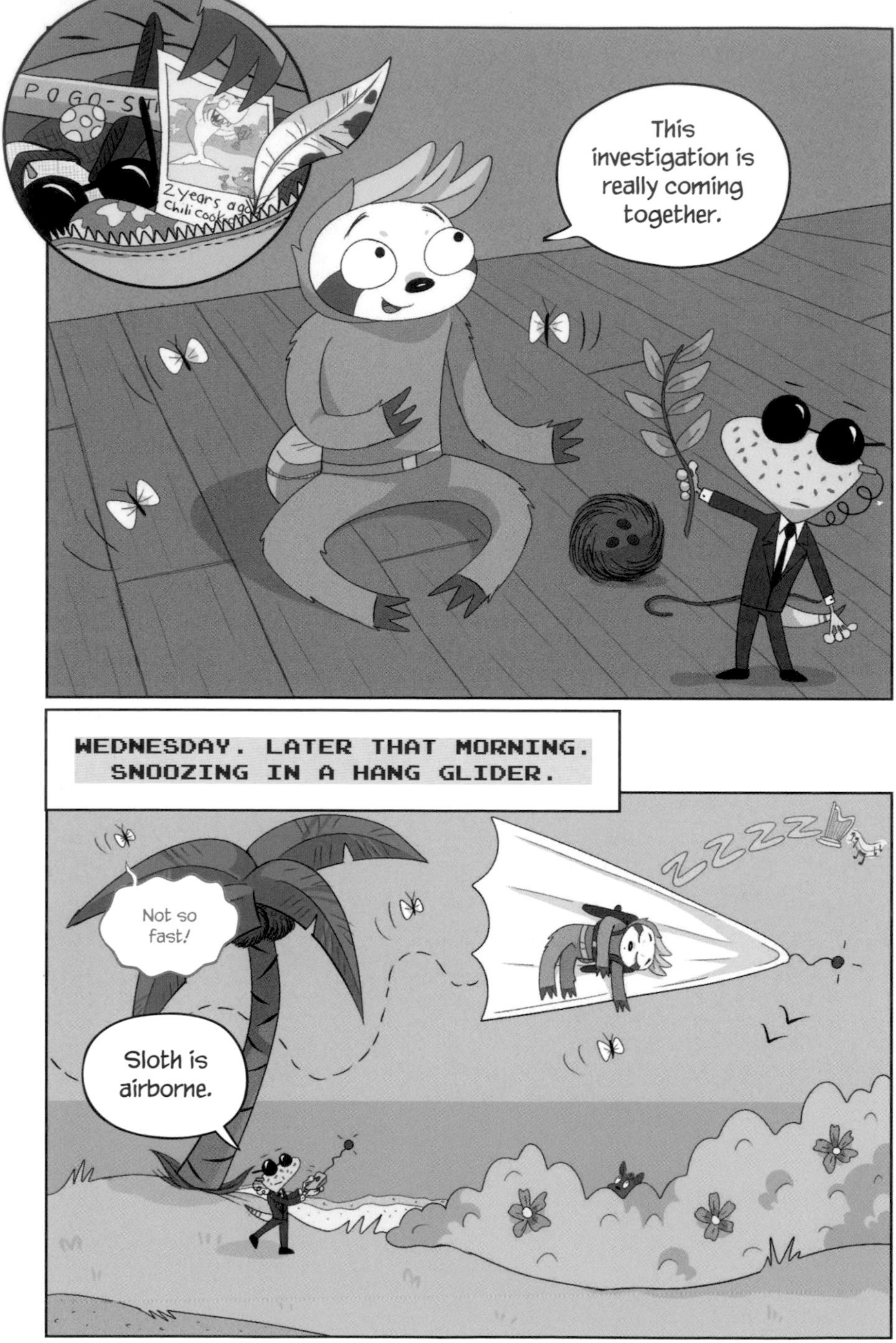
This investigation is really coming together.
WEDNESDAY. LATER THAT MORNING. SNOOZING IN A HANG GLIDER.
Not so fast!
Sloth is airborne.

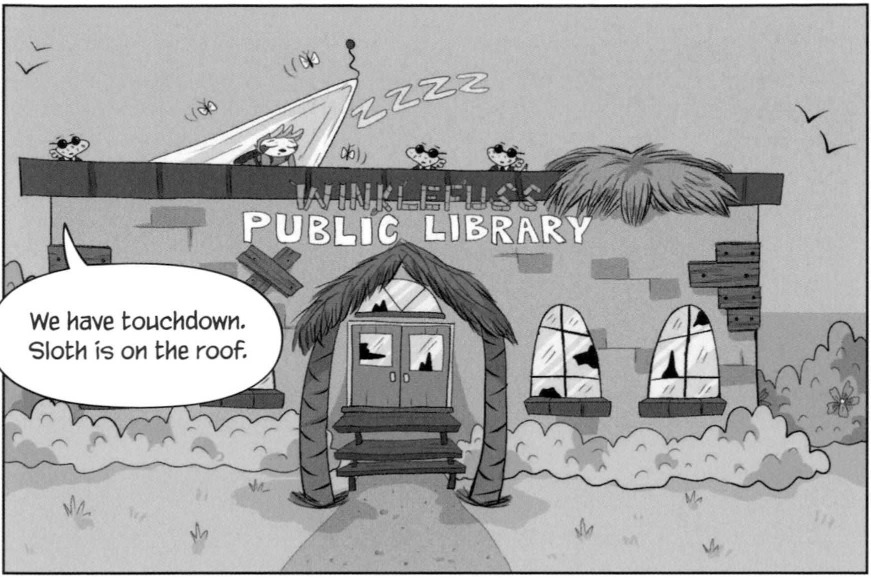
WINKLEFUSS
PUBLIC LIBRARY
ZZZZZ
We have touchdown. Sloth is on the roof.

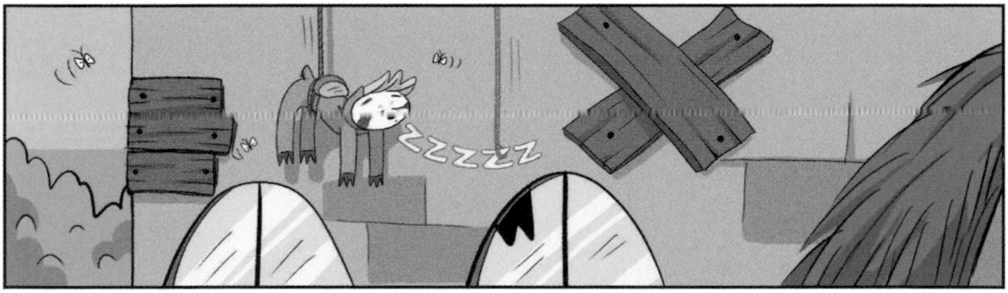
ZZZZZ

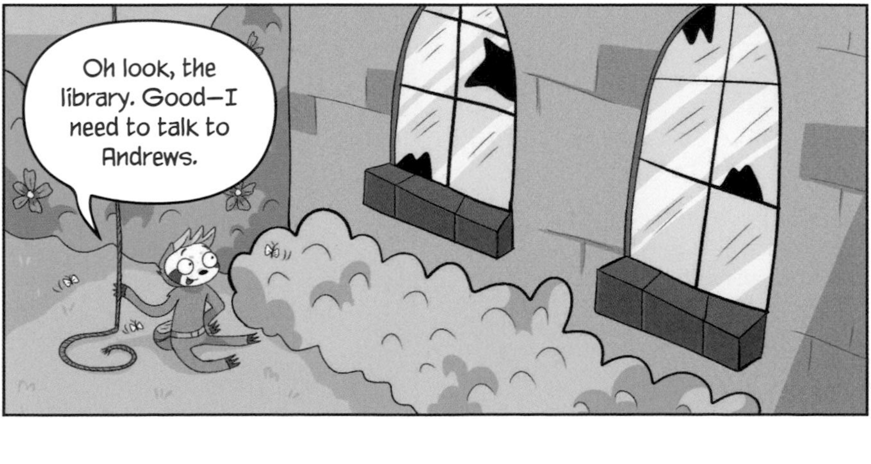
Oh look, the library. Good—I need to talk to Andrews.

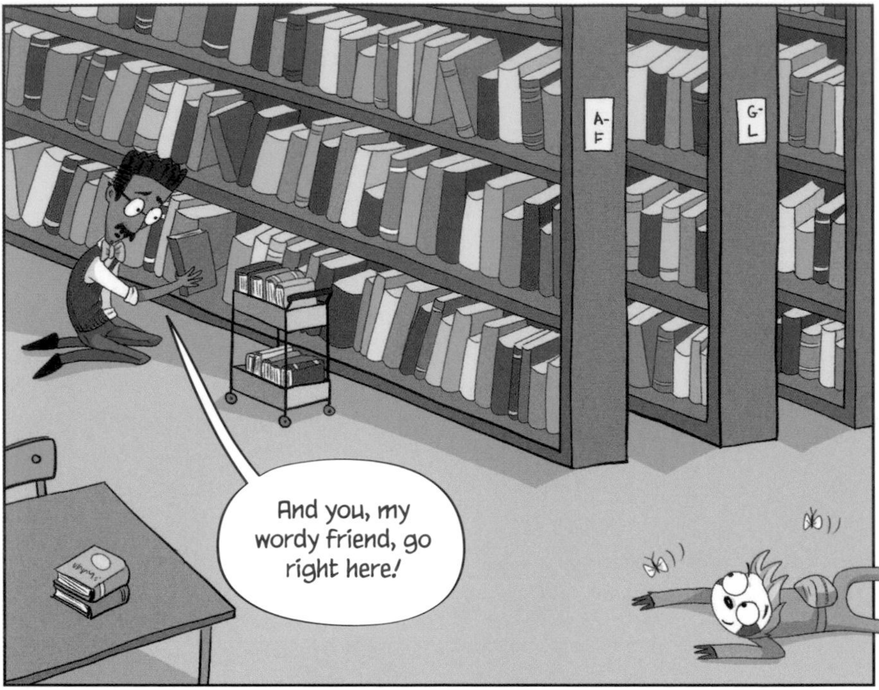
A-F
G-L
And you, my wordy friend, go right here!

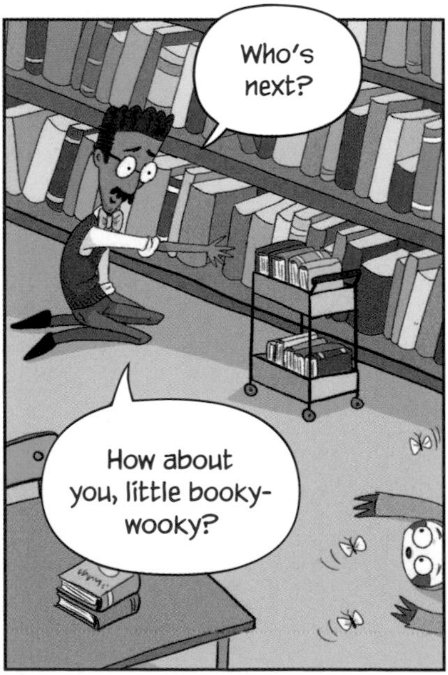
Who's next?
How about you, little booky-wooky?

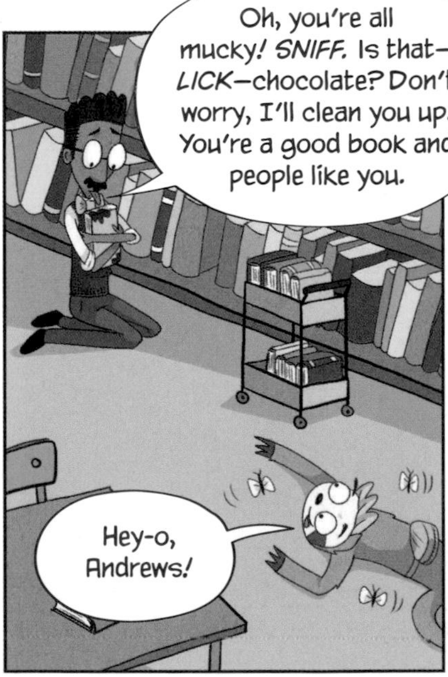
Oh, you're all mucky! SNIFF. Is that—LICK—chocolate? Don't worry, I'll clean you up. You're a good book and people like you.
Hey-o, Andrews!

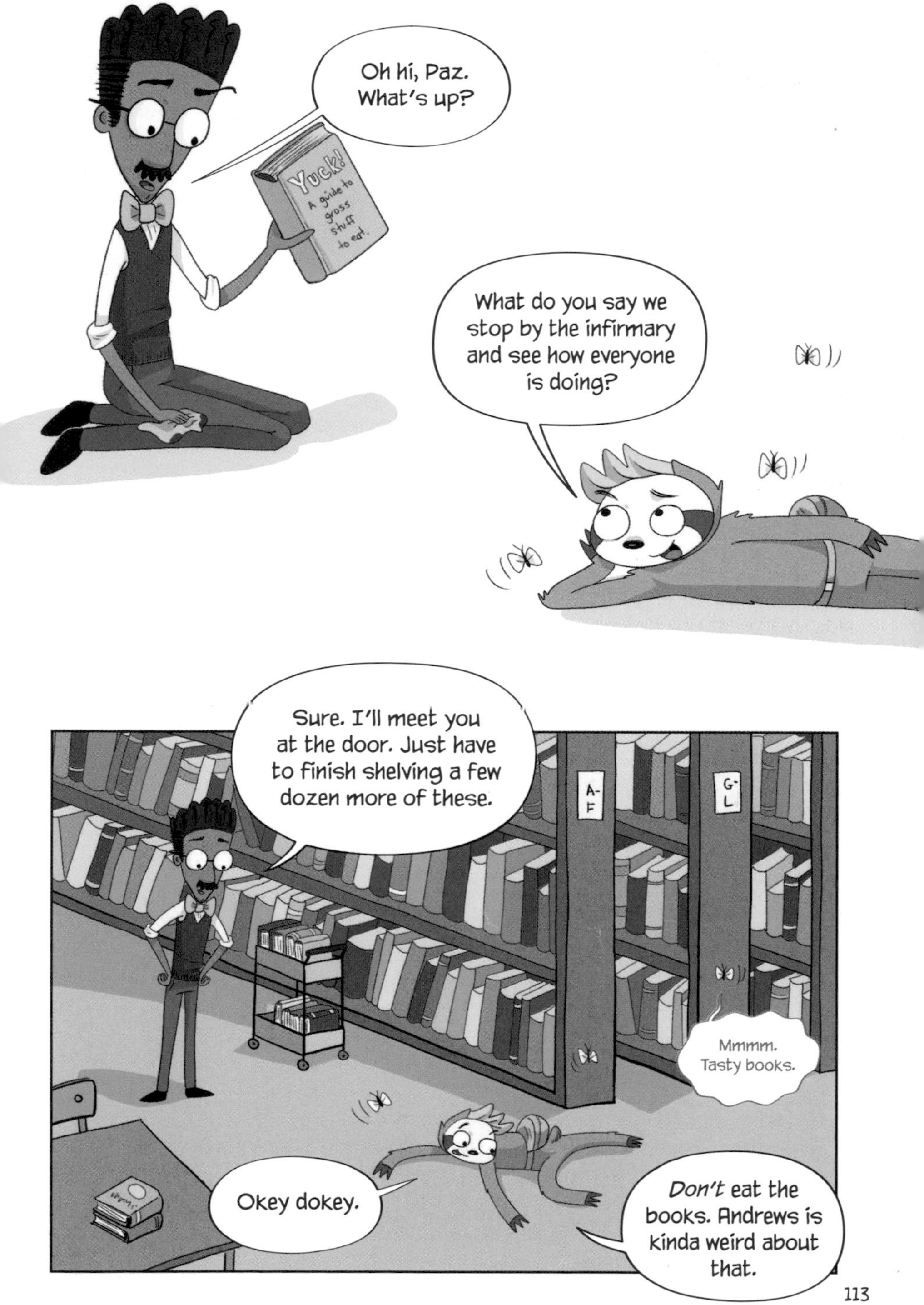

Oh hi, Paz. What's up?
Yuck! A guide to gross stuff to eat.
What do you say we stop by the infirmary and see how everyone is doing?
Sure. I'll meet you at the door. Just have to finish shelving a few dozen more of these.
A-F
G-L
Mmmm. Tasty books.
Okey dokey.
Don't eat the books. Andrews is kinda weird about that.

ONE HOUR LATER.

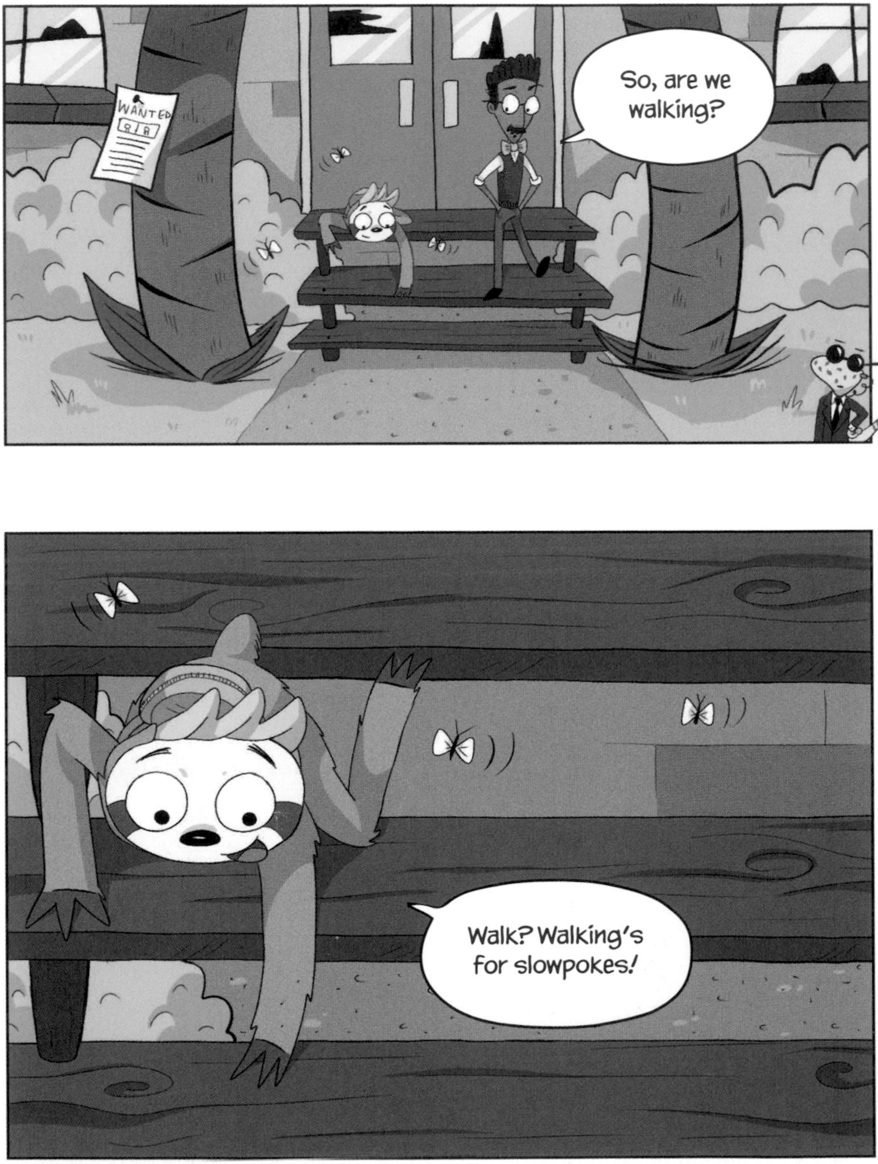
WANTED
So, are we walking?
Walk? Walking's for slowpokes!

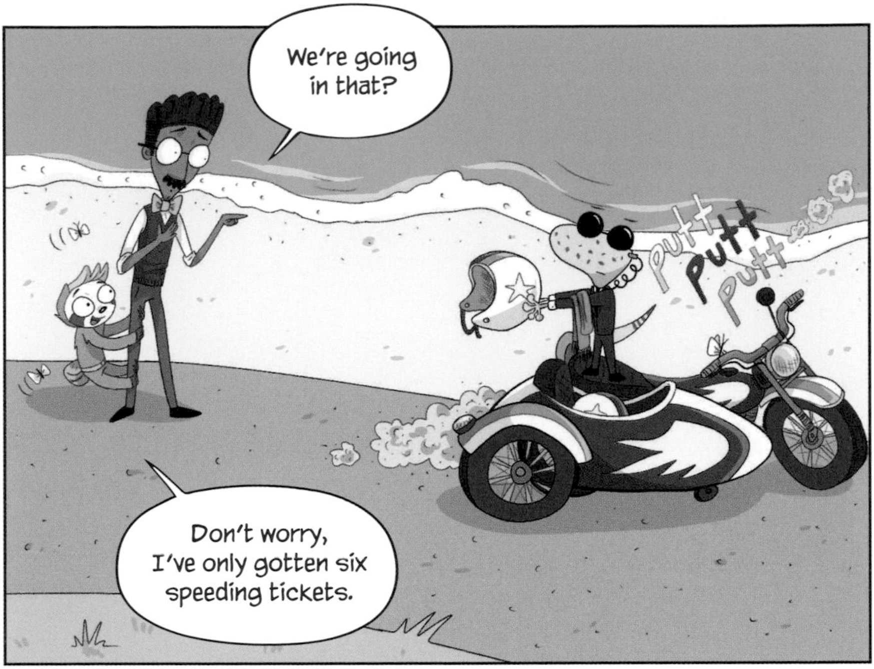
We're going in that?
putt putt putt
Don't worry, I've only gotten six speeding tickets.

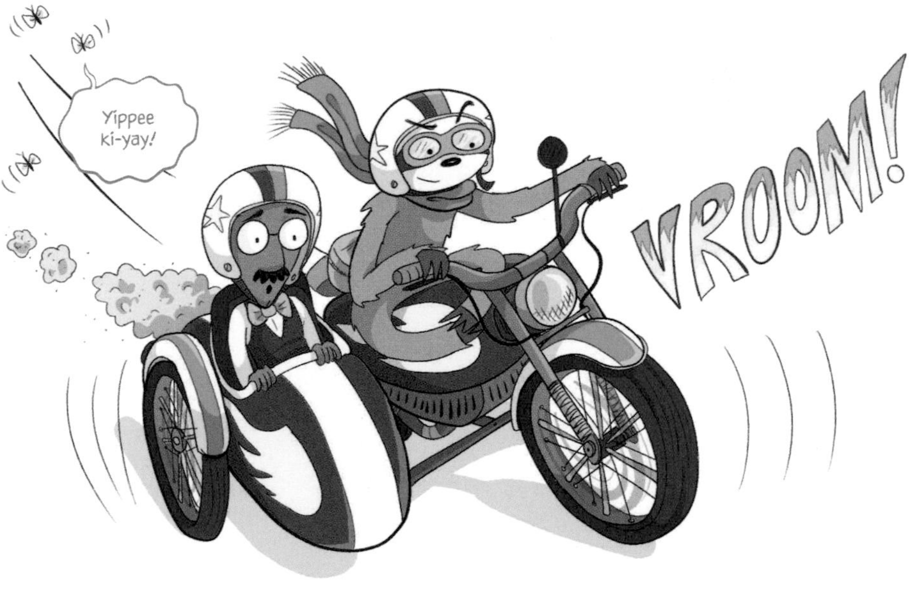
Yippee ki-yay!
VROOM!

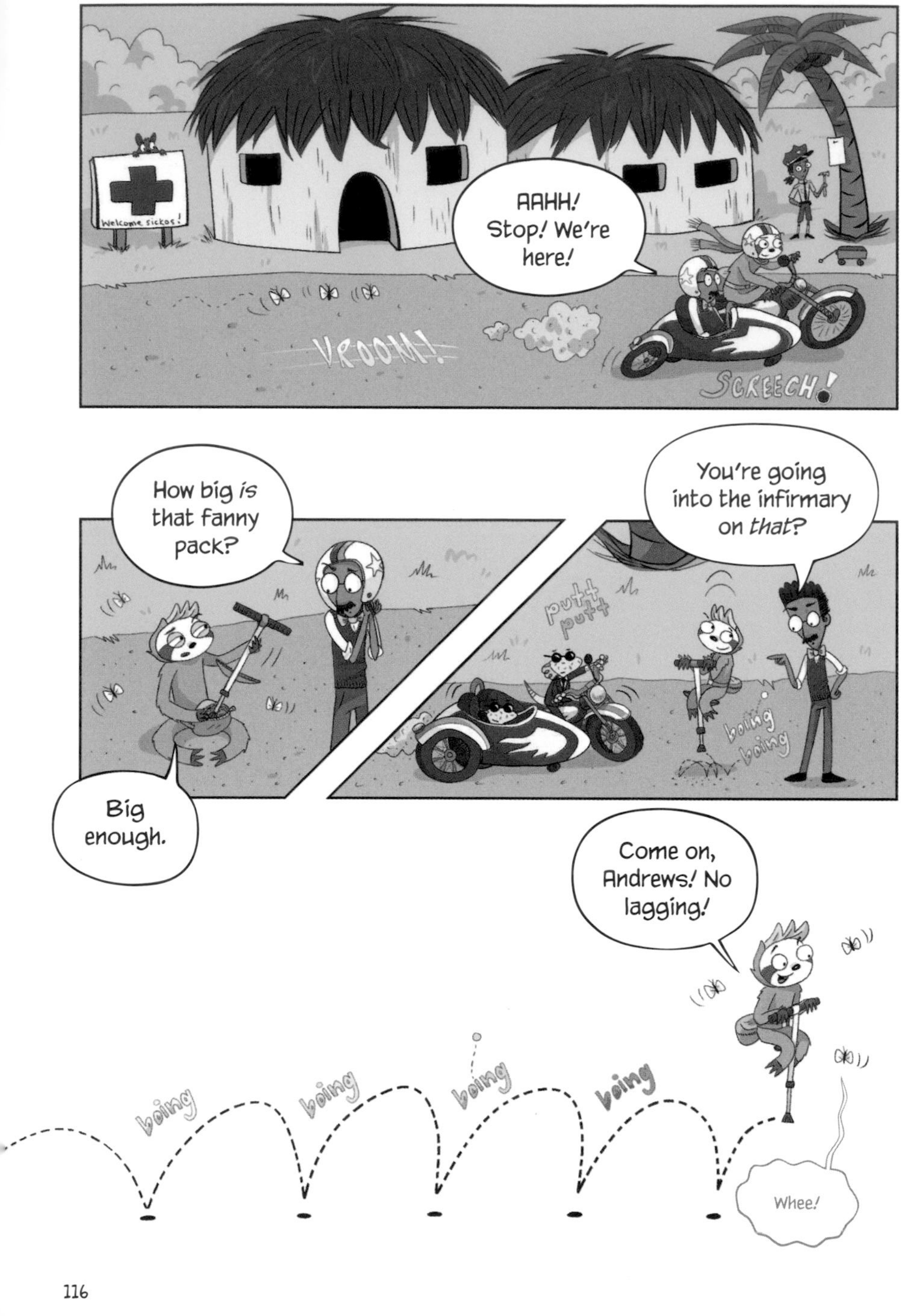
Welcome sickos!
AAHH! Stop! We're here!
VROOM!
SCREECH!
How big *is* that fanny pack?
Big enough.
You're going into the infirmary on *that*?
putt putt
boing boing
Come on, Andrews! No lagging!
boing
boing
boing
boing
Whee!

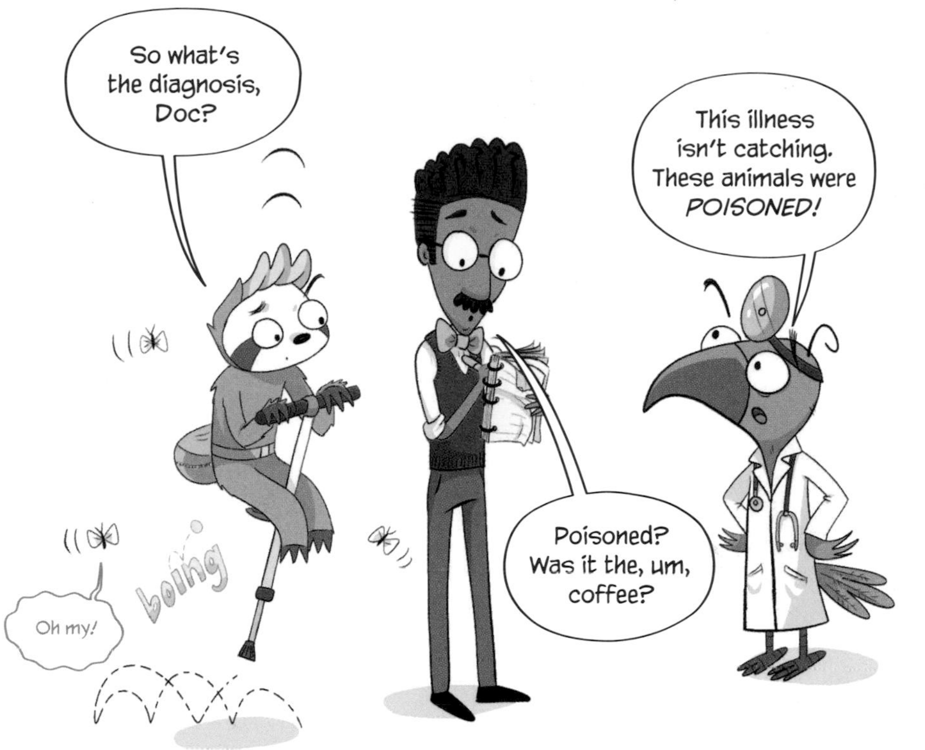
So what's the diagnosis, Doc?
This illness isn't catching. These animals were *POISONED!*
Oh my!
boing
Poisoned? Was it the, um, coffee?

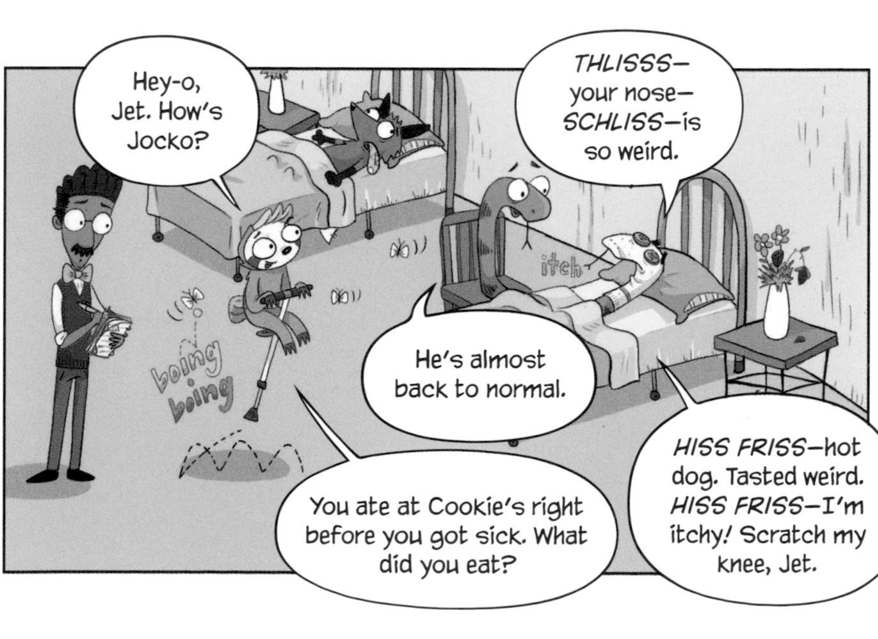
Hey-o, Jet. How's Jocko?
THLISSS—your nose—*SCHLISS*—is so weird.
itch
He's almost back to normal.
boing boing
You ate at Cookie's right before you got sick. What did you eat?
HISS FRISS—hot dog. Tasted weird. *HISS FRISS*—I'm itchy! Scratch my knee, Jet.

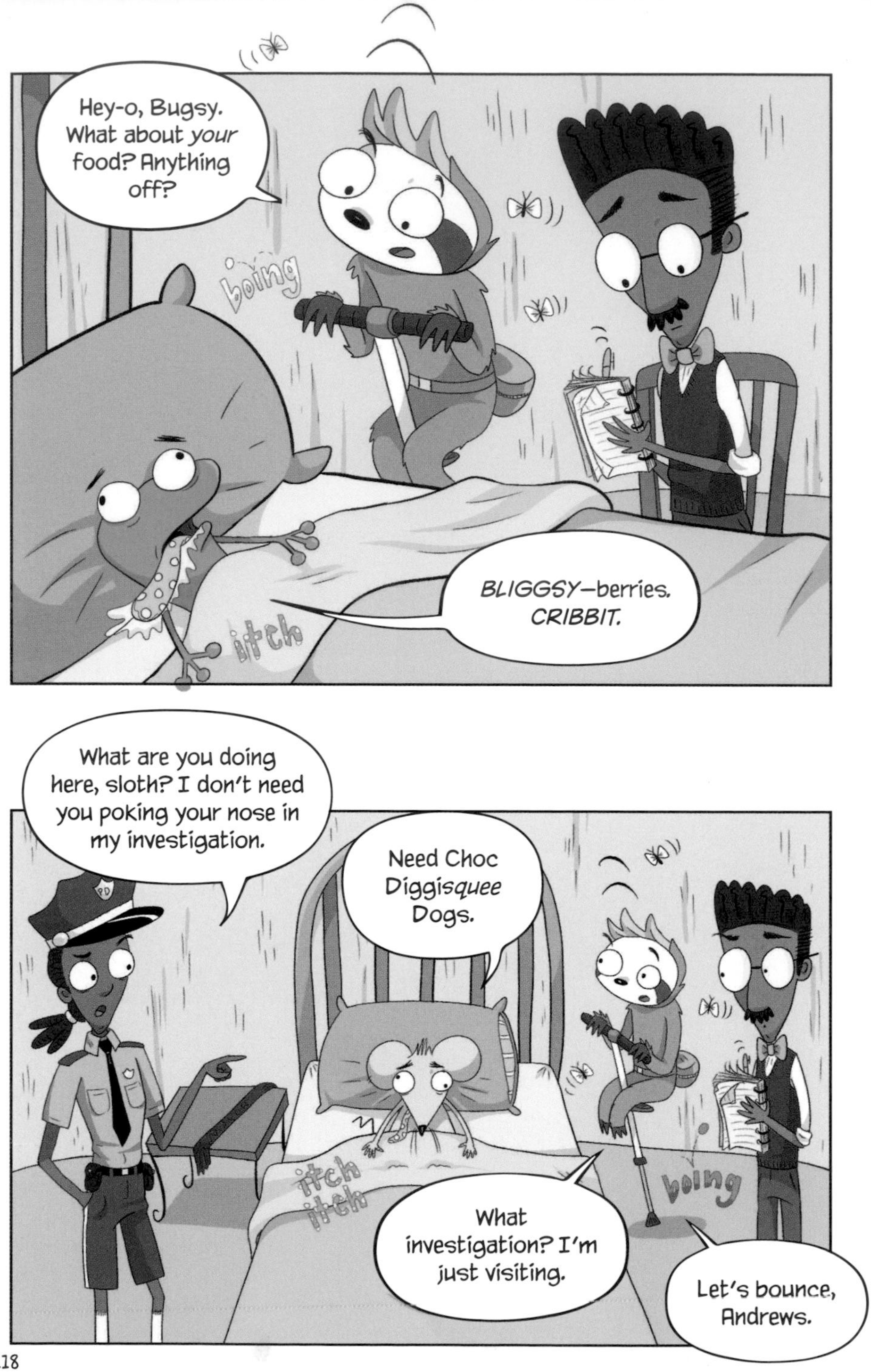
Hey-o, Bugsy. What about *your* food? Anything off?
boing
itch
BLIGGSY—berries. *CRIBBIT.*
What are you doing here, sloth? I don't need you poking your nose in my investigation.
Need Choc Diggi*squee* Dogs.
itch itch
boing
What investigation? I'm just visiting.
Let's bounce, Andrews.

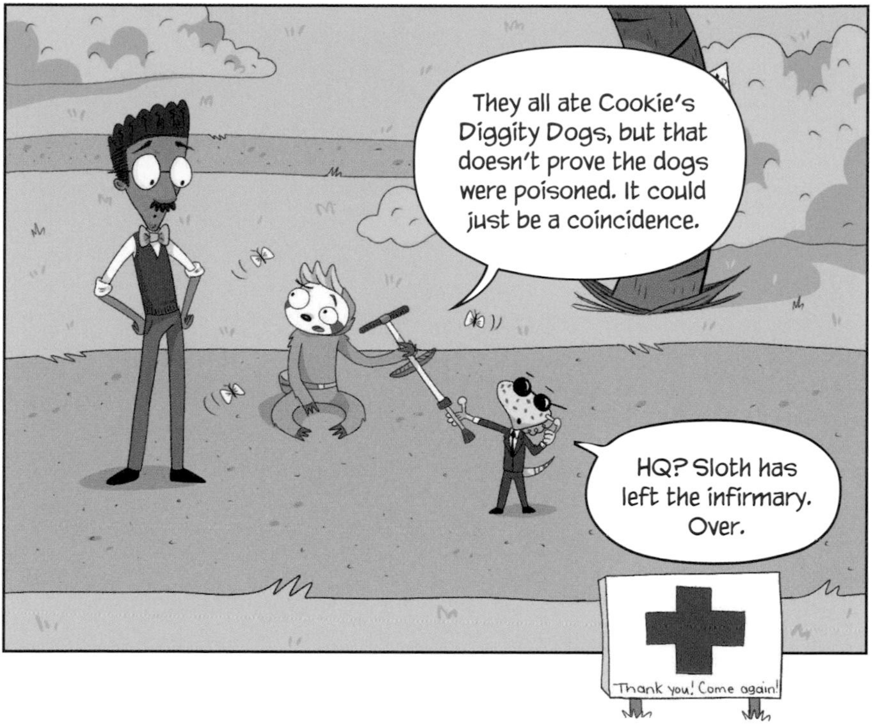
They all ate Cookie's Diggity Dogs, but that doesn't prove the dogs were poisoned. It could just be a coincidence.
HQ? Sloth has left the infirmary. Over.
Thank you! Come again!

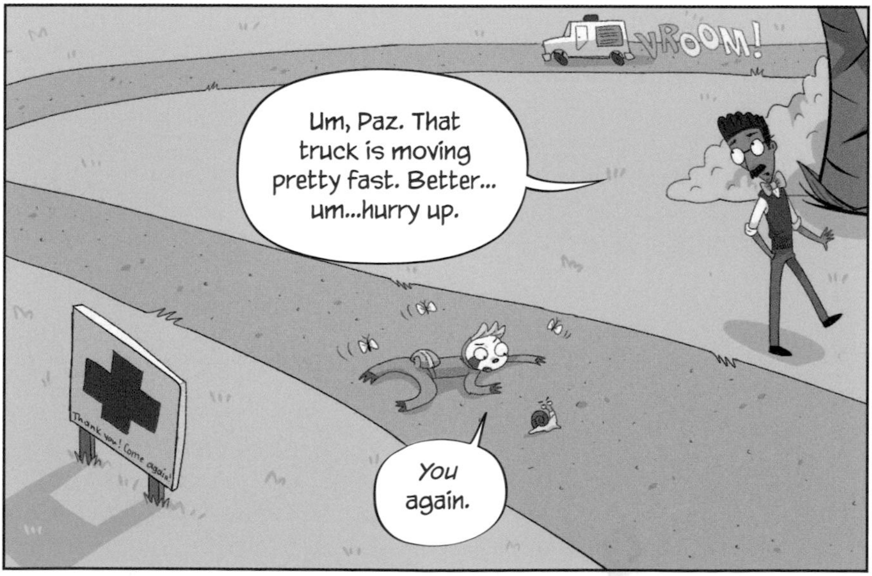
VROOM!
Um, Paz. That truck is moving pretty fast. Better... um...hurry up.
Thank you! Come again!
You again.

WINKLEFUSS GRAND PRIX 2: GRUDGE MATCH

THIS TIME IT'S PERSONAL.

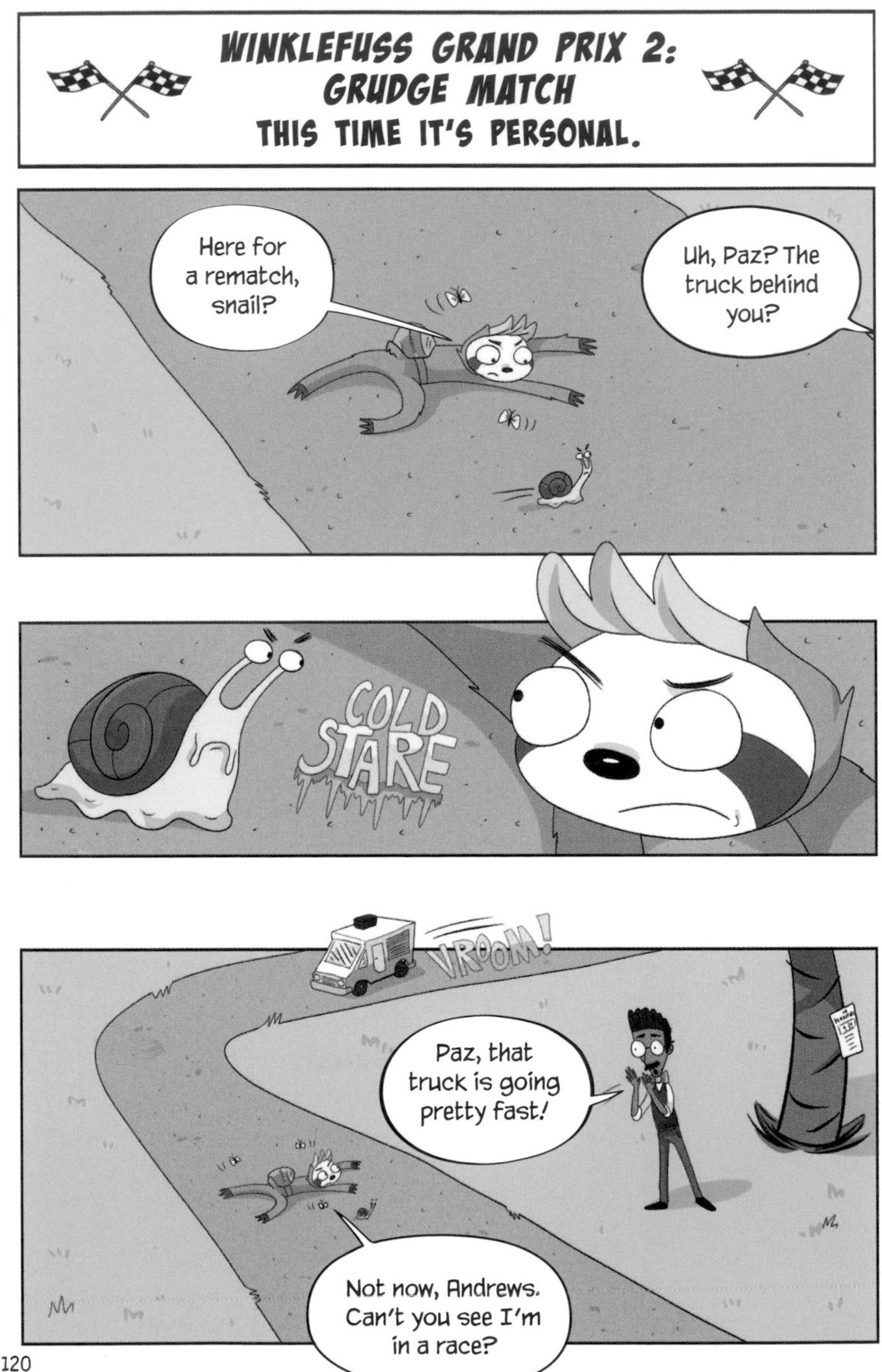
Here for a rematch, snail?
Uh, Paz? The truck behind you?
COLD STARE
VROOM!
Paz, that truck is going pretty fast!
Not now, Andrews. Can't you see I'm in a race?

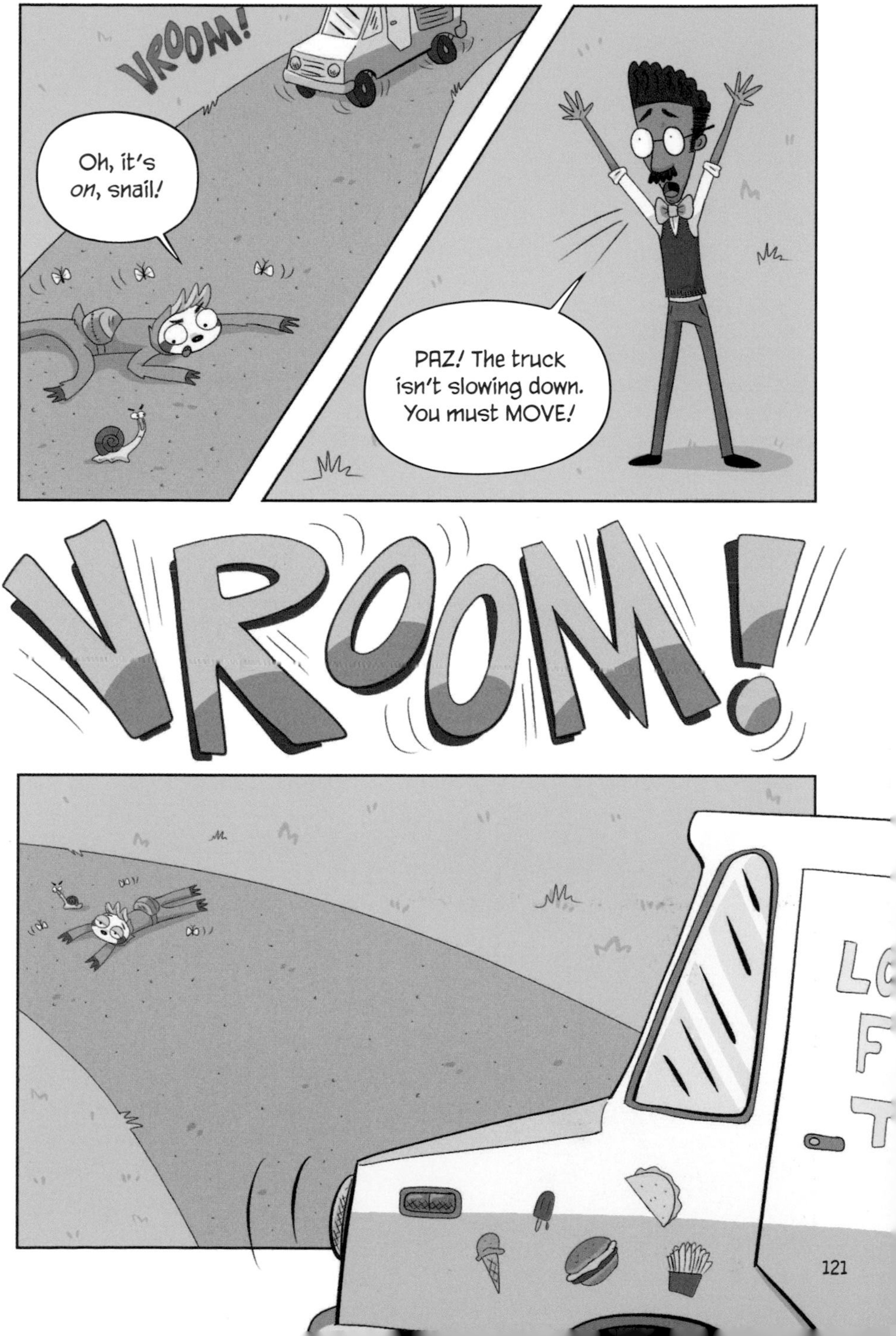
VROOM!
Oh, it's *on*, snail!
PAZ! The truck isn't slowing down. You must MOVE!
VROOM!

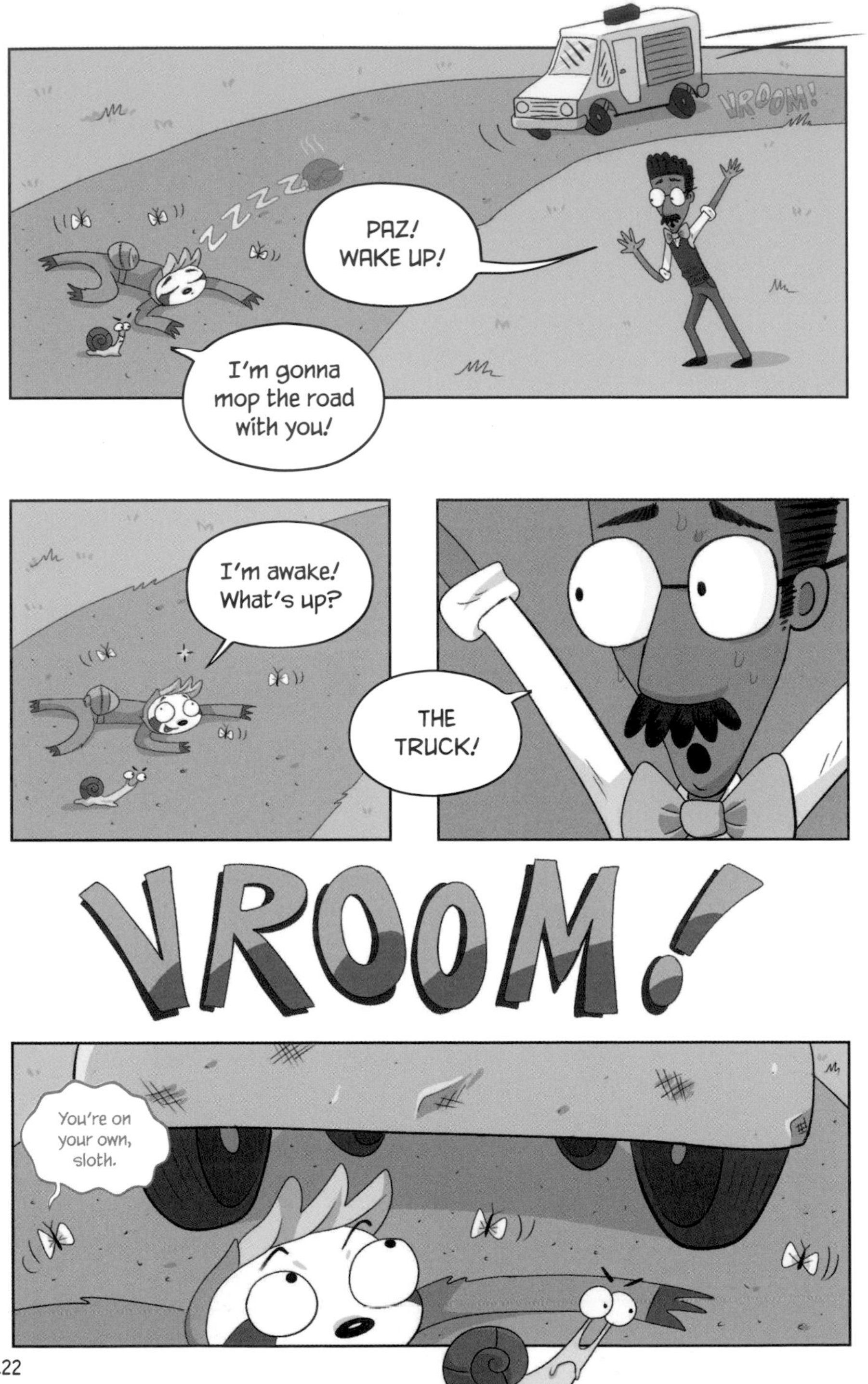
VROOM!
PAZ! WAKE UP!
I'm gonna mop the road with you!
I'm awake! What's up?
THE TRUCK!
VROOM!
You're on your own, sloth.

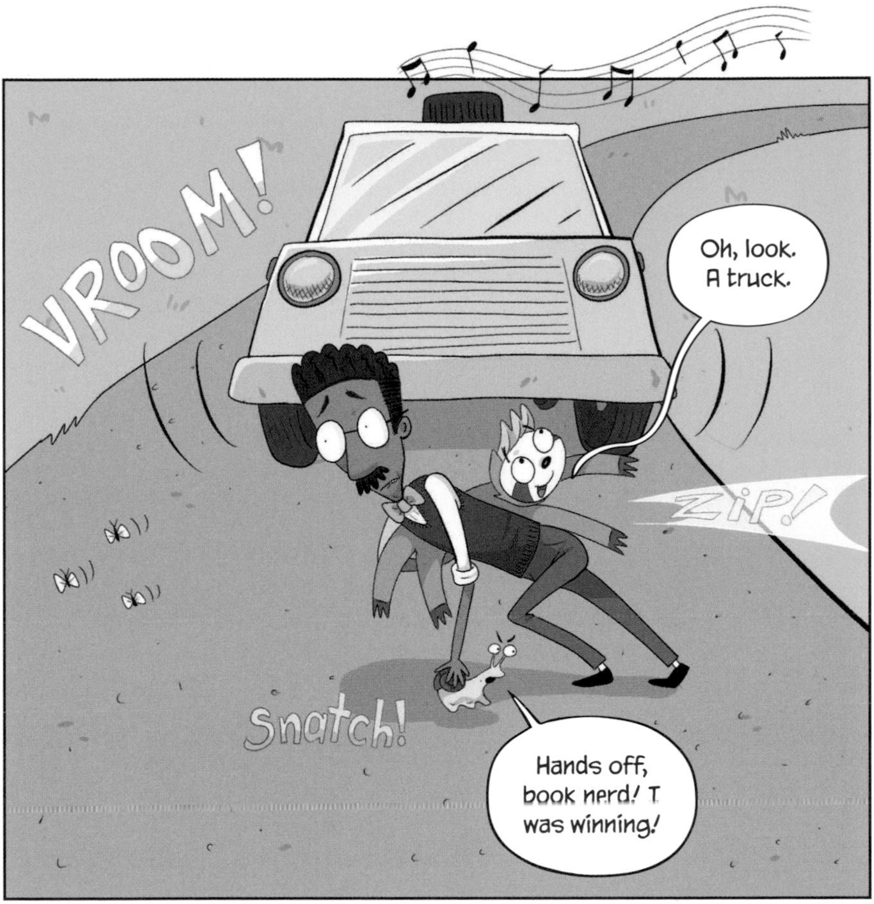
VROOM!
Oh, look. A truck.
ZIP!
Snatch!
Hands off, book nerd! I was winning!

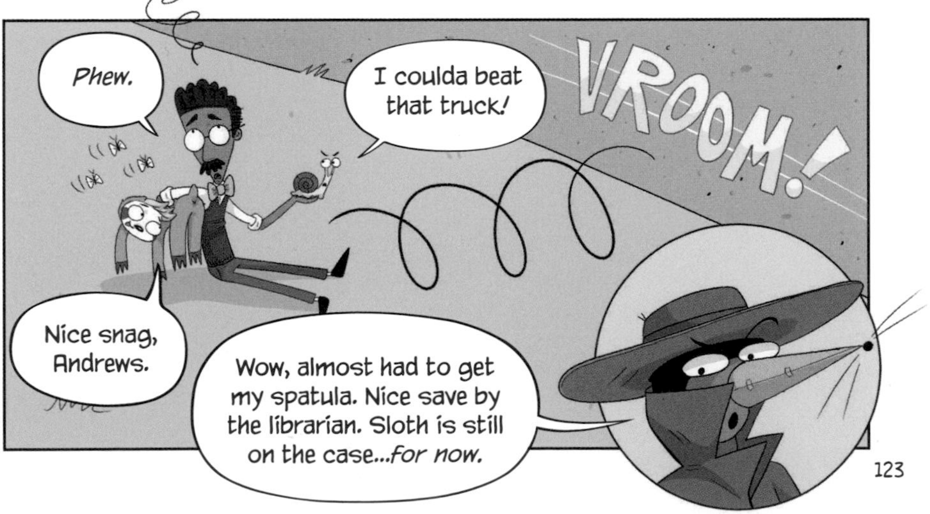
Phew.
I coulda beat that truck!
VROOM!
Nice snag, Andrews.
Wow, almost had to get my spatula. Nice save by the librarian. Sloth is still on the case...*for now.*

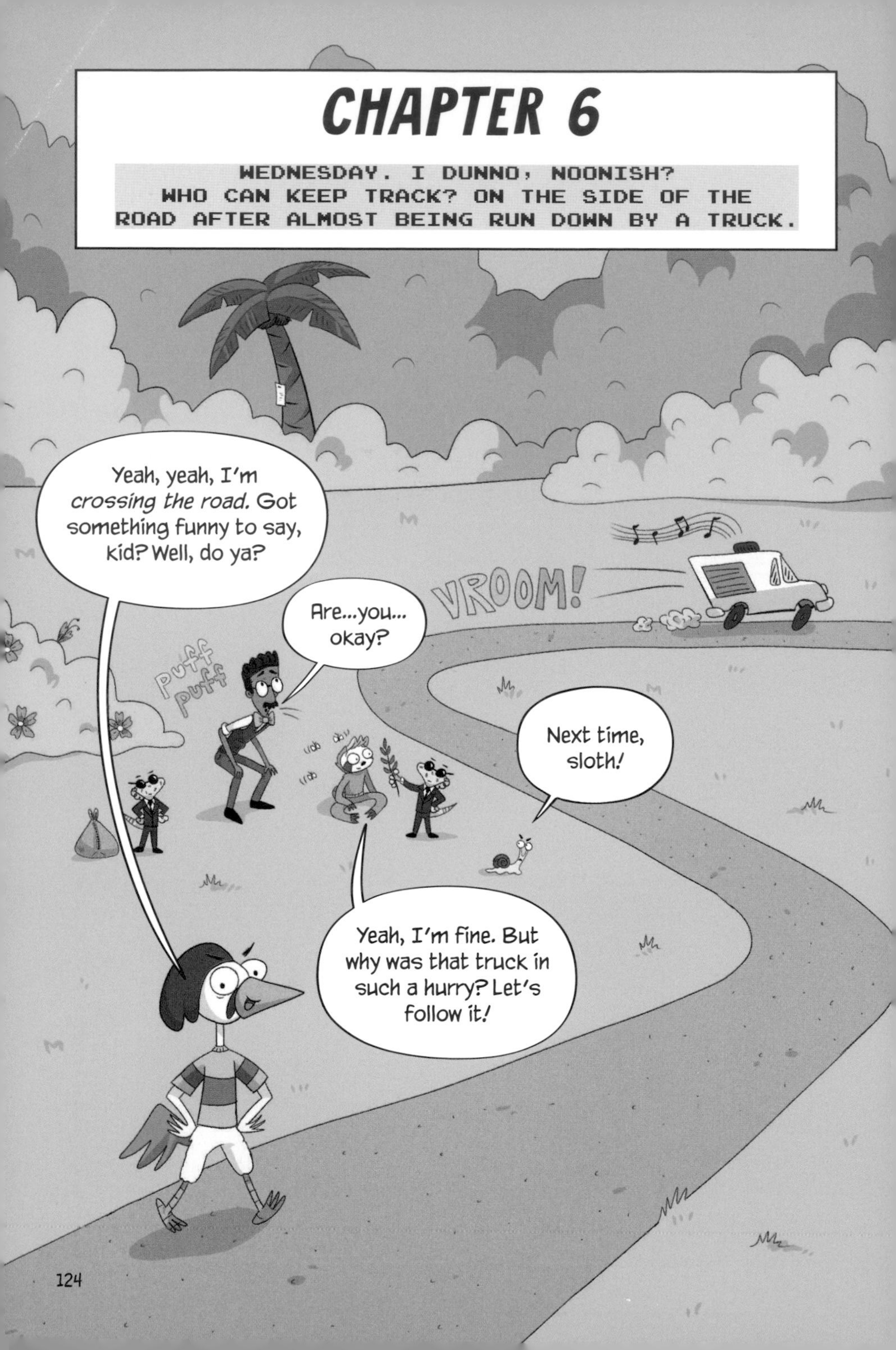
CHAPTER 6
WEDNESDAY. I DUNNO, NOONISH? WHO CAN KEEP TRACK? ON THE SIDE OF THE ROAD AFTER ALMOST BEING RUN DOWN BY A TRUCK.
Yeah, yeah, I'm *crossing the road.* Got something funny to say, kid? Well, do ya?
VROOM!
Are...you... okay?
puff puff
Next time, sloth!
Yeah, I'm fine. But why was that truck in such a hurry? Let's follow it!

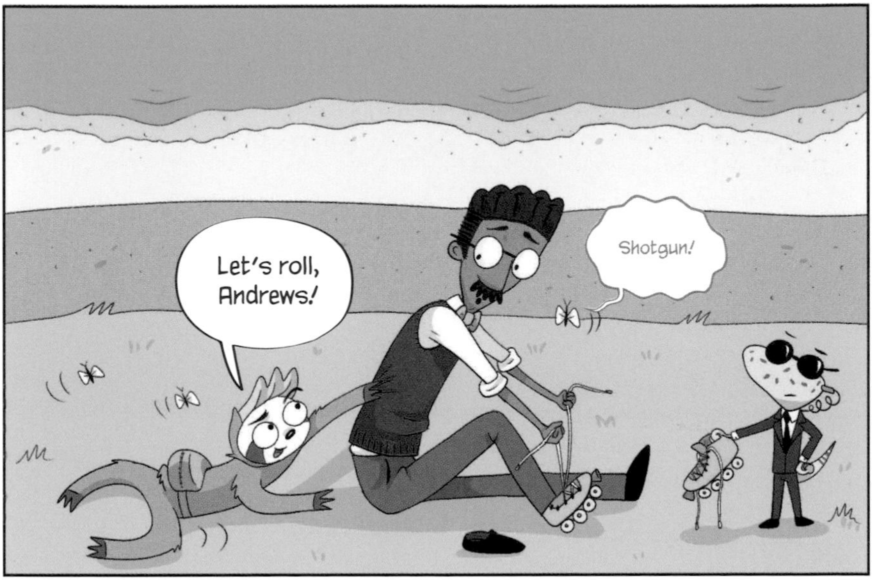
Let's roll, Andrews!
Shotgun!

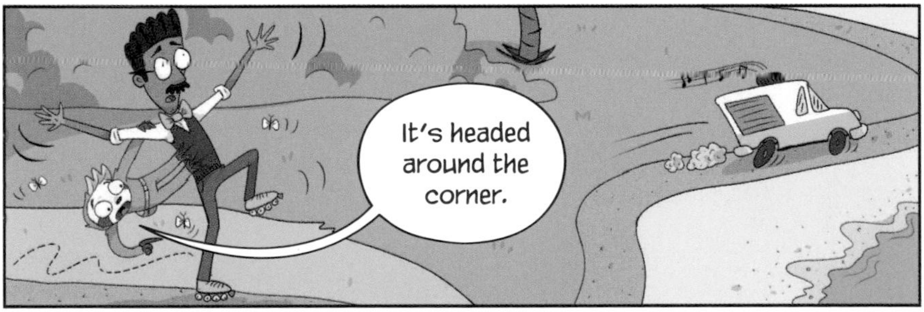
It's headed around the corner.

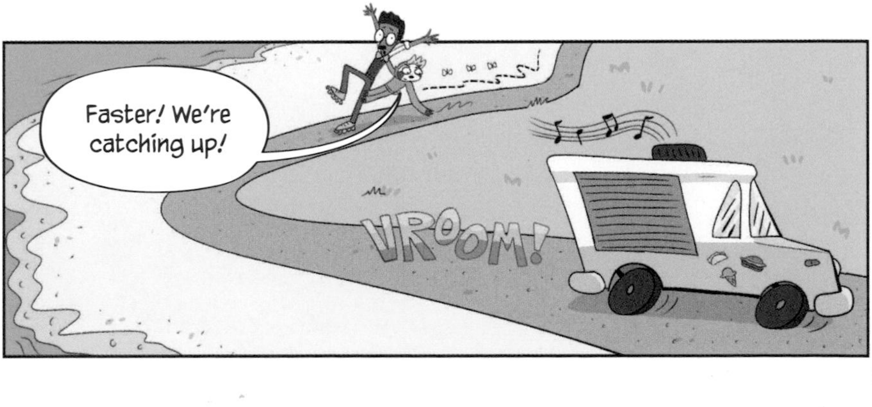
Faster! We're catching up!
VROOM!

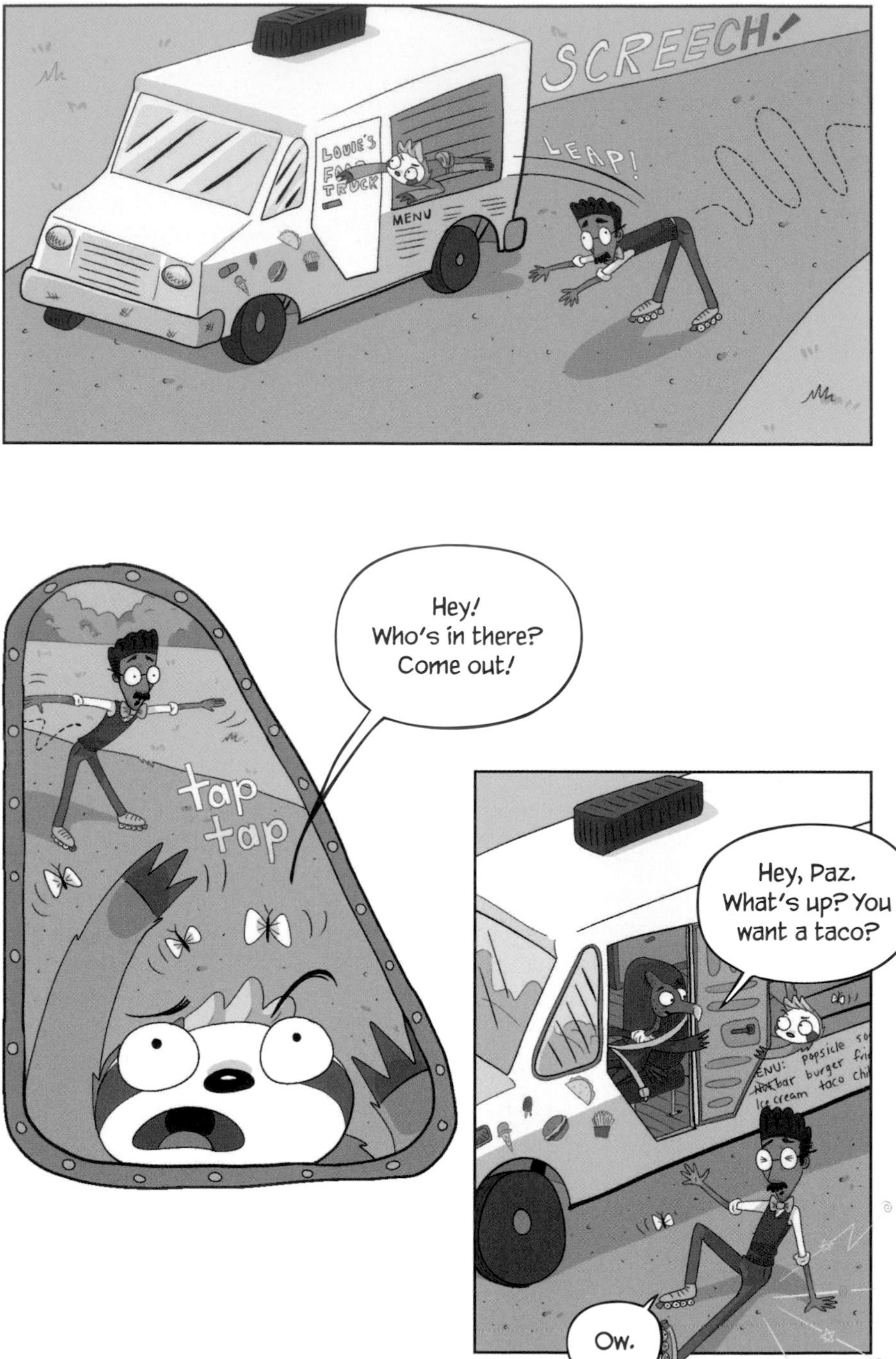
SCREECH!
LEAP!
MENU
Hey!
Who's in there?
Come out!
tap
tap
Hey, Paz.
What's up? You
want a taco?
Ow.

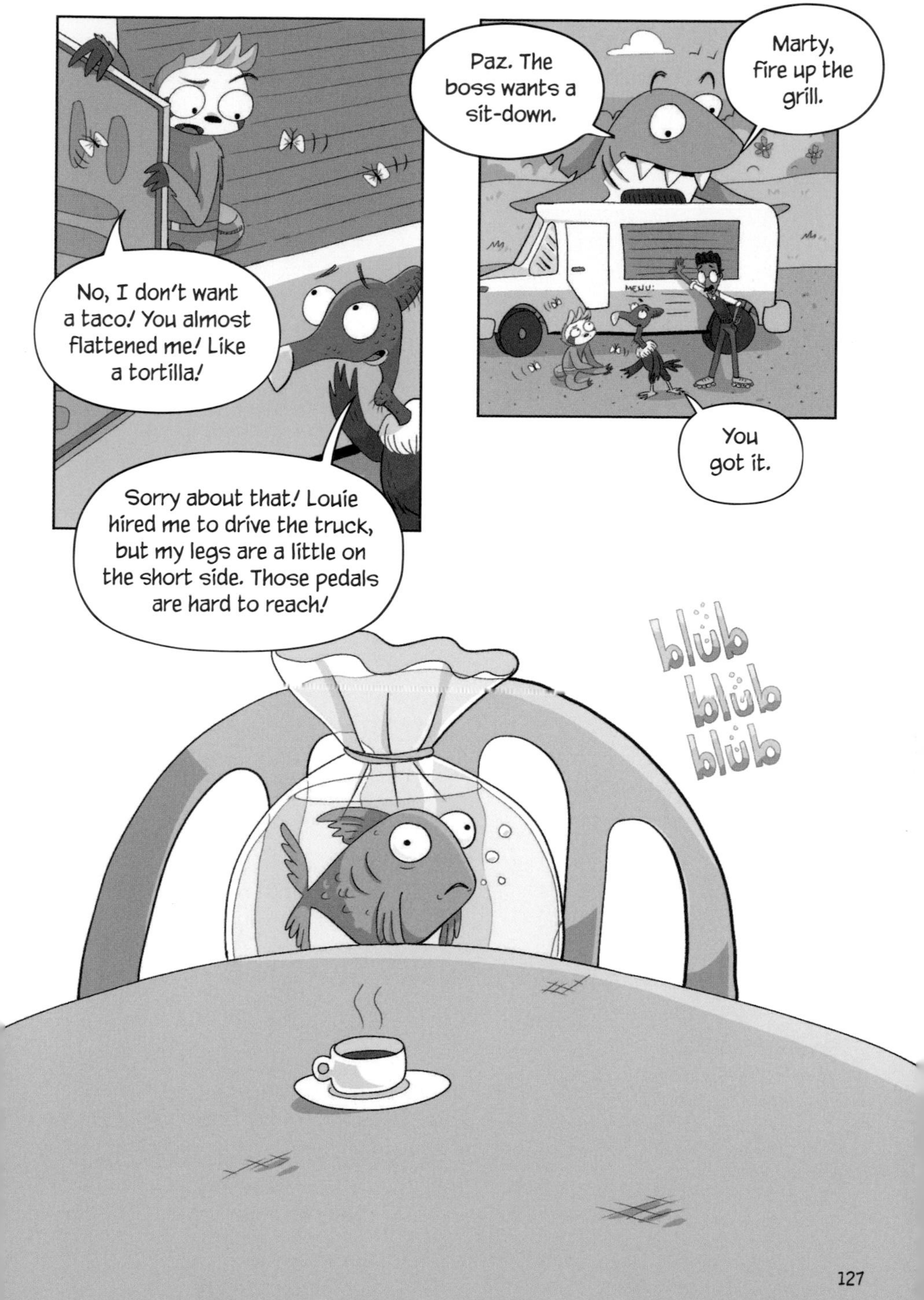
No, I don't want a taco! You almost flattened me! Like a tortilla!
Sorry about that! Louie hired me to drive the truck, but my legs are a little on the short side. Those pedals are hard to reach!
Paz. The boss wants a sit-down.
Marty, fire up the grill.
You got it.
blub
blub
blub

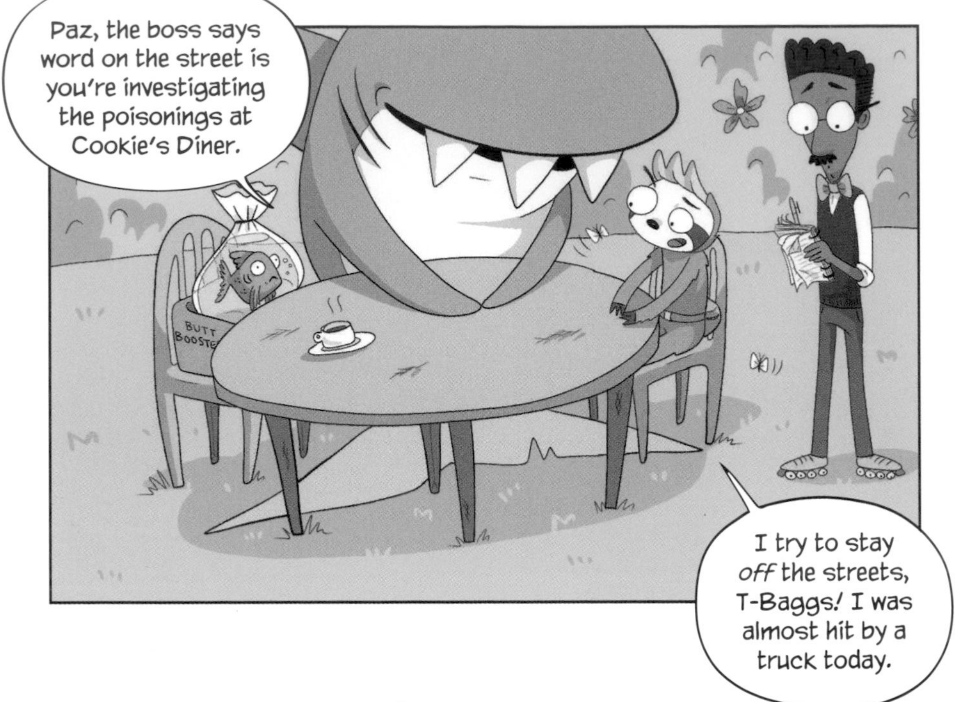
Paz, the boss says word on the street is you're investigating the poisonings at Cookie's Diner.
BUTT BOOSTE
I try to stay *off* the streets, T-Baggs! I was almost hit by a truck today.

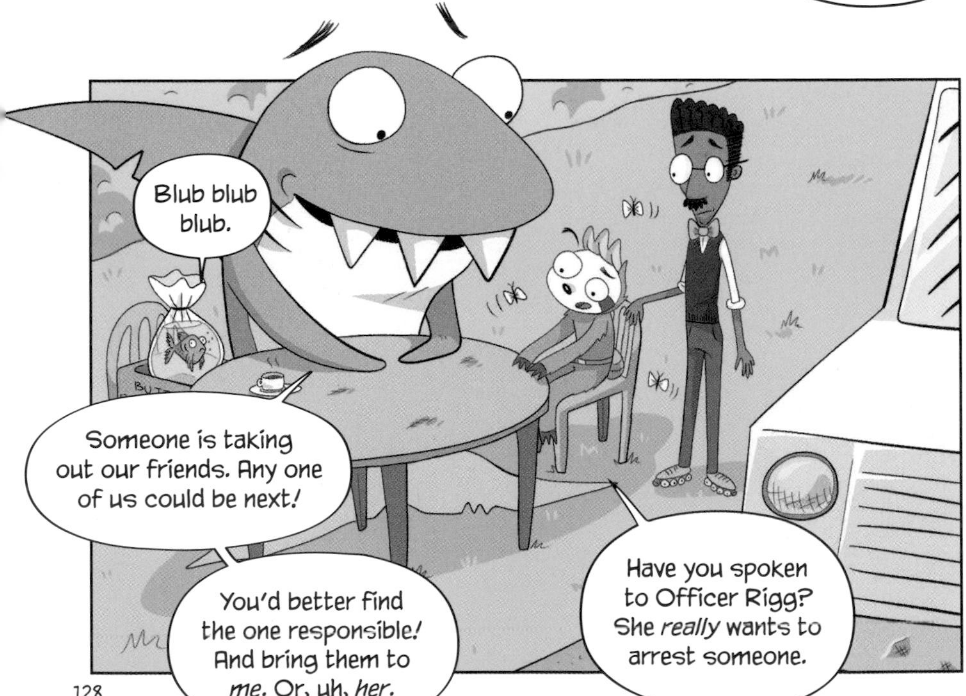
Blub blub blub.
Someone is taking out our friends. Any one of us could be next!
You'd better find the one responsible! And bring them to *me*. Or, uh, *her*.
Have you spoken to Officer Rigg? She *really* wants to arrest someone.

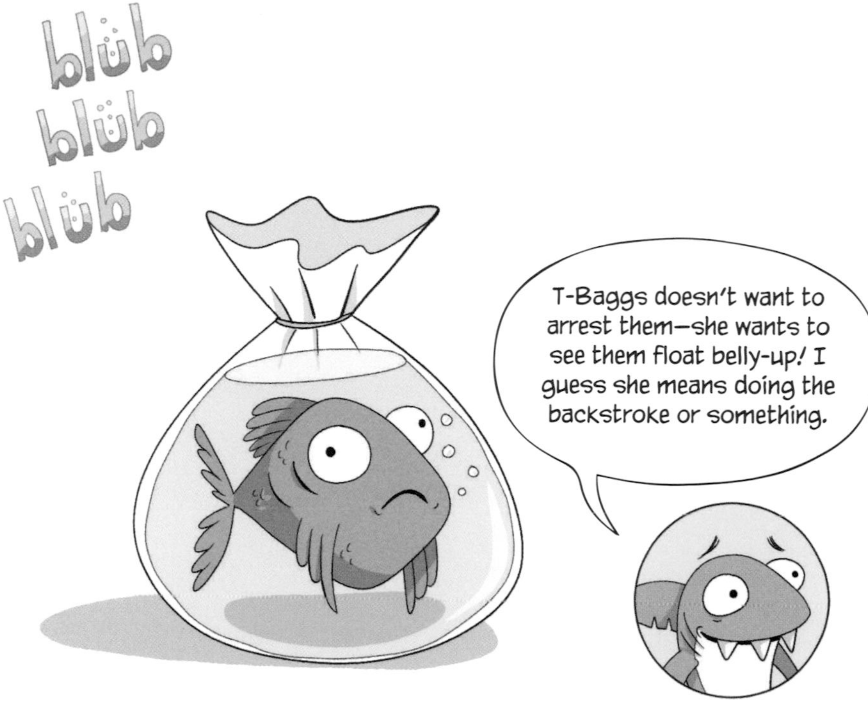
blub
blub
blub
T-Baggs doesn't want to arrest them—she wants to see them float belly-up! I guess she means doing the backstroke or something.

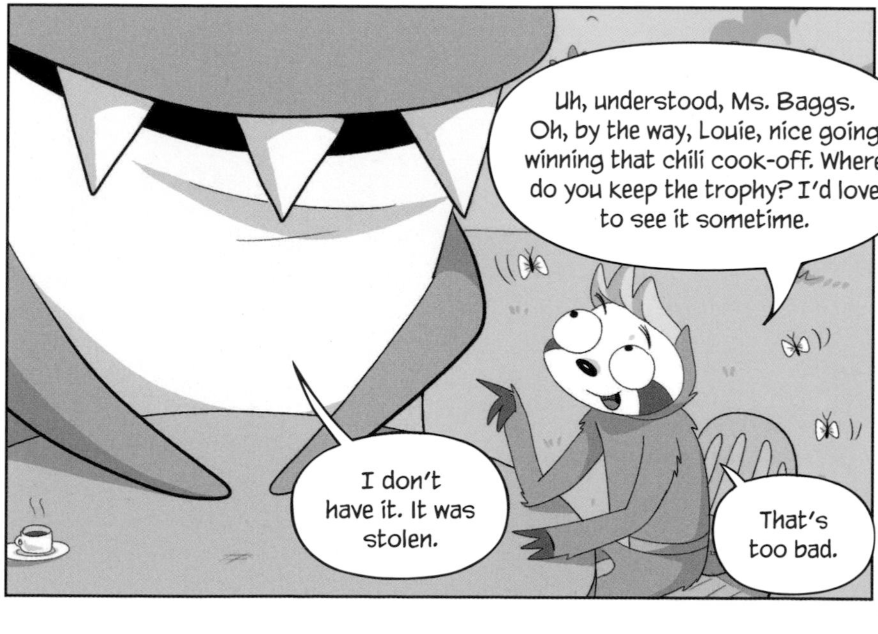
Uh, understood, Ms. Baggs. Oh, by the way, Louie, nice going winning that chili cook-off. Where do you keep the trophy? I'd love to see it sometime.
I don't have it. It was stolen.
That's too bad.

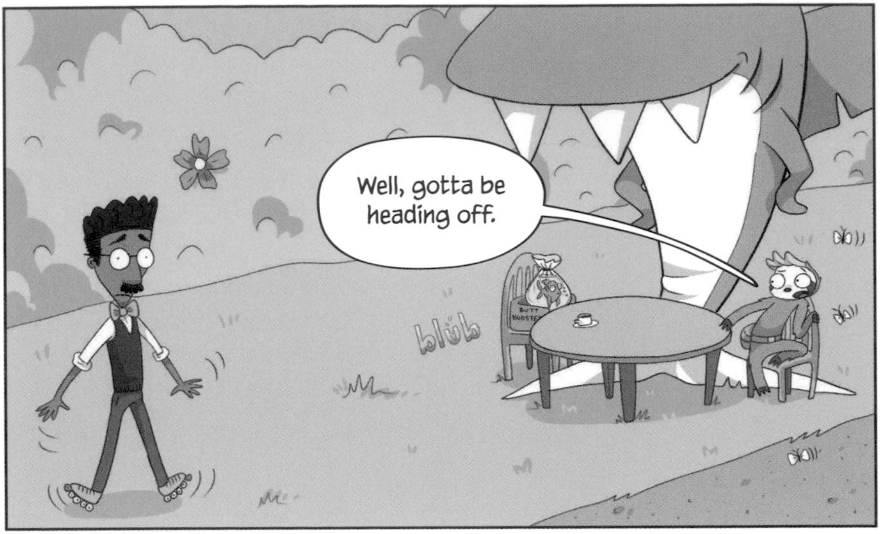
Well, gotta be heading off.
blub
BUTT BOOSTER

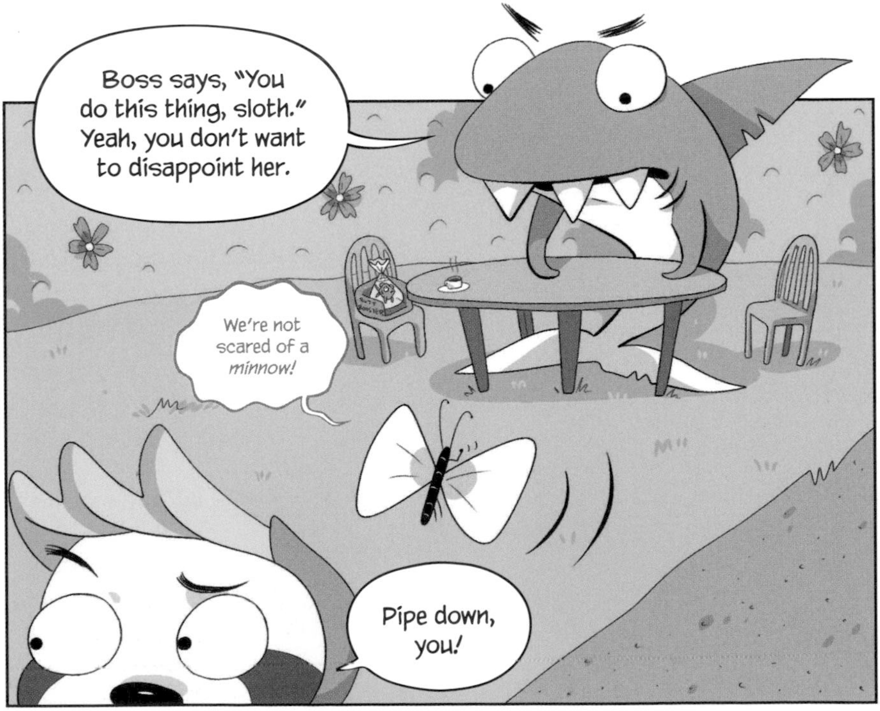
Boss says, "You do this thing, sloth." Yeah, you don't want to disappoint her.
We're not scared of a minnow!
Pipe down, you!

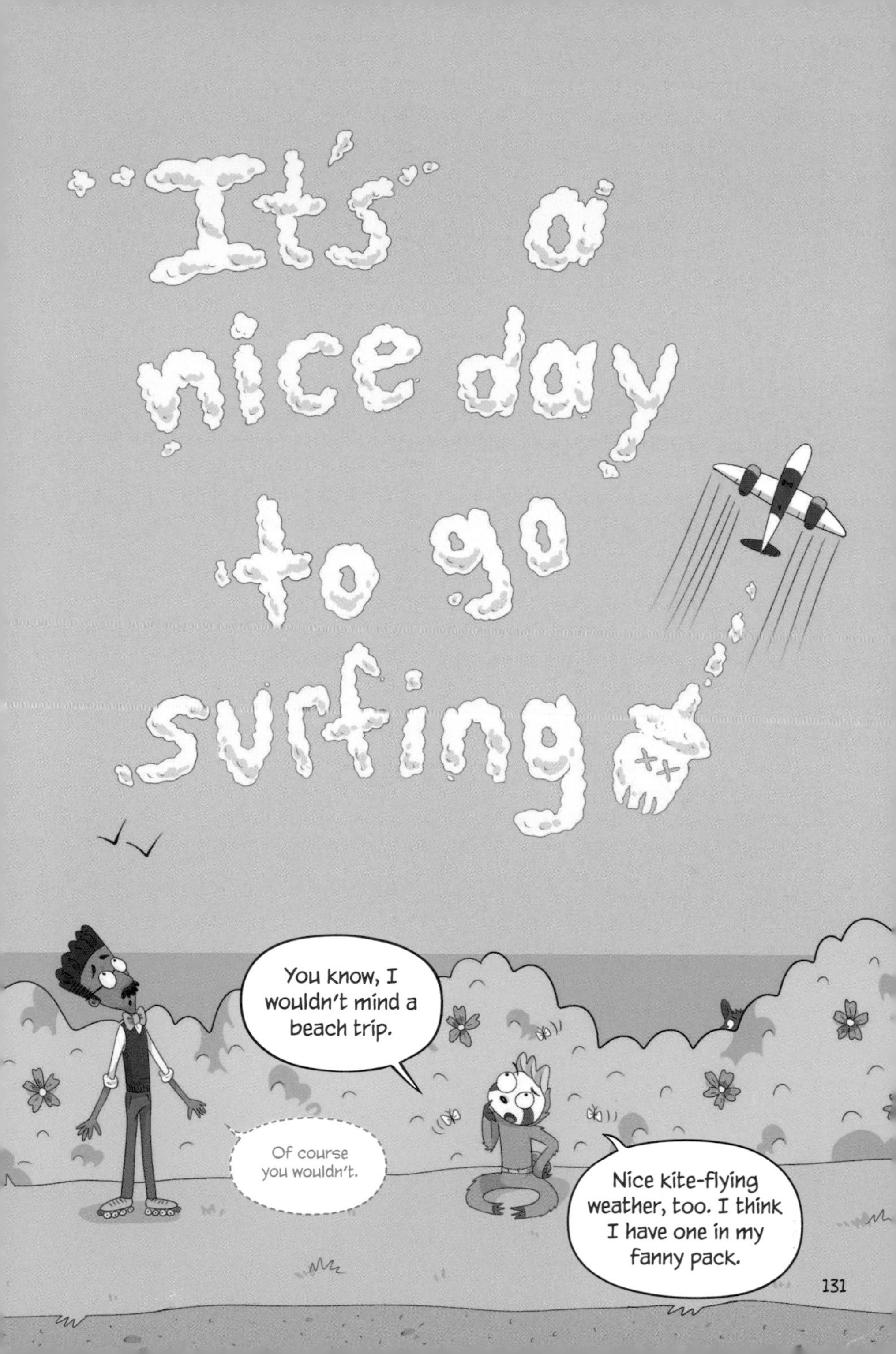
It's a nice day to go surfing
You know, I wouldn't mind a beach trip.
Of course you wouldn't.
Nice kite-flying weather, too. I think I have one in my fanny pack.

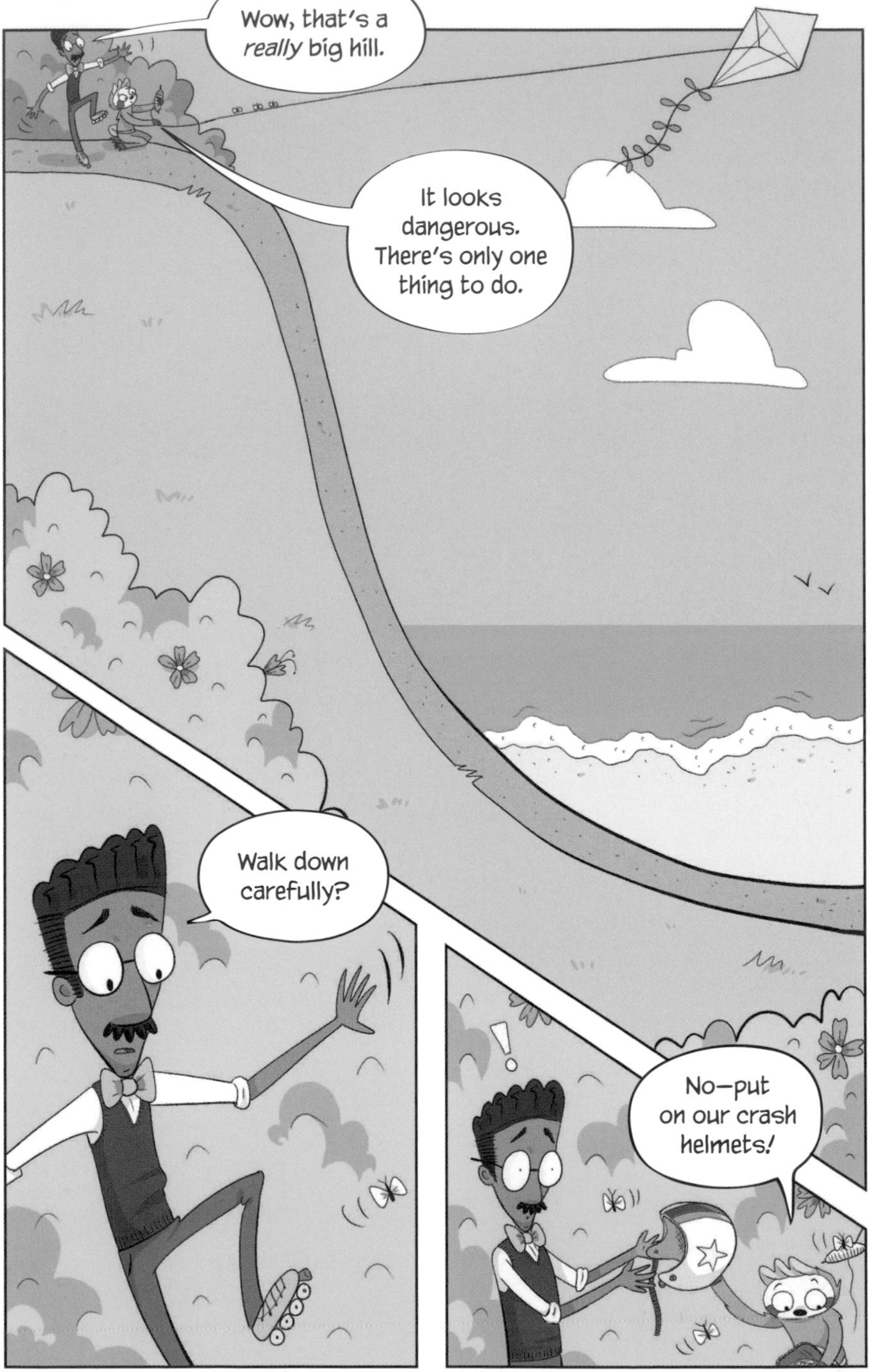
Wow, that's a *really* big hill.
It looks dangerous. There's only one thing to do.
Walk down carefully?
No—put on our crash helmets!

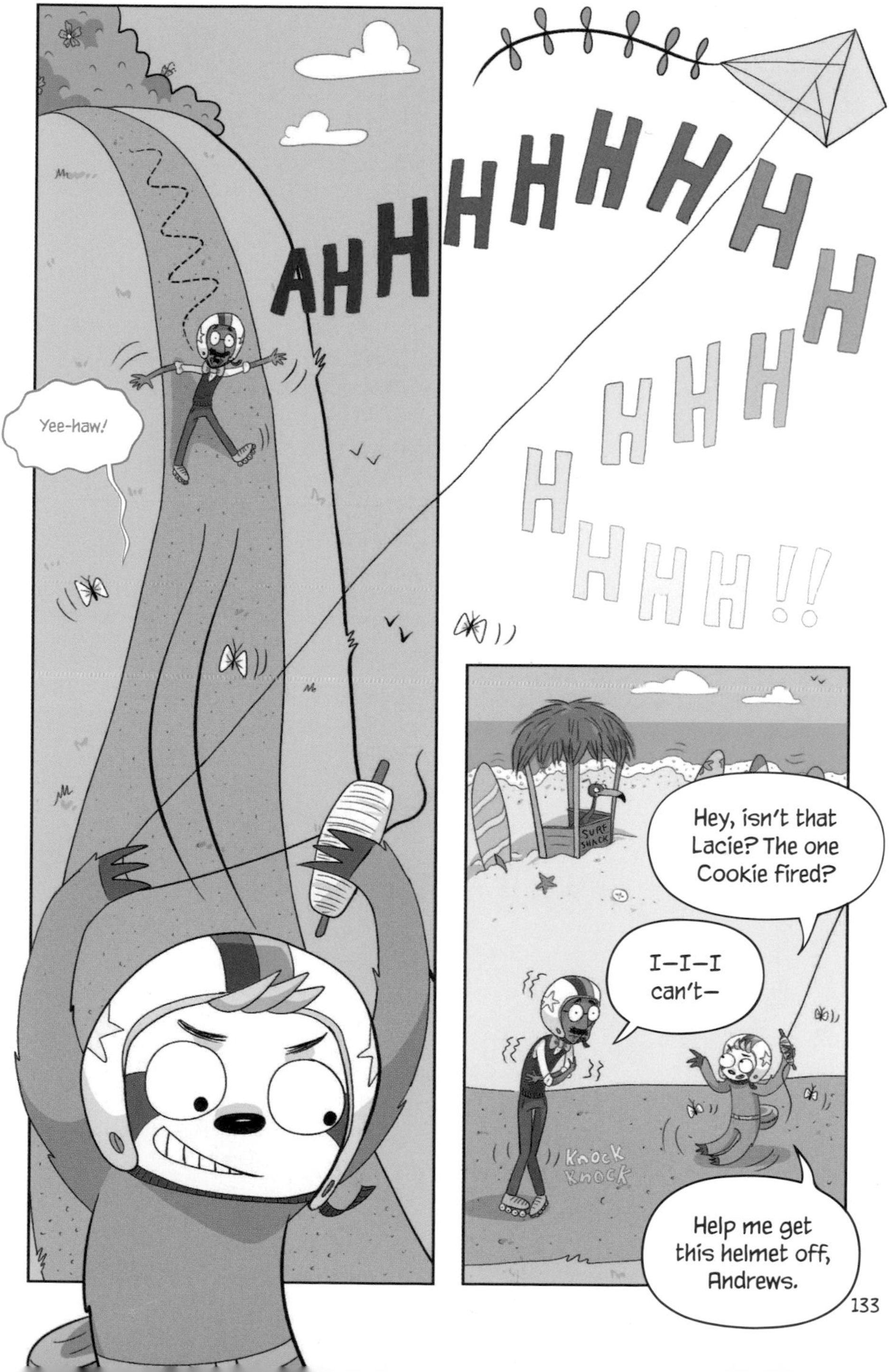
AHHHHHHHHHHHHHHHHHHHHH!!
Yee-haw!
SURF SHACK
Hey, isn't that Lacie? The one Cookie fired?
I—I—I can't—
KNOCK KNOCK
Help me get this helmet off, Andrews.

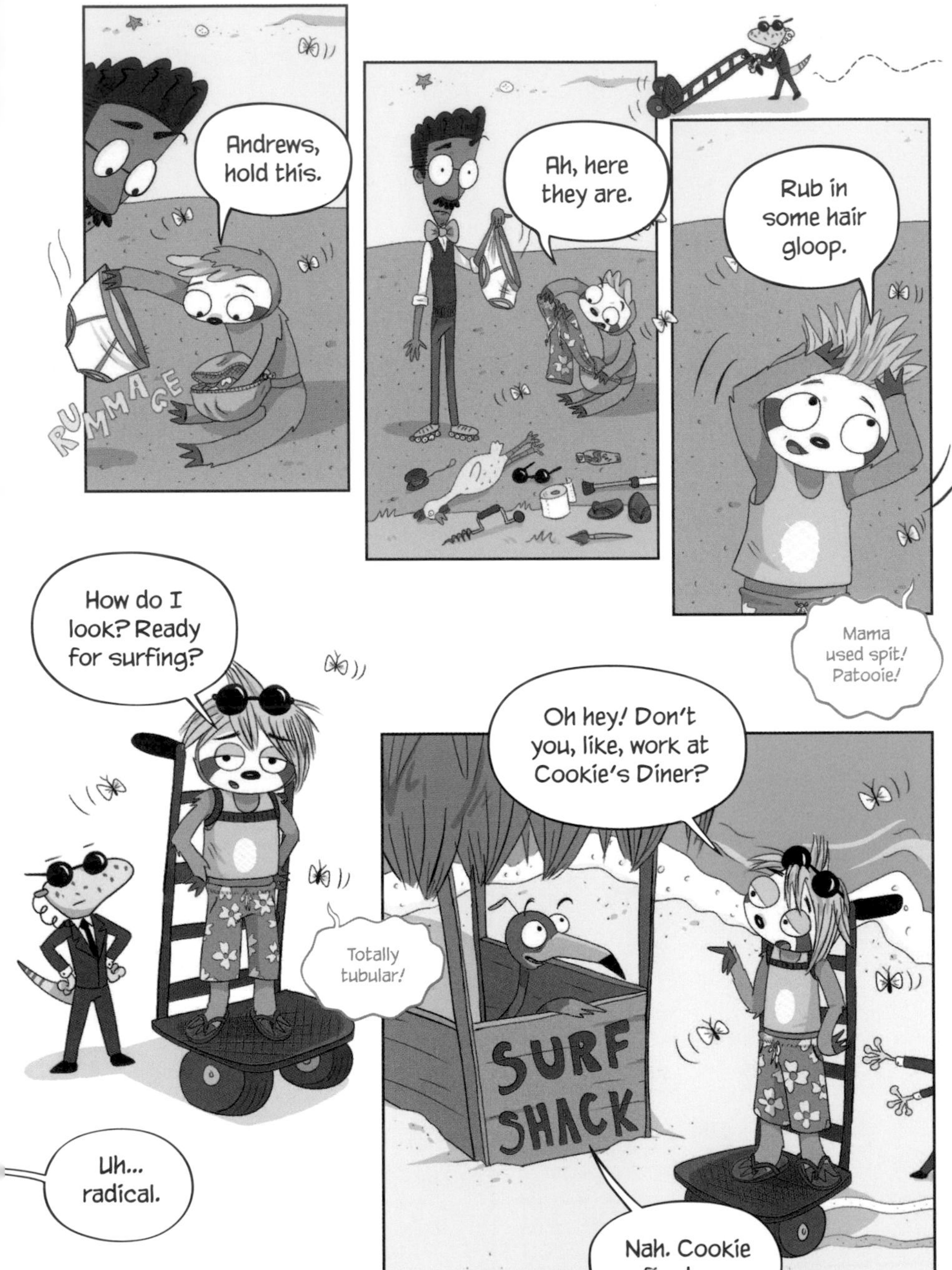
Andrews, hold this.
RUMMAGE
Ah, here they are.
Rub in some hair gloop.
Mama used spit! Patooie!
How do I look? Ready for surfing?
Totally tubular!
Uh... radical.
Oh hey! Don't you, like, work at Cookie's Diner?
SURF SHACK
Nah. Cookie fired me.

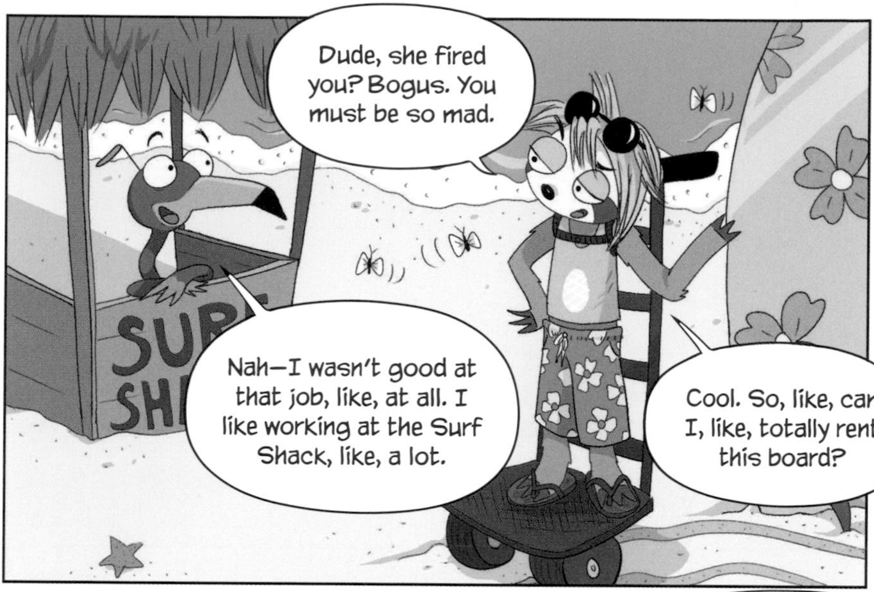
SURF SH
Dude, she fired you? Bogus. You must be so mad.
Nah—I wasn't good at that job, like, at all. I like working at the Surf Shack, like, a lot.
Cool. So, like, can I, like, totally rent this board?

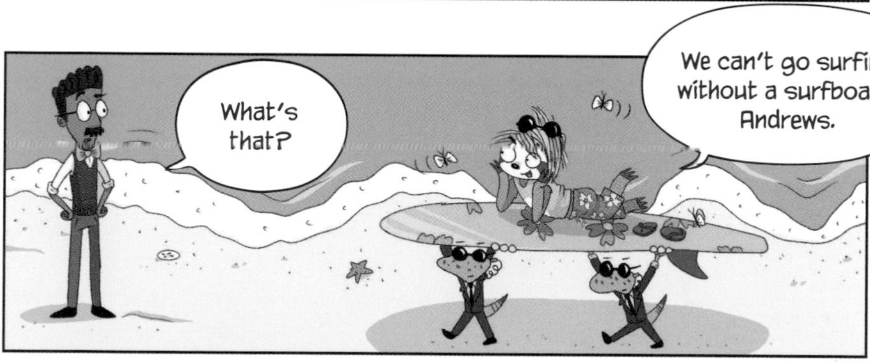
What's that?
We can't go surfing without a surfboard, Andrews.

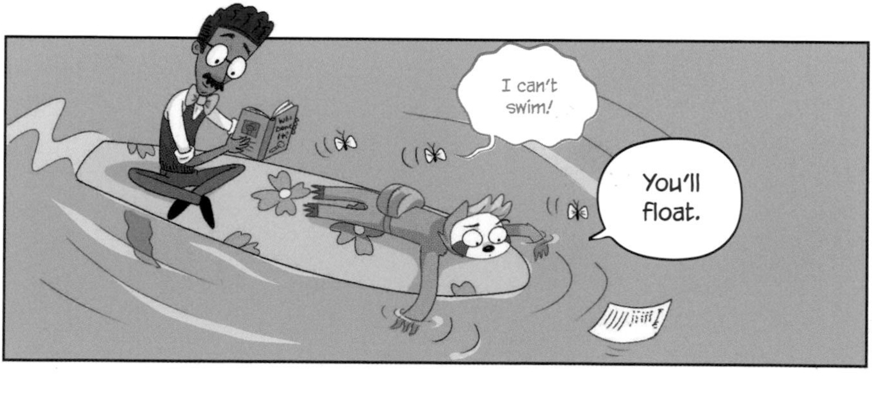
I can't swim!
You'll float.

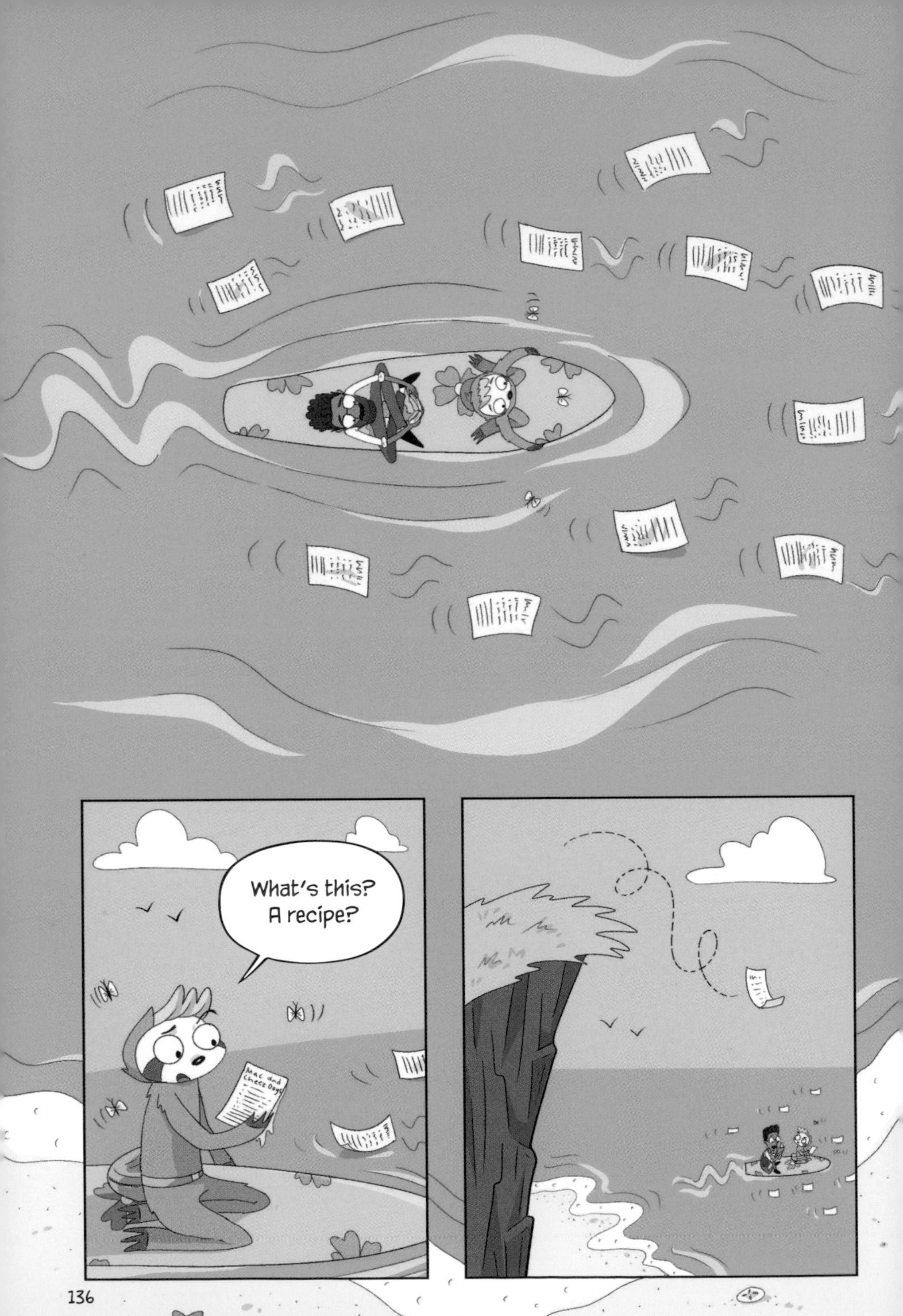
What's this?
A recipe?
Mac and Cheez Dogs

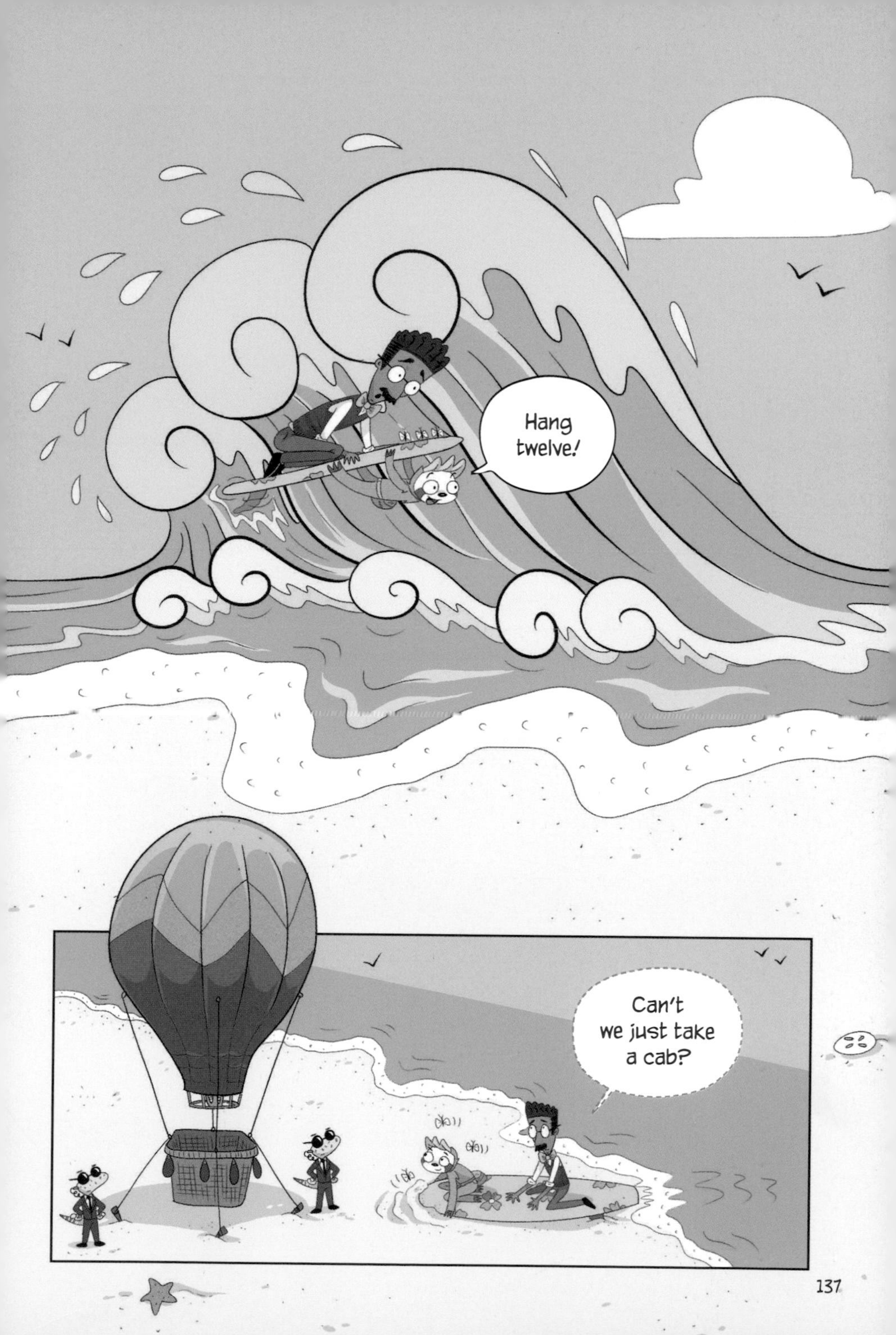
Hang twelve!
Can't we just take a cab?

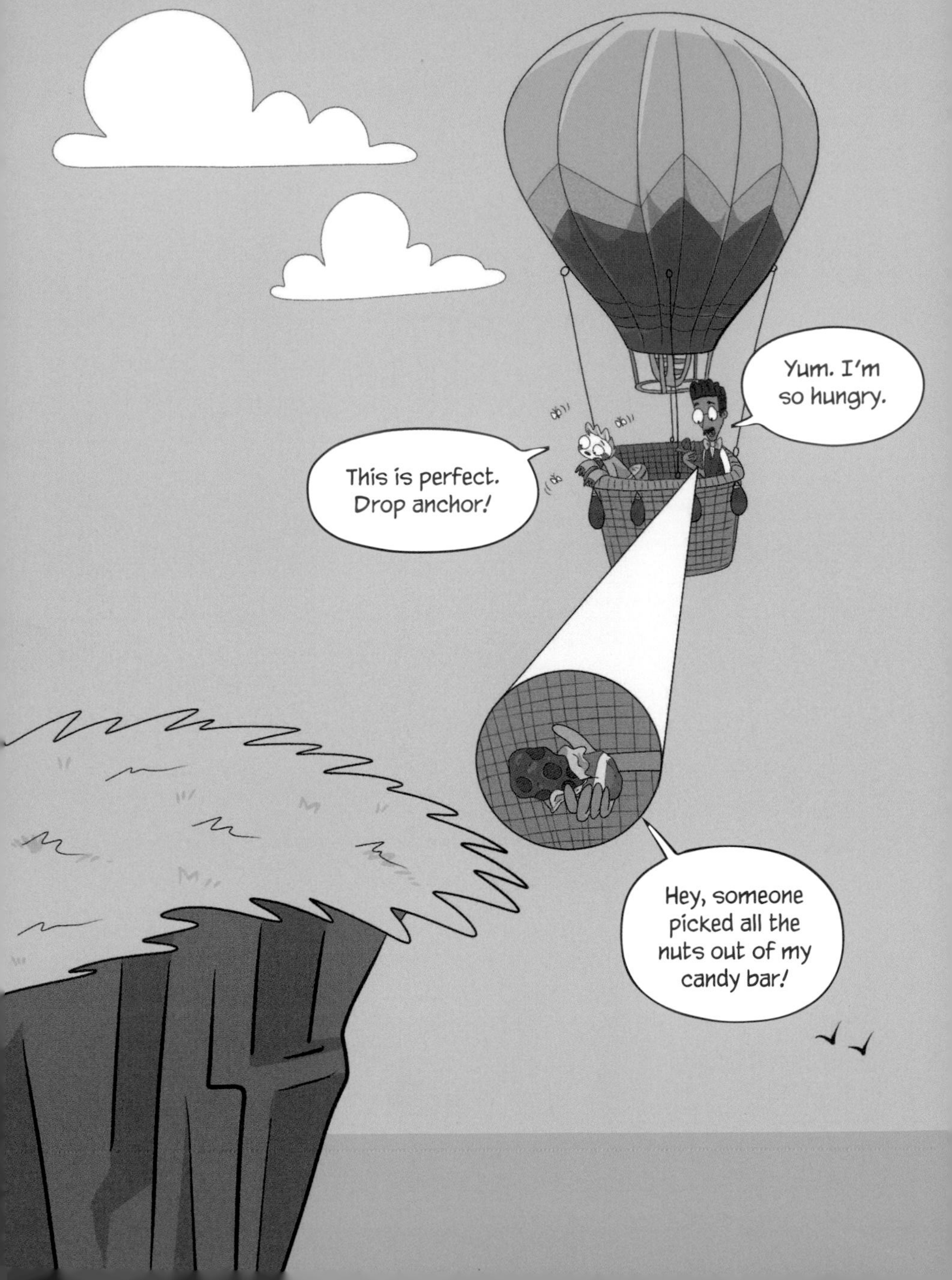
Yum. I'm so hungry.
This is perfect. Drop anchor!
Hey, someone picked all the nuts out of my candy bar!

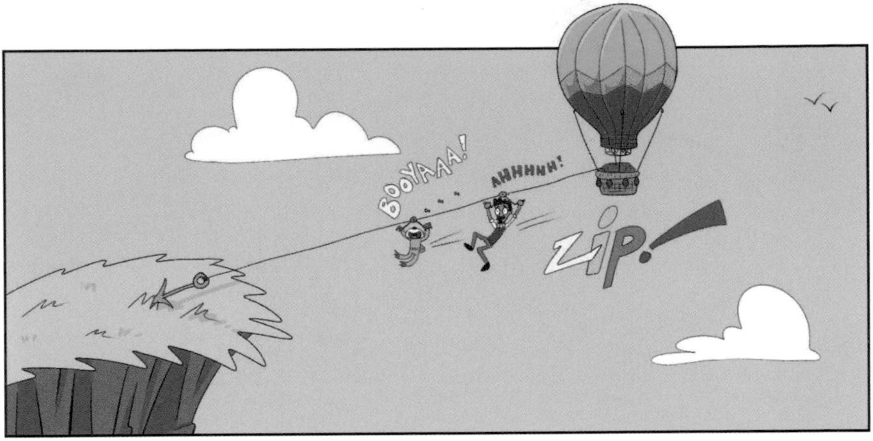
BOOYAAA!
AHHHHHH!
ZIP!

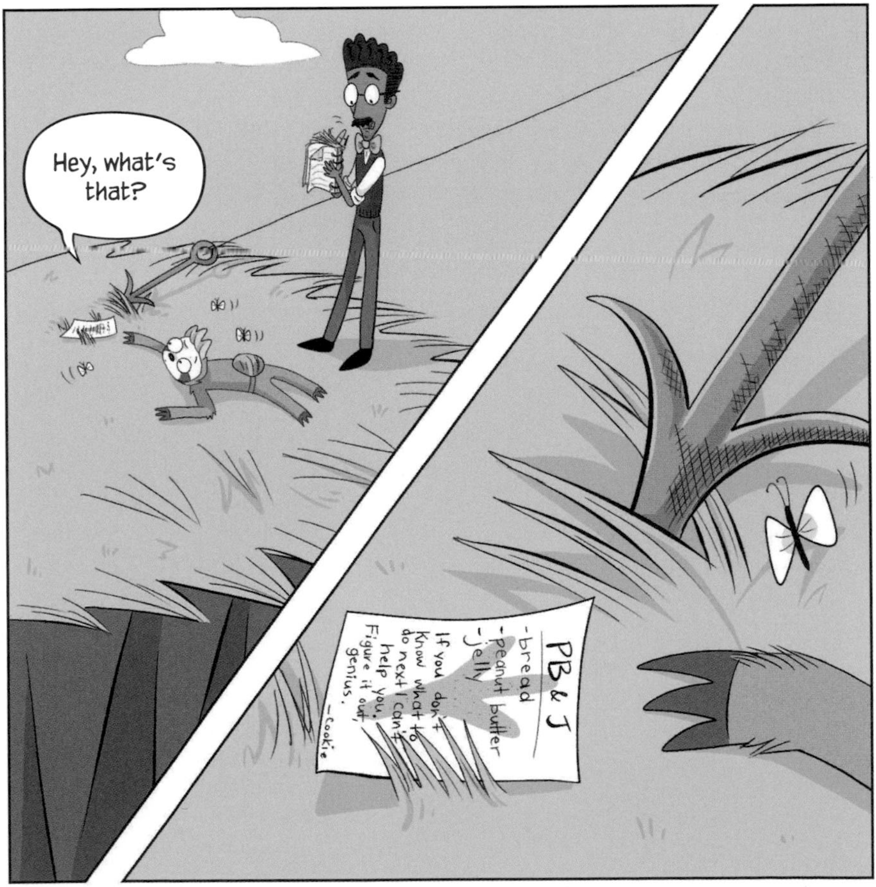
Hey, what's that?
PB & J
-bread
-peanut butter
-jelly
If you don't know what to do next I can't help you. Figure it out, genius.
-Cookie

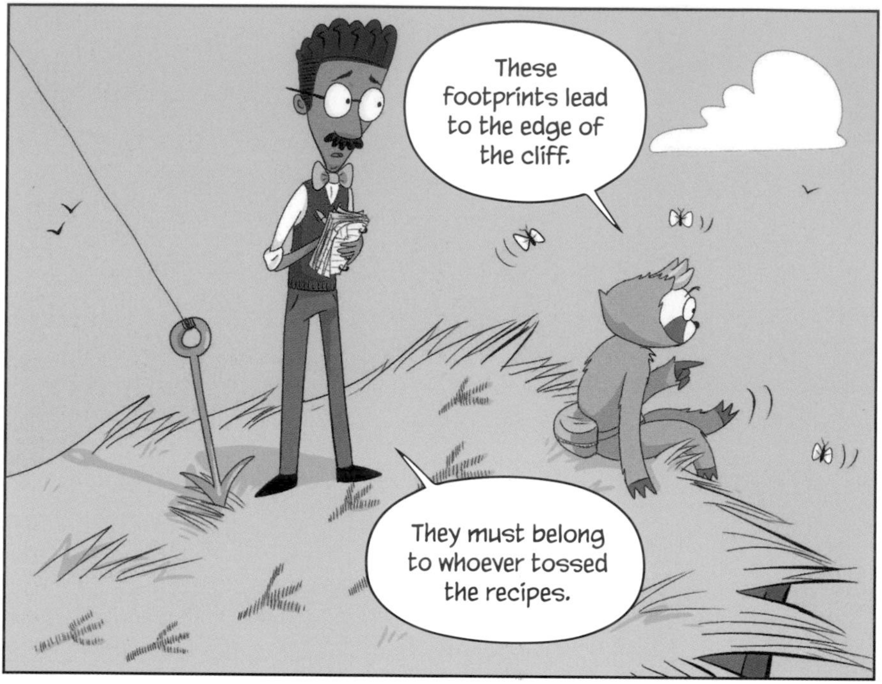
These footprints lead to the edge of the cliff.
They must belong to whoever tossed the recipes.

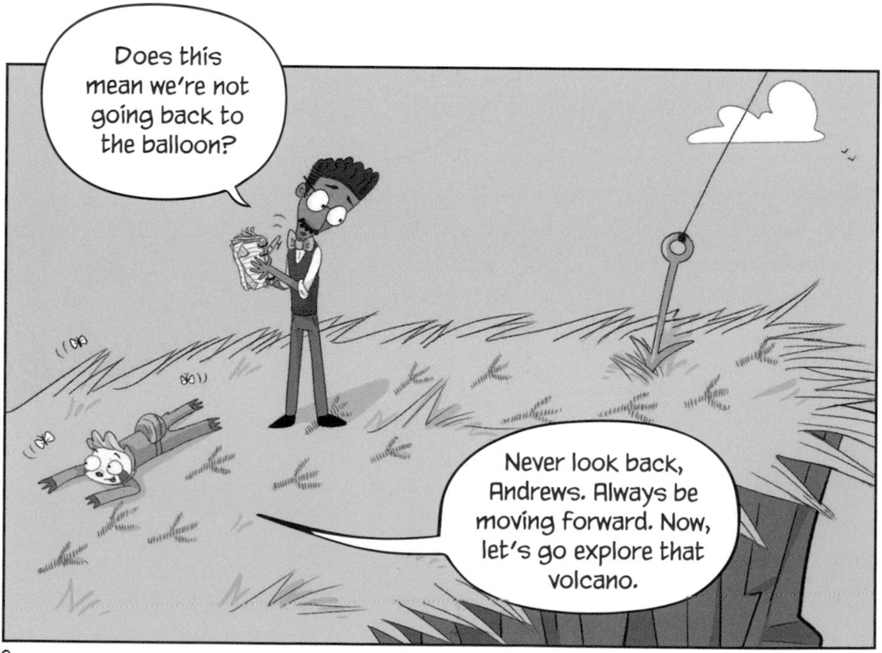
Does this mean we're not going back to the balloon?
Never look back, Andrews. Always be moving forward. Now, let's go explore that volcano.

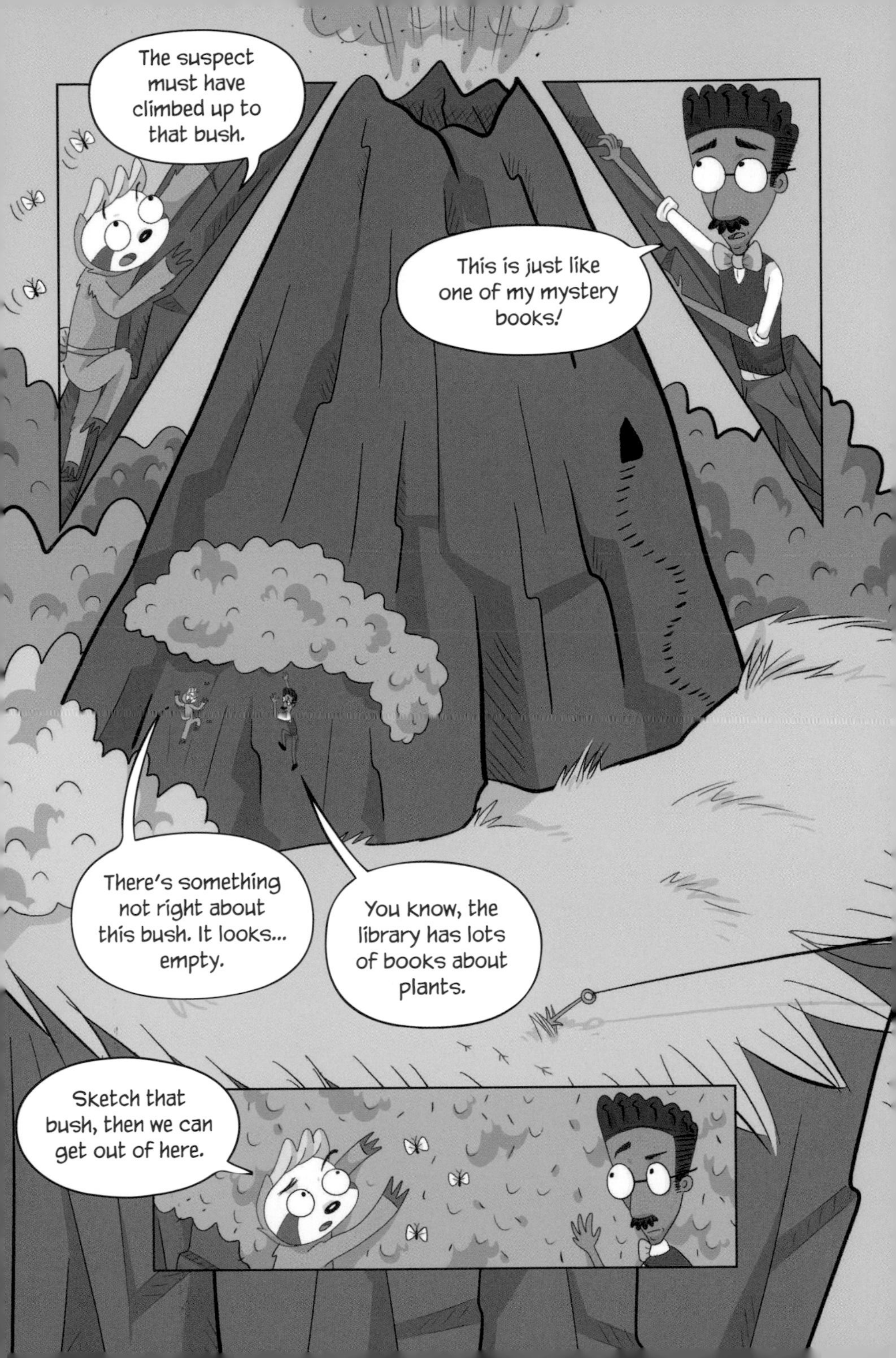
The suspect must have climbed up to that bush.
This is just like one of my mystery books!
There's something not right about this bush. It looks... empty.
You know, the library has lots of books about plants.
Sketch that bush, then we can get out of here.

CHAPTER 7

WEDNESDAY. LATE AFTERNOON.
DRYING OUT IN THE LIBRARY.

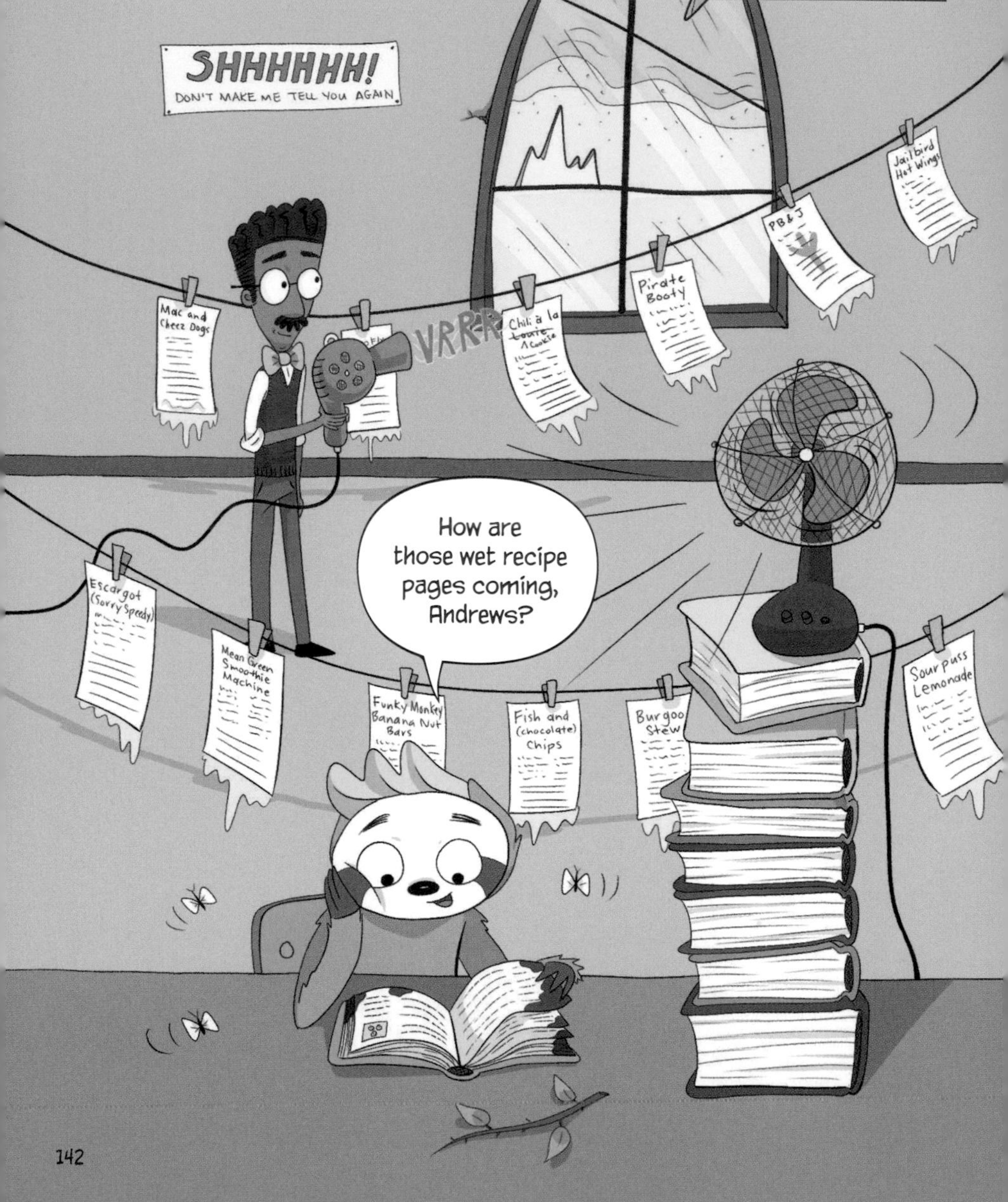

SHHHHHH!
DON'T MAKE ME TELL YOU AGAIN
Jailbird Hot Wings
PB&J
Pirate Booty
Chili à la ~~Louie~~ Cookie
VRRR
Mac and Cheez Dogs
How are those wet recipe pages coming, Andrews?
Escargot (Sorry Speedy)
Mean Green Smoothie Machine
Funky Monkey Banana Nut Bars
Fish and (chocolate) Chips
Burgoo Stew
Sourpuss Lemonade

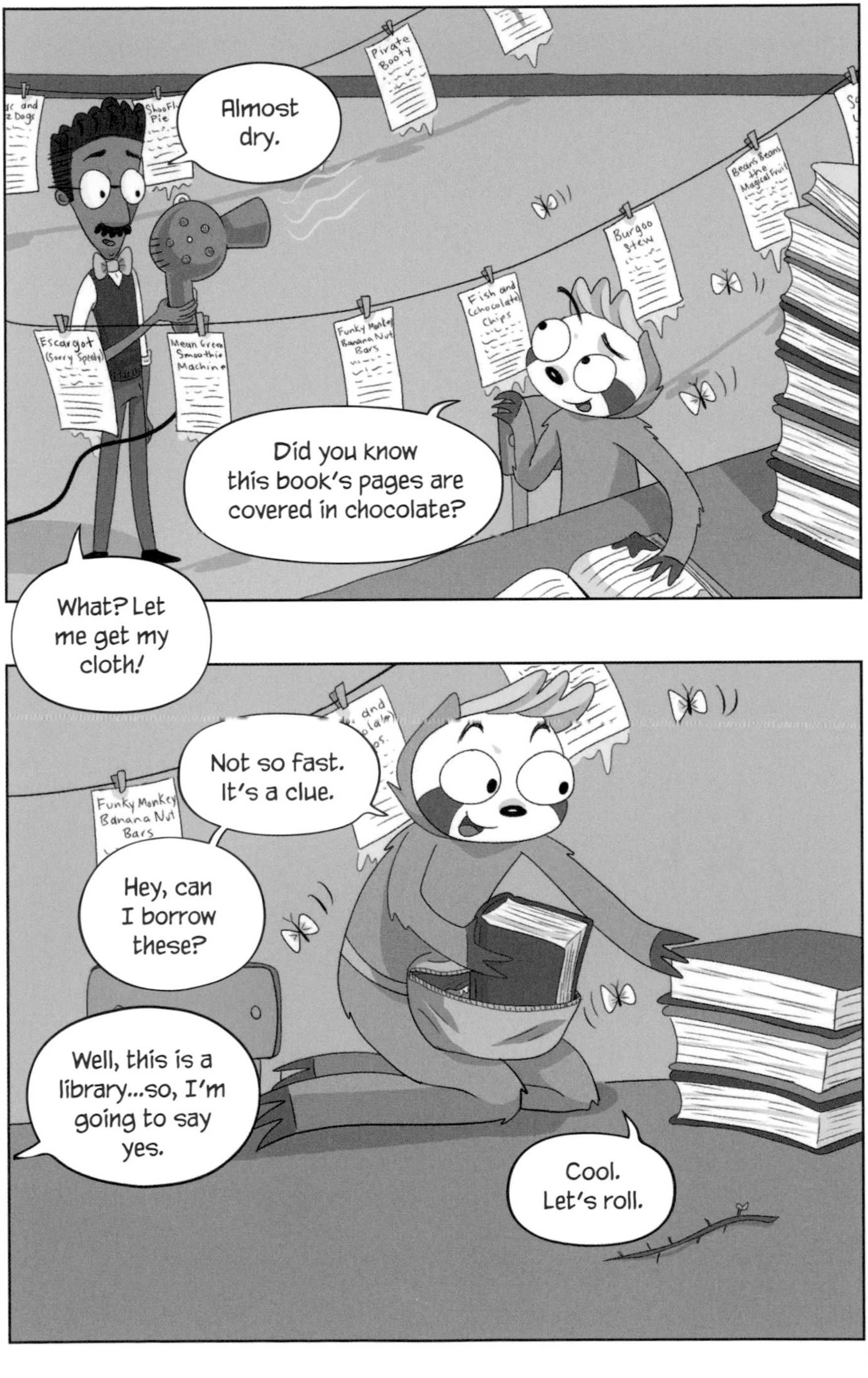
Pirate Booty
Shoofly Pie
Almost dry.
Beans Beans the Magical Fruit
Burgoo Stew
Fish and Chocolate Chips
Funky Monkey Banana Nut Bars
Escargot (Sorry Speedy)
Mean Green Smoothie Machine
Did you know this book's pages are covered in chocolate?
What? Let me get my cloth!
Not so fast. It's a clue.
Funky Monkey Banana Nut Bars
Hey, can I borrow these?
Well, this is a library...so, I'm going to say yes.
Cool. Let's roll.

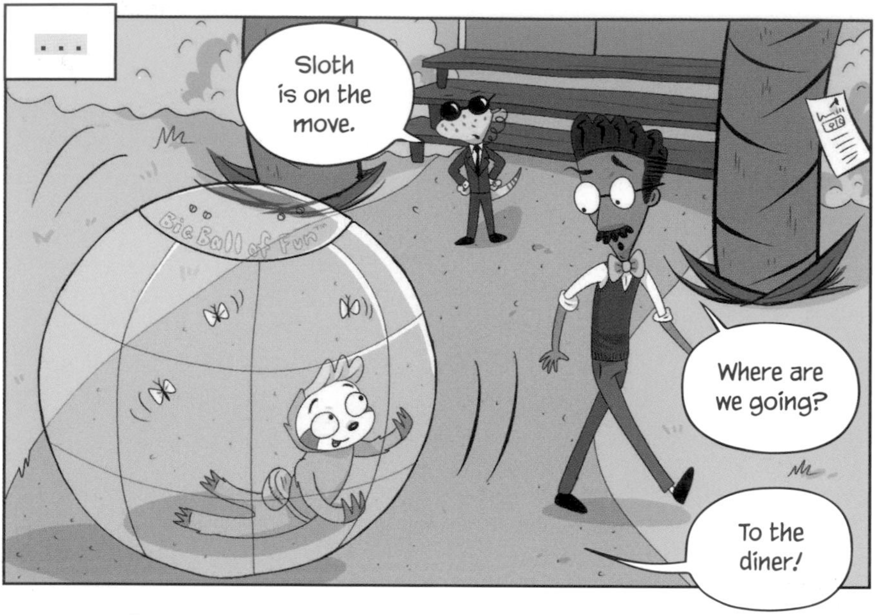
. . .
Sloth is on the move.
Big Ball of Fun™
Where are we going?
To the diner!

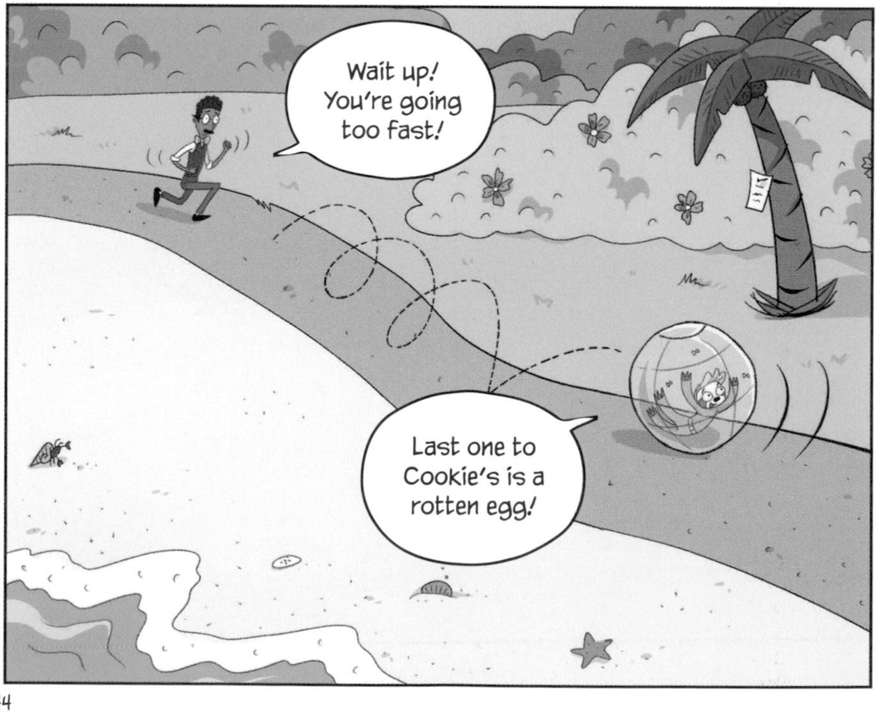
Wait up! You're going too fast!
Last one to Cookie's is a rotten egg!

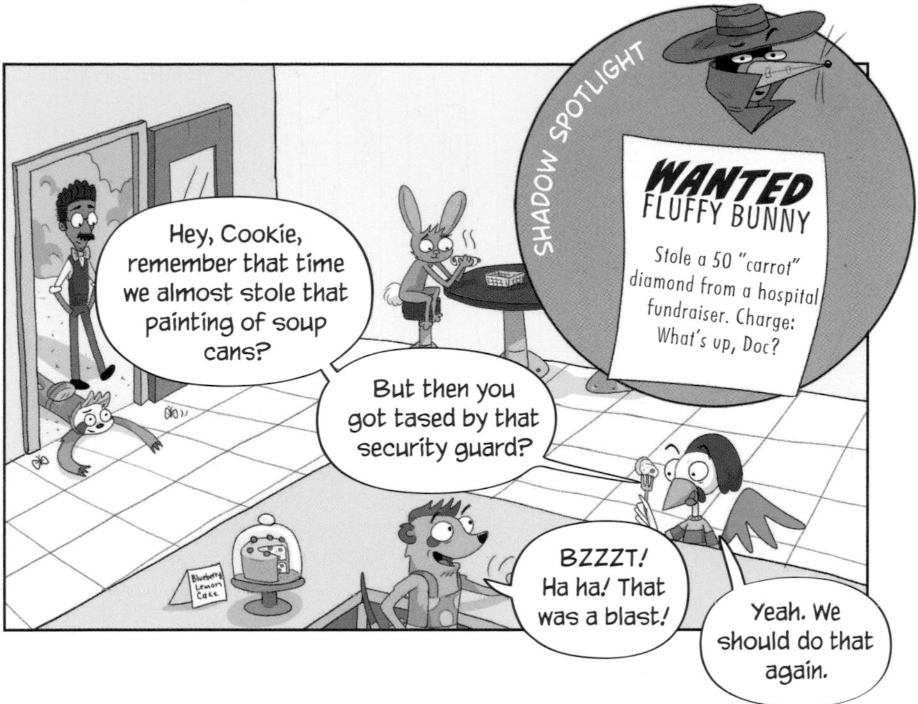
SHADOW SPOTLIGHT
WANTED
FLUFFY BUNNY
Stole a 50 "carrot" diamond from a hospital fundraiser. Charge: What's up, Doc?
Hey, Cookie, remember that time we almost stole that painting of soup cans?
But then you got tased by that security guard?
BZZZT! Ha ha! That was a blast!
Yeah. We should do that again.
Blueberry Lemon Cake

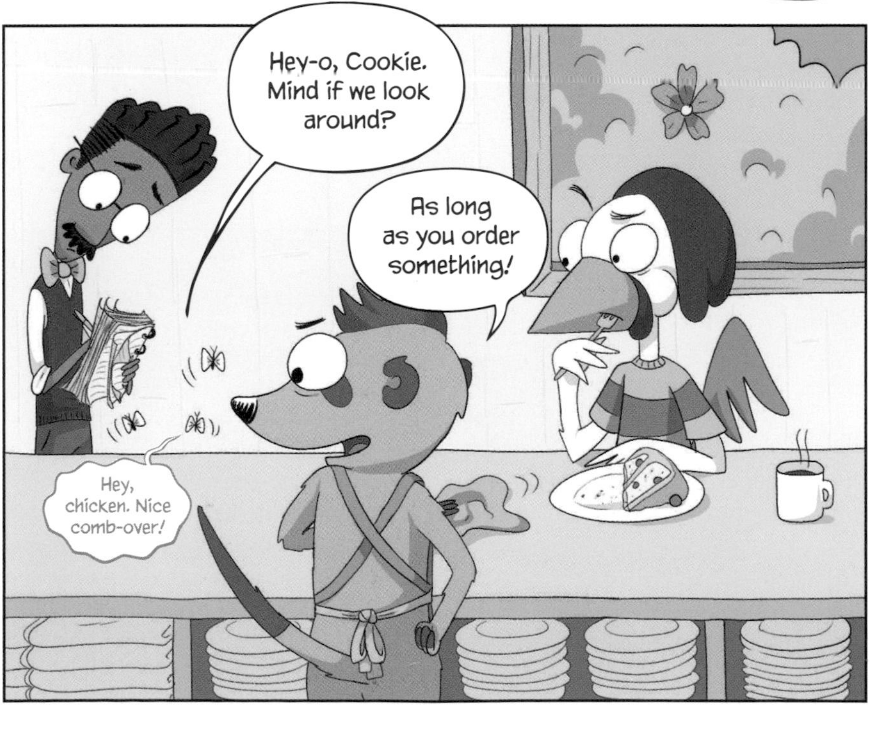
Hey-o, Cookie. Mind if we look around?
As long as you order something!
Hey, chicken. Nice comb-over!

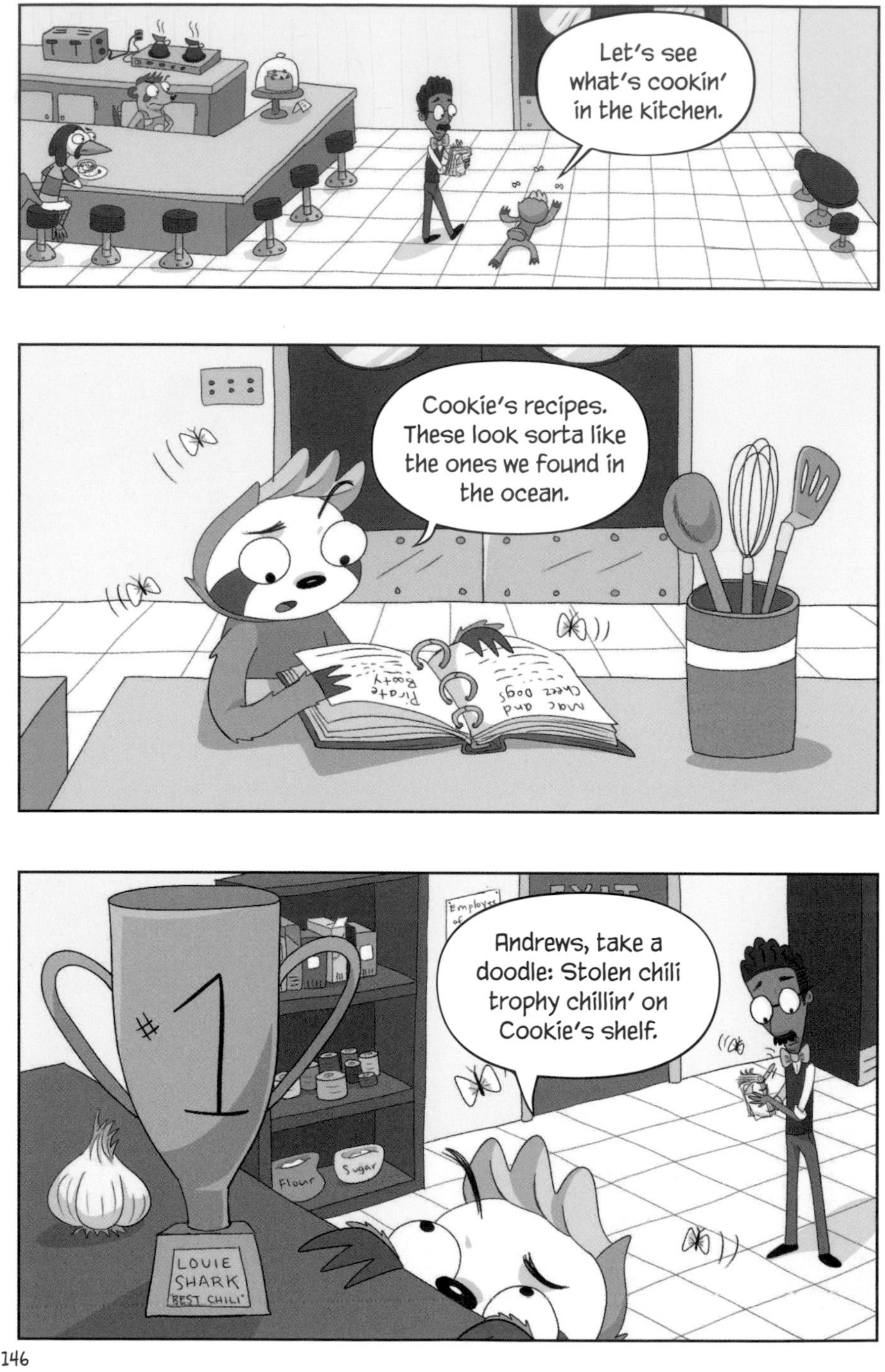
Let's see what's cookin' in the kitchen.
Cookie's recipes. These look sorta like the ones we found in the ocean.
Pirate Booty
Mac and Cheez Dogs
Andrews, take a doodle: Stolen chili trophy chillin' on Cookie's shelf.
#1
LOUIE SHARK BEST CHILI
Flour
Sugar

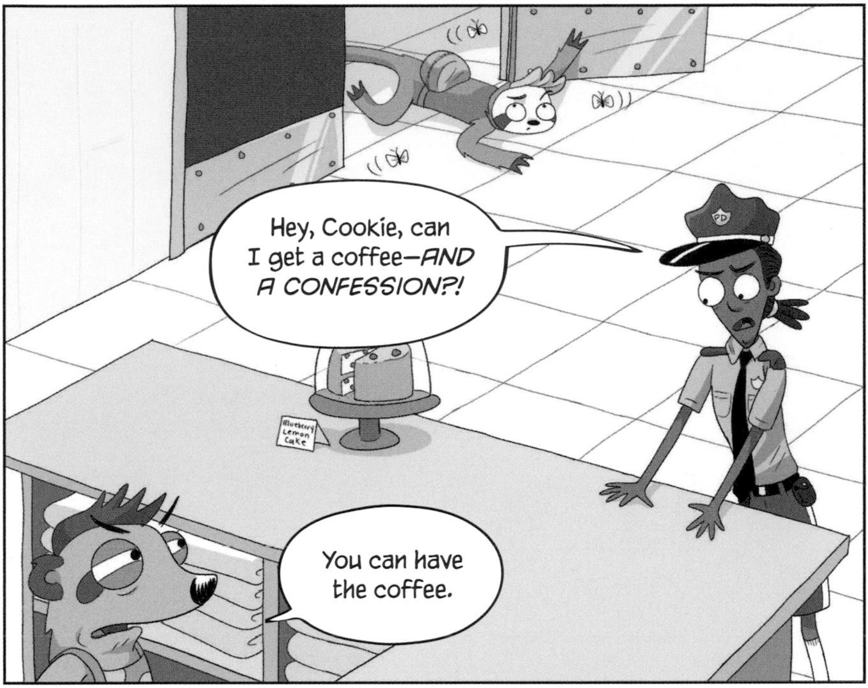
Hey, Cookie, can I get a coffee—*AND A CONFESSION?!*
Blueberry Lemon Cake
You can have the coffee.

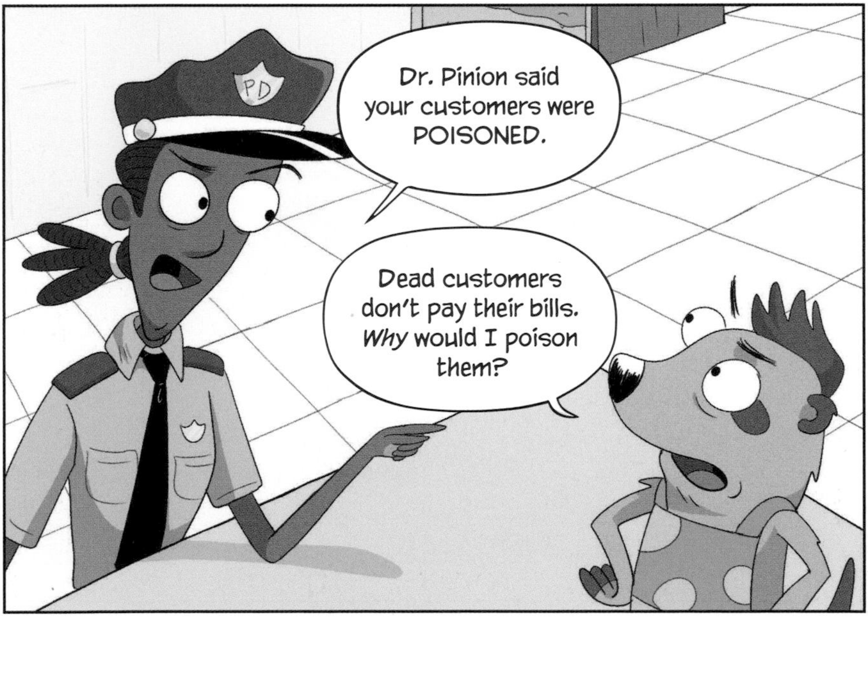
Dr. Pinion said your customers were POISONED.
Dead customers don't pay their bills. *Why* would I poison them?

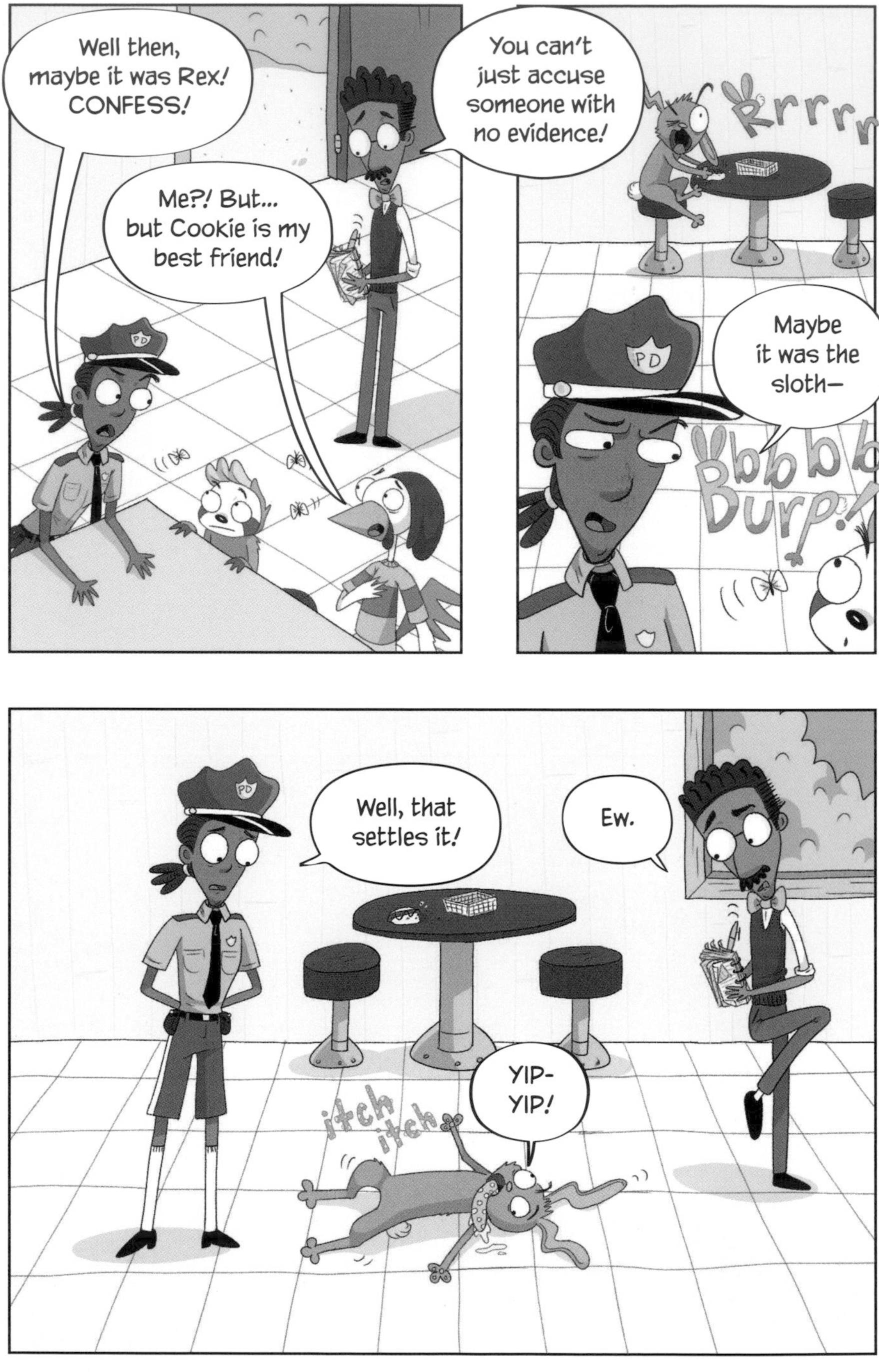
Well then, maybe it was Rex! CONFESS!
Me?! But... but Cookie is my best friend!
You can't just accuse someone with no evidence!
Rrrrrraaaaaaa
Maybe it was the sloth—
Bbbbba
Burp!
Well, that settles it!
Ew.
YIP-YIP!
itch itch

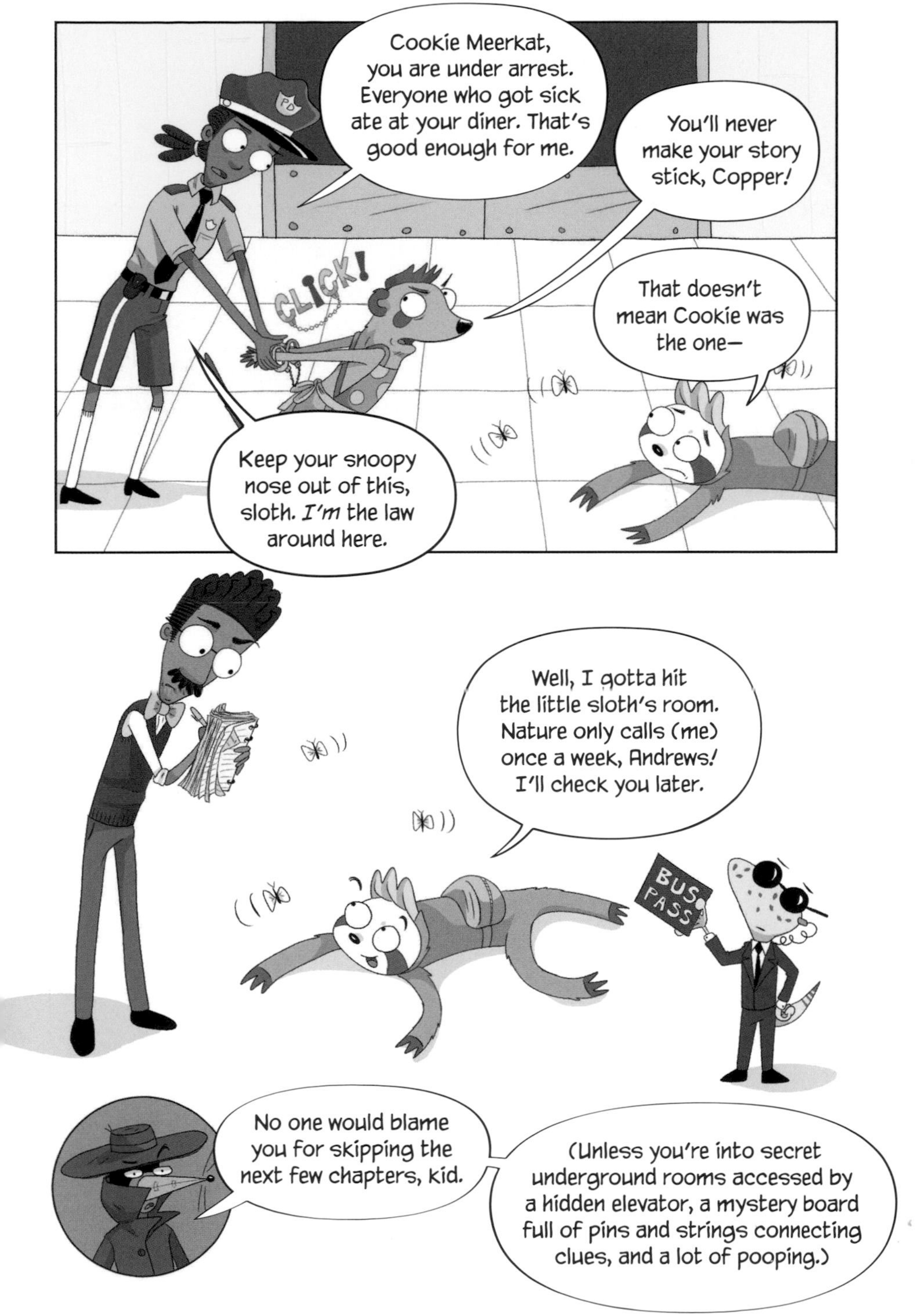
Cookie Meerkat, you are under arrest. Everyone who got sick ate at your diner. That's good enough for me.
You'll never make your story stick, Copper!
CLICK!
That doesn't mean Cookie was the one—
Keep your snoopy nose out of this, sloth. *I'm* the law around here.
Well, I gotta hit the little sloth's room. Nature only calls (me) once a week, Andrews! I'll check you later.
BUS PASS
No one would blame you for skipping the next few chapters, kid.
(Unless you're into secret underground rooms accessed by a hidden elevator, a mystery board full of pins and strings connecting clues, and a lot of pooping.)

CHAPTER 8

WEDNESDAY. EARLY EVENING.
THE OUTHOUSE OUT BACK OF THE TREEHOUSE.

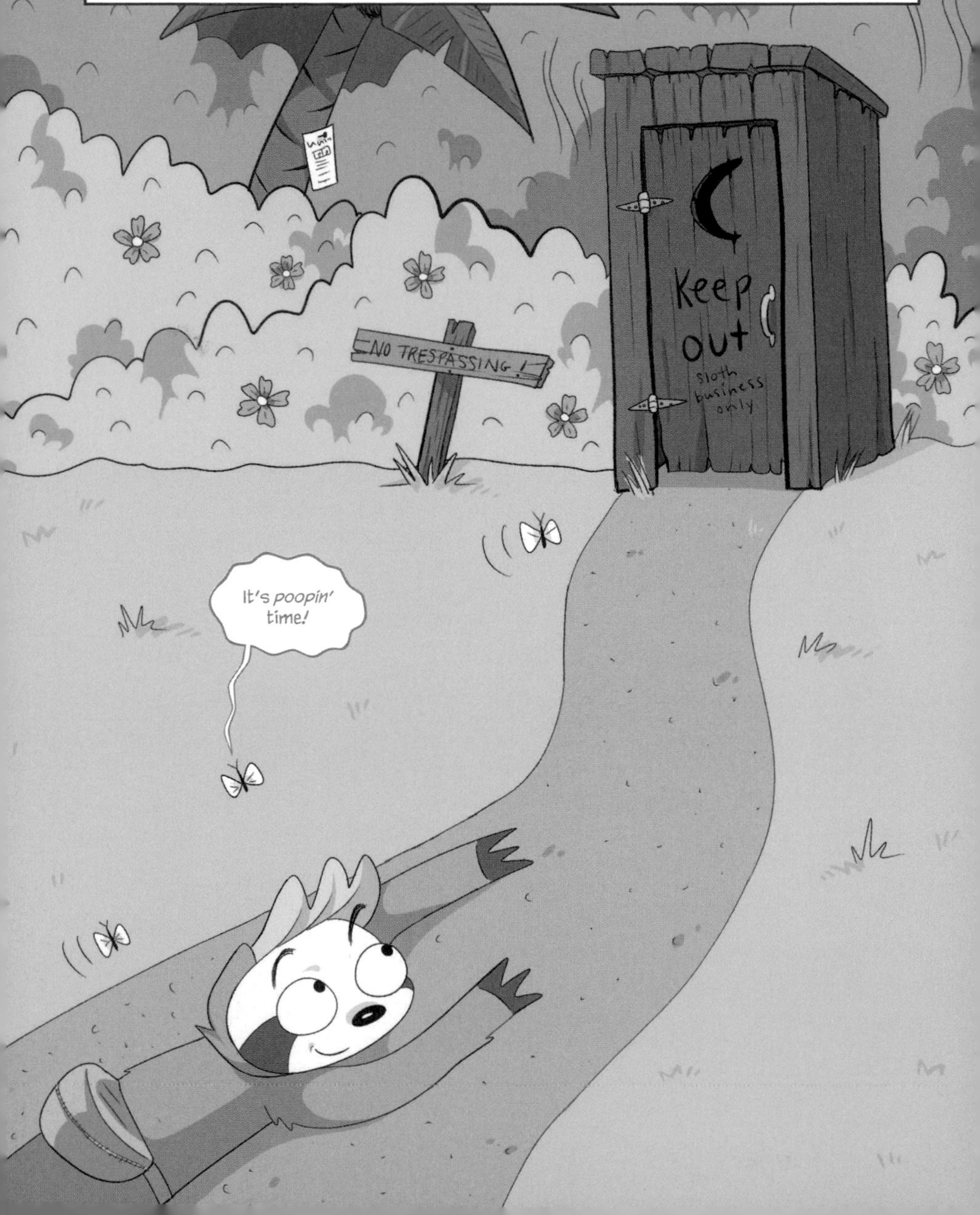
NO TRESPASSING!
Keep out
sloth business only
It's *poopin'* time!

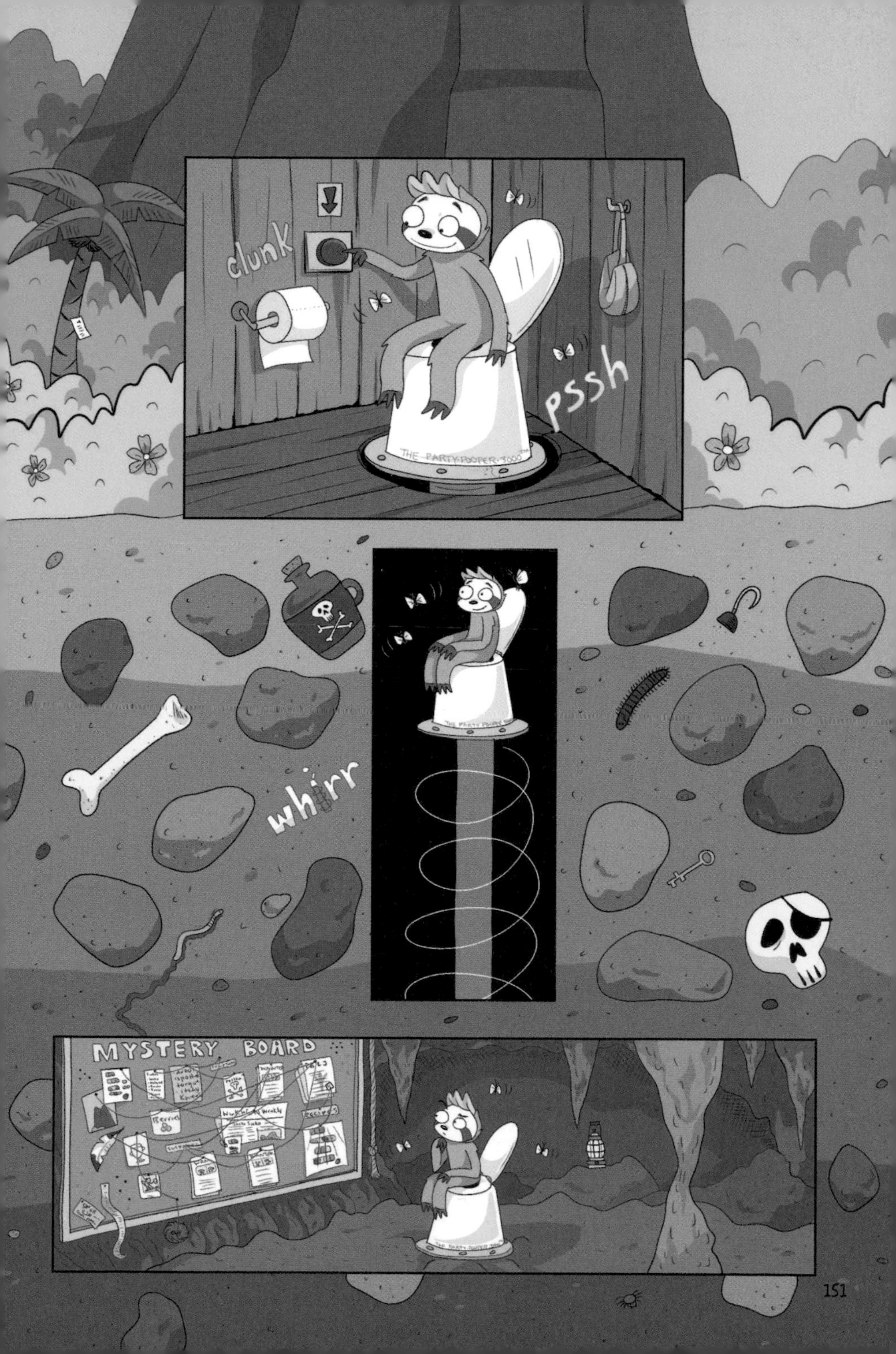
clunk
pssh
THE PARTY POOPER 3000
whirr
MYSTERY BOARD

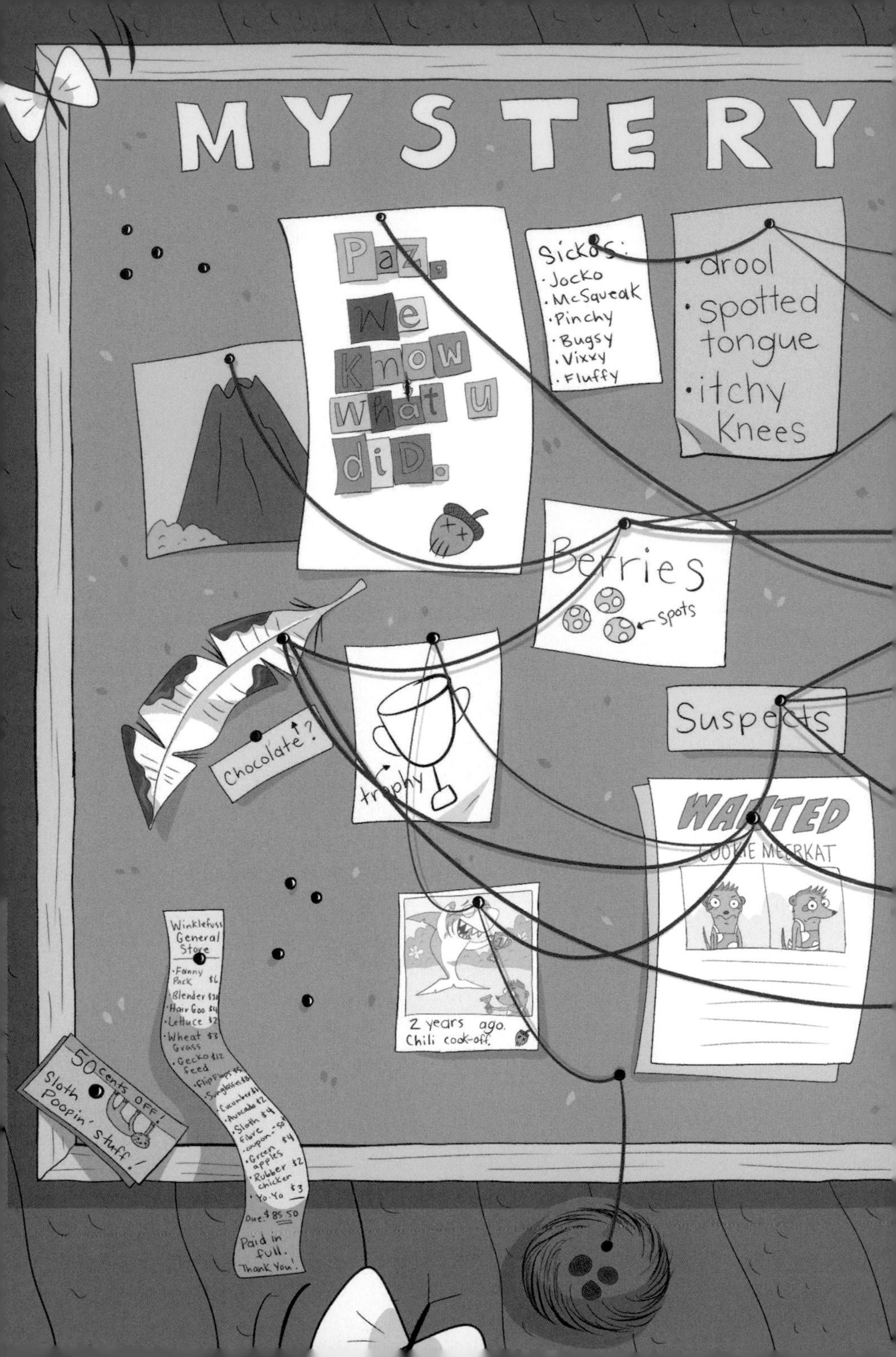
MYSTERY
Paz, We Know what u diD.
Sickos:
· Jocko
· McSqueak
· Pinchy
· Bugsy
· Vixxy
· Fluffy
· drool
· spotted tongue
· itchy Knees
Berries
spots
Chocolate?
trophy
Suspects
WANTED
COOKIE MEERKAT
2 years ago. Chili cook-off.
Winklefuss General Store
· Fanny Pack $6
· Blender $3
· Hair Goo $4
· Lettuce $2
· Wheat Grass $3
· Gecko feed $12
· Flip Flops $5
· Sunglasses $8
· Cucumber $1
· Avocado $2
· Sloth Fibre $4
· coupon -50¢
· Green apples $4
· Rubber chicken $2
· Yo-Yo $3
Due: $85.50
Paid in full. Thank You!
50 cents OFF! Sloth Poopin' Stuff!

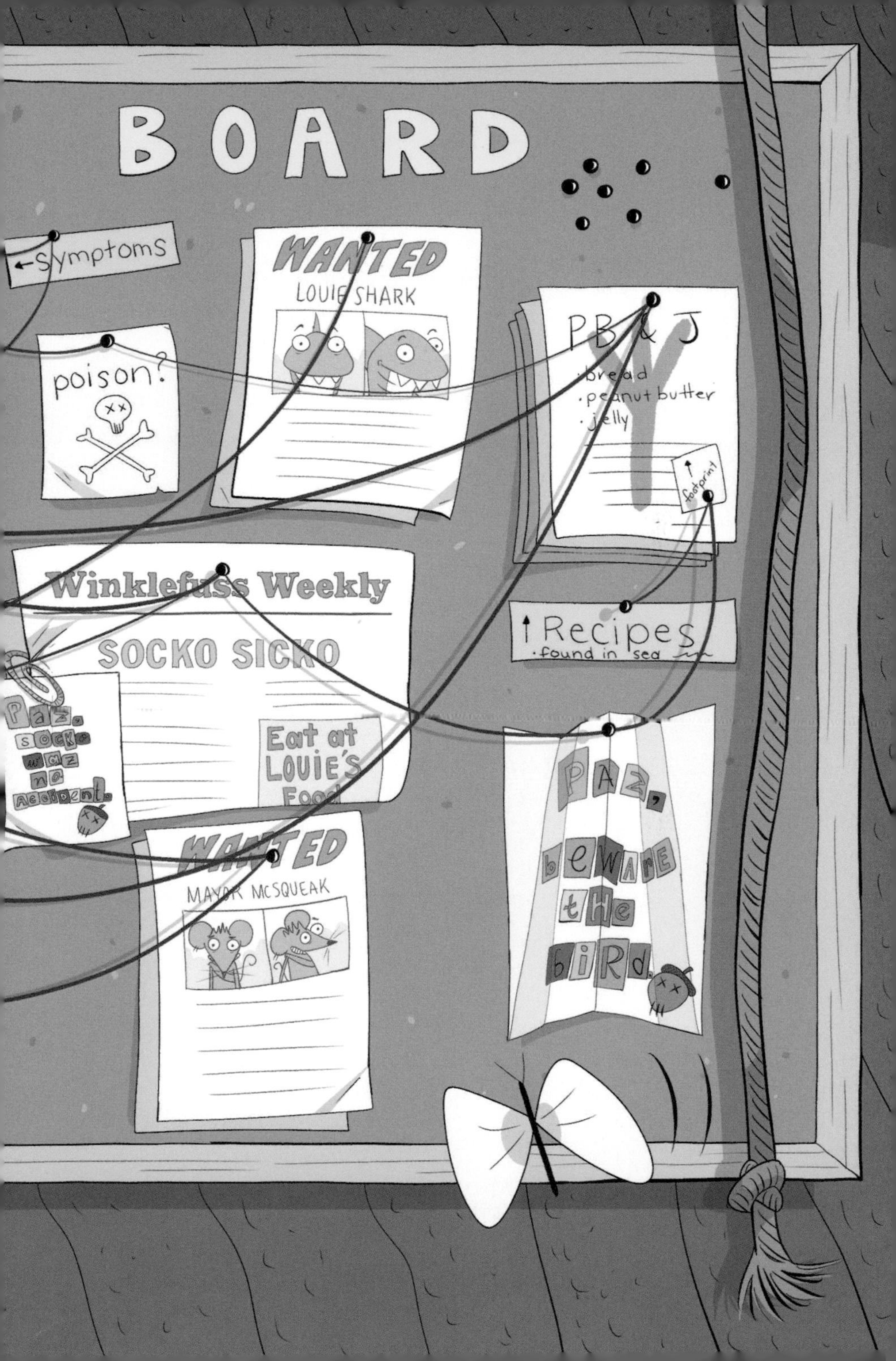
BOARD
←Symptoms
poison?
WANTED
LOUIE SHARK
PB&J
·bread
·peanut butter
·jelly
↑ footprint
Winklefuss Weekly
SOCKO SICKO
Eat at LOUIE'S Food
Paz, socko waz no accident.
↑Recipes
·found in sea
WANTED
MAYOR MCSQUEAK
Paz, beware the bird.

CHAPTER 9

WEDNESDAY. IT'S UNDERGROUND—
WHO KNOWS? AFTER DINNERISH? ON THE POOPER.

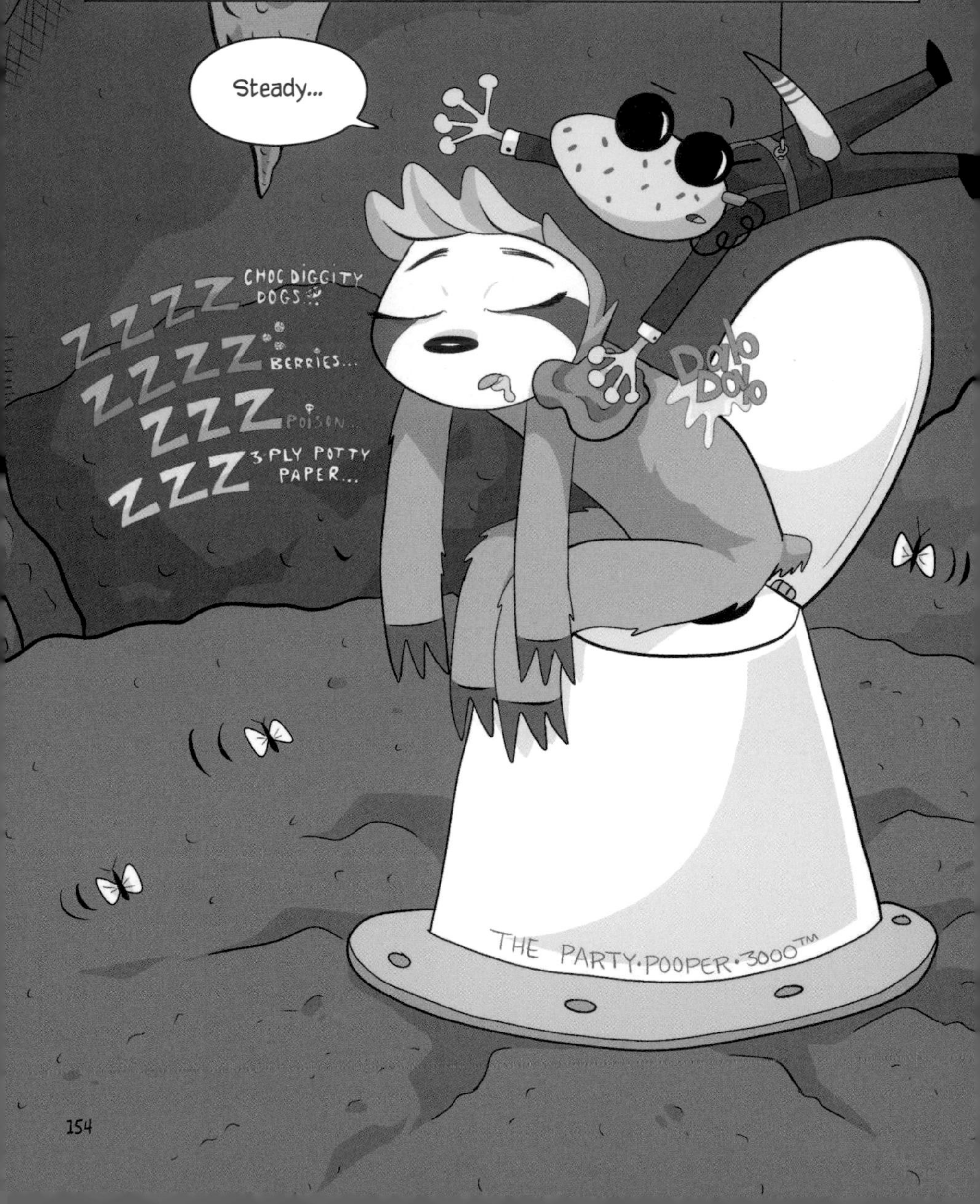

Steady...
ZZZZZ CHOC DIGGITY DOGS...
ZZZZZ BERRIES...
ZZZ POISON...
ZZZ 3-PLY POTTY PAPER...
Dolo Dolo
THE PARTY·POOPER·3000™

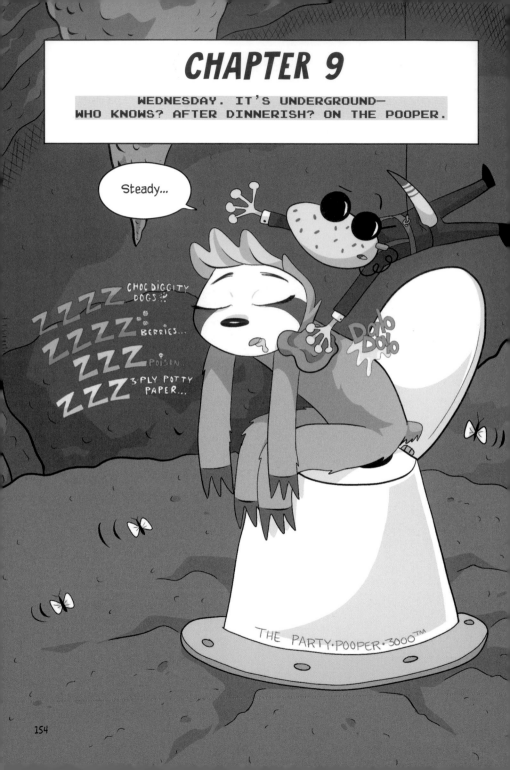

CHAPTER 10

WEDNESDAY? THURSDAY? WHO CAN TELL?
DARK O'CLOCK. STARING AT THE MYSTERY BOARD
AND TAKING CARE OF BUSINESS.

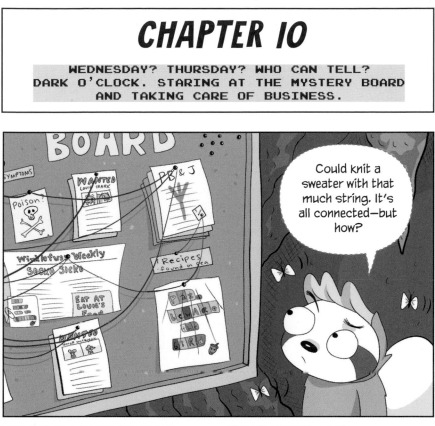

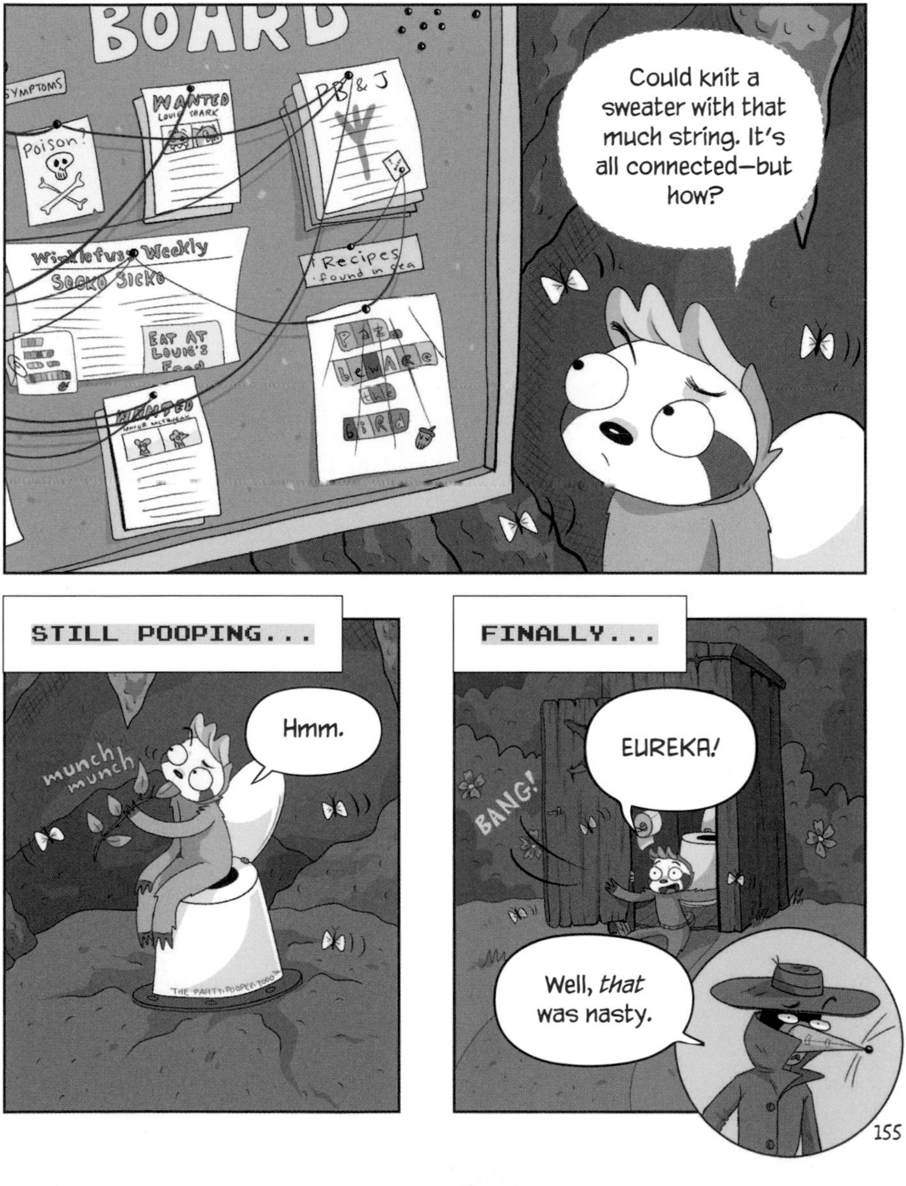
BOARD
SYMPTOMS
Poison?
WANTED
PB&J
Winklefuss Weekly
Socko Sicko
Recipes found in sea
EAT AT LOUIE'S
Could knit a sweater with that much string. It's all connected—but how?
STILL POOPING...
munch munch
Hmm.
THE PARTY POOPER 2000
FINALLY...
EUREKA!
BANG!
Well, *that* was nasty.

CHAPTER 11

THURSDAY. BRIGHT AND EARLY.
ABOUT FIVE POUNDS LIGHTER AND READY TO ROCK.

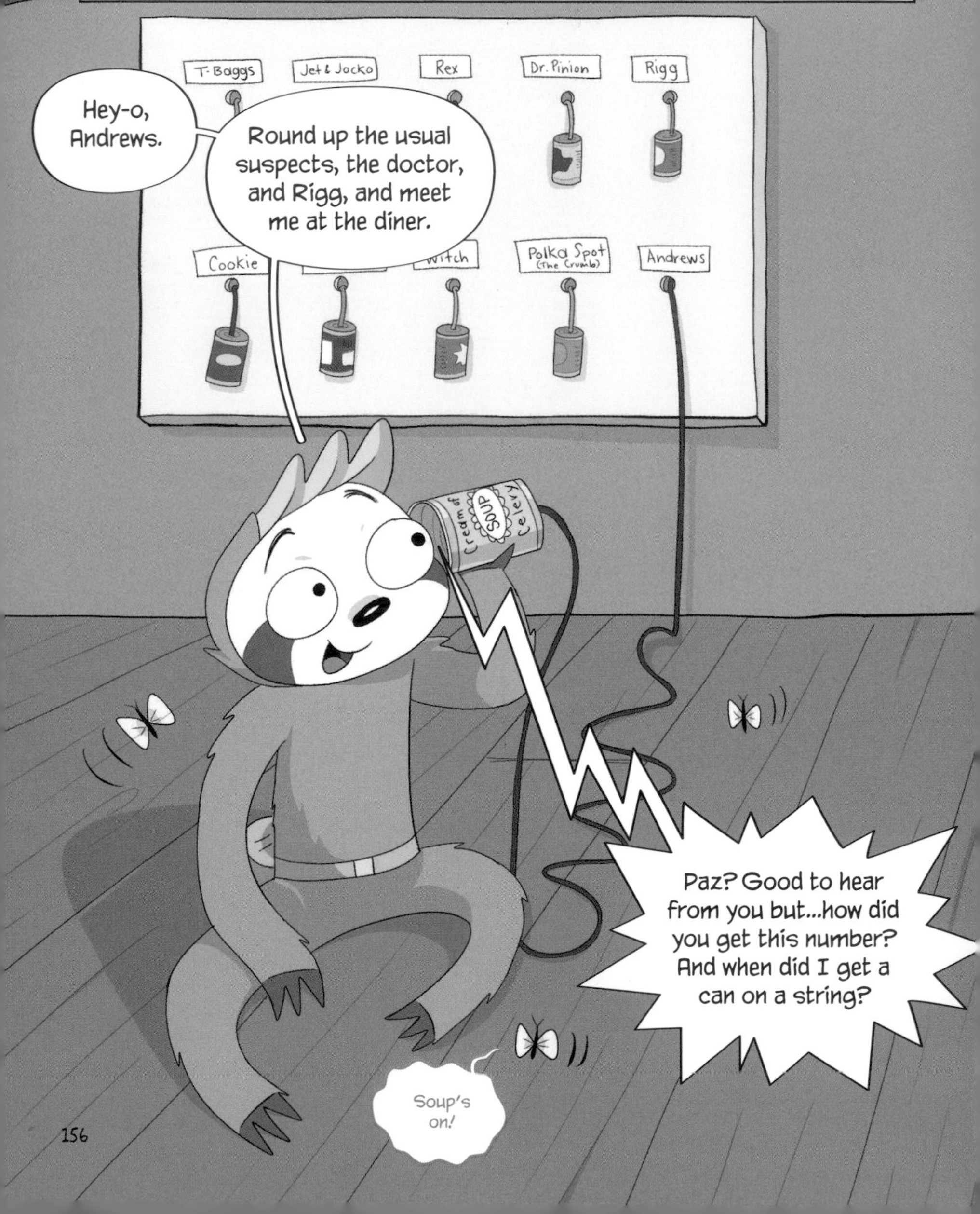
T-Baggs
Jet & Jocko
Rex
Dr. Pinion
Rigg
Hey-o, Andrews.
Round up the usual suspects, the doctor, and Rigg, and meet me at the diner.
Cookie
Witch
Polka Spot (The Crumb)
Andrews
Cream of SOUP Celery
Paz? Good to hear from you but...how did you get this number? And when did I get a can on a string?
Soup's on!

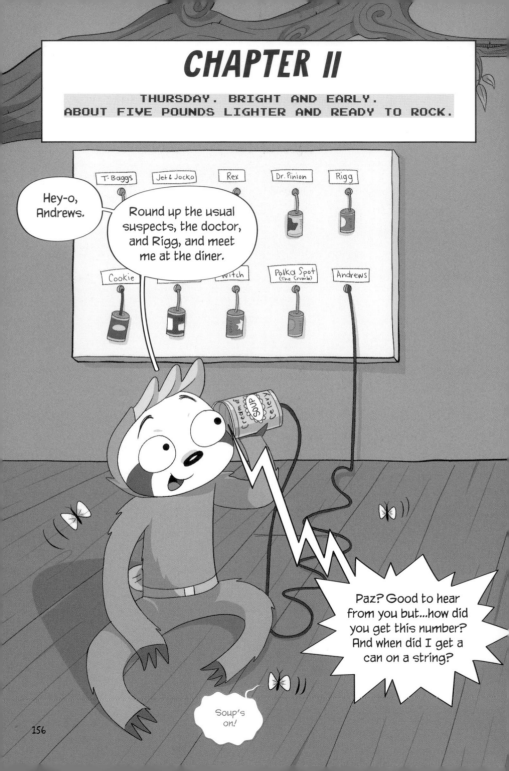

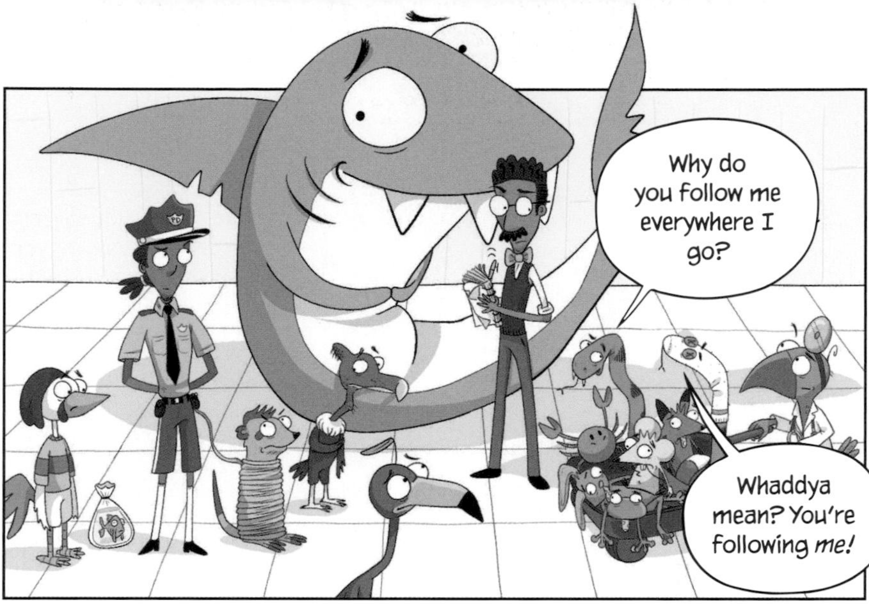
Why do you follow me everywhere I go?
Whaddya mean? You're following *me!*

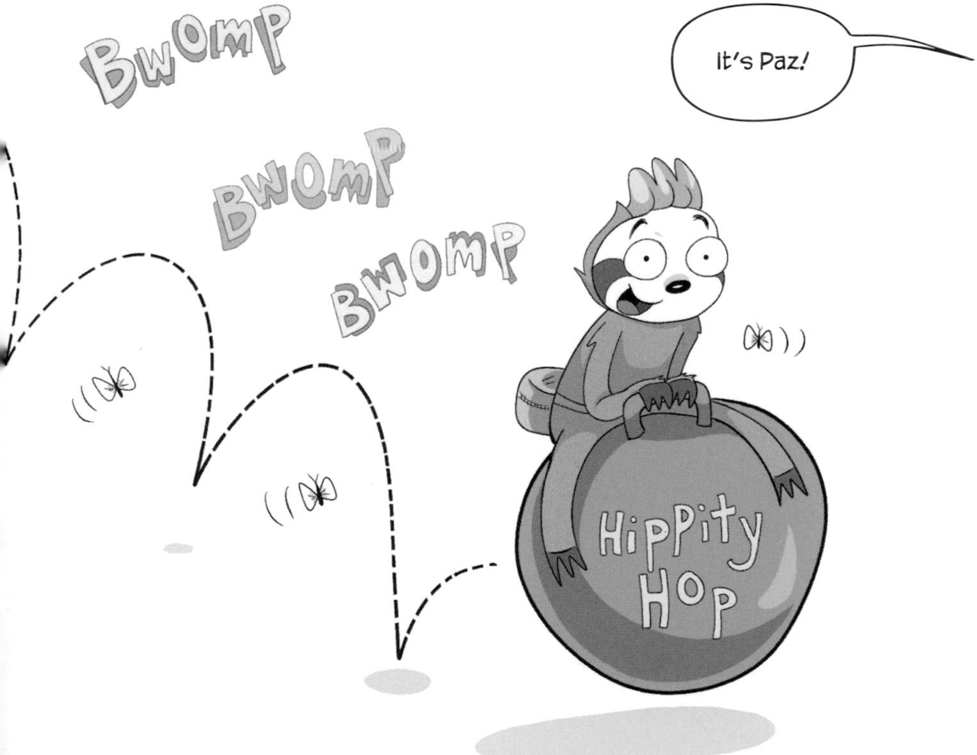
It's Paz!
BWOMP
BWOMP
BWOMP
HIPPITY HOP

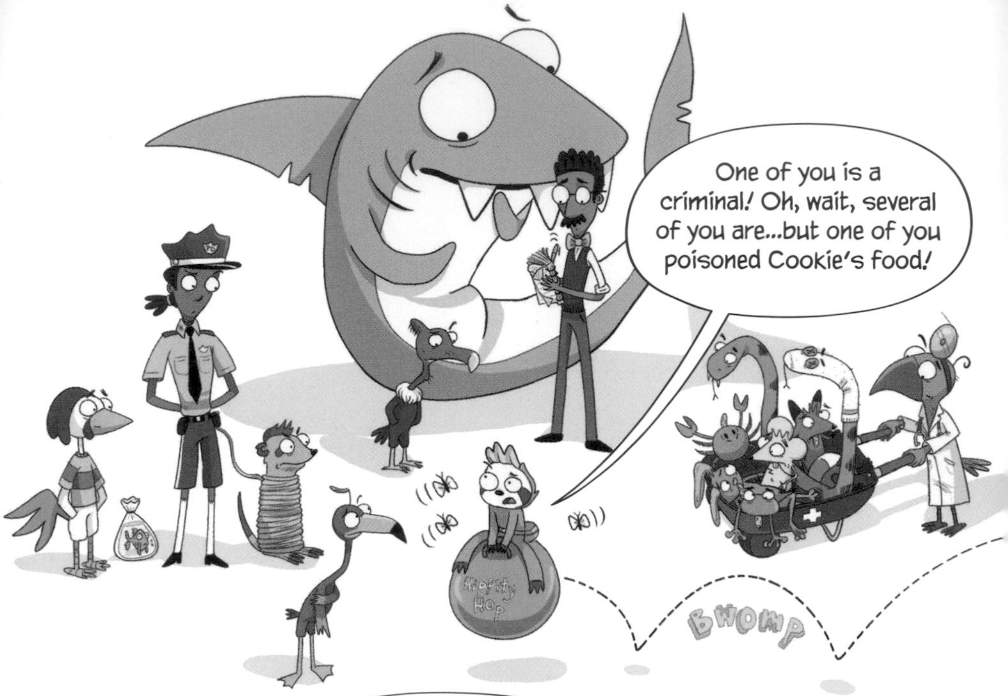
One of you is a criminal! Oh, wait, several of you are...but one of you poisoned Cookie's food!
Hippity Hop
BWOMP

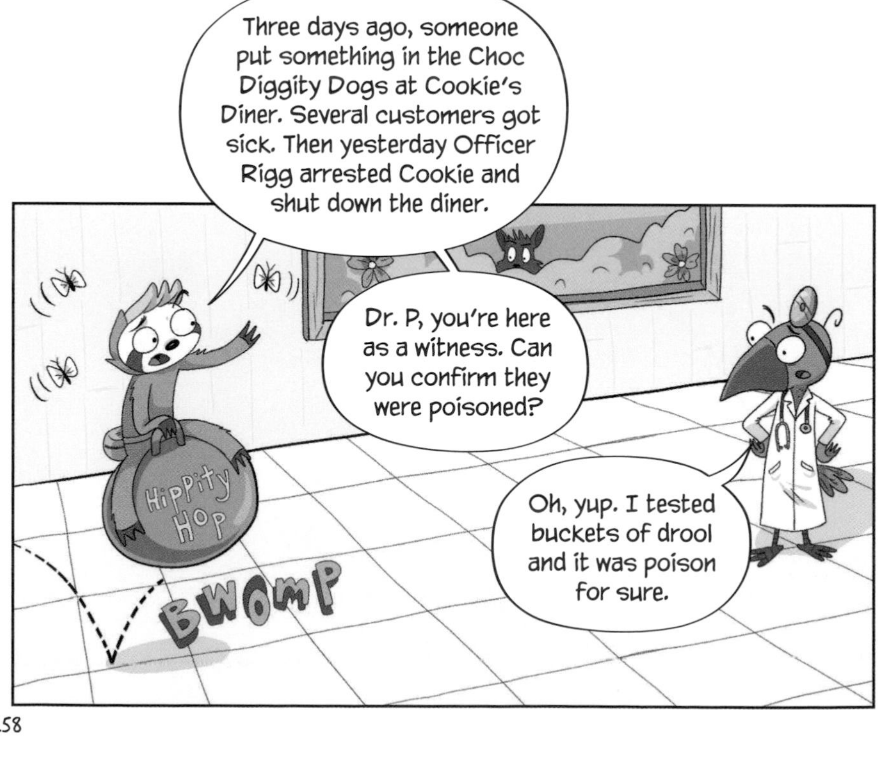
Three days ago, someone put something in the Choc Diggity Dogs at Cookie's Diner. Several customers got sick. Then yesterday Officer Rigg arrested Cookie and shut down the diner.
Dr. P, you're here as a witness. Can you confirm they were poisoned?
Oh, yup. I tested buckets of drool and it was poison for sure.
Hippity Hop
BWOMP

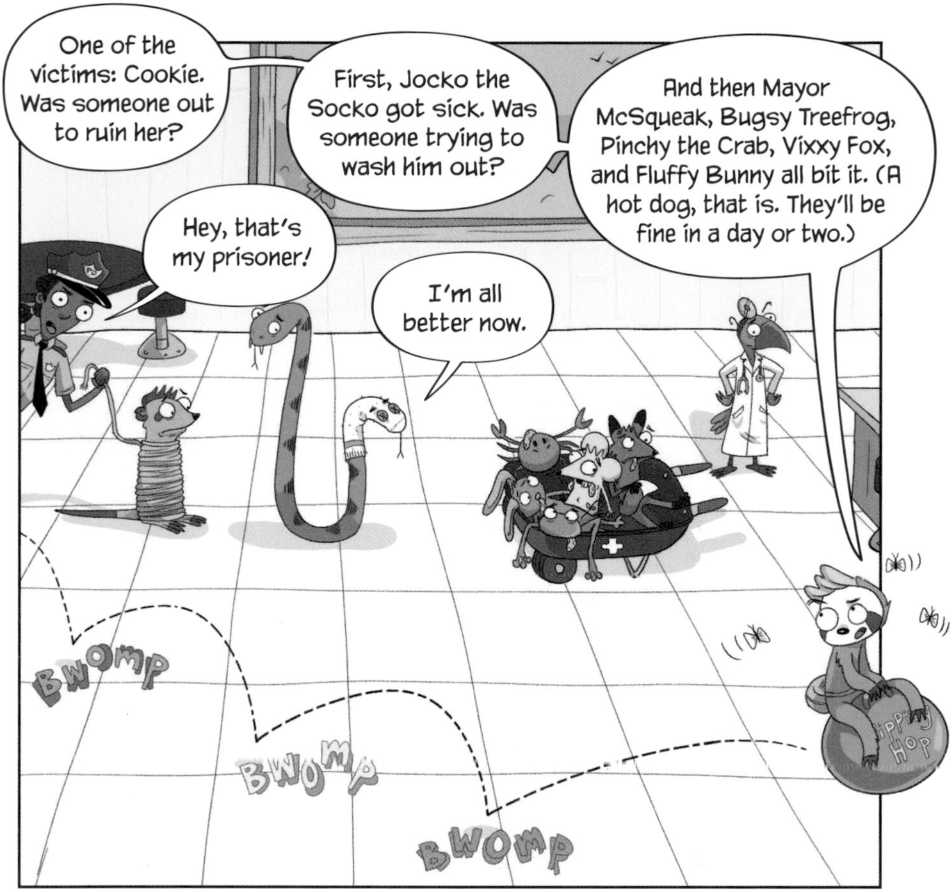
One of the victims: Cookie. Was someone out to ruin her?
First, Jocko the Socko got sick. Was someone trying to wash him out?
And then Mayor McSqueak, Bugsy Treefrog, Pinchy the Crab, Vixxy Fox, and Fluffy Bunny all bit it. (A hot dog, that is. They'll be fine in a day or two.)
Hey, that's my prisoner!
I'm all better now.
BWOMP
BWOMP
BWOMP
Hippity Hop

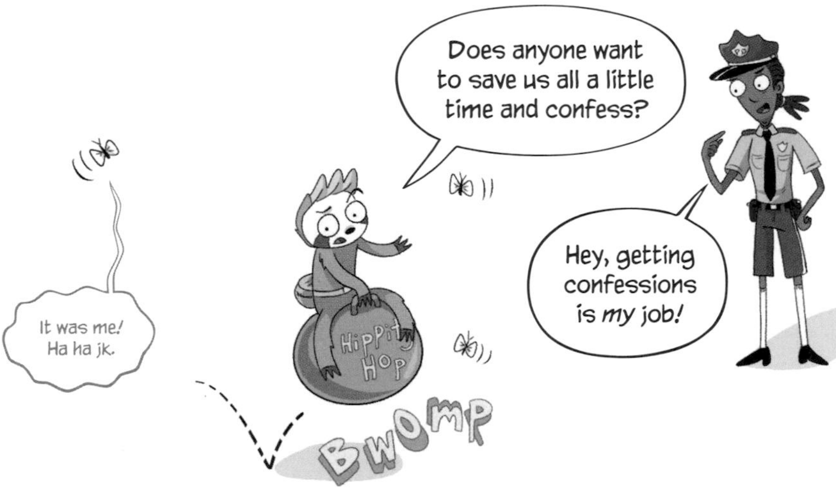
Does anyone want to save us all a little time and confess?
Hey, getting confessions is *my* job!
It was me! Ha ha jk.
Hippity Hop
BWOMP

THE SUSPECTS

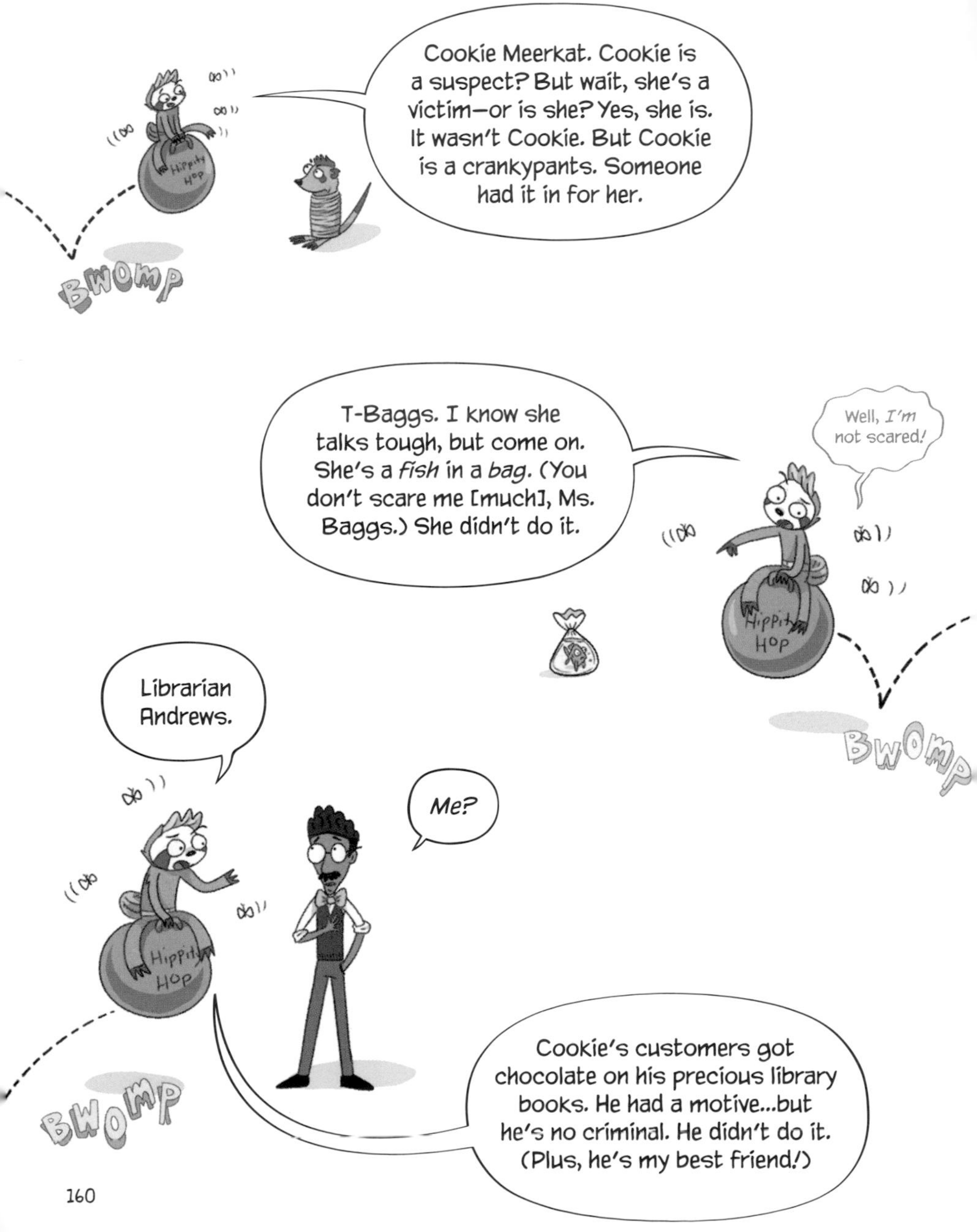
Cookie Meerkat. Cookie is a suspect? But wait, she's a victim—or is she? Yes, she is. It wasn't Cookie. But Cookie is a crankypants. Someone had it in for her.
Hippity Hop
BWOMP
T-Baggs. I know she talks tough, but come on. She's a *fish* in a *bag*. (You don't scare me [much], Ms. Baggs.) She didn't do it.
Well, *I'm* not scared!
Hippity Hop
BWOMP
Librarian Andrews.
Me?
Hippity Hop
BWOMP
Cookie's customers got chocolate on his precious library books. He had a motive...but he's no criminal. He didn't do it. (Plus, he's my best friend!)

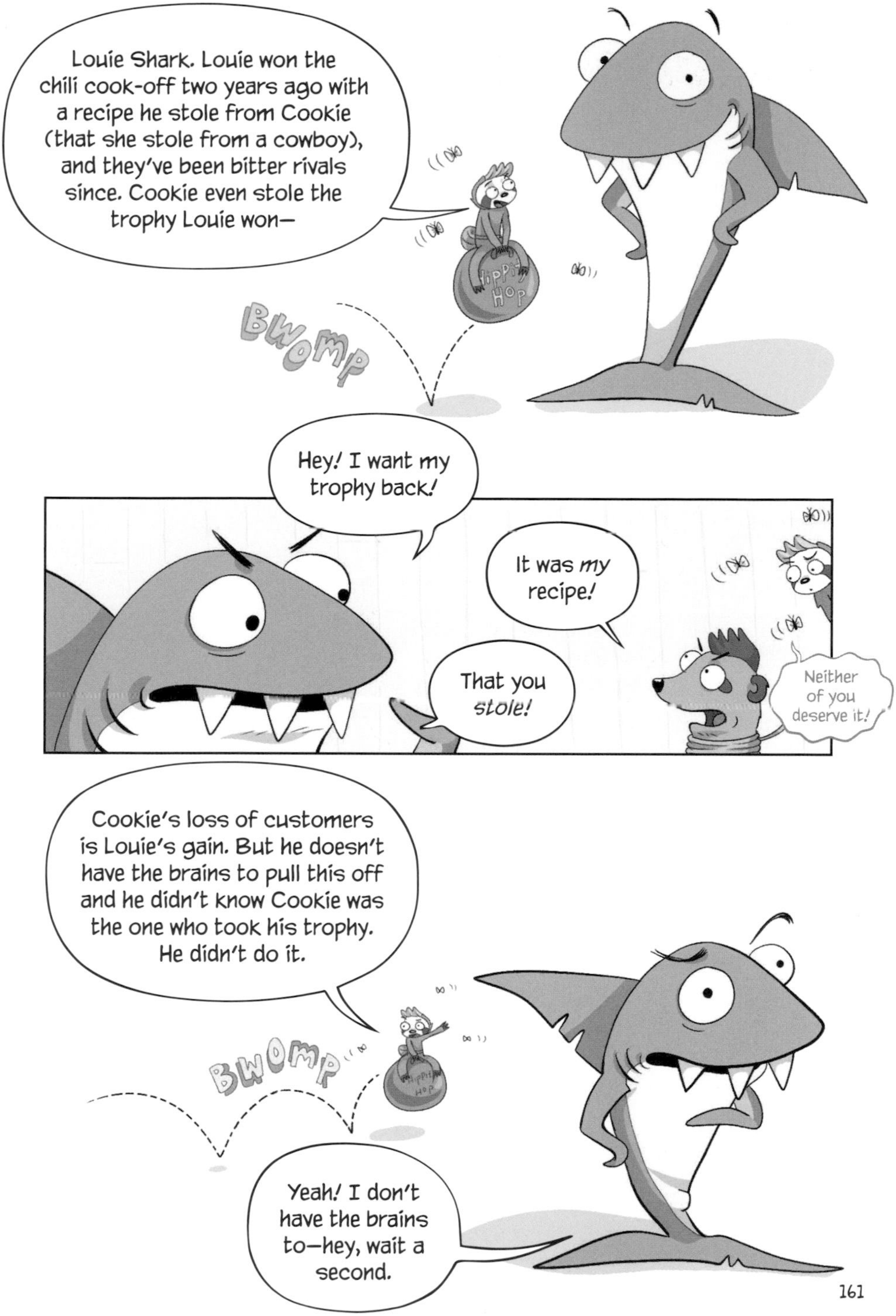
Louie Shark. Louie won the chili cook-off two years ago with a recipe he stole from Cookie (that she stole from a cowboy), and they've been bitter rivals since. Cookie even stole the trophy Louie won—
BWOMP
Hey! I want my trophy back!
It was *my* recipe!
That you *stole!*
Neither of you deserve it!
Cookie's loss of customers is Louie's gain. But he doesn't have the brains to pull this off and he didn't know Cookie was the one who took his trophy. He didn't do it.
BWOMP
Yeah! I don't have the brains to—hey, wait a second.

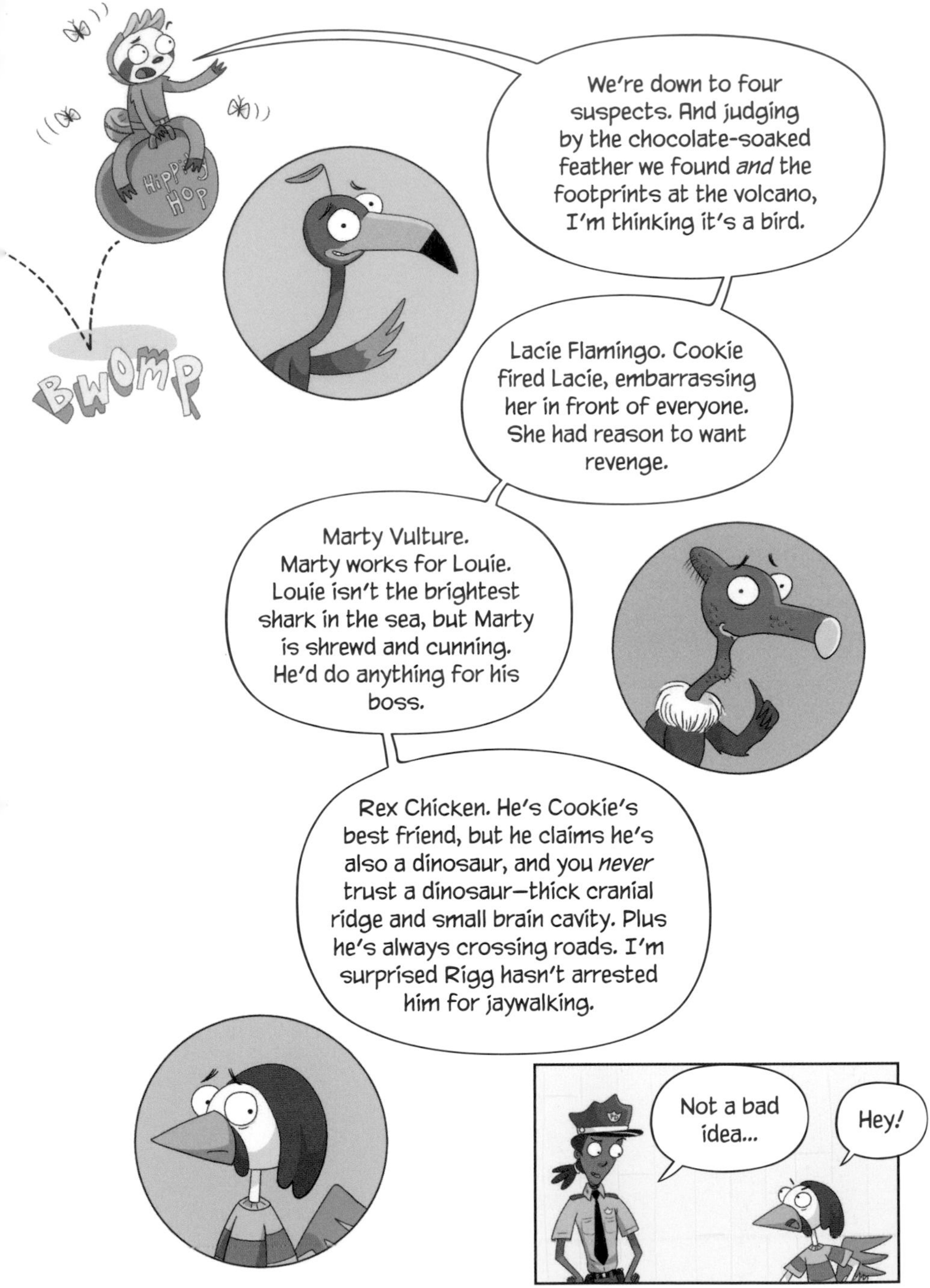

We're down to four suspects. And judging by the chocolate-soaked feather we found *and* the footprints at the volcano, I'm thinking it's a bird.
HIPPITY HOP
BWOMP
Lacie Flamingo. Cookie fired Lacie, embarrassing her in front of everyone. She had reason to want revenge.
Marty Vulture. Marty works for Louie. Louie isn't the brightest shark in the sea, but Marty is shrewd and cunning. He'd do anything for his boss.
Rex Chicken. He's Cookie's best friend, but he claims he's also a dinosaur, and you *never* trust a dinosaur—thick cranial ridge and small brain cavity. Plus he's always crossing roads. I'm surprised Rigg hasn't arrested him for jaywalking.
Not a bad idea...
Hey!

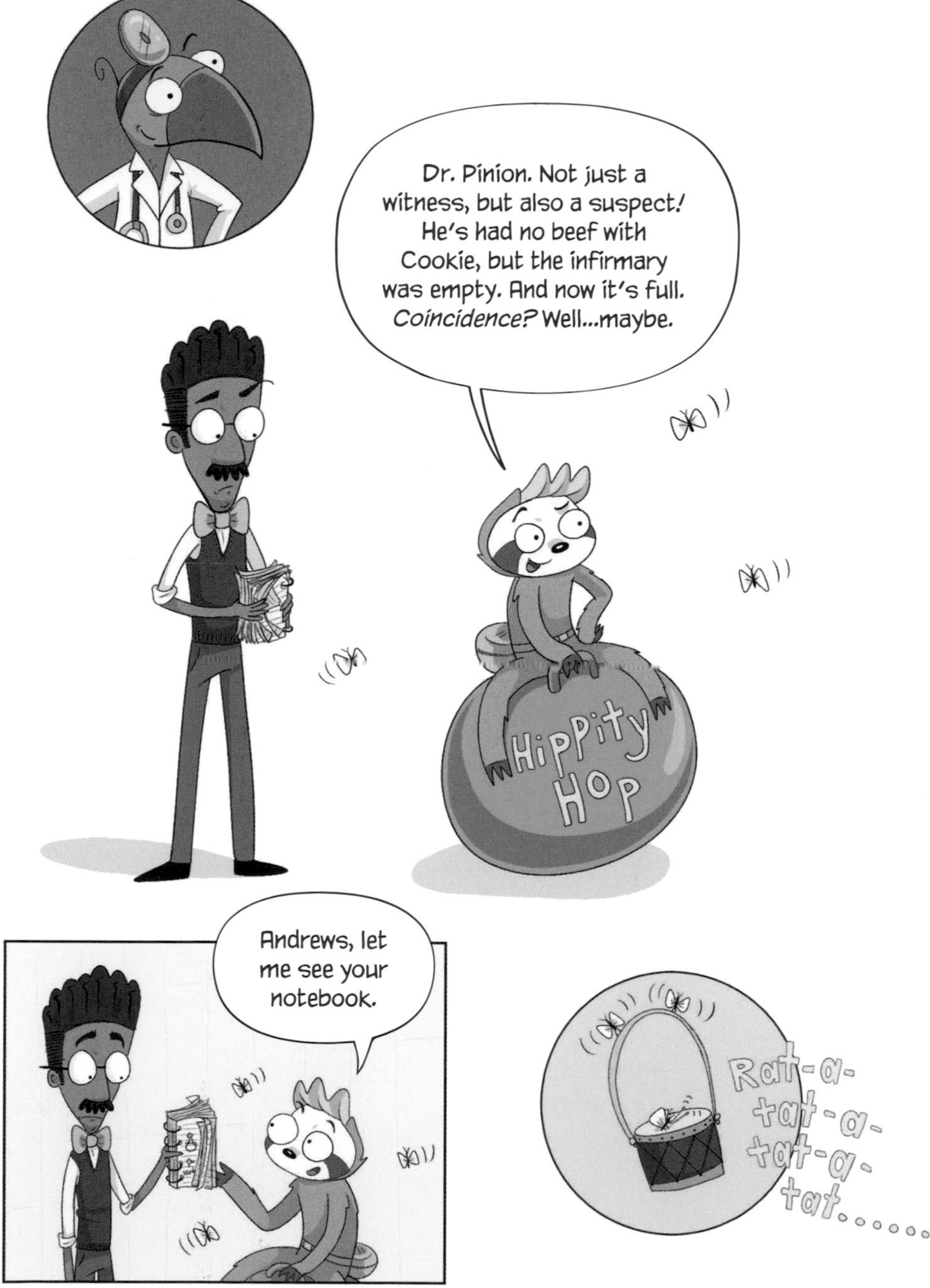
Dr. Pinion. Not just a witness, but also a suspect! He's had no beef with Cookie, but the infirmary was empty. And now it's full. *Coincidence?* Well...maybe.
Hippity Hop
Andrews, let me see your notebook.
Rat-a-tat-a-tat-a-tat......

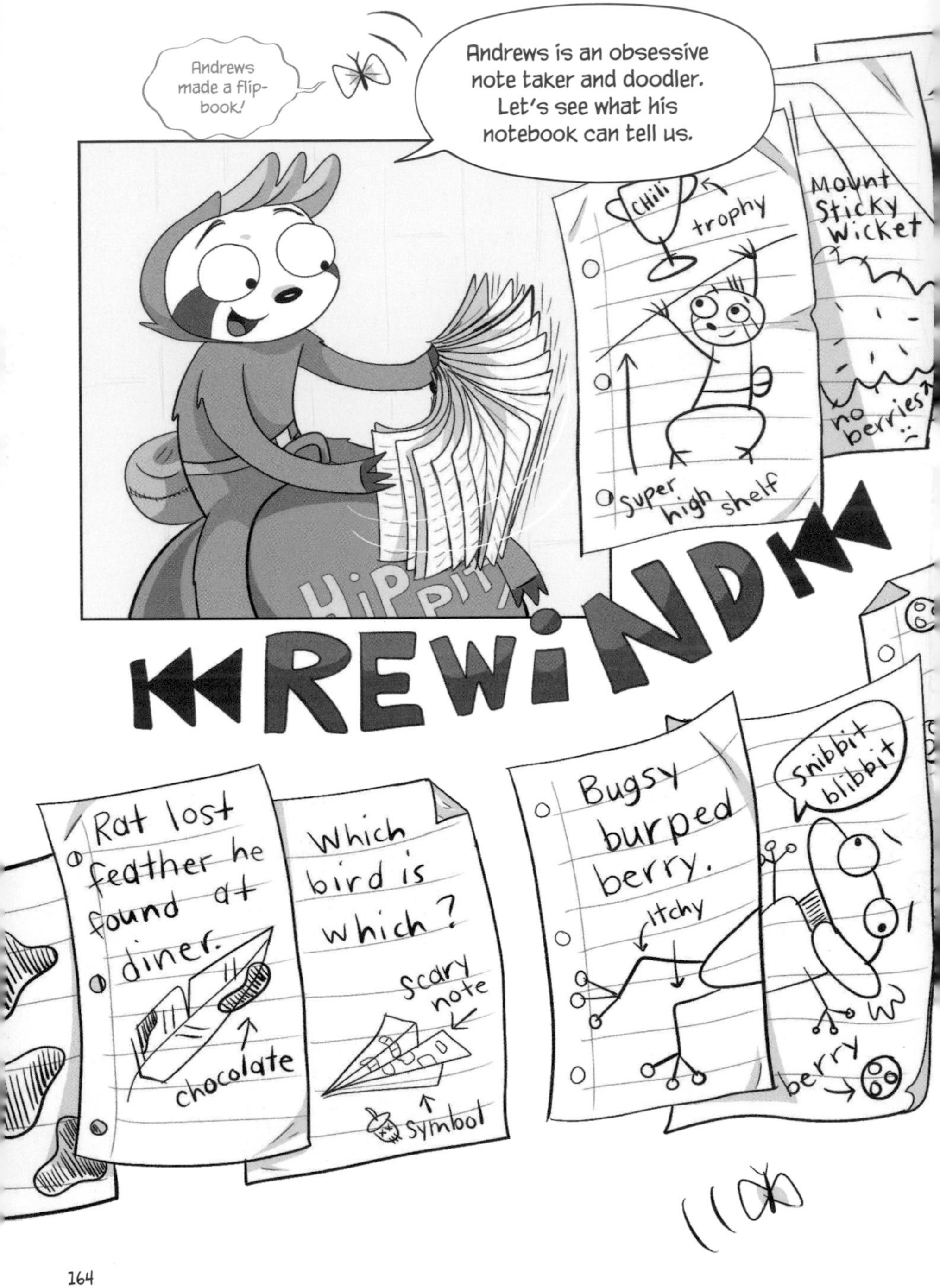
Andrews made a flip-book!
Andrews is an obsessive note taker and doodler. Let's see what his notebook can tell us.
CHILI
trophy
super high shelf
Mount Sticky Wicket
no berries
REWIND
Rat lost feather he found at diner.
chocolate
Which bird is which?
scary note
symbol
Bugsy burped berry.
Itchy
snibbit blibbit
berry

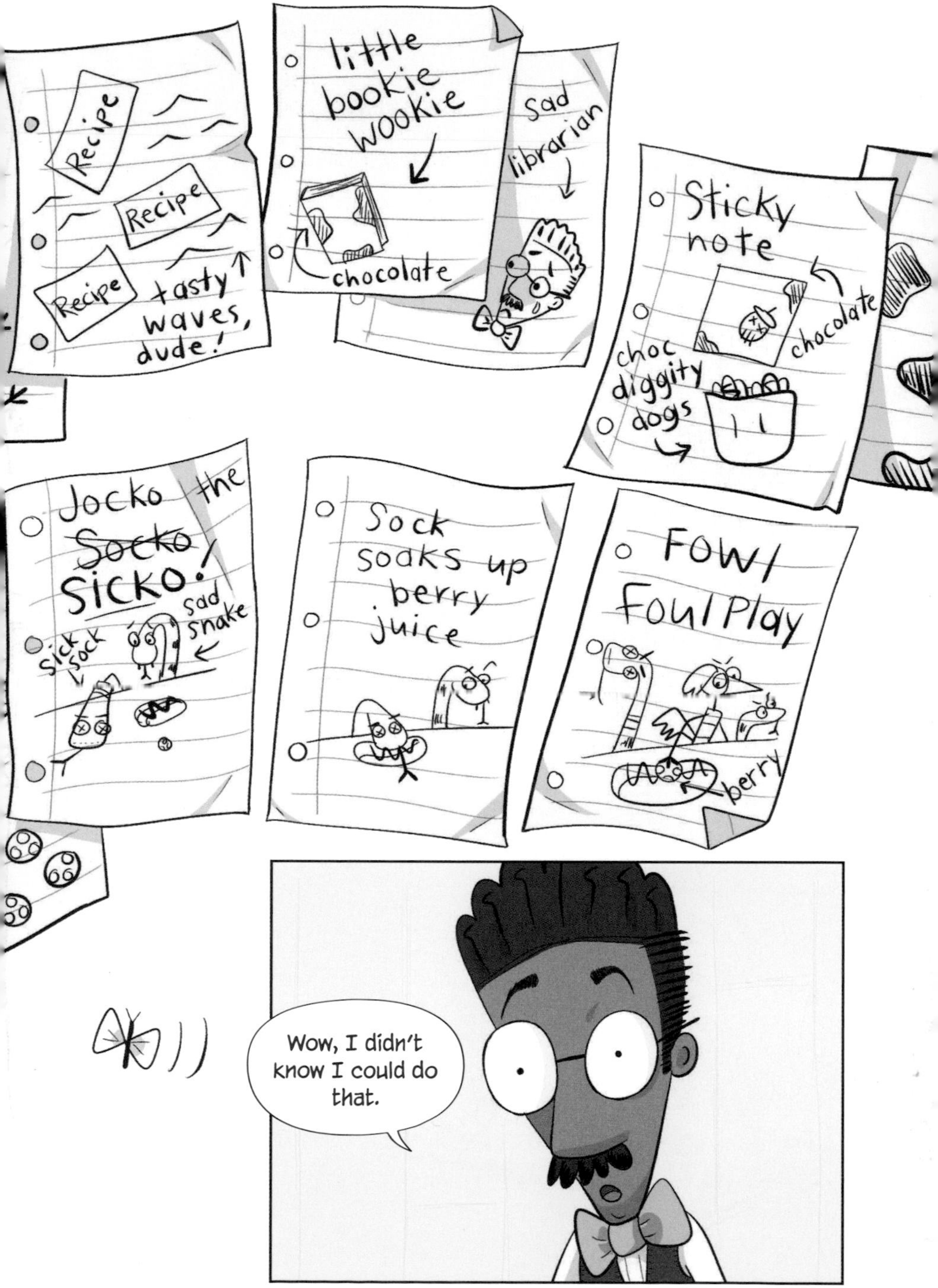
Recipe
Recipe
Recipe
tasty waves, dude!
little bookie wookie
chocolate
Sad librarian
Sticky note
chocolate
choc diggity dogs
Jocko the Socko SICKO!
sick sock
sad snake
Sock soaks up berry juice
FOWl FoulPlay
berry
Wow, I didn't know I could do that.

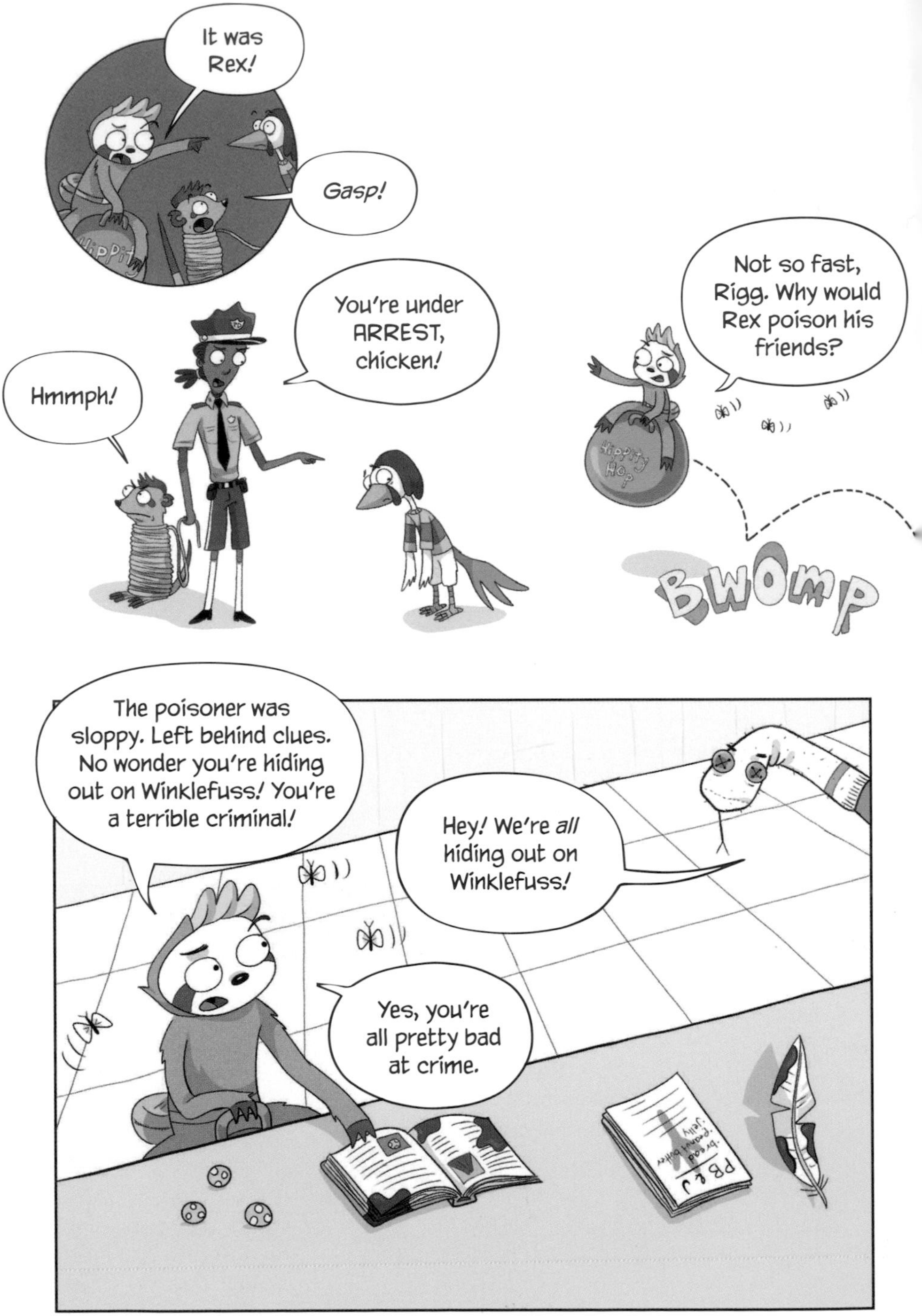
It was Rex!
Gasp!
You're under ARREST, chicken!
Hmmph!
Not so fast, Rigg. Why would Rex poison his friends?
Hippity Hop
BWOMP
The poisoner was sloppy. Left behind clues. No wonder you're hiding out on Winklefuss! You're a terrible criminal!
Hey! We're *all* hiding out on Winklefuss!
Yes, you're all pretty bad at crime.

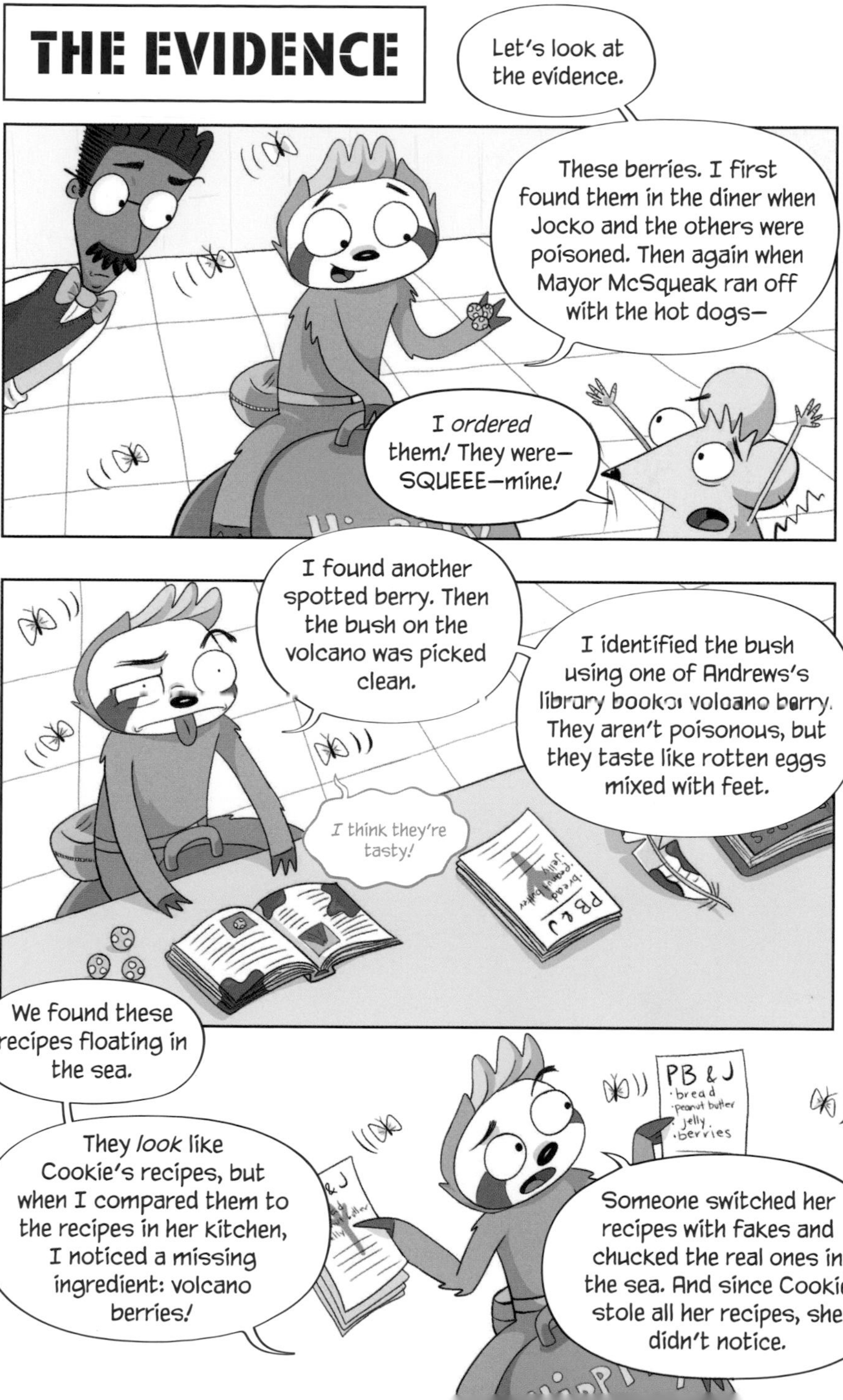
THE EVIDENCE
Let's look at the evidence.
These berries. I first found them in the diner when Jocko and the others were poisoned. Then again when Mayor McSqueak ran off with the hot dogs—
I *ordered* them! They were—SQUEEE—mine!
I found another spotted berry. Then the bush on the volcano was picked clean.
I identified the bush using one of Andrews's library books: volcano berry. They aren't poisonous, but they taste like rotten eggs mixed with feet.
I think they're tasty!
PB & J
·bread
·peanut butter
·jelly
·berries
We found these recipes floating in the sea.
They *look* like Cookie's recipes, but when I compared them to the recipes in her kitchen, I noticed a missing ingredient: volcano berries!
Someone switched her recipes with fakes and chucked the real ones in the sea. And since Cookie stole all her recipes, she didn't notice.

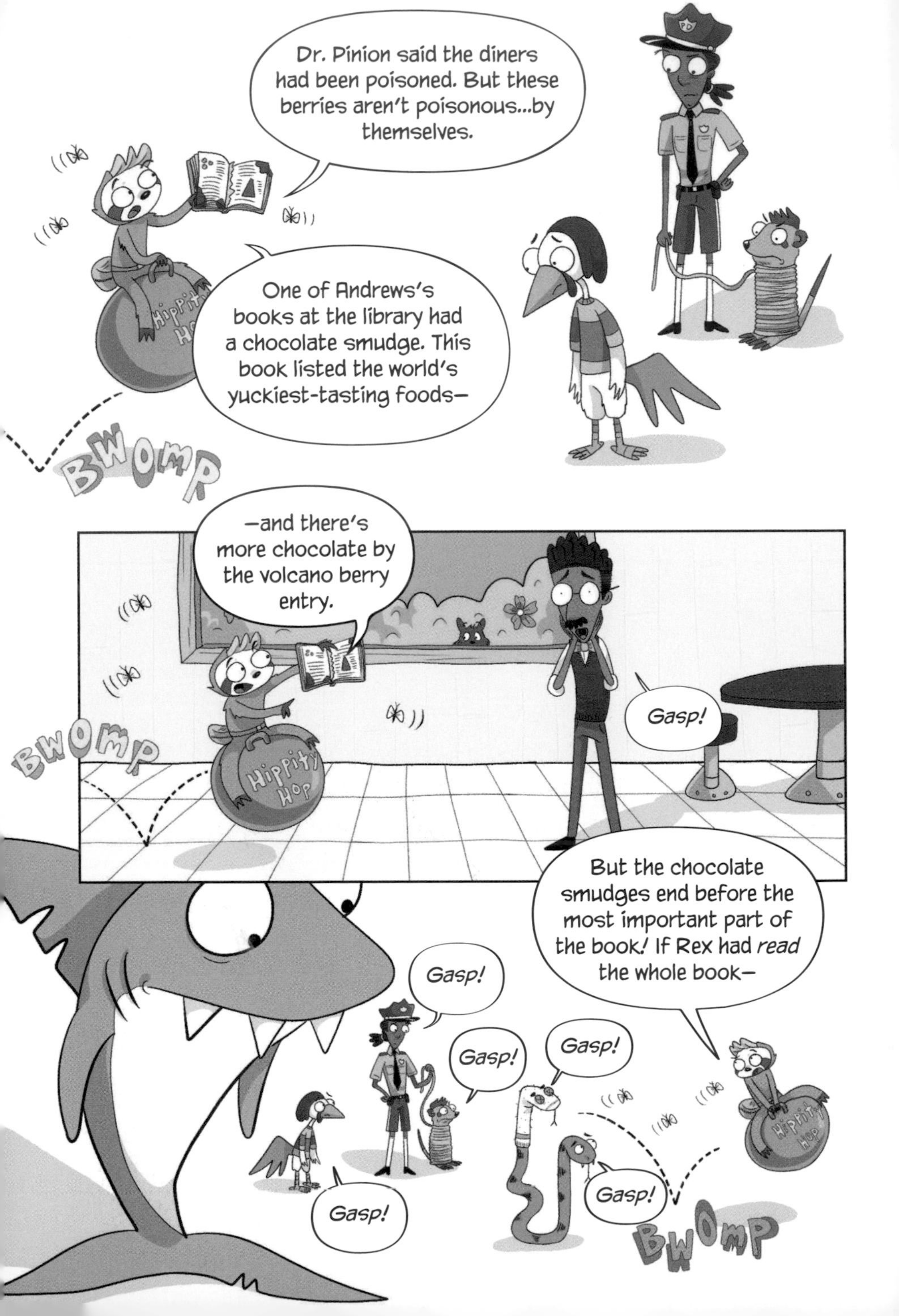
Dr. Pinion said the diners had been poisoned. But these berries aren't poisonous...by themselves.
One of Andrews's books at the library had a chocolate smudge. This book listed the world's yuckiest-tasting foods—
BWOMP
—and there's more chocolate by the volcano berry entry.
Hippity Hop
BWOMP
Gasp!
But the chocolate smudges end before the most important part of the book! If Rex had *read* the whole book—
Gasp!
Gasp!
Gasp!
Gasp!
Gasp!
Hippity Hop
BWOMP

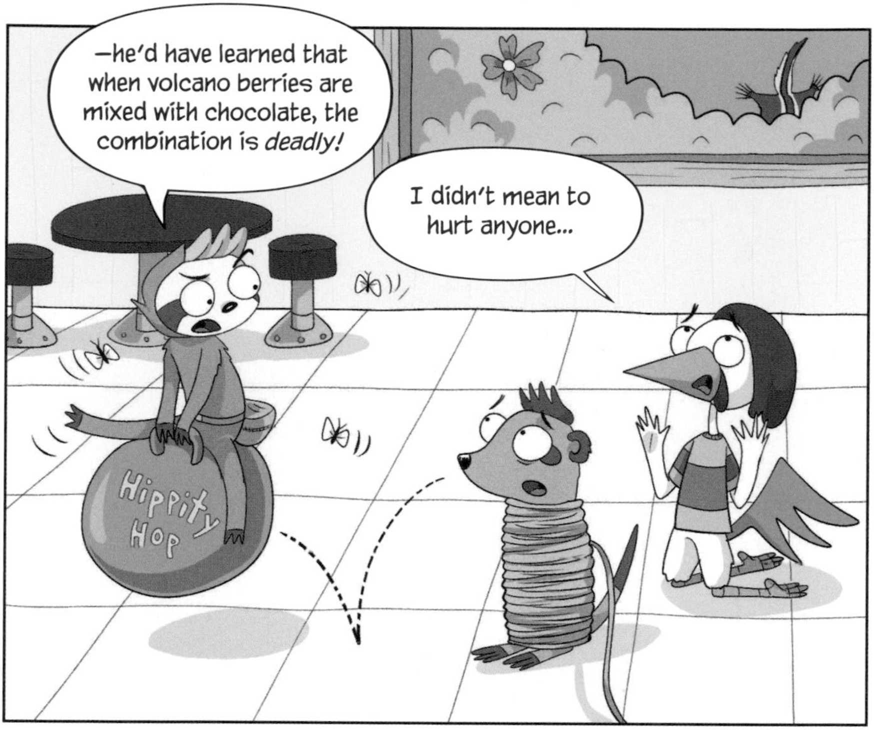
—he'd have learned that when volcano berries are mixed with chocolate, the combination is *deadly*!
I didn't mean to hurt anyone...
Hippity Hop

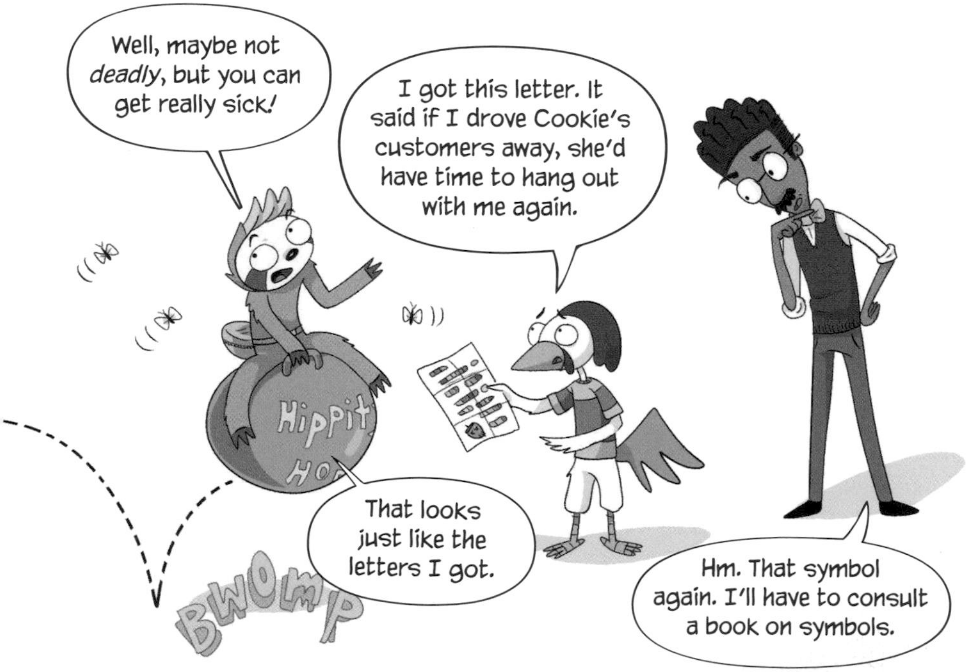
Well, maybe not *deadly*, but you can get really sick!
I got this letter. It said if I drove Cookie's customers away, she'd have time to hang out with me again.
Hippit
Ho
That looks just like the letters I got.
BWOMP
Hm. That symbol again. I'll have to consult a book on symbols.

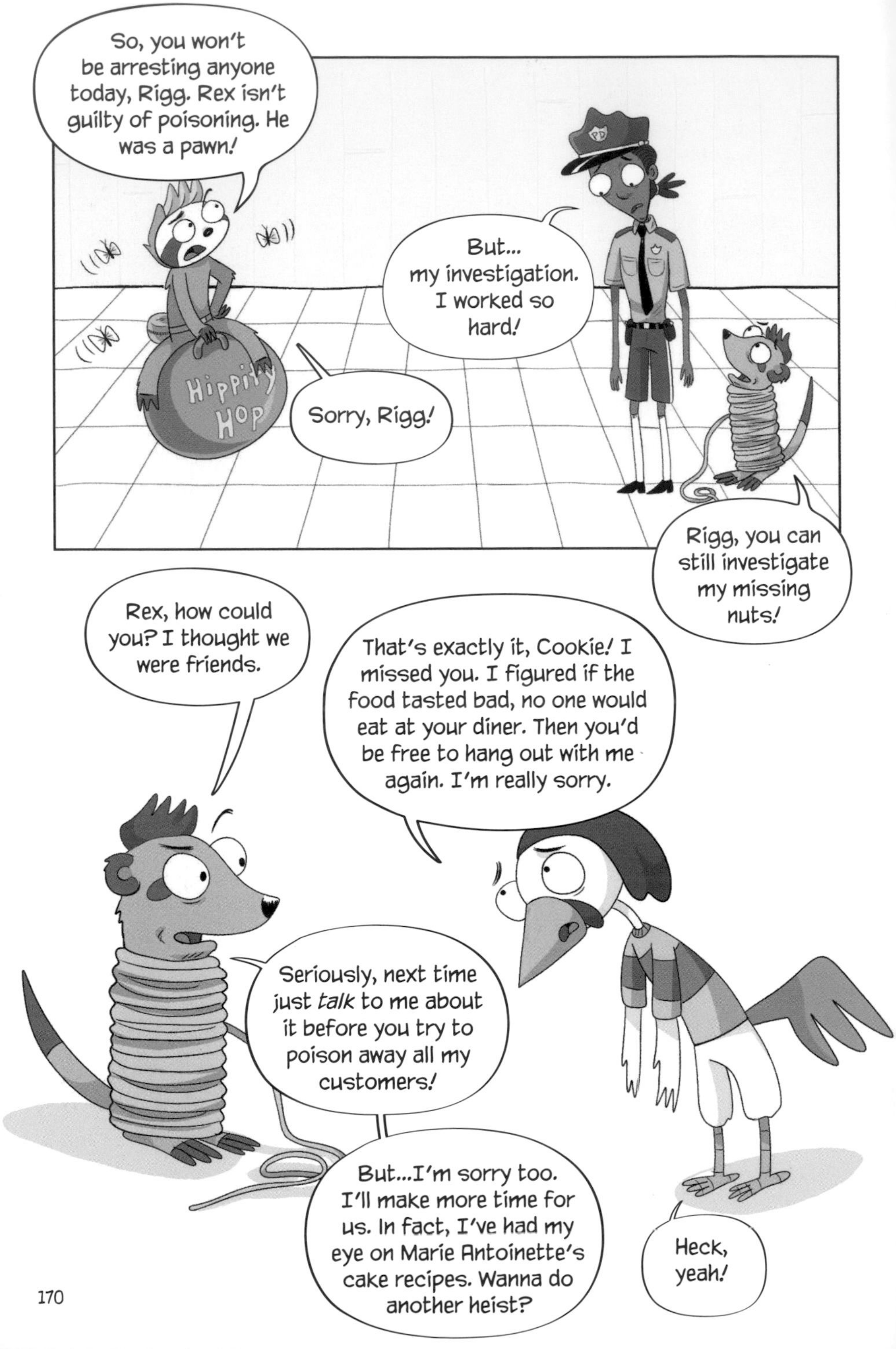
So, you won't be arresting anyone today, Rigg. Rex isn't guilty of poisoning. He was a pawn!
But... my investigation. I worked so hard!
Sorry, Rigg!
Hippity Hop
Rigg, you can still investigate my missing nuts!
Rex, how could you? I thought we were friends.
That's exactly it, Cookie! I missed you. I figured if the food tasted bad, no one would eat at your diner. Then you'd be free to hang out with me again. I'm really sorry.
Seriously, next time just *talk* to me about it before you try to poison away all my customers!
But...I'm sorry too. I'll make more time for us. In fact, I've had my eye on Marie Antoinette's cake recipes. Wanna do another heist?
Heck, yeah!

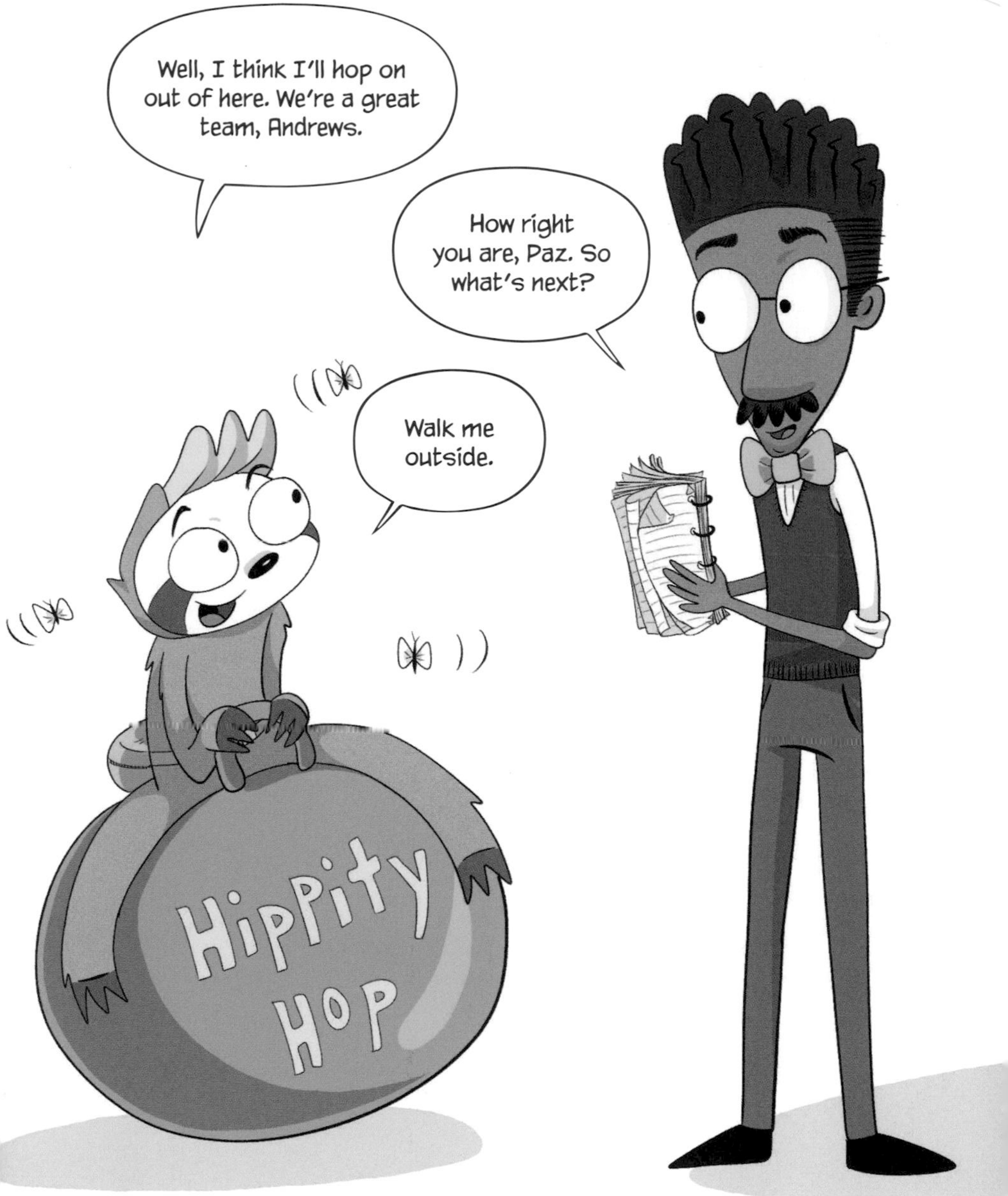
Well, I think I'll hop on out of here. We're a great team, Andrews.
How right you are, Paz. So what's next?
Walk me outside.
Hippity Hop

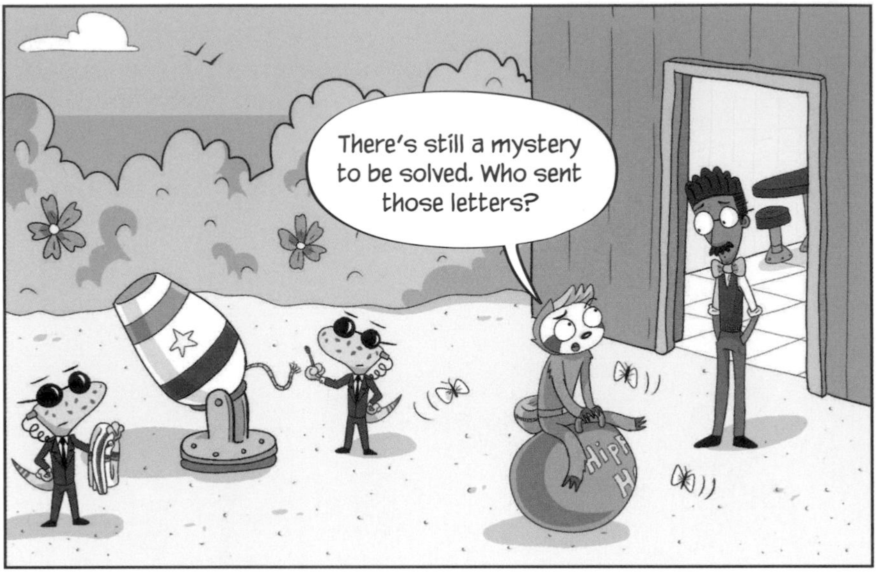
There's still a mystery to be solved. Who sent those letters?

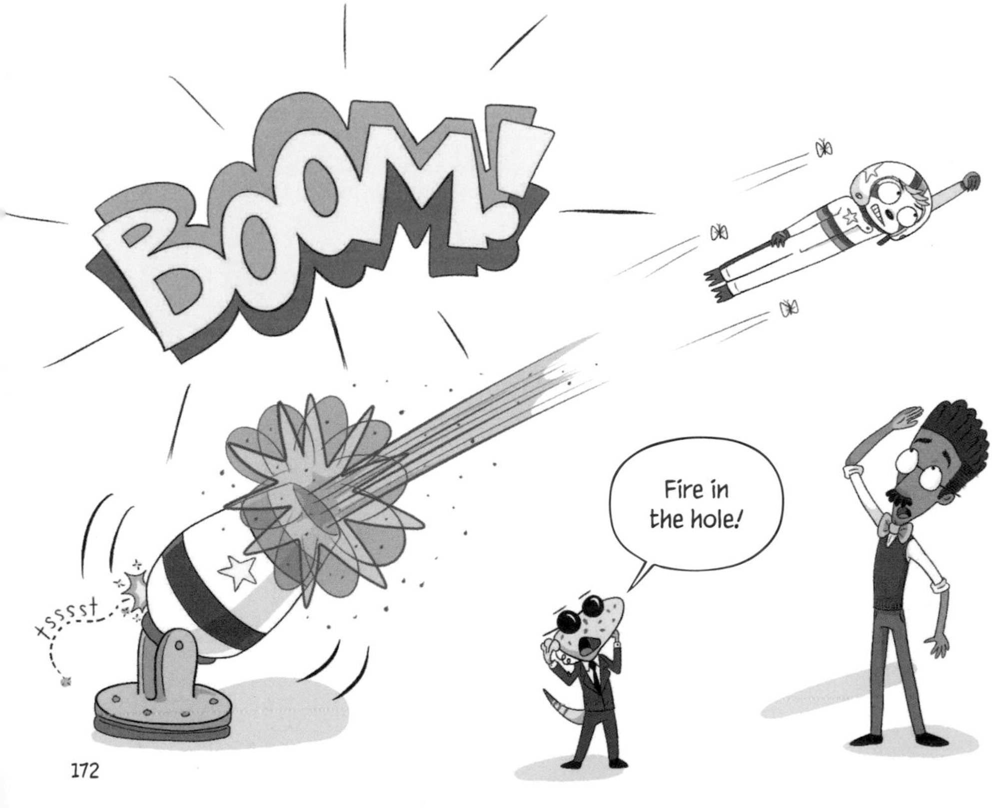
BOOM!
tssssst
Fire in the hole!

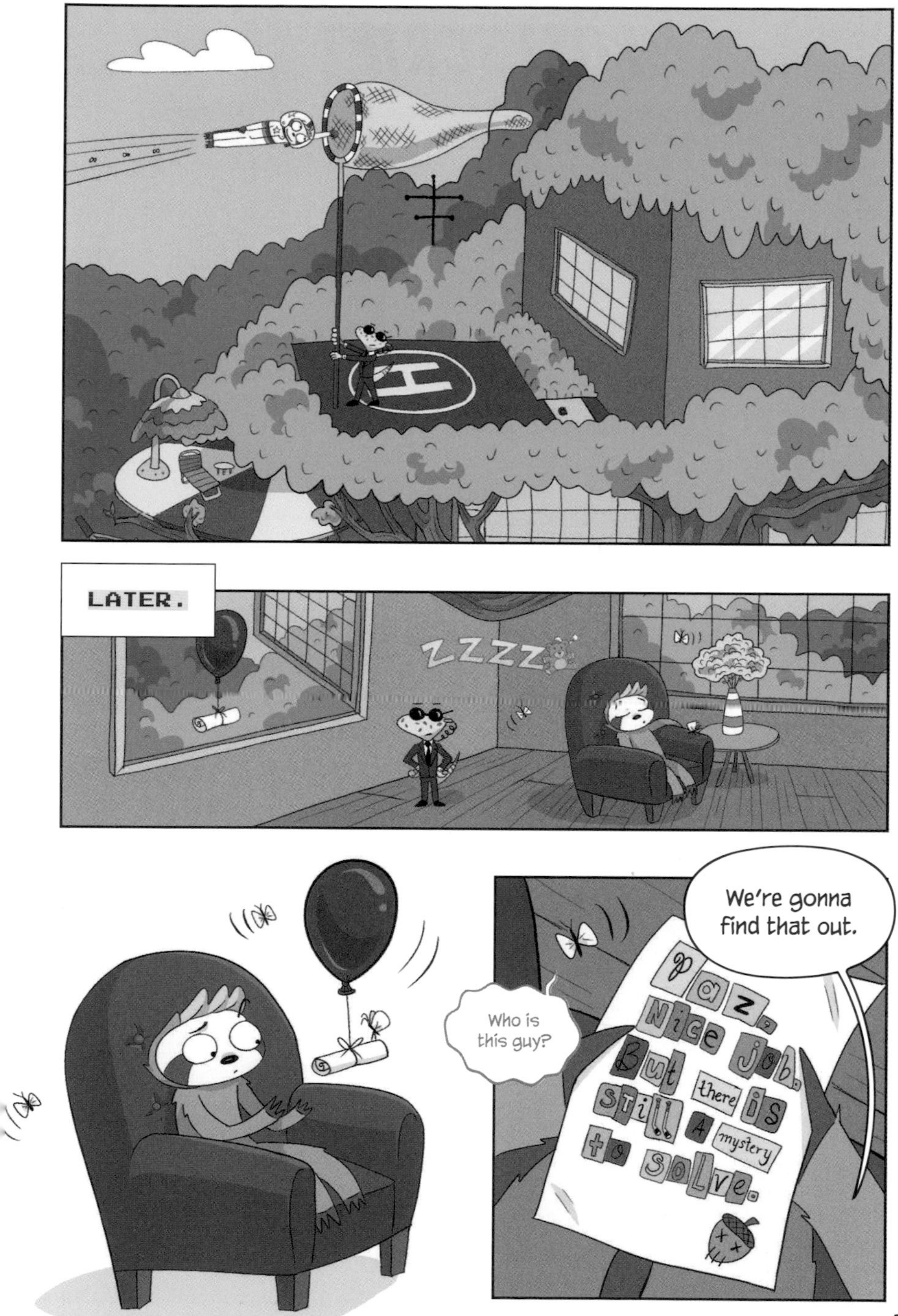
LATER.
ZZZZ
Who is this guy?
Paz, Nice job. But there is still a mystery to solve.
We're gonna find that out.

POSTSCRIPT

(BECAUSE EPILOGUES ARE FOR SNOOTY BOOKS)
AFTER THE INVESTIGATION IS COMPLETE. SOME TIME THE NEXT MORNING. SIX DAYS UNTIL POOPING.

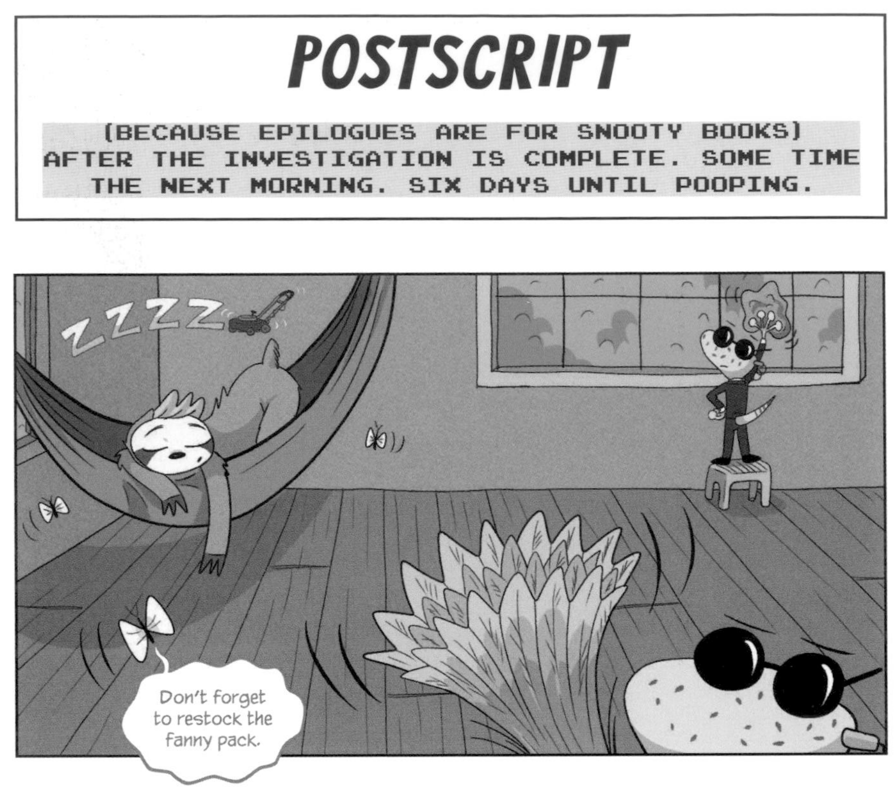

ZZZZ
Don't forget to restock the fanny pack.

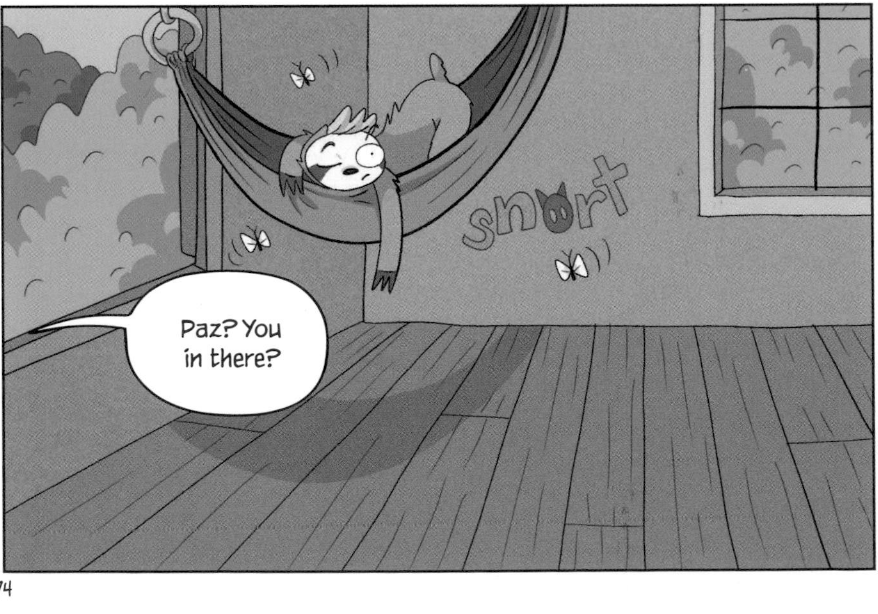

snort
Paz? You in there?

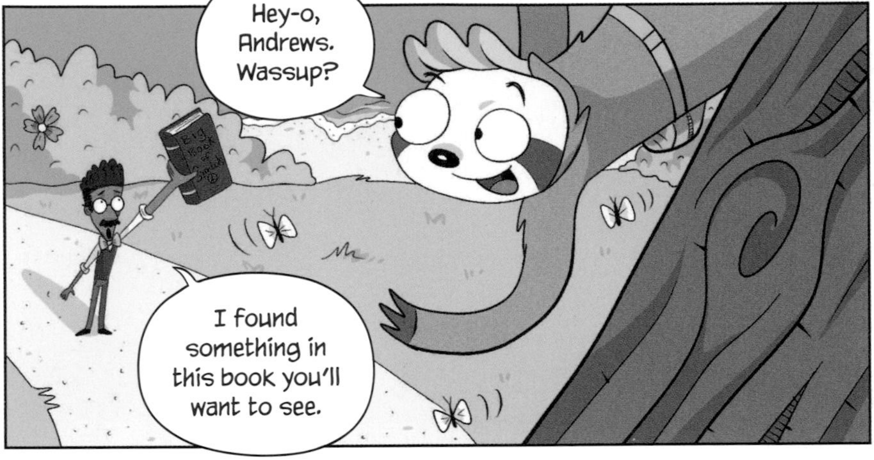
Hey-o,
Andrews.
Wassup?
I found
something in
this book you'll
want to see.

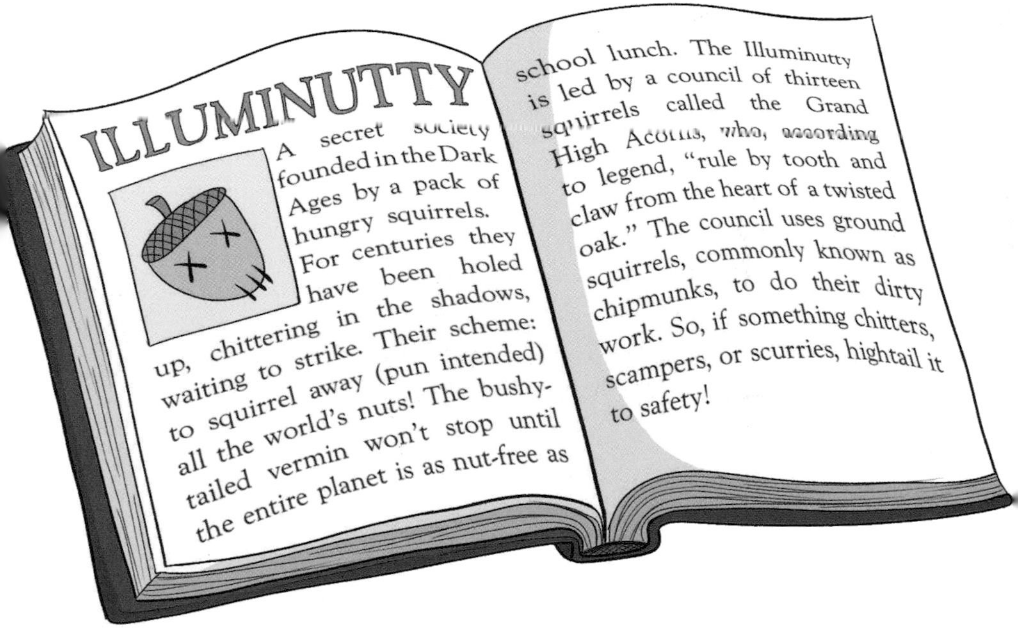

ILLUMINUTTY

A secret society founded in the Dark Ages by a pack of hungry squirrels. For centuries they have been holed up, chittering in the shadows, waiting to strike. Their scheme: to squirrel away (pun intended) all the world's nuts! The bushy-tailed vermin won't stop until the entire planet is as nut-free as school lunch. The Illuminutty is led by a council of thirteen squirrels called the Grand High Acorns, who, according to legend, "rule by tooth and claw from the heart of a twisted oak." The council uses ground squirrels, commonly known as chipmunks, to do their dirty work. So, if something chitters, scampers, or scurries, hightail it to safety!

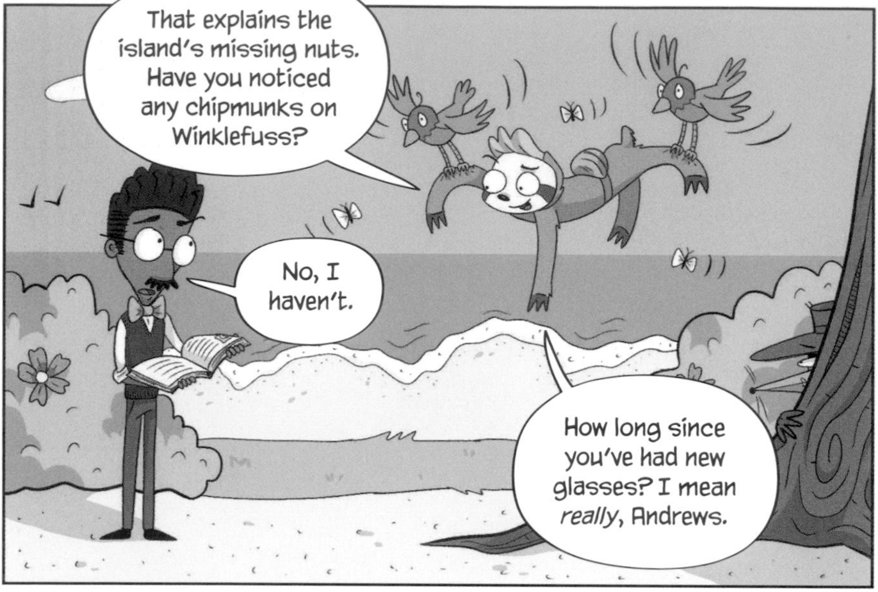
That explains the island's missing nuts. Have you noticed any chipmunks on Winklefuss?
No, I haven't.
How long since you've had new glasses? I mean *really*, Andrews.

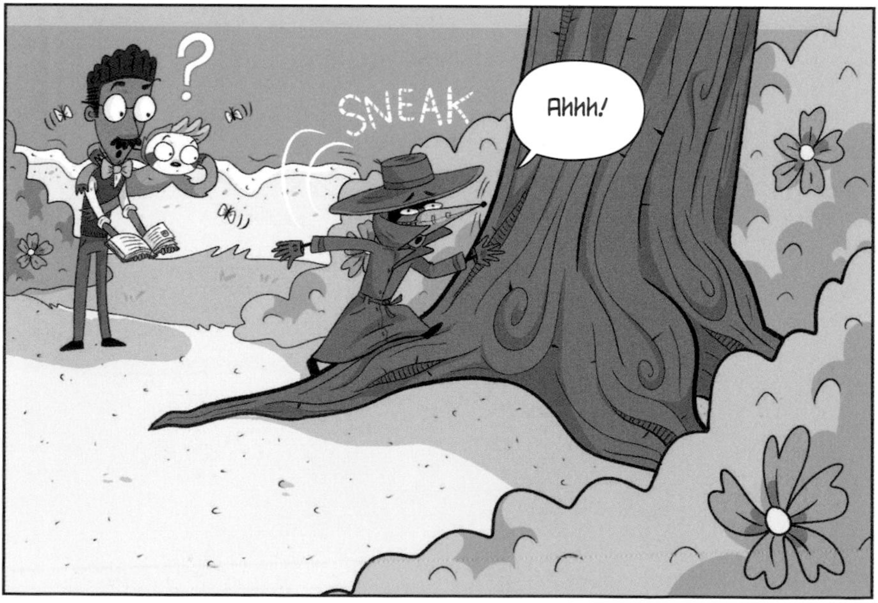
?
SNEAK
Ahhh!

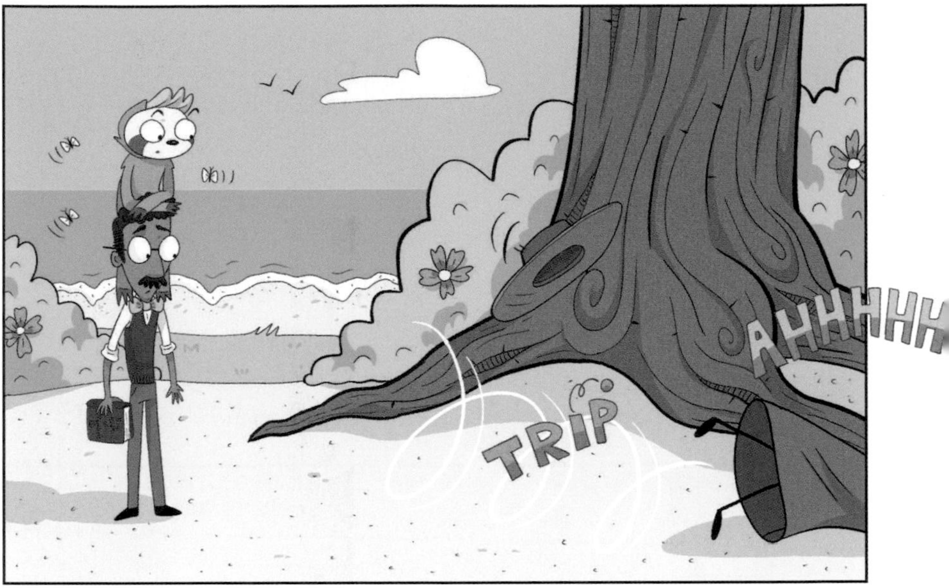
AHHHHH
TRIP

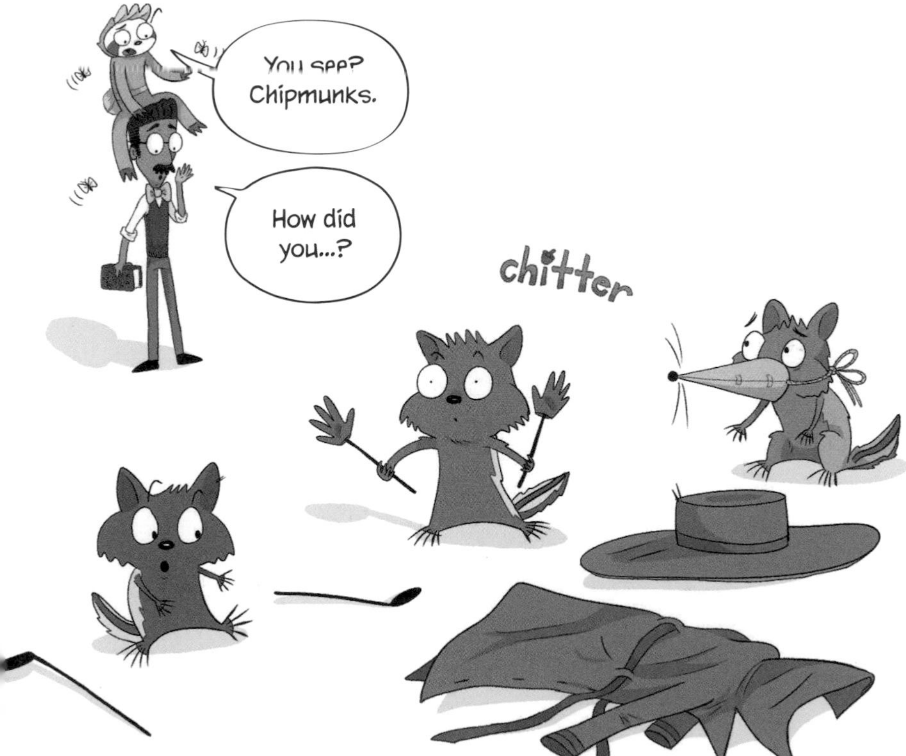
You see?
Chipmunks.
How did you...?
chitter

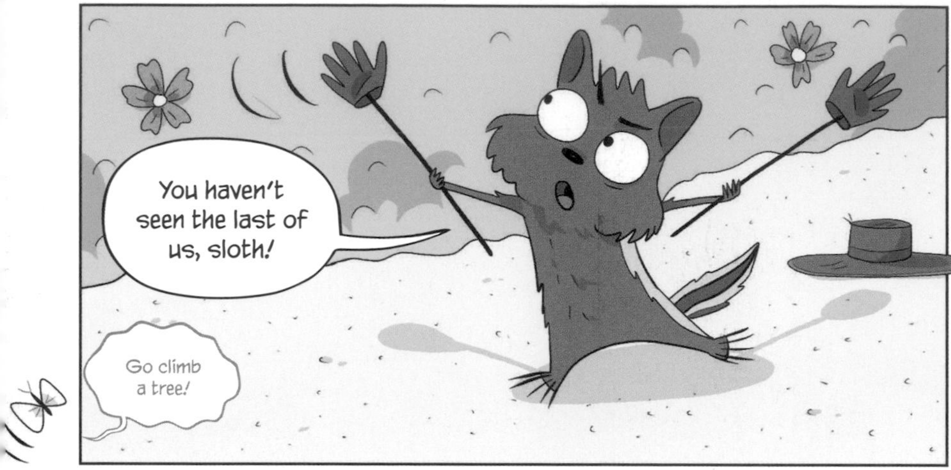
You haven't seen the last of us, sloth!
Go climb a tree!

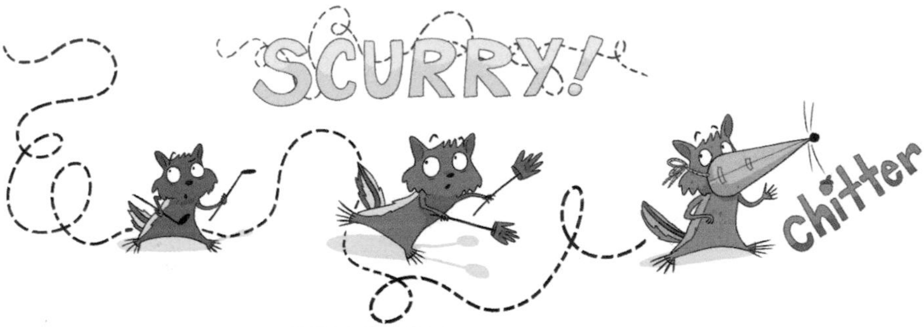
SCURRY!
chitter

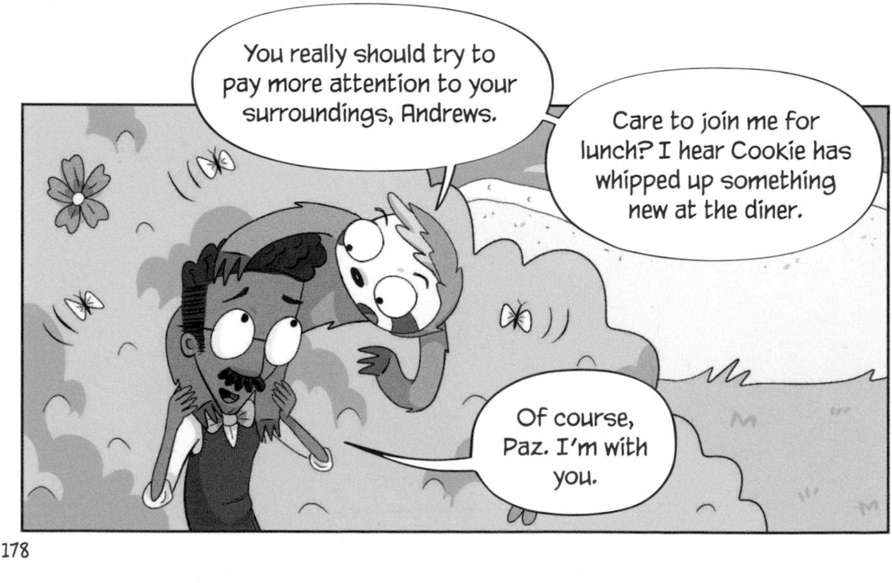
You really should try to pay more attention to your surroundings, Andrews.
Care to join me for lunch? I hear Cookie has whipped up something new at the diner.
Of course, Paz. I'm with you.

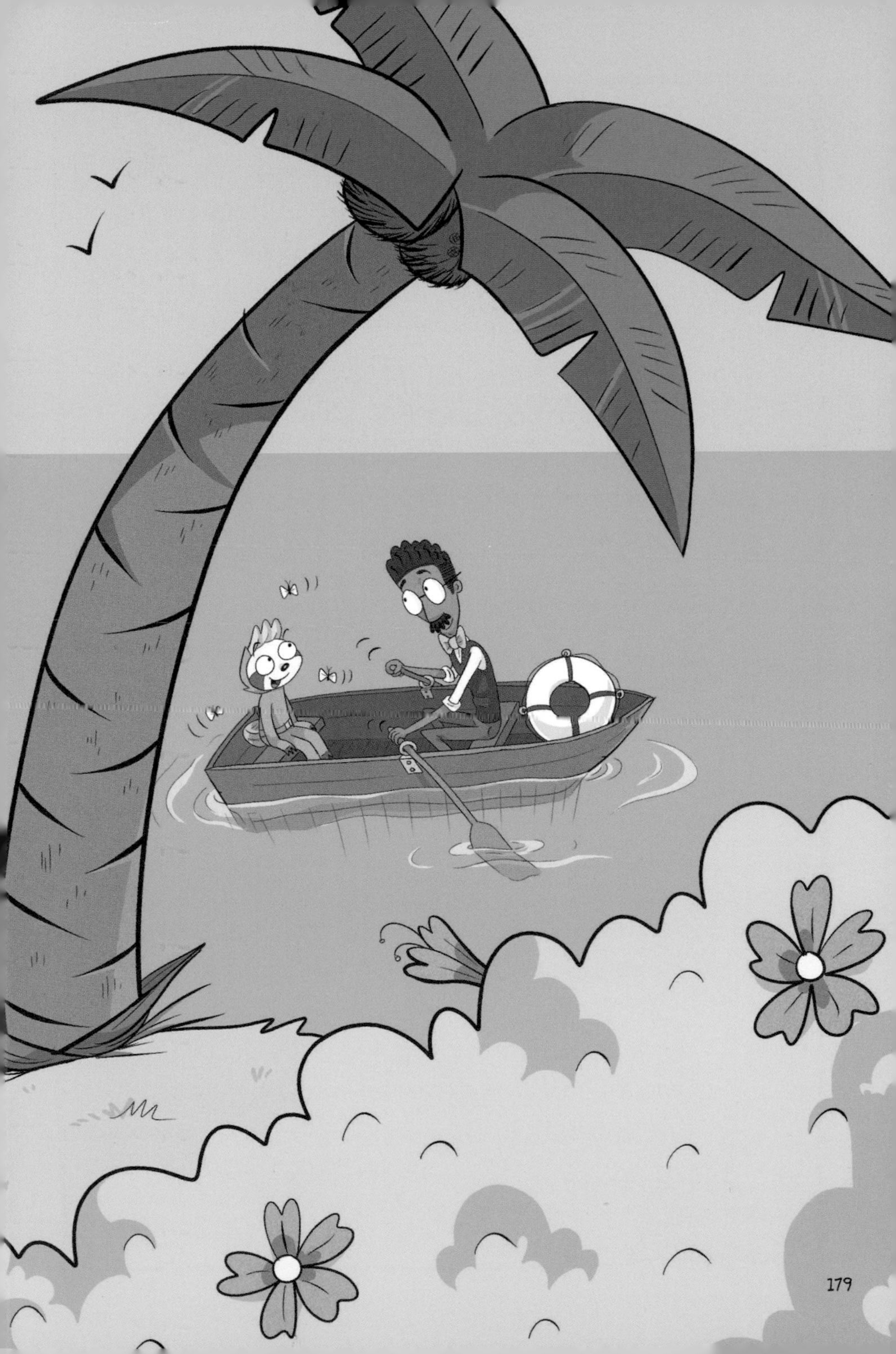

Winklefuss Public Library

Come check out our books!

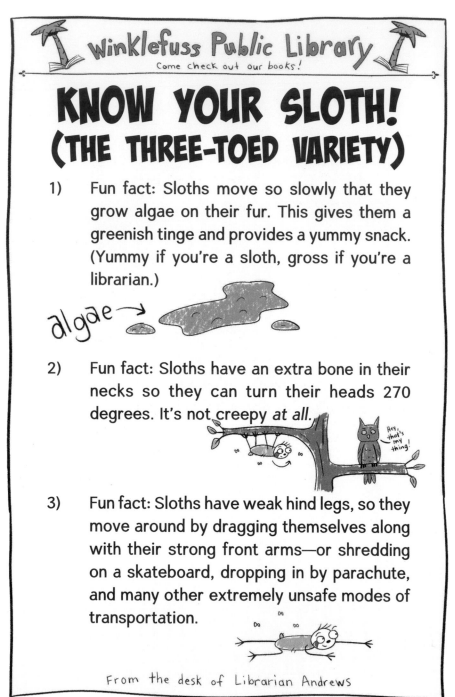

KNOW YOUR SLOTH!
(THE THREE-TOED VARIETY)

1) Fun fact: Sloths move so slowly that they grow algae on their fur. This gives them a greenish tinge and provides a yummy snack. (Yummy if you're a sloth, gross if you're a librarian.)

algae

2) Fun fact: Sloths have an extra bone in their necks so they can turn their heads 270 degrees. It's not creepy *at all.*

Hey, that's my thing!

3) Fun fact: Sloths have weak hind legs, so they move around by dragging themselves along with their strong front arms—or shredding on a skateboard, dropping in by parachute, and many other extremely unsafe modes of transportation.

From the desk of Librarian Andrews

Winklefuss Public Library

Come check out our books!

4) Fun fact: Sloths only poop once a week, which is usually the only time they come down from their trees—unless they're investigating crimes.

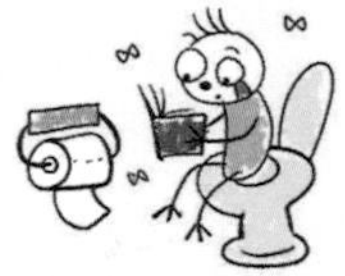

5) Fun fact: A sloth's fur is home to up to 120 moths! These moths live their entire adult life in the sloth's fur. Female moths lay their eggs in the sloth's poop, which is both super gross and really fascinating! (A sloth's fur can also be home to hundreds of scarab beetles, mites, lice, ticks, and biting flies. When you're a sloth, you're never alone!)

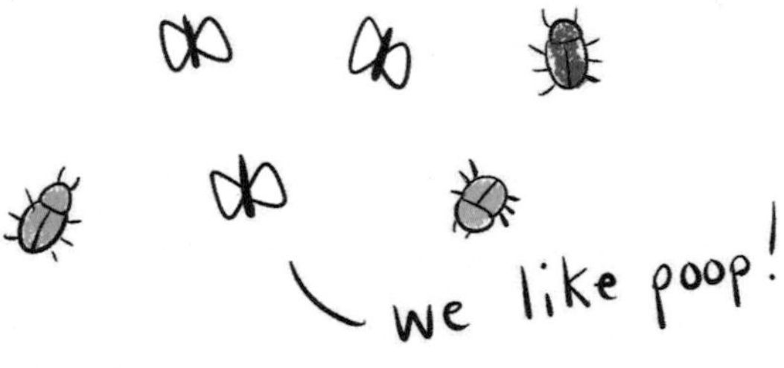
we like poop!

From the desk of Librarian Andrews

HOW TO DRAW PAZ

1. Draw two circles for the eyes.

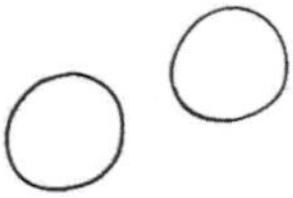

2. Draw an oval for the nose.

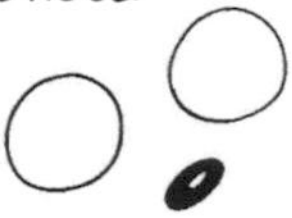

3. Draw the face.

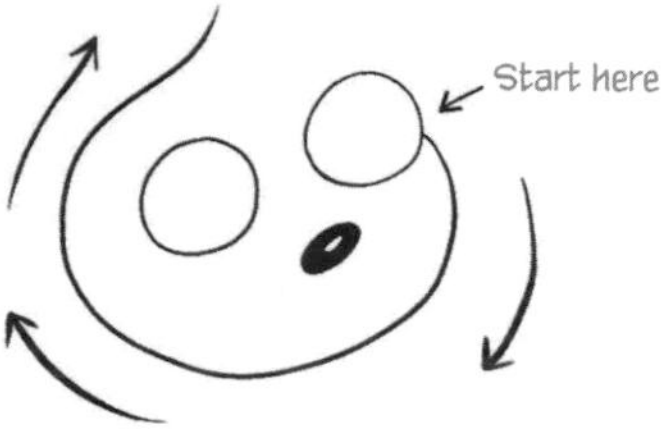
Start here

4. Finish the hairline.

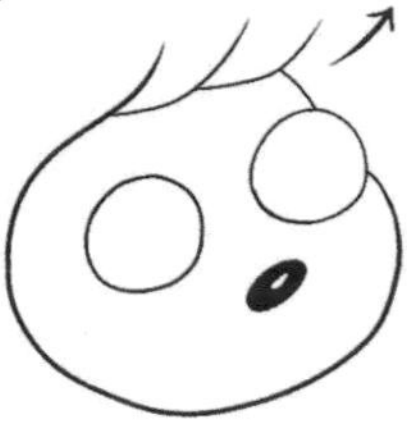

5. Add the furry bits.

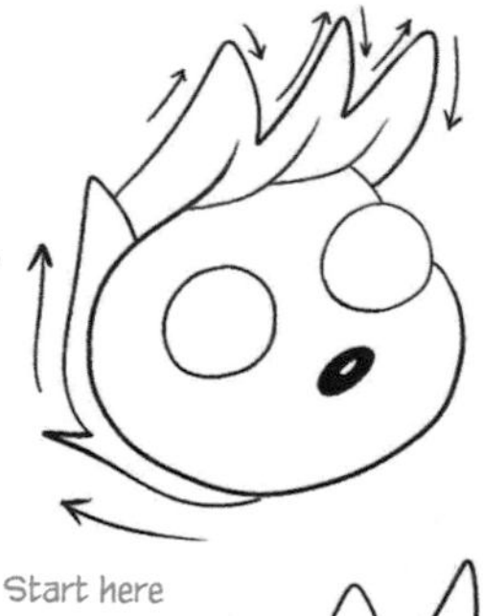
Start here

6. Add details.

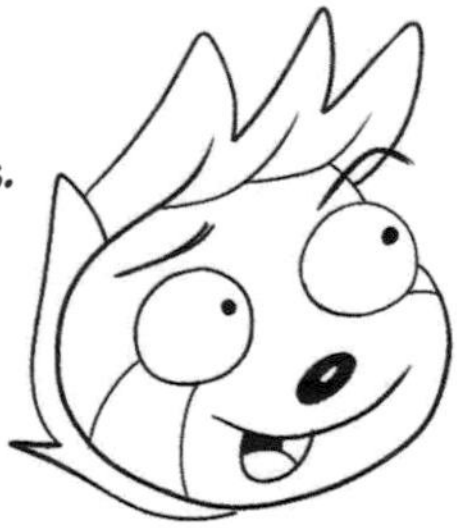

7. Add a torso.

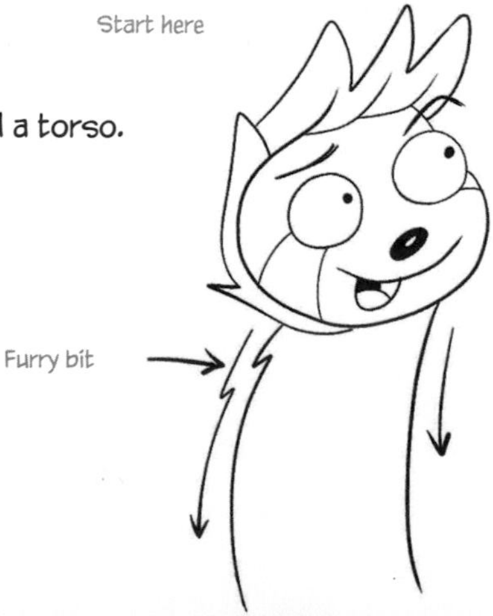
Furry bit

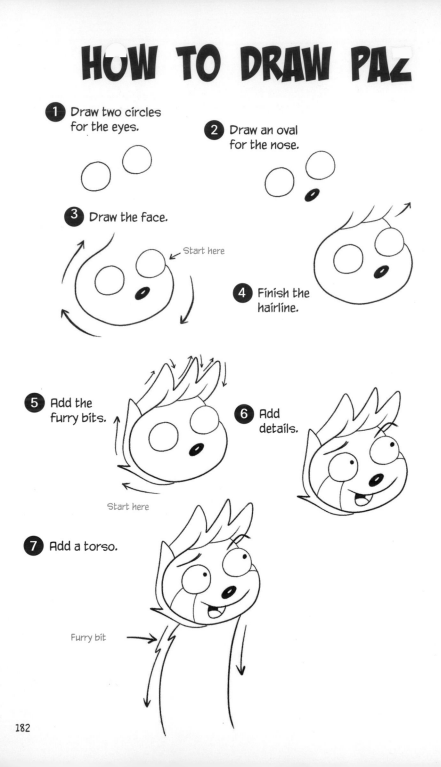

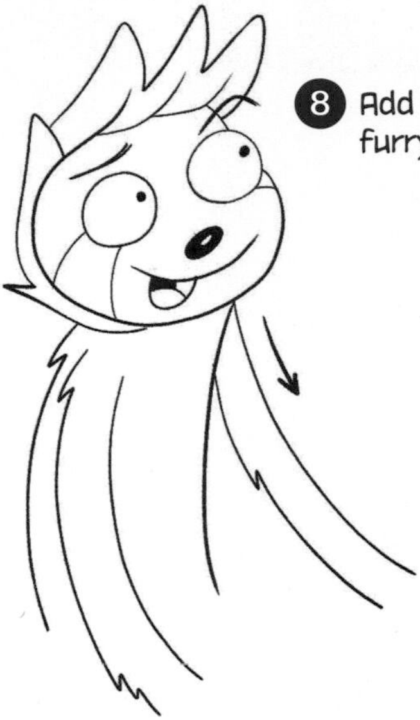

8 Add long furry arms.

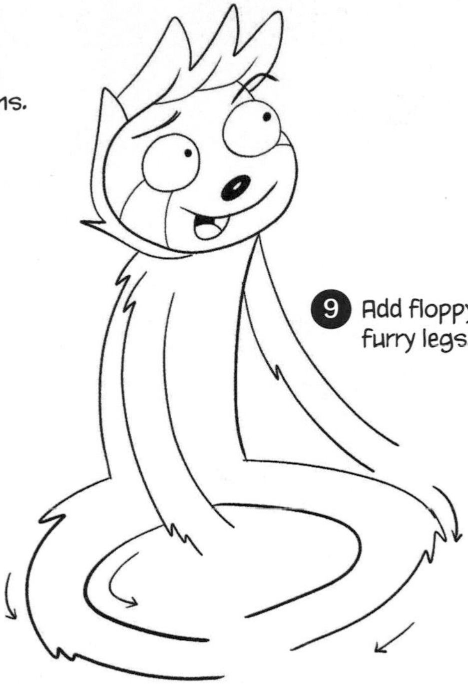

9 Add floppy furry legs.

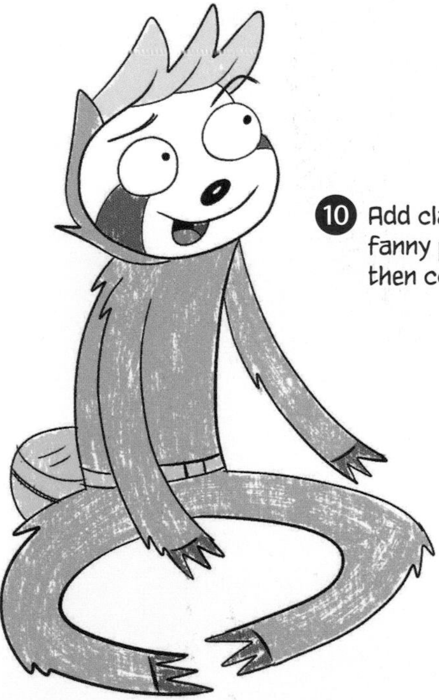

10 Add claws and fanny pack and then color!

11 Don't forget the moths!

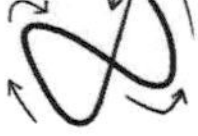

a Draw a sideways figure eight.

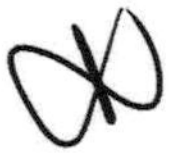

b Draw a thick line down the center.

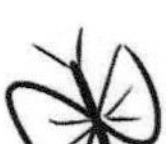

c Add details.

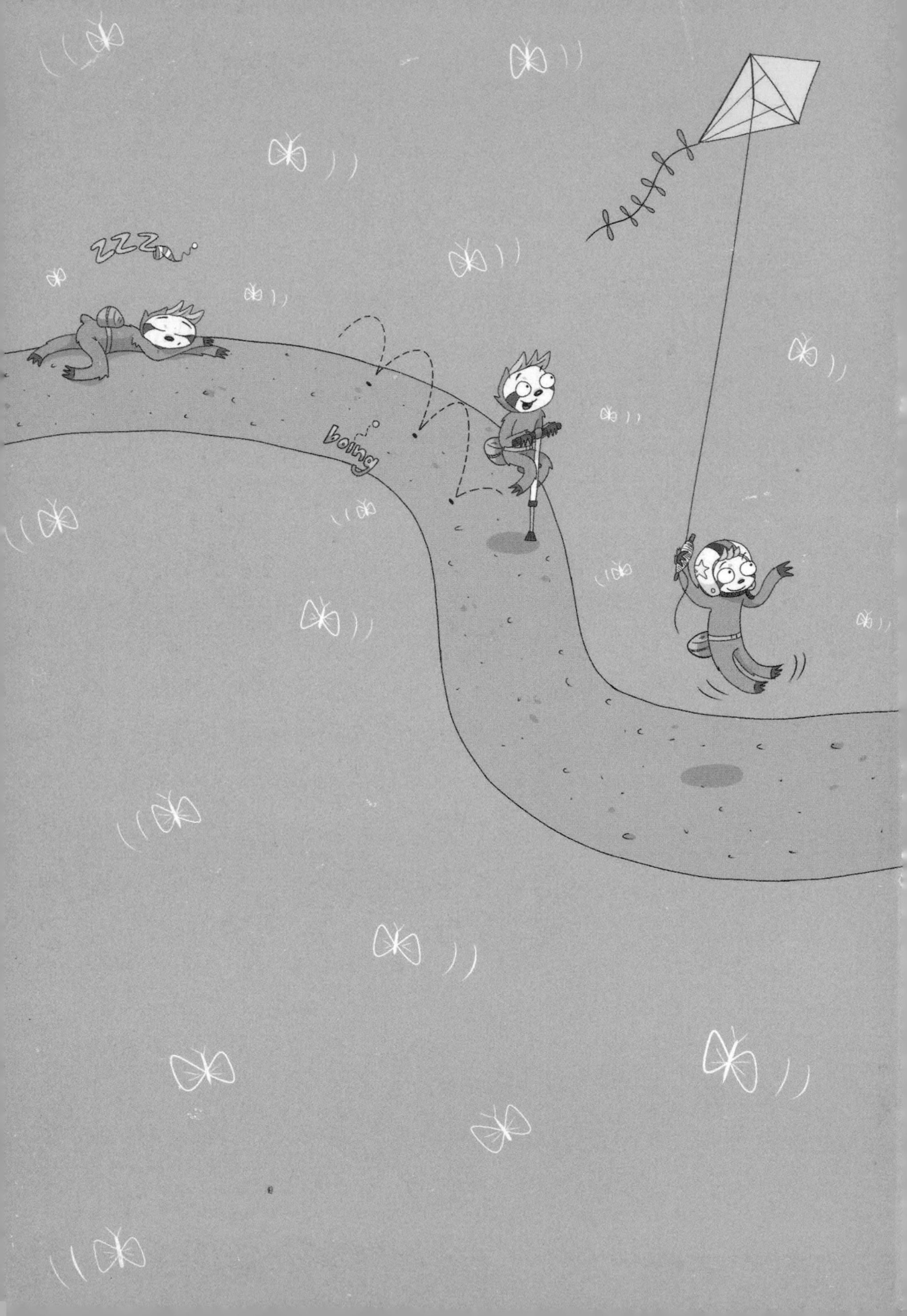
ZZZ
boing